Praise for *Fallen*

"Beautifully written, intensely passionate, and
gripping, *Fallen* grabbed me from the first sentence
and didn't let go. It's *The Matrix*, *Blade Runner*, and
The Terminator rolled into a riveting love story and made
better. Perfect. A must-read by an author who keeps
you on the edge of your seat."

—Linnea Sinclair,
RITA Award–winning author of *Shades of Dark*

BOOKS BY CLAIRE DELACROIX

Fallen
Guardian

Guardian

CLAIRE DELACROIX

tor paranormal romance

A TOM DOHERTY ASSOCIATES BOOK
NEW YORK

This is a work of fiction. All of the characters, organizations, and events portrayed in this novel are either products of the author's imagination or are used fictitiously.

GUARDIAN

Copyright © 2009 by Claire Delacroix, Inc.

A Tor Book
Published by Tom Doherty Associates, LLC
175 Fifth Avenue
New York, NY 10010

www.tor-forge.com

Tor® is a registered trademark of Tom Doherty Associates, LLC.

ISBN 978-0-7653-5950-6

First Edition: October 2009

Printed in the United States of America

0 9 8 7 6 5 4 3 2 1

For Kon,
as always.

Guardian

"But still, the fates will leave me my voice, and by my voice I shall be known."

—The Cumaean Sibyl

From *THE REPUBLICAN RECORD*
January 11, 2100
Download version 2.03

President Matheson Dead

NEW D.C.—President Richard Matheson died early this morning, passing peacefully in his sleep at the New White House. The First Lady made the discovery shortly after 0500. By 0600, Vice President Morris Van Buren had been sworn in as the sixty-fourth president to occupy the Oval Office. He also assumed the candidacy for the upcoming presidential race for the Heartland Party in President Matheson's stead.

An official seven-day period of mourning for President Matheson has already commenced. The funeral will be conducted at New D.C. Cathedral on January 18 at 1100, followed by a procession to Arlington National Cemetery. A public viewing of the President lying in state will be offered by live vidcast, beginning tomorrow at 0600.

Representatives from the Republic's allies have already begun to arrive in New D.C. Citizens should be aware that all transit systems in the New D.C. area have moved to Red Alert status due to the presence of these dignitaries. Travelers can expect delays and extra inspections throughout the greater metropolitan area.

It is anticipated that tens of thousands of citizens will line the route from New D.C. Cathedral to Arlington National Cemetery on Monday to bid a final farewell to this popular leader. Those planning to attend should be aware that the route is secured and that all who enter the area will be scanned in the interest of security. The live vidcast of the ceremony will begin at 1000, commencing with the official biography of President Matheson.

Associated Articles in Today's Download:

Vidcast of Morris Van Buren Taking the Oath of Office
Condolences from World Leaders
President Richard Matheson: A Dynamic Leader for
  Our Times
Funeral Procession Route and Security Measures
Presidential Candidate Maximilian Blackstone Seizes
  Lead in Advance Polls

I

Near New Seattle
Friday, February 12, 2100

SHE WAS being watched.

The woman known only as Twenty-three felt her pulse quicken. The hair prickled on the back of her neck, and she tried to tell herself that the glance she felt was only passing.

It wasn't. Someone was scrutinizing her.

She'd kept her head down as she lit the tall candles in the chapel, trying to be as nondescript as possible. She'd moved slowly, so as to not attract attention, but the weight of that gaze had made her want to run.

Someone knew her secret. Conviction made her heart race and her hands shake.

Twenty-three was a shade, and shades officially had no secrets.

Shades—those humans who had failed the Sub Human Atomic Deviancy Evaluation, or S.H.A.D.E.—forfeited their citizenship and rights because of their birth defects. They became the property of the Republic and were destined to labor unseen for the collective good of the Republic's citizens.

It was the duty of shades to remain invisible, the better to ensure that no norm was reminded of the existence of slavery in the Republic. But someone was keenly watching Twenty-three. Her mouth went dry—she knew how the Daughter Superior would react toward any shade who defied convention.

Twenty-three had to avoid suspicion on this night of nights. Her mind, for once, was clear. Someone had made a mistake in issuing her daily sedation for the past two days, because she hadn't been given any. She didn't care who or why.

Her chance had finally come.

Twenty-three was sick of lies and sick of servitude. The haze of indifference had risen slowly from her mind, leaving her with a clarity of thought that was shocking. She'd seen more in the last twenty-four hours than she'd noticed in the Citadel in years.

It was time to reveal herself.

The chapel was filled with strangers and the unusual hum of conversation. Once every four years, guests were allowed into the Citadel of the Daughters of the Light of the Republic to act as witnesses, and on this night, those guests had come.

Twenty-three knew that the Daughters would have preferred to have denied access to others, but the selection of the official Oracle of the Republic had to be witnessed by outsiders to appear legitimate.

Appearances were key, for the selection had already been made. This ceremony was a lie. Twenty-three shouldn't have been surprised when she had stumbled upon the rehearsal the day before. This entire ceremony, which witnesses would endorse with their presence, would be a sham.

But then, she already knew that nothing in the refuge of the Daughters was as it appeared. The only mercy was that no one knew that she had seen the truth. Sometimes it paid to be invisible. Sometimes the shadows—or the shades—were the true witnesses.

It was wrong to feign the revelation of the true Oracle.

It was wrong to ensure that a false Oracle could take the honored place.

And Twenty-three, who had been told years before that she was destined to be the one true Oracle, found the deceit offensive. She wasn't going to let the acolyte Teresa usurp the place that was destined to be hers.

It was time for Twenty-three to act. She felt awake and alive, vital, as if she'd rediscovered a lost key to herself. She'd almost forgotten the power of her undrugged body.

Yet at the same time, she felt naked and exposed, certain that someone would see the truth before she could prove her abilities. She feared that watchful gaze.

The eyes of the Republic, after all, were everywhere.

Cloaked from head to toe in black, veiled and gloved, Twenty-three should have blended with the shadows. She should have been invisible.

But the weight of that gaze was relentless.

She was keenly aware of the men who had been allowed into the Citadel for this ceremony. At all other times, the Citadel was a refuge of women for women only. The low resonance of men's voices in the crowd was foreign and titillating.

Was it a man who watched her? Something quivered deep inside her, something that she knew would have found disapproval from the Daughters. It was a seductive hum, a pleasurable tingle, and one that Twenty-three might have enjoyed under other circumstances.

She'd felt this sensation before, this buzz of awareness. That time, it had been accompanied by a pearly opalescent light, a light that ran like quicksilver and resonated with the same hum. She closed her eyes and remembered, shivering with delight.

Angelfire.

The source of her power and the root of her faith. The angels wouldn't abandon her now, not when triumph and justice were so close.

Twenty-three returned to her place at the perimeter of the chapel, folded her hands, and dipped her head. She was just another shade in the shadows, another anonymous figure in the line of similarly clad attendants.

Still, she knew she was watched.

Twenty-three straightened slightly and looked for the bold culprit. Her gaze collided immediately with that of a man, the only one who stared directly at her.

And only at her.

Twenty-three's heart stopped cold.

He stood at the back of the assembled crowd, seeming to

think that the others would overlook his presence. The idea
was ridiculous. He was almost radiant in his vitality, his golden
hair gleaming, his eyes glowing like sapphires. Among the
poorly nourished and burdened citizens of the Republic, he
was a magnet for every eye.

Never mind that he dressed with such verve. He wore a
faux-leather cloak, so deep an indigo that it was nearly black,
high black boots, and long black gloves. There was a froth of
white at his throat, a fine ruffled shirt with a striped silk cravat. His vest was sleek and zipped up the front, defining the
muscled breadth of his chest, and made of faux-leather in
midnight blue.

He had to be affluent, then.

Successful.

Of course. It wasn't easy to gain a witness pass. It probably took creds or connections or both. There were senators
in the crowd—Twenty-three had heard the Daughters brag-
ging about their number this time.

But this man was no senator. He didn't have the smug satisfaction of a politician, much less the bulk of one who ate
frequently and well at the expense of others. Twenty-three
doubted that this man would ever tell others what they wanted
to hear. To the contrary, she suspected that he preferred to
surprise people.

There was an intriguing hint of mischief in his smile.

And a knowing glint in his eyes.

The gem in the pin that held his cravat in place was large
and faceted, large enough to catch the light at a distance. It was
blue, maybe a sapphire, but couldn't compete with the brilliant blue glimmer of his eyes. His fair hair was tied back in
a queue, as luxuriant as spun gold. He was clean-shaven, and
made no pretence that he was doing anything other than what
he was doing.

He watched her openly.

Twenty-three knew he couldn't truly see her. Her features
were hidden behind her veil, but she feared that his bright
gaze could pierce those shadows. She knew he couldn't even

see her eyes given the distance between them, but she felt as if he could read her thoughts.

As if he knew how she felt.

As if he could see the trickle of perspiration running down her bare back or smell the heat rising from her skin. Could he know that her heart was racing? That there was a shimmer spreading through her lower body? That she was awake for the first time in years? Twenty-three's mind filled with questions but she couldn't avert her gaze from his. Awareness strung taut between the two of them, increasing the hum in her ears.

Would he thwart her plan?

She was snared. She felt dizzy. Her hood—which she despised because it was hot and suffocating—might have been infested with angry bees. She couldn't look away from the stranger, couldn't dispel the sense that he knew all of her secrets.

Twenty-three wondered who he was.

She wondered what he wanted.

She was afraid she knew. Hunters dressed in such sturdy garb, although not usually with such flamboyance. The stranger was a magnificent male animal, broad-shouldered and confident, as shrewd and stealthy as a predator.

A hunter.

A *shade* hunter.

She fought her urge to cover her sleeved left forearm with her right hand. The tattoo that condemned her was there, the tattoo that had been modified but not removed.

Twenty-three closed her eyes and surreptitiously rubbed the middle of her forehead. It was a habit that always eased her worries, maybe because it reminded her of what she had survived. Maybe because it reminded her of that white cleansing light. She rubbed her forehead and breathed deeply.

That hum gained resonance within her, driving every thought from her mind. There was only the thunder of her heart and the insistent reverberation, and her memory of this strange feeling.

She'd had it before, a long time ago.

She'd had it when she met the angels.

They were coming.

Twenty-three beckoned to the light that filled her mind, knowing that it brought salvation. She called to the angels, welcoming them in her thoughts. She would be the next Oracle, chosen before witnesses, and the plan of the Daughter Superior would be foiled.

Hers would be the perfect exit from this refuge of lies.

The angels knew best.

The music, the hymn, the incense, and the candlelight combined to deepen the spell that enfolded Twenty-three. When the acolytes entered the chapel, Twenty-three saw a line of angels floating toward her.

They were hardly angels, these ambitious and privileged young women who would do anything to secure the position of Oracle. They would even lie, but Twenty-three's heart was filled with truth.

The truth of angel-song.

Twenty-three heard the low cadence of the men's voices when the visitors sang. She heard one voice in particular, one that wound into her ears, cast a net around her heart, tangled with that persistent hum and sparkled like an army of fireflies.

His.

She saw the spark of the divine radiating from that bright-eyed hunter, watched as the brilliant light that seemed to emanate from him flooded the chapel.

She was awed by the radiance.

The light touched her, caressed her, awakened her. Twenty-three felt the tide rising within her. She shook from head to toe, her body slipped out of her own control. She knew what was going to happen, and embraced it. She heard Sonja clucking softly in warning, as if that old crone had sensed the tumult in Twenty-three.

She ignored Sonja. This was no time for caution.

This was the moment to believe.

Twenty-three knew the angels would soon claim her tongue, that they would possess her and command her and pour their truth into the ears of the witnesses. With their words would come her freedom. She trusted them, explicitly and implicitly. Twenty-three surrendered everything to them.

Again.

And the vision ripped through her, relentless and potent, blinding with its brilliance and truth, indifferent to what preconceptions were destroyed in its path.

RAFE WAS bored.

The Citadel of the Daughters of the Light of the Republic was the last place he would have expected to find himself, yet he was present all the same. His infernal palm had been so insistent about his attendance that he had heeded its summons, if only in the hope of shutting it up.

He doubted that would work. He'd had nothing but trouble with the computer display inlaid in his left hand, yet he had seen that other citizens had no similar challenges.

His routinely pinged him with news downloads that he had never bought; it provided hotlinks to data that he thought should be secured for those with higher clearance than he possessed; it had capabilities beyond those of the other citizens he'd met. He knew that there were applications installed on his palm that weren't common, that might even be illegal.

Generally, he ignored the palm, and silently loathed it.

He'd often felt as if someone was trying to compel him to follow an agenda that wasn't his own, instead of his spending another night in another pleasure fringe.

His personal affinity was for the pursuit of pleasure. He enjoyed the discovery of new sensations—new tastes, new scents, new stimuli—and could happily have lost himself in completing his inventory of the possibilities available to the human body. If each sensation lost its appeal quickly, that only increased his hunger for more new experiences.

His palm, though, had other ideas.

And those ideas had brought him to the Citadel, under protest.

His gaze trailed repeatedly to one cloaked shade, following her gestures as she lit the candles. She was the only thing of interest in this hovel of solemnity and austerity. He had no doubt of her gender—he knew his weakness well enough and no amount of dark cloth could fool him.

He wondered what she looked like under that veil.

She was tall and slim, and her hand appeared to be finely boned. Even more, she had a strong presence even in silence. Rafe was intrigued.

Was it because he had never sought pleasure with shades? It was one of the few possibilities that he hadn't explored, maybe because he disliked the idea of one partner not being agreeable to an intimate union. He knew there were plenty of norms who didn't have that concern, who kept attractive shades as personal sex slaves.

Not Rafe. He much preferred a joyous coupling, and the possibilities that joy created.

Had he ever believed otherwise? He probed his memory again, half certain of what he would find and not surprised when he came up against that black void of silence. He remembered nothing beyond the previous October, although every dalliance and experiment since then was vivid in his recollection.

There was a black wall of silence in his mind, a barrier as impenetrable as the security walls on netherzones that kept shades separated from norms.

That void in his mind defied his sense that he had once had thousands of detailed memories. He recalled a falling star and a conviction that its descent marked his loss of memory, but that made no sense. More important, he wanted that elusive data back. He sensed that it was there, but access was forbidden to him.

Not unlike the Republic's netherzones.

Where had his memories gone? It was a puzzle he wasn't sure he'd ever solve.

It was, after all, easier to surrender himself to pleasure.

Rafe's eyes narrowed as his shade began to twitch in the shadows. She looked as if she would have a convulsion.

No one else seemed to notice.

He supposed that he should be thinking about his mission, the one that his palm harassed him about completing. That task should be at the fore of his thoughts.

It hadn't yet been, partly because Rafe resented the sense that he was obligated to pursue a mission he didn't welcome or understand. That mission also seemed to require his presence in places he would have preferred to have avoided.

Like this Citadel, with its dedication to the ideals of poverty, chastity, and obedience carved over its entry. Rafe couldn't see the appeal of any one of that trio.

There were a lot of things about the Citadel of the Daughters of the Light of the Republic that annoyed Rafe. He didn't like that the child he was supposed to retrieve was apparently hidden here. He didn't like the tightly controlled access, or the injuncture against the presence of men. He hadn't liked that there was only one way to get inside the Citadel—by becoming a witness to this ritual—and he definitely hadn't appreciated that his palm had conjured a witness pass when he might not have bothered.

Rafe hadn't been particularly surprised by the revulsion he felt when greeted by the unctuous Daughter Superior, or his sense that she was lying to all of them. She was a toad of an old bureaucrat—squat and wide, self-satisfied and toxic—but she was more venomous than any reptile could have been.

The other Daughters, scurrying and nervous, weren't much better. The whole place stank of deception.

He watched the shade, sensing that she watched him back, and felt a familiar heat grow within him.

He was just anxious to get to Hood River's pleasure fringe.

Rafe's mysterious and unwelcome assignment was to save a child harvested at birth by the Society of Nuclear Darwinists, now recorded dead by the Republic's databases. Rafe knew that Delilah was alive, and that nine years before, she had been hidden at this Citadel. He knew that she was the child of Lilia Desjardins, whom he remembered meeting the previous October.

His task was to find Delilah and install her as the official Oracle of the Republic.

His palm and his memory were both emphatic about that.

The details of how precisely he was to achieve that end were not at all clear. He knew nothing about the child, except that she had once been assigned the number E562008 by the Republic. He didn't understand the process of appointing an Oracle, much less the necessity of it—he simply knew that the choice would be made on this night. He couldn't remember how he'd gotten this task, or why he felt such an imperative to complete it.

How could he even be certain that Delilah was still in this place? How could he find her, if she was? The acolytes, all robed identically in white, were so numerous and so indistinguishable from each other that his task seemed hopeless.

Too bad the prospect of failure filled him with such fear.

Too bad he couldn't remember the consequences. He checked the time on his palm with impatience, then watched his shade shake more violently.

The indifference of the Daughters irritated him and made him more determined to intervene.

The Daughter Superior ended the hymn, then lifted her veil and smiled. "Welcome, guests, to our humble refuge . . ."

A large woman to Rafe's left began to speak into her palm. "This is Reverend Billie Jo Estevez, and I'm here on location at the Citadel of the Daughters of the Light of the Republic."

Her words were sufficiently loud that Rafe could hear them. The other citizens glanced toward her in wonder. The Daughter Superior cleared her throat with gusto, but the reverend continued to speak.

Rafe was amused by the toad's disapproval.

"As many of you know, the new Oracle will be chosen on this night and we are just about to see which of these hundred young women have the ear of the divine . . ."

The Daughter Superior raised her voice. "We are honored to have the Reverend Billie Jo Estevez among our witnesses this evening," she said, almost hissing the words.

The company turned to look openly at the reverend, their expressions a mingling of awe and admiration. The Daughter Superior and the reverend glared at each other for an electric moment, but the reverend ceased her broadcast.

Rafe's shade, meanwhile, began to shake violently and sway. He took a step toward the aisle.

The Daughter Superior was oblivious. "On this night, one of our children will show herself worthy of great honors." Her voice was low and rich, so resonant that it carried over the hushed company. "For it is writ *'I am the Alpha and the Omega' says the Lord God, who is and who was and who is to come, the Almighty.'*"

"Amen," murmured the assembly as one.

"Hallelujah," declared the reverend. She lifted her left hand and Rafe understood that she was snatching a live vidcast of the ceremony. From the fury that briefly lit the Daughter Superior's eyes, that detail hadn't been negotiated in advance.

The shade twitched. Her suffering took Rafe away from his own concerns, had him pushing toward the aisle. He knew it, but he was almost ready to defy the toad's notion of how everything should proceed.

He wanted the ceremony done so he could leave. He wanted to return to his own agenda. Rafe felt that familiar restlessness grow in him, the sense that he sought an elusive something that he never quite managed to grasp. Whatever he desired, he certainly wouldn't find it in this austere Citadel, with its wholesale rejection of everything that made life worthwhile.

Within moments, Rafe learned just how wrong that assumption was.

THE SHADE shook more violently, as if having a seizure. One of the older Daughters moved toward the trembling shade and put a hand on the black-shrouded figure's shoulder. She bent and murmured quietly to the trembling shade, although it seemed to make little difference.

Rafe scanned the motionless acolytes once again, his irritation rising. They all looked the same. If Delilah was still here, he'd never find her. His assigned mission was a foolish one.

Maybe that was a good enough reason to abandon it.

Terror rolled through him at the very thought, and he was irritated by his inability to remember the root of his fear.

The Daughter Superior continued to quote Scripture. *"When I saw him, I fell at his feet as though dead. But he placed his right hand on me, saying, 'Do not be afraid; I am the first and the last, and the living one. I was dead, and see, I am alive forever and ever; and I have the keys of Death and of Hades.'"*

The Daughter Superior raised her voice to a command. *"Now write what you have seen, what is, and what is to take place after this."* She placed her hands together and lifted them high before herself, bowing her head at the same time so that her brow touched the tips of her index fingers. "Let us hear then, of what was, what is, and what will be."

"Amen!" cried the reverend.

The Daughter Superior's lips tightened ever so slightly.

Then she pivoted and lifted her hands toward the young women enshrouded in white. "Speak to me, my children," she urged, "and share with me what you know. Tell me what message the angels bring to you, what portents you have for the future of the Republic of the United States of the Americas."

Rafe saw her turn slightly to the left, as if she guessed who would speak first. But how could the favor of the divine be known in advance?

It couldn't, unless the Oracle had already been chosen.

Interesting.

One acolyte began to step forward.

But just then, the black-shrouded shade fell through the ranks of the young women in white, writhing on the floor and moaning. Her seizure had started at an inappropriate time and Rafe moved down the aisle, intending to defend her.

The young women parted and retreated, squealing with horror that they had been touched by a shade. The witnesses murmured in consternation. The Daughter Superior looked fit to spit sparks. The older Daughter who had consoled the shade scowled with what might have been disappointment, but didn't approach the shade again. Rafe was disgusted by the array of responses.

If she was an epileptic, someone should ensure that she survived her seizure. Rafe pushed the people ahead of him aside as the shade moaned loudly and writhed before the altar.

"For goodness' sake!" the Daughter Superior declared and moved to grasp the shade by the ankle. She hauled the shade like a sack of grain across the altar, obviously meaning to cast her out of the chapel. The shade twisted, oblivious to this treatment.

The black hood fell away, baring the shade's face to view.

And Rafe's heart stopped cold.

Her hair was shaved close, dark stubble covering her head, but her gender was as undeniable as her beauty. Her face was heart-shaped, her eyes blue and thickly lashed. The similarity between her features and those of Lilia Desjardins was unmistakable.

Delilah.

She couldn't have been anyone else.

She ripped her ankle from the Daughter Superior's grasp with a violent jerk and hissed like a feral cat. "Do not impede the will of the angels!"

Her voice was commanding and deeper than Rafe had expected. Feminine yet powerful.

The Daughter Superior backed away, then pointed imperiously at her. "Someone, restrain this shade! Immediately!"

Delilah braced herself on her knees and hands, looking up at the assembly. Her hair was wild, her eyes wide. She was shaking, but the intensity of her gaze commanded every eye. Her pupils were enormous. Rafe could see the full curve of her breasts and one bare taut nipple through the disheveled neck of her robe.

Delilah was a woman, not a child, and she was nude beneath her robes. Rafe's assignment showed sudden promise. She stared directly at him, holding his gaze captive.

The assembly was as transfixed as he was.

Then Delilah raised her voice, speaking with such authority that the disconcerted witnesses were silenced as one:

> *Matheson is dead, unjustly so;*
> *His killer was the first to know.*
> *Ambition demanded sacrifice,*
> *A President has paid the price.*
> *The Republic's days are condemned*
> *If the villain remains unnamed.*
> *Justice must begin on high*
> *Lest all be scattered like ashes dry.*

Delilah wasn't having a seizure. She was having a vision. Rafe understood instantly that this was real, this was the genuine power of the Oracle, and that realization shook him.

She shouted, shook, then stood with her arms stretched toward the heavens and her head tilted back. Her pose was triumphant and Rafe was sure she shimmered slightly in the candlelight.

Angelfire.

Her prophecy was enough to make him believe in the unbelievable.

Silence claimed the chapel, all eyes fixed upon her. Delilah's pale skin and her shaved head were potent reminders of her slave status.

Yet possessed of the abilities of an oracle, all the same.

Rafe was fascinated. He'd been chasing sensation and pleasure, everything illusory and fleeting, while this, this was genuine. His hair tingled at its roots as if there was a charge of electricity in the air and he could have sworn that he felt the presence of the divine. Her power was real and his assigned quest was imperative.

Rafe realized, a bit late, that the Oracle was the prize he'd been seeking all along.

The assembly, meanwhile, was seized by a ripple of unease that spoke volumes. The Daughter Superior sputtered, seeking a smooth recovery from what had obviously not been planned. The acolytes had withdrawn to the perimeter of the chapel and huddled together in horror.

Delilah lowered her chin and eyed the crowd, her gaze brilliant with challenge. She smiled slightly. "Praise be to the wisdom of the angels."

"Amen," said the old Daughter who had soothed her.

Instead of echoing the blessing, the company took a step backward in fear. Could the citizens of the Republic accept that anything of merit came from the netherzones?

Rafe knew the answer a moment later. The Daughter Superior moved sternly toward Delilah and the witnesses began to murmur in consternation. The older Daughter at the periphery surveyed the responses of the witnesses with a sly smile.

Then she began to laugh.

Her laugh was maniacal and highly pitched, tinged with madness. It filled the chapel, echoing like a laugh from another world. The flames danced wildly atop the candles, seemingly responding to the sound. They burned higher and higher, stretching tall in defiance of every expectation.

The laughing Daughter abruptly blew at the flames. The candles were extinguished as one and the chapel was plunged into impenetrable darkness.

And silence.

Within a single heartbeat, the guests began to push for the doors in panic.

Rafe shoved them aside, trying to get to Delilah. He knew from the look on the Daughter Superior's face that she would retaliate against Delilah for her vision. He knew that the truth of the Oracle revealed would be buried.

And Delilah with it.

Would his assigned quest be a failure before it had begun?

Rafe felt the unwelcome press of time. He regretted every

dalliance, every moment he had lingered, every whore, every drink, every meal, every sensation he had pursued on his journey west. He regretted his wholehearted embrace of sensory pleasure and his dedicated exploration of his body's response to stimulus.

He had to fix his miscalculation.

He had to save Delilah.

Identification Beads Become Mandatory

GOTHAM—IN a move that has been widely anticipated, the Senate today approved new legislation introduced by the President, making the embedded identification beads mandatory for each citizen of the Republic above twelve years of age. The glass bead, which contains a nanochip carrying biographical information for the citizen in question, is embedded beneath the skin on the back left of the neck and can be read with an external scanner. Beads will be installed over the next year during each citizen's annual physical examination. The embedding requires only a local anaesthesia and is not painful.

Identification beads were first proposed by Nicholas Blackstone, then Vice President, during the border crisis that became known as the Great Alien Scare five years ago. At that time, Mr. Blackstone presented the idea in the Republic's interest of providing a secure means of identifying legitimate citizens. The technology has been used for decades to track livestock in breeding programs and domestic pets, and has proven both its versatility and its reliability. Since stepping into the presidency in 2014, shortly after the protests from civil rights groups terminated any hope of the identification bead being used on the general populace, Blackstone has repeatedly lobbied for what he calls the "good sense of using this technology for the Republic's benefit."

President Blackstone cited last year's nuclear incidents in Texas and Louisiana as the impetus for this increased security in his appeal to the Senate. "Times have changed, but our response to new threats has lagged behind the times.

The time has come to ignore the naysayers who would keep our borders porous and put our families at risk. This small glass bead can easily ensure that our perimeter is secure, by guaranteeing that official documentation cannot be so readily forged or trafficked. The citizens of the Republic must know that they are safe within their homeland in order to function effectively." Upon news this morning that the legislation he had sponsored was passed by both houses, President Blackstone indicated that he had expected nothing less. "The Senate knows that I have vowed to give citizens confidence in the future and that I will deliver upon my promise. It is time for the Republic to be strong."

Identification beads have been embedded in all military personnel since 2013, as part of their indoctrination into the service. General Michael O'Donnell of the Marine Corps states categorically that there are no reports of any negative health effects and that, in fact, the identification beads have simplified security measures on military bases as well as provided more reliable data. He cited the example of scanners installed in the lintels of doorways in all military buildings, which automatically log the arrival and departure of individual personnel. "There is no question of who is where, and no doubt as to the integrity of the data," he said. "That saves us a tremendous amount of verification, and eliminates duplicate efforts. We can use those resources to better defend the Republic."

There are rumors of military personnel complaining about a lack of privacy, but no individuals in the service were available to comment. An unidentified source confirmed that black market versions of the beads do exist, but that they are readily distinguished from the official identification beads and so do not pose a formidable obstacle to security.

Related Articles in Today's Edition:

II

THE WITNESSES were frightened, having received more than they expected from this ritual, and rushed toward the doors. Rafe was trying to move against them and making little progress, given their numbers and their fear.

"I apologize for the rude interruption," the Daughter Superior said, her voice booming with authority. "And beg for your indulgence." Her voice carried the tinge of command and the witnesses halted instinctively.

A match was struck, flaring in the darkness, and the Daughter Superior lit the first candle again. The witnesses turned and stared.

She smiled at the assembly. "I beg you return to your places." There was an undercurrent of steel to her tone, an expectation that she would be obeyed.

In the light of that one candle, Rafe saw that Delilah and the crone were gone.

The Daughter Superior lit the other candles in succession, exuding confidence that she would be obeyed. "Our Citadel has great need of maintenance in these troubled times," she said smoothly, and Rafe felt the crowd's mood settle. "The winter wind rushes through the chinks in the log walls and causes us no end of discomfort. I apologize that you were compelled to share our discomfort on this night of nights."

Rafe knew that Delilah couldn't have disappeared so quickly, not unless the refuge had a netherzone with an access in the chapel.

And that wouldn't be the only access. If the netherzone ran beneath the complex, there would be others.

Rafe eased toward the doors. His mood had improved remarkably. He felt sharper and more focused than he had in months.

Well, in as long as he could remember.

All he had to do was find a netherzone access. His experience in the dark corners of the Republic appeared to be part of a plan, one that he'd forgotten, as had his fascination with picking locks and exploring forbidden activities.

It would be easy to steal Delilah out of this hovel.

As he drew near the double doors, Rafe heard the bolt slide home on the other side. He leaned his weight against the wooden portal, but it was secured from the outside.

He was stuck with the witnesses, at least until they observed what the Daughter Superior wanted them to see. Rafe leaned against the door, folded his arms across his chest, and willed the old toad to hurry.

Who knew what would happen to Delilah while he was detained?

He didn't want to think about it. He had a hard time hiding his disdain for the Daughter Superior, as he disliked the idea that anyone would dismiss truth to serve her own purposes. Anyone with eyes would have seen that Delilah had the true gift of an oracle.

Yet she had been banished and would be punished or destroyed, without a whimper of protest from these so-called witnesses.

The injustice of it all incensed Rafe. It infuriated him as nothing else had. He forced himself to be temperate.

For the moment.

"Please excuse the enthusiasm of the little one," the Daughter Superior said, her sweet tone grating on Rafe. "Some of our shades are affected by the powerful abilities of the unnamed Oracle within our ranks." The Daughter Superior sighed and appealed to the witnesses. "I am sorry to have you so strongly reminded of the extent of our charitable work."

Rafe seethed as the company swallowed these lies.

The ritual began again, but he was skeptical of its merit.

That same young woman, already indicated by the Daughter Superior, stepped forward once more. She made some thin prophecy about the glorious future of the Republic, one that utterly lacked the power of the shade's prophecy.

It was false.

It was rehearsed.

There was no fire to her words and Rafe knew that the angels didn't speak through her.

Anyone should be able to see the truth, but only Rafe apparently did. He understood then the Daughters of the Light of the Republic preferred to silence the true Oracle. Perhaps they wanted to control the Oracle. Perhaps they disliked the unpredictability of a true gift of foresight.

Perhaps they had been bought.

He didn't much care for the details. He wasn't enamored of the Republic and its policies, but the future could only be dark with a false Oracle in place. He'd heard her prophecy and he believed it.

Delilah was the true Oracle and he'd see her established in her rightful place. One glimpse had made him a believer. He wouldn't think about how highly the odds were stacked against him and Delilah. He wouldn't think about who their opponents might be.

Not yet.

It would be sweet to defeat the Daughter Superior.

WHEN THE witnesses were finally released, Rafe kept to the perimeter of the group. He walked to one side of the corridor that led to the exit, sliding his fingers surreptitiously along the paneling. His heart skipped when he found the access he was seeking. One panel in the wooden wall didn't quite line up with its fellows.

"My hat!" he exclaimed with alarm, looking about himself for the supposedly missing garment.

"Easily forgotten on this night," said a citizen beside him.

"I should say," muttered another. "I'll never volunteer for this duty again."

"When I think of the cred," seethed the first, exhaling noisily through his teeth.

The second nodded in sympathetic agreement.

Rafe nodded as well, then strode back toward the chapel. When the guests had all filed past him, he stepped into the shadows and waited a moment. A Daughter walked past him, following the witnesses, perhaps to ensure that they all left. Rafe didn't doubt that they'd be counted on departure.

And the tally would come up one short.

He didn't have much time.

Once the corridor was empty, he returned to the suspect panel. Rafe's fingers quickly found the hidden latch. He depressed it and his heart leapt when a half-height door opened.

Narrow stairs led downward.

Rafe quickly ducked into the darkness and closed the panel behind himself. He smelled the familiar mix of kitchen waste, human sweat, and devastation, and knew he hadn't found a mere closet. He held up his palm and its faint blue light illuminated the crude set of stairs that descended into the earth.

The device had given him nothing but trouble and he was gratified to find it useful for once, if not useful as it had been intended to be.

He'd take what he could get.

When Rafe reached the base of the stairs, he heard women's voices in the netherzones ahead. They were arguing, the tone of one hinting at restraint, the other young and strident and determined. Low and feminine.

He could guess not only the identities of the two women, but which voice belonged to which woman. Rafe grinned, confident in the divine plan and his ability to fulfill it, and strode into the shadows.

En route, he pulled his laze, ready for anything.

INSTEAD OF emerging triumphant, Twenty-three was dragged from the darkened chapel by Sonja. She bit and fought, without gaining any advantage, the older woman showing surprising strength.

She was flung on the floor of the netherzones beneath the kitchen. The scent of rotting potato peelings mingled with the acid chemical tinge of spoiled protein-paks. The smell of sewage permeated all of the netherzones of the refuge, underscored by the scents of mold and wet earth. The floor was pounded dirt in the netherzones, the space as redolent as a damp cellar.

It was Twenty-three's world and she loathed it.

The smell—and the implication that she was trapped forever in the nightmare of her life—could have been enough to make her despair. Despite her vision, she was back in this hellhole, consigned to the darkness again.

Instead, it made her angry.

Sonja had locked her in the small storage room, the one where the cleaning supplies were kept, one lantern swinging from the hook on the ceiling.

The angels were gone.

But Twenty-three had had a vision, and the prophecy was strangely clear in her thoughts.

As was the urgency it had awakened within her.

Who was Matheson?

What was she supposed to do about his death, even if he had been murdered? The prophecy left her tingling and electrified, though, filled with new determination.

She had to escape.

Being back in the netherzones meant that no one had given credence to her prophecy. Being back in the netherzones meant there would be hell to pay for what she'd done. She didn't look forward to the Daughter Superior's pronouncement.

Twenty-three peeled off her dark robes and chucked them aside, irritated with the oppressive weight of the cloth. She rattled the door and peered through the crack at the netherzone beyond.

Ferris was watching the door, nibbling on his fingernails as he had a tendency to do. He was obscured by shadows, his dark clothes blending into the darkness around the edges, his posture so still that he could be easily overlooked.

Ferris was another of the shades at the refuge, a lanky boy of fifteen or so, one who had no ability to speak. He was sufficiently well behaved that he was seldom drugged or tied down. His presence as the only male in a refuge of women was a puzzle, one that Twenty-three had never solved.

Ferris wore shoddy clothes, worn and dirty, and boots that barely fit his feet. His dark hair hung uncut over his shoulders and his brown eyes were haunted. There was a scar on his throat that his shirt didn't always disguise and a faint shadow of stubble on his chin.

He wasn't called Ferris by the Daughters, of course, but he knew his name and had displayed it on his palm one day for Twenty-three. The memory of his confidence could still send a pang through her—Twenty-three was achingly jealous that Ferris had a name.

He probably remembered his family, as well.

"I suppose I'm in trouble," Twenty-three whispered through the door. "Again."

Ferris nodded and shrugged. He flicked a glance behind himself, then came to the door.

"I need to leave, Ferris, and you have to help me."

Ferris looked stricken. He shook his head and frowned.

"But I'm the Oracle and they'll disguise that truth. I have to leave to follow my destiny. You have to help me."

Ferris dropped his gaze.

"Wait a minute. You should come too. You're growing into a man, Ferris. What will they do with you? Men can't stay here."

Ferris swallowed, but didn't move.

"What if they sell you?"

Ferris breathed more quickly.

Twenty-three knew it wasn't fair, but she had to invoke his worst fear. "What if they give you back to the Society? What if they do that, Ferris? You can't just *wait*."

Ferris caught his breath, wild fear in his eyes. He still

didn't move and Twenty-three was furious that he would be so stubborn.

The Daughters didn't deserve his loyalty.

"I thought you were my friend," she hissed at him. "I thought we could stay friends." Ferris dropped his gaze. "Help me, Ferris. Please. You have the key, don't you? Sonja always trusts you to help her. Help me this time. All you have to do is unlock the door and look away."

Ferris' lips tightened and he turned his back on her.

Why wouldn't he help her? Twenty-three rattled the door. Ferris was her friend. He had always been her friend.

Then Twenty-three understood. That Ferris refused to help her could only mean that he was afraid.

"What did they do to you?" Twenty-three whispered and Ferris flicked a fearful glance over his shoulder. "How did they threaten you? You know it's a lie, Ferris. You know that they're just trying to control you." He licked his lips nervously and looked down, but she knew he was listening. "You should come with me. We could run away together. You have nothing left to lose and neither do I." He flicked a glance at her, his eyes filled with hope, and Twenty-three was certain he would agree.

Sonja had to appear right behind him in his moment of indecision.

"He knows I don't lie," the old woman said, revealing what she'd overheard. Sonja unlocked the door and pushed it open. She tapped a syringe as she filled it from a vial with a familiar label.

Ivanofor.

Twenty-three hated that drug more than the others. It stole her will and left her little control over her body. Worse, Ivanofor left her mind untouched, so that she was acutely aware of everything that happened around her.

But couldn't do anything about it.

The lack of control, the inability to do anything but observe and understand—while others abused her body or conducted experiments upon it—was sheer torture.

Twenty-three backed away, her hands up. She knew she had to fool Sonja and spoke slowly. She wasn't supposed to have missed her sedatives. "I don't need more medicine," she said, letting her words slur.

Sonja snorted. "I know you didn't have your medication this morning. Yesterday either. Don't think you have me fooled."

Twenty-three stuck to her ruse. "I don't understand . . ."

"You understand too much, that's always been your problem. And now, they all know it too." Sonja's eyes glinted as she glared at Twenty-three. "Giving that prophecy was a stupid choice, made in the wrong place to the wrong witnesses."

As was so often the case, Sonja was pragmatic and sane in private. It was a complete contrast to how wild and incoherent she could be when the other Daughters were present. Twenty-three had noticed long before that Sonja's most compelling displays of madness were made for the Daughter Superior. Her wild laugh, for example, was only heard in the Daughter Superior's company.

Nothing in the Citadel was as it seemed.

At least Sonja's practical manner was evidence that they three were alone. Sonja probably would have said that they two were alone, for Ferris, as a shade, didn't count.

Oddly, Twenty-three seemed to count to Sonja. It had always been that way, but Twenty-three had never figured out why.

"I'll be good." Twenty-three eased backward, certain of what was coming. She kept her tone childish and her words simple, still hoping the older woman would be deceived. Ferris stood in the doorway as Sonja entered the room. He clenched his fists and unclenched them repeatedly in his agitation.

He knew what was coming too, as well as the price of defiance.

"It's for your own good," Sonja said. "There's no point in defying me and you know it. You might as well make this easier for both of us."

Twenty-three wasn't convinced. She wondered whether the grate was unlocked. The exterior door on the kitchen had a grate that locked over it to secure shades. It wasn't always locked, since most of the shades were too drugged to escape and the Daughters had become complacent.

She wasn't sedated.

Yet. There might be a tiny window of opportunity, if she could just get past Sonja.

Ferris kept his gaze averted from her nudity and the back of his neck was ruddy. Most of the shades were nude in the netherzones, so Twenty-three didn't know why he was shy around her. She knew he had a violent dislike of the sight of blood.

"You won't get away," Sonja murmured, her gaze still fixed on the filling syringe. "You're smart enough to know that by now."

Ferris fidgeted as he looked between the two women.

"I don't understand you." Twenty-three feigned a yawn and pretended to be exhausted. "Can I sleep now?"

Sonja gave Twenty-three a sharp look. "You're a lousy liar, child, and I wasn't born yesterday."

"I don't understand." Twenty-three stayed at the back of the room. Sonja would have to come to her, which meant she'd leave the doorway. Twenty-three could get past her, trip Ferris, then run for freedom.

She'd only get one chance. She dropped her gaze to hide her anticipation and let her mouth go slack.

"If you were going to lie, you should have lied tonight, to the Daughter Superior." Sonja pulled the syringe out of the vial. The needle shone gold in the lantern's light. She gave Twenty-three a hard look. "Have I taught you nothing about appearances in all these years?"

"What are app-app-appearances?" Twenty-three asked, speaking slowly and in a confused tone.

Inwardly, she seethed.

She should be luckier than this.

Anyone should be luckier than this.

Sonja snorted. "Too late for that game, child." She strode

toward Twenty-three, the needle held high, leaving the doorway.

She took one step.

Two.

Three.

Four.

Twenty-three lunged at the older woman, giving her a shove on the way. Sonja stumbled and Twenty-three ran for the doorway. Ferris recoiled, putting his hands before his face.

He was going to let her go!

Twenty-three could taste liberty. She grabbed the door frame and saw the glint of light at the top of the stairs to the kitchen.

But Sonja was fast and Sonja was strong. She leapt after Twenty-three and locked one arm around the younger woman's neck. Her forearm pressed against Twenty-three's windpipe. Twenty-three choked and stumbled, and that moment of weakness was enough.

Sonja flung Twenty-three to the floor with surprising force. The breath was driven out of Twenty-three's lungs when she landed on her back. She hit her head on the floor and saw stars. In that one beat of her disorientation, Sonja stepped astride her and sat down across her hips.

Sonja was solid and determined. Twenty-three flailed, but it was too late. Sonja's weight held Twenty-three captive as she drove the needle into Twenty-three's belly. Twenty-three struggled, swinging her arms and kicking with all her might. She knew it was futile, but was unable to stop herself. She couldn't dislodge Sonja's weight, but still she tried.

The old woman was just too heavy.

"Not fair!" Twenty-three roared, abandoning her guise of being stupid.

Sonja threw the syringe across the floor. It clattered in the corner as Sonja slapped Twenty-three hard across the face. The pain made her gasp.

"Don't make it worse!" the old woman hissed, her features sharp as she leaned close to whisper. "Do you think they can't hear us? Do you think they don't *listen?*"

Twenty-three was shocked to silence by the older woman's words. She felt the familiar lethargy of the Ivanofor slide through her body and hated it. She felt betrayed by her own body as her muscles slackened. It would only be moments before she couldn't even be able to speak coherently.

But her mind would be normal, unfettered, chafing at the injustice. She despised this drug and knew the Daughters chose it on purpose. They wanted their shades to be cognizant of their captivity and of the Daughters' power over them. They were sadistic and evil.

Twenty-three hated them all.

Especially Sonja.

Sonja sat back then, confident that the drug had taken effect. Twenty-three could barely move. A great roar of fury built within her, but she couldn't make a sound.

Meanwhile, Sonja scolded her. "I've tried to teach you. I've tried to persuade you to show some sense. Do you think it's an accident that you're a shade who is so different from all the others? You didn't come to us the same way. You were brought to me, and I took you in out of mercy. It hasn't been easy to keep the other Daughters from noticing you and your differences."

Twenty-three listened, because she had no choice.

Sonja leaned closer. "Do you think it's easy to hide a person being hunted by the Republic? Do you think it's easy to make a child disappear? Do you imagine for a moment that you could have survived these nine years without my help?"

Twenty-three's skepticism must have shown because Sonja's eyes flashed.

Her words came low and hot with anger. "If you imagine so, then think again. I've kept you safe, but you threw that all away tonight. I thought you were smart enough to understand who was your ally, but perhaps I underestimated you." Her eyes narrowed. "Do you really think it was an accident that you didn't get your sedatives for the past two days?"

Twenty-three stared at the older woman in shock.

"Yes. I managed that. It wasn't a mistake. I thought you might be able to escape if you were lucid. I thought you might be able to slip unobserved from the Citadel in the activity to-night. I thought it was time to give you an opportunity." Sonja grimaced. "But no. You had to draw attention to yourself. You had to destroy my plan for you. You had to alert them all to the jewel in the dung heap."

Twenty-three tried to argue her case, but all that came from her lips was an incoherent moan. She wanted to spit. She wanted to fight, to defend herself, to run.

Instead, she lay captive on the floor, held powerless by an old woman armed with a syringe. If Sonja had had a plan for her, the old woman should have told her about it.

It wasn't her fault that the angels had come to her.

"There is no turning back, no way to change the course of events." Sonja stood and pointed a gnarled finger at Twenty-three. "Make no mistake, child, this choice was yours."

Twenty-three made a gurgling sound of protest.

"There is *always* a choice," Sonja snapped. "You felt the vi-sion coming. You must have. So powerful a prophecy doesn't come unannounced. Do you think I don't know?"

Twenty-three could only glare at the old woman.

Sonja dropped her voice to a growl. "You knew, and you chose to let it claim you, in a public meeting, in front of the Daughter Superior. You could have held back until you were in a safer place. You could have trusted me, you could have let things be resolved easily, but you left me with no choice."

Twenty-three wanted to argue. Why should she have trusted Sonja? Why should she believe that Sonja would do anything other than what she always did, that she would come with any-thing other than that cursed drug? How could she have known Sonja's plan without being told it?

"You had the third eye," Sonja leaned close to hiss and Twenty-three's heart stopped cold that the old woman knew this part of her truth. "Just because it was removed doesn't mean that the power of foresight it gave you is gone."

How did Sonja know Twenty-three's secret? There was no scar from the removal of her third eye, no physical evidence remaining of its existence.

Did Sonja know about the angels too?

Even more important, what was Sonja going to do about it?

"We could have resolved this quietly." Sonja shrugged as she stood. "Now, *she* won't let it be any other way. Optimism has betrayed you." She shook her head. "You should have known, child, that hope has no place in this world."

Sonja stepped back and looked down at Twenty-three, pity in her expression. "So, now you must die."

Twenty-three saw a silver flash as Ferris passed a kitchen knife to Sonja. She struggled to scream as Sonja came to her side and lifted the knife high.

No! Sonja bent over her.

Maybe the old woman *was* mad.

Maybe the Daughters wouldn't let their plan to install a false Oracle be so easily thwarted.

Twenty-three wanted to save herself, but the drug held her in its potent grasp. All she could do was watch. Even Ferris simply watched. There was no one to help her, no chance of salvation. She would die in this hellhole, just as she had been compelled to live in it.

That silent scream of rage grew to a crescendo within her.

"Good-bye, Twenty-three," Sonja whispered. The blade gleamed. Twenty-three panicked as the knife descended toward her.

She was powerless to Sonja's whim.

She was going to die, before she had ever had the chance to live.

Worse, there was nothing she could do about it.

THE BOY'S reaction stopped Rafe from intervening.

Rafe lurked in the shadows of the netherzones and watched the scene in the lit storeroom. There were shades working beneath the kitchen, but their eyes were glazed and their motions mechanical. Unless he stood in their way, they were oblivious to his presence.

When they found him in their path, they simply halted and waited for the obstacle to be removed. Their despondency tore at Rafe's heart, given all that life had to offer to humans, but he had other obligations in this netherzone.

The light was meager, with just one lantern in the storeroom where he had discovered the older woman and Delilah. There was a faint glimmer pouring down the stairs from the kitchen above.

He'd arrived in time to hear part of their discussion, to hear the old woman chiding Delilah and to see Delilah's splendid nudity. She was lean and strong, her breasts and hips sweetly curved. He'd stopped cold at that sight, shocked again that the child he was charged to defend was a woman.

And what a woman. She was unlike any he'd seen or savored. Delilah's beauty was sharp and dangerous, as admirable as a skillfully made knife honed to precision. She was both younger and leaner than her mother, but still graced with full feminine curves.

Temptation made flesh.

She was too pale and too thin, but her defiance and her beauty struck him to the core. It was abominable that she should have been consigned to darkness and servitude.

It was outrageous that her voice would be silenced.

Delilah had bolted suddenly, her eyes wild with fear and determination in the line of her lips. Rafe thought about catching her, but the old woman had moved with surprising speed. She'd flung Delilah down hard and jammed the needle into her stomach.

There was affection in her diatribe, so Rafe assumed that the syringe contained a sedative. And the boy, the boy's gaze was both locked on Delilah and filled with yearning. If he didn't love Delilah, Rafe understood nothing of people.

Rafe held his position in the shadows, watching as Delilah went limp. Her eyes were bright as the woman lectured her and he guessed that she understood what was happening.

She simply couldn't do anything about it.

Hideous.

When the old woman raised the knife, Rafe pulled his laze and stepped closer, intending to intervene.

But the boy, the boy who gazed at Delilah with undisguised adoration, watched impassively. That made Rafe hesitate.

The boy wasn't surprised.

Or afraid for Delilah.

Rafe froze. He'd already removed the safety on his laze, but the boy's reaction made him wonder what he was truly witnessing. If the boy had to choose between the old woman and Delilah, Rafe was certain he would choose Delilah.

Which meant that this assault had been planned.

Which meant that the older woman was not killing Delilah, or even injuring her seriously.

What *was* she doing?

Delilah moaned as the blade sliced into the back of her neck.

The location of the incision and its shallow cut told Rafe everything he needed to know. He'd been right to wait.

Rafe watched as the old woman worked with the expertise of one familiar with a knife. She pushed her fingers into the wound, worked the identification bead loose from Delilah's neck, and withdrew it with triumph. The glass bead was slick with blood but glistened in the light when the old woman tossed it onto the floor.

The boy crushed it under the heel of his boot.

The old woman had bidden Twenty-three farewell, because Twenty-three—evidently the name used for Delilah in this place—was ceasing to exist.

Brilliant. Rafe watched, wondering what identity the old woman would give Delilah.

The answer was so startling that he nearly revealed himself.

III

WITHOUT RISING to her feet, the older woman then drew the sharp edge of the knife across the back of her own neck.

Rafe was shocked, then realized her intention.

Her own blood flowed over her hands and she grimaced, though Rafe didn't know whether it was due to frustration or to pain. She slashed at her neck more aggressively to make the wound deeper and her face paled. She looked much older, but no less resolved. Rafe understood that the angle made it difficult for her to free her own identification bead—what she lacked in dexterity, she made up for with sheer will.

With trembling fingers, she worked the glass bead out from beneath her flesh. She held it toward the boy, her manner imperious. He had fetched a bottle and opened it hurriedly. He splashed a clear liquid across the identification bead.

Rafe caught a whiff of alcohol.

The older woman shoved the wet bead under Delilah's skin with strong fingers. Rafe winced, knowing the alcohol would burn in the wound. Delilah's entire body shook, despite the muscle relaxant she'd been given. The old woman held the wound closed with one bloody thumb.

Her own blood trickled down her throat in a crimson river as the old woman sutured Delilah's wound. The boy anticipated her needs with an efficiency that made Rafe wonder how many times they had done this before.

Every occupant of the Republic had an identification bead embedded in the back of the neck. The bead contained the identity of the individual, as well as key biographic details.

No one could hide in the Republic without rewriting the information on that identification bead.

Or exchanging the identification bead for another.

Both processes were illegal, of course, but that didn't mean they never happened. Rafe was intrigued to find the law being broken with such calm confidence within the Citadel of the Daughters of the Light of the Republic.

Did the old woman act alone, or was she completing an assignment? What else happened in this remote place, beyond the watchful gaze of the Republic? And what made the Daughters so certain that they could break the law without repercussion?

From the exchange in the chapel, he was fairly certain that this old woman was outside of the Daughter Superior's confidence.

Or was that an act?

Like the sham of choosing the Oracle?

Delilah had closed her eyes, and Rafe thought he saw the sparkle of tears on her cheeks. He would have guessed that she felt betrayed and frustrated. But it was a clever scheme, one that would give her an identity other than her own; one that would help Rafe to hide her.

The boy hadn't intervened because the exchange was for Delilah's benefit.

The old woman, meanwhile, wiped her hands once Delilah's wound was closed and bandaged, but didn't rise to her feet. She removed the probe from her palm, and lifted Delilah's limp left hand. She meshed their left hands together so that the gap between the third and fourth fingers touched.

Their skin didn't quite make contact, because the probe from the old woman's palm snicked into the port in Delilah's palm, located at that spot.

She was datasharing with Delilah. The old woman tapped at her own palm, programming a download.

The boy averted his gaze, the back of his neck turning red. Rafe could understand his shyness—it was rare to witness a datashare. Many citizens regarded a datashare to be as

intimate as sex—maybe more so, because there were no secrets that could be hidden from an inquisitive palm. Lovers
often used the datashare as a final surrender and mark of com-
mitment, although Rafe had never permitted anyone to inter-
act with his unruly palm.

But there was no joy in this particular union. The older
woman was brisk and efficient, while Delilah was livid.

He could see the truth in her flashing eyes.

She probably would have compared this datashare to a
rape.

And in a way, it was. The older woman had to be changing
the data on Delilah's palm to match the identification bead.
She would be eliminating Delilah's identity, replacing it with
her own.

Bead and palm would concur that Delilah was the old
woman.

Rewriting the identification sector on the palm wasn't a legal operation, and Rafe wasn't even certain where one would
buy the bootleg software to make the transition possible.

Which meant that the old woman had prepared for this
moment.

For how long?

Rafe was impressed by the scheming necessary to violate
the Republic's laws so efficiently, and to do so without having raised suspicion. The faint blue light of the displays of the
two palms gave the old woman's features a diabolical look as
she tapped in her commands. Her palm clicked and beeped as
it executed the exchange. She took the time to be thorough
and Rafe appreciated that she was making his quest so much
simpler.

It would be easier to hide Delilah with a different identity.

In the shadows, Rafe could still see the dark number tattooed on Delilah's left forearm. That tattoo worried him. It
would be the only evidence of her former shade status, and
one glimpse of it by an authority would condemn her, under-
mining everything the old woman was doing.

How was he going to get rid of her tattoo?

There were surgeons who specialized in such work, but

reconstructive surgery took time and money. Rafe had no time to spare. Did the old woman have a plan for the tattoo too? If so, Rafe would have liked to have known what it was.

Rafe had a moment to dread the possibilities, a heartbeat to wonder whether the Republic truly was oblivious to the old woman's scheme, then the old woman pulled out her probe.

"All of the circles must be closed, child," the old woman whispered, her eyes filled with fire. "I know you can hear me so I bid you listen."

Delilah opened her eyes the merest slit and Rafe saw the bright light of her anger.

She didn't yet realize the gift she'd been given.

"Few know where the power of prophecy lurks," the old woman continued in a low tone that Rafe had to strain to hear. "I have it. You have it. It is not an easy blessing to endure, but its truth must be protected. It cannot be defended in a place like this—only hidden." She sighed. "But you revealed it, and eyes have seen. I am giving you every advantage I can, even though the odds are formidable." She swallowed. "It won't be easy, but Ferris will help you. This is the only choice."

Delilah's eyes glittered.

The old woman pursed her lips. "On this day, I had a vision myself, but I wasn't so stupid as to let anyone witness it. Dangerous gifts should be disguised. That's why I said you should have lied. In this place, in this time, it would have been the prudent choice." She half laughed. "But I'm not so old that I don't remember what it's like to not care about prudence."

The old woman dug in the pocket of her robe and removed a bundle of dried leaves, knotted with twine. "I work the old way, with the old tools. Maybe it's safer that way." She glanced around herself then, her move so sudden that she might have heard something.

She stared directly at Rafe and he froze.

He expected her to raise an alarm.

Instead, she nodded and turned her attention back to Delilah. "Maybe it's not. Maybe neither of us are truly prudent." She shrugged. "Maybe that's the price of the gift. Maybe the divine truly does work in mysterious ways."

She tied the cluster of leaves to Delilah's wrist, firmly but gently. "This is my last gift to you," she said, that affection returning to her tone. "This is what came to me earlier today, a sign that the end was not only coming but had arrived. All along, I knew that you might be the one. You have proven it to me, but you shall have to prove it to many to gain your rightful place. I have done my part, at least." She bent and kissed Delilah's cheek. "May God be with you, child."

Delilah closed her eyes.

The older woman pushed to her feet. She pulled another vial from her own pocket, one with different markings from the first. The boy made a wordless protest, but if he would have intervened, the old woman's glare stopped him cold.

"All the circles must be closed, Ferris," she told him softly, as she filled another syringe. "You know what to do."

The boy fidgeted.

She gave him a hard look. "Don't you?"

He swallowed and nodded, standing straighter.

"Then don't betray me now." Her voice softened. "Don't betray she who was known as Twenty-three."

Ferris set to work. He moved around the room with the bottle of alcohol, splashing its contents on rags and wooden boxes until it was empty. Rafe saw that flammable items were strategically positioned around the perimeter of the small room.

Accident or design? Rafe could guess.

Meanwhile, the old woman stood directly under the lantern. She filled the syringe, then lifted the hem of her skirts. She poked at her ankle, found the blue shadow of a vein, then slid the needle into it with assurance. She emptied the syringe and winced as she pulled the needle out of her skin.

She straightened and squared her shoulders, flinging the syringe into the shadows with defiance.

The boy stifled a sob, but the old woman put a hand on his head and ruffled his hair. "It is done," she said with some tenderness. "My time was nearly over anyway. Finish what we have begun."

He nodded, his tears scattering.

"You will find allies in the most unlikely of places." Her voice dropped. "Protect yourself, Ferris. You will not survive *them* again."

The boy caught his breath, then the old woman kissed his cheeks in turn. This show of affection between a norm and a shade was surprising, but then, it was unwitnessed by other norms.

She even called him by a name. Ferris.

The old woman closed her eyes and looked suddenly fatigued. Rafe guessed that she was feeling the effect of whatever drug she had given herself.

Ferris collected the syringes and the bottles, putting them into the waste compressor on the far side of the netherzones. Rafe stepped into deeper shadows when the boy left the storeroom.

Tears ran unchecked over Ferris' cheeks as he fulfilled the old woman's plan. Rafe remained out of his way, watching. Ferris lifted Delilah to one shoulder and carried her to the foot of the stairs, placing her gently there. The boy was stronger than he looked.

And just as smitten as Rafe had imagined. He leaned down to look at Delilah, touching her cheek with a fingertip, but she kept her eyes resolutely closed. The boy caught his breath, seemingly struck right to the heart by her rejection.

Rafe knew her choice was deliberate.

Once Delilah had been moved away, the old woman lifted down the lantern and removed the shade. She tossed the lantern toward an alcohol-soaked rag and it shattered, the fire leaping to the new fuel. Rafe knew he didn't imagine the triumph in the glance she cast upward.

"Let this abomination be destroyed," she whispered with vigor.

Then she fell to her knees and folded her hands before herself. She began to recite the Lord's Prayer as the flames burned higher and hotter all around her. He saw her silhouetted in orange, heard the anger in her voice, and knew he would never forget the sight of her.

"Our Father, who art in heaven,
Hallowed be thy name . . ."

Rafe understood. She was killing herself, to disguise the fact that her identification bead was gone. It would take time to identify a burned body, time to establish what identity Delilah had taken, time that gave Delilah a chance to flee.

She'd done all she could for Delilah.

She'd done more than most. Her sacrifice was humbling.

Rafe would do the rest.

The flames burned, high and bright, the old woman's voice resonating in the netherzones.

"Thy kingdom come, thy will be done
On earth as it is in heaven . . ."

Ferris slammed the door to the storeroom and locked it from the outside. Darkness engulfed the netherzones, darkness lit on the edges with the fire's orange glow. He choked back a sob as he stepped away, and tried to rub the tears from his face.

Rafe stepped squarely into his path, keeping him from returning to Delilah's side. The boy froze in shock.

"Well done," Rafe said softly. "But I'll take her from here."

The boy's gaze dropped to the muzzle of Rafe's laze.

"For thine is the kingdom,
The power, and the glory . . ."

There was a moment while they assessed each other, a moment while the fire in the storeroom crackled to an inferno.

Rafe removed the safety from his laze and knew the boy heard the click. Ferris gritted his teeth and relaxed his stance, unhappy with his choice but having made it. Rafe eased closer to Delilah as Ferris watched with obvious resentment.

The old woman's voice became more vehement as she finished the prayer.

"For ever and ever . . ."

Rafe reached Delilah's still form, his fingertips grazing her hip, just as the wooden walls of the storeroom were engulfed in flames. The alcohol and tinder were catching, raging with furious flames. The netherzones lit with brilliant orange so suddenly that Rafe blinked. Ferris flinched as he ducked away from the burning storeroom.

"Amen!" the old woman roared.

Then an explosion rocked the building.

An explosion?

Rafe looked upward in confusion.

He sensed motion, pivoted, saw Ferris leaping toward him and fired.

TWENTY-THREE WANTED to scream but she couldn't. She couldn't speak, she couldn't move, she couldn't make a sound. Her body was drugged, but her thoughts flew like quicksilver.

She had given a prophecy at the wrong time.

Sonja had given her a new identity.

Sonja was killing herself in an auto-da-fé, one that would eliminate every trace of evidence of what she had done. The fire raged in the storeroom just yards away, the sparks already dancing toward the old wooden walls.

A roar had shaken the building overhead, rattling the structure to its foundations. The ceiling still vibrated over their heads and Twenty-three feared that the netherzones would collapse.

And she would die within its debris.

Worse, the golden hunter had found her. Twenty-three was terrified. It would be better to die in this inferno than to be sent to the research labs of the Society of Nuclear Darwinists.

She'd narrowly escaped that fate once before.

She saw Ferris attack the hunter, but knew it was a bad idea. The hunter was armed and dangerous, while Ferris had only passion on his side. She wanted to shout a warning, but knew she couldn't.

The hunter, in contrast to herself, wasn't paralyzed.

He pivoted and fired at Ferris so quickly that Ferris didn't have the chance to touch him. Twenty-three closed her eyes against the brilliant white blast from his laze and feared the worst.

But there was no cry of pain.

There was no smell of burning flesh.

Twenty-three opened her eyes to find Ferris backed against the far wall of the netherzones. His shirt was singed on his right shoulder and there was a laze mark smouldering on the wall behind him. His eyes were wide and he was breathing quickly. Twenty-three could almost smell his fear. The fire in the storeroom crackled three steps away from him, lighting his face with orange and yellow.

He didn't move.

"I said I would take her from here," the hunter repeated calmly. He still kept his laze trained on Ferris, and Twenty-three understood that he had missed on purpose.

Why? Why had he let Ferris live?

The hunter flicked a triumphant glance her way, his eyes dancing, and Twenty-three's mouth went dry. She was keenly aware of his masculinity and his vigor, never mind the intoxicating glimmer of his eyes.

His confidence alone could have beguiled her.

But she didn't know what he wanted.

She was nude on the netherzone floor, and glad that she couldn't feel its dampness, couldn't smell the wet earth. Would he shoot her naked? Would he rape her? She supposed it would be a blessing to not be able to feel that violation.

It would be horrible to endure, helpless to defend herself.

She would have preferred to have run, even if she'd been hunted and cornered and attacked. She would have preferred to have had a chance.

"Here. Now." The hunter spoke tersely, beckoning Ferris

with his laze. Before Twenty-three could imagine his scheme, he removed his cloak with one hand and cast it over her body. It obscured her vision, engulfing her in darkness and scent.

The hunter smelled clean, of soap and fresh air, an evocative combination that reminded Twenty-three all too clearly of the days before she had come to the Citadel.

Before she worked in darkness and filth.

She was certain that the faux-fur must be soft and warm, but she was numb. It was bad enough to smell cleanliness, and the scent brought tears to her eyes.

She had lost so much. Could she truly lose more?

Didn't the angels care?

Ferris rolled her in the cloak under the hunter's instruction, and fastened it closed. When the hood fell back, Twenty-three saw that his hands were shaking and his face was red. When he was done, she was on her back, staring up at the golden hunter.

He smiled at her and she was sure he winked.

As if they were coconspirators.

No. As if he knew that her mind raced unchecked but her body was paralyzed.

What else did he know about her? Twenty-three remembered how he had watched her, how the brilliant light had seemed to emanate from him in the chapel, and wondered again who he was.

Meanwhile, the hunter gestured with his laze and Ferris stepped back with reluctance. The hunter picked up Twenty-three as if she weighed nothing at all and cast her over his shoulder. He backed up the stairs, keeping his laze trained on Ferris. "Keep back," he murmured, his voice so low that Twenty-three barely heard it.

Ferris whimpered and took a step forward. The hunter fired at his feet and Ferris leapt back again.

"No one will stop me now," the hunter said with a quiet determination that made Twenty-three shiver. "Don't imagine otherwise."

He spun at the top of the stairs, as light on his feet as a dancer, or an athlete. Twenty-three glimpsed Ferris gazing after them, his hands twitching, and feared what he would do.

The hunter checked the main floor and didn't look back. He strode through the kitchen with purpose, heading straight for the back door. He kicked the grate but it was locked.

"Close your eyes," he said tersely and Twenty-three realized he was talking to her.

He was more observant than most. She'd have to remember that.

She did as she was told, then heard the searing blast of the laze being fired. He kicked the grate again and she heard the creak as it opened. The lock was smoking when he stepped through the door, and Twenty-three realized he'd shot off the lock.

She would have liked to have done that herself.

Her excitement rose when she saw the kitchen door behind them. He was carrying her away from this place! She wished she could feel the cool caress of the night—it always lifted her spirits with the promise of freedom.

On the other hand, she was captive and helpless, claimed by a hunter whose scheme couldn't be good.

She refused to be pessimistic. There *was* room for hope in the Republic, despite what Sonja said. Somehow she would escape the hunter. Somehow she would fulfill her destiny.

She wished she knew how much Ivanofor Sonja had given her, how much time she had to endure the paralysis before the drug's effects wore off. She chafed to run, to seize this opportunity, and hated that the hunter would be making all of her decisions in the short term.

She doubted he'd make the same ones she would make, but she'd have to live with it.

At least she'd be away from the Citadel by the time she could run on her own.

He strode into the clearing beyond the kitchen and halted as if surprised. Twenty-three expected the darkness to close around them and hide them, but instead the clearing was ablaze with light. It could have been midday instead of midnight. The hunter pivoted to look as if he was also confused. She had a dizzying glimpse of the entire complex consumed in flames.

The Citadel was burning. The sight defied belief. Twenty-three couldn't make sense of it. The fire in the netherzones couldn't have spread that far that fast.

A second explosion echoed from the far end of the dormitory, sending new plumes of fire and smoke into the night. The hunter ducked and swore, sheltering her with his body.

When he straightened, Twenty-three saw flames rise from the dormitory.

Had the Citadel been bombed? The evidence before her eyes made her wonder, though she couldn't imagine why. She would have liked to have destroyed the place, but didn't imagine anyone with the power to do so would agree.

Except that the Citadel *was* burning.

The hunter took one look at the fire and swore vehemently. He ran, ducking lower as he headed for the protective cover of the surrounding forest. Twenty-three's weight slid from his shoulder to his left arm but he didn't slow down.

She understood that he wasn't in league with whoever was responsible for the destruction.

Women screamed far behind and she looked over his shoulder. Daughters and acolytes streamed from the buildings in their white robes. They milled in the courtyard, not knowing where to turn. The buildings burned so quickly that they might have been anointed with alcohol, just like the storeroom in the netherzones.

To Twenty-three's shock, men appeared in the shadows, men in black pseudoskins with their helms down. *Men?* In the Citadel? They weren't firefighters because they did nothing to halt the blaze. They wore uniforms, though, and could have been policemen or military men.

Why did the hunter run? Everyone knew that the Society of Nuclear Darwinists—and its shade hunters—worked in unison with the Republic.

But this hunter ran away from the Republic's troops.

A man in black cornered one of the acolytes as Twenty-three watched. The pair was silhouetted against the flames, their actions evident even from a distance. The distraught woman fell to her knees, hands clasped before herself as if she prayed for salvation.

There was none to be had. The man waved his palm over her neck, then checked its display.

Twenty-three caught her breath. He'd scanned her identification bead.

He was looking for someone.

Her mouth went dry in realization of the gift Sonja had given her.

Then the man fired his laze directly at the acolyte's head, shocking Twenty-three. It wasn't an accident. He held the blast until her body had fallen, been destroyed beyond recognition and stopped twitching.

Then he targeted another woman, repeating the exercise.

Meanwhile, Twenty-three's captor ran.

Why the hunt? As much as Twenty-three disliked the spoiled and demanding acolytes, none of them deserved this fate. She wondered what Sonja had seen in her vision earlier in the day, whether she had guessed what was coming.

She wanted to unknot that bundle of leaves immediately, to read what Sonja had prophesied, but couldn't.

They were close to the forest's shadows when Twenty-three heard the dogs. She panicked at the sound.

Only shade hunters used hunting dogs—and they used them to harvest shades. She had always suspected that the Society kept its dogs hungry. They were vicious beasts, trained to maim and kill fugitive shades, which by law deserved no clemency.

Twenty-three was a shade and now she was a fugitive. She had the tattoo to prove her shade status, regardless of what identity Sonja had given her.

Twenty-three peered over the hunter's shoulder. She saw Ferris at the threshold of the kitchen door. She saw his lips set as he crossed the broken grate and made himself a fugitive as well.

He hadn't heard the dogs.

She wanted to warn him and strained to scream with everything she had. She couldn't make a sound. Twenty-three was terrified for him.

Ferris loped after the hunter, his old satchel swinging from his shoulder and his boots slapping against the ground. He moved faster now that his choice was made, speeding from a walk to a run.

It wasn't enough.

The dogs leapt around the corner of the kitchen building, growling and snapping. Ferris glanced back, his terror clear, too late to save himself.

Twenty-three fought to scream a warning.

It was futile, but she couldn't just watch Ferris be shredded alive.

THE CITADEL had been constructed in a U shape, the buildings surrounding a courtyard on three sides. The kitchen was at the tip of one arm and the dormitory formed the entire opposite arm. The chapel was in the far corner, forming the junction between the dormitories and the base of the U. The land was cleared for maybe a hundred feet around the Citadel, then deep forest closed tightly around the clearing. The only road cut through the woods directly to that front entrance, which was on the outside at the base of the U.

Once he stepped out the kitchen door, Rafe realized that he was just inside the central courtyard. He was shocked to see the fire so widespread and faltered momentarily. The chapel was in flames, even though the fire that Ferris had lit in the kitchen netherzones couldn't have spread that quickly.

When the second explosion rocked the dormitory, Rafe understood what he had heard earlier.

The Citadel was being bombed.

Why? By whom?

The force of the second explosion made the end of the dormitory collapse. The adjacent structure fell like a line of dominoes until roof of the chapel fell in. Only the bell tower arching high over the entrance remained standing, like a defiant finger pointing heavenward.

Plumes of smoke billowed into the night sky, disappearing into the low clouds, as the fire leapt from one building to the next. It was a conflagration, and Rafe could already see that there'd be nothing left standing. The best that could be hoped for was that the forest wouldn't catch. To his relief, the court-yard was filling with women from inside the Citadel.

Helmeted men in black pseudoskins emerged from the smoke and shadows. Rafe watched in dawning horror, seeing that they were scanning identification beads before executing women, and guessed their mission.

They sought one specific woman.

Delilah.

Rafe bolted. The blaze of the buildings eliminated any shadows that might have hidden his escape. He couldn't hide. He couldn't disappear. He could only hope he wouldn't be seen and run as fast as he could.

Rafe swung Delilah down into his left arm, hoping to hide her presence with his own silhouette, and ran with all his might for the forest's protective shadows.

He hated that he couldn't help the other women. He was a good shot, but Rafe knew that he was vastly outnumbered. He couldn't fight with a sedated Delilah on his shoulder. He couldn't save her if he was dead or even injured in the defense of others.

He had to complete his mission and trust that he was serving the greater good.

Rafe had no real choice, but he didn't have to like it.

The darkness of the forest seemed impossibly far away. His body was pumping with adrenaline and he was running faster than ever, but Rafe felt exposed and vulnerable.

The dogs barked from behind him. Rafe heard the men shout to each other as the hounds were released. He reached for his laze, because dogs could be fast, even as he hurled himself onward.

He heard the women scream, the lazes being fired with sickening regularity, and the hungry crackle of the fire.

He heard the shout when he was spotted, and then the snarl of a dog in pursuit. He heard the pad of those canine feet, closing fast.

He felt more than heard Delilah's increased anxiety.

He glanced back to find Ferris running toward them, a satchel on his shoulder and determination in his expression.

And Rafe understood. The old woman had bidden Ferris to complete her plan.

To help Delilah.

His command that the boy stay put was nothing compared to that.

A dog had separated itself from pack that came around the end of the kitchen. The hound lunged after the boy, fangs bared, spit dripping.

The hunter was right behind it, but there was no leash. The dog's shape was silhouetted against the blaze, its teeth shining as it leapt for Ferris' back.

The dog was unrestrained and trained to kill.

Rafe spun, aimed his laze, and fired.

The shot must have grazed Ferris, or at least surprised him, because he stumbled.

The dog's body fell heavily to the ground.

It twitched once and didn't move again.

Ferris caught his footing and ran for Rafe, his eyes wide with terror.

The hunter behind the dog swore and pulled his own laze.

He aimed at Rafe, but wasn't quick enough.

Rafe took him down a heartbeat after the dog.

Then he ran while he still had a chance.

Rafe had a feeling he wasn't going to be bored again anytime soon.

IV

RAFE WAS too angry to care what Ferris did, but wasn't surprised to hear the boy's footsteps close behind him.

There would be more hunters and more dogs, fast in pursuit, and this would be Rafe's only chance to disappear. It would be his only chance to hide Delilah.

It might not be good enough.

Fear was a sensation he would have been happy to avoid. It shot through him, filling his body with energy and chilling him at the same time.

Rafe had two fugitive shades to hide and defend, and he had shot a norm in cold blood. Any possibility of disguising his presence was gone. They were three fugitives—with a team of the Society's shade hunters and their dogs hot on the scent.

Never mind the commandos who had bombed the refuge. When those men finished executing every woman at the refuge without finding Delilah, Rafe knew what they'd do.

They'd expand the hunt.

His mission could have been going better. Rafe would be lucky to survive it, let alone complete it successfully.

Not for the first time, he wondered whom he was working for and what he had done to be put in such a situation. How had he earned this mission? How was he supposed to fulfill it? And why was he so terrified of failure?

That bank of silence in his mind didn't allay his fears.

Rafe forced himself to think positive. There was a chance that he'd left the hunters behind, a slight possibility that he'd lost the dogs. There was a glimmer of hope that he'd left the commandos behind.

He didn't slow his pace. He had to cover as much distance as possible, as soon as possible. He had to get farther faster to have any chance. The undergrowth snatched at his clothing, brambles tearing at his skin, but he didn't dare slow down.

The forest was an abomination, a wasteland of death and destruction. Rafe had never been in the wilderness, at least not as far as he recalled, and he disliked the sense that it offered true solitude. He didn't like the eyes of the Republic, but he did like the press of humanity around him. He liked the hustle and bustle of cities, no matter how dirty they were. He liked the sense that there was more than met the eye, that there were netherzones and pleasure fringes and lost corners of humanity to explore.

This forest offered none of that. It brooded and it troubled him. It might have been empty, completely lacking in human life. He might have been the first to step into it—or the last. He had a definite sense that his presence wasn't welcome.

Yet he didn't feel entirely unobserved.

The large trees were all dead, all devoid of leaves and many with blackened bark. A number had fallen over the years, lying dark and rotten on the forest floor. They were silent sentinels to what had been a place of vitality and life.

Their dark shadows were interspersed with raw young growth. It was all scrubby and yellow, weeds and bracken and brambles, none of it much taller than Rafe. A thick coating of ash had fallen over the forest, and Rafe's boots disturbed it as he walked. When he broke the surface, the ash rose like a cloud of gnats. He could smell it, knew he was breathing it, and refused to consider whether it was the radioactive fallout from the destruction of New Seattle.

And there was silence. Rafe had a sense that there should be animals in the forest, birds maybe, but this woodland was as silent as a tomb.

Rafe hated it with a virulence that surprised him. It made him think of death and annihilation, reminded him of a festering wound. He thought this might be how the world would be in the absence of the human race. Rafe didn't want to think about that prospect. For all their follies and weaknesses, he liked people. He wanted forests like this to disappear, not the human race, but hadn't the first idea how to make that happen.

The forest made him think of failure.

But what was behind them was worse.

The chapel tower fell with a crash as if to enforce that thought, the bell giving one last melancholy peal as it hit the earth. The fire at the Citadel burned so brightly that it illuminated Rafe's path even at this distance.

The reverb of laze shots was persistent.

It began to rain then, an icy, slithering rain that slanted out of the sky and soaked Rafe to the skin. At least the rain dampened down the ash. For the first time, Rafe was irritated with sensation, annoyed with discomfort, and impatient with the limitations of his body. He was furious that he couldn't even recall how he had come by this quest.

Especially as it might be the last thing he ever did.

Rafe saw a stream to his left, the running water glinting in the firelight. He strode into it and the cold water soaked through his faux-leather boots almost immediately. He didn't care. His boots would chafe his feet when wet, but he didn't care about that either.

The water would disguise his scent, and he needed every advantage he could get. Rafe strode onward, indifferent to the rolling stones underfoot, ignoring how much noise Ferris made, and dared to hope that his luck would change.

If nothing else, his situation couldn't get worse.

He believed that only until his palm chimed.

THE GOLDEN hunter had shot a norm.

Without hesitation.

Even more incredibly, he'd shot a shade hunter in order to save a fugitive shade.

Twenty-three was shocked, so shocked that she couldn't make sense of what she'd seen. If she hadn't seen it herself, she wouldn't have believed it. Hunters, in her experience, were competitive and utterly self-motivated, but not to the point of doing injury to each other.

She tried to figure out what she'd missed, what detail would solve the mystery, but had no success. He hadn't just wounded the other shade hunter—no, that man was as dead as his hunting dog. It hadn't been staged either—she'd smelled the burned flesh.

If her captor wasn't a shade hunter, then who was he?

At least he was surefooted. He moved with surety on the forest floor, even with the ash disguising whatever laid beneath. He didn't jostle her, but carried her as if she were a precious burden.

Maybe the Society wanted her alive.

But if he worked for the Society, surely he would have turned back to meet his fellows—instead of shooting one of them.

He was strong too, and he was determined. She liked that he hadn't hesitated to destroy the grate over the kitchen door, and that he was quick with his laze. There was a lot to admire about this mysterious man.

It would have been better to have known his motives.

Why had the hunter saved Ferris?

Her captor was a predator and a kidnapper, a man confident in his abilities. Given how accurately and quickly he'd killed the shade hunter, that confidence was deserved.

Why had he saved her?

Was he her ally or her enemy?

As the rain beat upon the leaves of the forest and the cool shadows cloaked the three of them, as the hunter strode to some unknown destination with an unknown motivation and Ferris ran behind, Twenty-three did the only thing possible.

She slept.

And a potent memory filled her dreams.

Later, she would wonder whether it was a portent of another kind.

Or maybe a message from an old friend.

THE LONELIEST child in the world has a new friend.
   Rachel.
   Rachel is beautiful. Rachel is kind. Rachel has stolen the

child away from the mill where she had to work so hard, where days blended into nights and the years ran together.

Rachel is unlike anyone she has ever known.

Rachel laughs.

Rachel smiles.

Rachel gives her hugs and touches her with affection.

Rachel makes her feel something funny, like a bubble in her belly. Rachel says that's happiness.

She only wants more.

There was only one bad thing that happened with Rachel, but it made her prettier. The ugly bump on her forehead is gone.

It barely hurt and besides, she saw the angels. Seeing the angels made it easy to bear the pain.

Rachel says soon she'll be a norm.

Rachel is magic.

Rachel has bought her ice cream. Rachel has bought her a wig with long dark hair, and promises that her own hair will grow and look the same. Rachel buys her pretty clothes. Rachel holds her hand. Rachel talks to her and takes her into the city.

Maybe Rachel is her mother.

The lonely child holds this idea close to her heart, keeping it safe and secret. Rachel is everything a mother should be, everything she has imagined her mother would be. Life with Rachel is a dream come true and she doesn't want to break the spell by asking too many questions.

Everything is perfect until the hunter comes.

She sees him right away. There is something about hunters, something that draws the eye. She can always spot them. Rachel calls it a learned response, but the lonely girl doesn't understand.

She spots this hunter.

Rachel says it's okay, but it's not.

He follows them all day. He sits in the restaurant where they eat and watches them. Just that he's there means that she doesn't want dessert. Not even ice cream. Nothing tastes good anymore.

She feels the shadow of bad things following them.

He trails behind them when they go back to the motel. She remembers the stars overhead. She remembers the sound of the cicadas. She remembers the skip of Rachel's pulse. She remembers the flicking red sign of the motel.

Vacancy.

Even when they're safe in the room, even when Rachel says they're safe, she knows he is out there. Waiting. It's not safe. No one is ever safe when there are hunters around. There is a lump in her throat and she can't sleep.

It is late when there is a knock on the door. It's a soft knock, but both she and Rachel hear it. They might both have been waiting for it. She doesn't want Rachel to answer the door.

But Rachel crosses the room to look through the peephole.

The little girl closes her eyes in terror. She knows what hunters do, where they go. She knows that they take and they destroy, but Rachel is brave. Rachel is strong.

Rachel opens the door.

She sees his silhouette, framed in the doorway with that red light beating behind him.

He is dangerous. He braces on hand on the door frame and leans in to whisper to Rachel. He is confident, dressed in sturdy gear, armed with two lazes and a smile intended to charm. His hair is dark and his complexion tanned. She still sees that smile in her dreams.

In her nightmares.

She knows better than to trust him.

She will never forget him.

But Rachel invites him into the room. Rachel smiles and laughs. Rachel says that the girl is asleep, to ignore the girl. Rachel touches his arm and the hunter's smile changes.

It makes the girl's heart race in fear.

It makes her want to hide.

She makes herself breathe in and out, in and out, in and out, all the while fearing that the hunter will hear her pounding heart.

Rachel draws the curtain to hide the big bed from the cot.

She pulls the hunter into that hidden space, her words low and husky. They chuckle together and make strange sounds. Zippers slide. Clothes fall. Someone catches a breath.

But the girl isn't asleep.

She opens her eyes and watches the shadows. She listens. And finally, she creeps from her cot to look.

She peeks around the edge of the drape. She knows she shouldn't look, knows she shouldn't see, but she is curious and fearful.

Rachel is kissing the hunter. He is half naked, alien and masculine and strong. Rachel is sitting in his lap, her skirt pushed up and his hand beneath the hem. They move as if Rachel is riding him. The hunter closes his eyes and groans. Rachel whispers, touches, kisses.

The hunter shouts and falls back. He is panting, but doesn't open his eyes.

And Rachel looks directly at the girl, so sure of the girl's location that she realizes she wasn't hidden at all.

"Run!" Rachel mouths.

The girl is trained to obey. Her body moves at the command, but she cannot leave Rachel. She cannot leave her friend with the hunter. She cannot run away, alone.

She shakes her head.

Rachel's eyes blaze. The little girl is shocked. Rachel has never been angry with her. Rachel has never scolded her.

Doesn't Rachel love her anymore?

The hunter awakens. Rachel moves to block his view, but it is too late. He shoves her aside. He has seen the girl.

Worse, he has seen her tattoo.

He roars and snatches at the girl.

She leaps backward. He's big. He's strong and he's fast. She squeals and scurries, trips over her own bed.

Rachel grabs the hunter from behind. Now she shouts "Run!"

"That's a fugitive shade!" the hunter cries and throws Rachel aside. She stumbles, fights him, and he hits her across

the face. Rachel falls, spinning even then to shield the child from him.

He catches her by the back of her dress, intending to fling her aside.

"Run!" Rachel screams.

This time, the girl runs to the door. She hears the dress rip and looks back as she pulls open the heavy door. The room is cast in flickering red light, but no one is chasing her anymore.

The hunter is staring at Rachel's back.

Rachel has closed her eyes and looks both sad and tired.

The hunter smiles. "One shade or another, it's all the same to me."

He pulls a syringe from the pouch on his belt. Rachel struggles. She fights and bites and screams. She is no match for the powerful hunter. He flings her on the bed and holds her down with one heavy hand.

Then he plunges the needle into her stomach.

Rachel, beautiful Rachel, still fights, but he steps back to watch. He puts his hands on his hips, watching her fight the drug. He smiles with a confidence that makes the girl shiver, then moves to lie on top of Rachel.

"One more for the road," he says.

Rachel shudders and falls still. Her eyes are open, though, wide open and fixed on the little girl.

A tear slides down her cheek.

The girl takes a step into the night, torn by her love for Rachel and her fear of being alone.

Rachel is still and her eyes are closed. She is sleeping, or maybe dead. The little girl stares as her heart breaks.

The hunter grunts, then lifts himself from Rachel. He fastens his pants, then reloads the syringe from a bottle.

He pulls the needle free and steps toward the door. His gaze fixes on the child.

"Next," he murmurs with that cold smile.

She knows where he will take her.

She knows how the story will end.

*She knows that this might be her only chance, understands
that this is the chance Rachel has paid to give her.*

This time, she runs.

TWENTY-THREE AWAKENED to find the hunter still running,
herself still captive on his shoulder. She couldn't tell if it was
darker or lighter, much less how much time had passed. She
still couldn't move her body, still couldn't influence her own
fate.

But she saw Rachel in her mind's eye, as clearly as if nine
years had dissolved in the blink of an eye.

Run.

There had been a time when she had had a friend.

When she had had a chance.

That chance had been lost, but Twenty-three had another
one. Maybe Rachel was warning her to make the most of opportunity. Maybe Rachel was reminding Twenty-three of the
risks, or insisting that her sacrifice not be wasted.

It didn't matter which it was—they were all reminders that
Twenty-three didn't need. She watched and she listened, her
impatience growing as she waited for her chance to shape her
own fate.

IN THE main room of a nondescript residential unit on the periphery of Nouveau Mont Royal, Adam Montgomery considered his bootleg desktop. It was a unit worthy of the circus
where his partner, Lilia Desjardins, worked, built of scrap
parts and contraband devices. Officially, it didn't exist, but it
gave Montgomery the ability to send messages to those within
his network of fallen angel volunteers.

Like Rafe.

Attuned to pirate frequencies, it should have only received
messages from a select array of individuals, all of whom
were known and trusted by Montgomery.

Despite that, it had received a missive marked URGENT,
from point and person unknown. The desktop indicated that

there was an attached vid-file. Even more ominous was the message's title:

DECISION TIME

Who could know codes to even send him a message without knowing who he was? Why would the sender's identity be cloaked?

Was it his superior, Tupperman, working from an insecure location? Montgomery couldn't believe it. Tupperman would have warned him.

Was it a phish, seeking more information from Montgomery, which he would unwittingly supply just by opening the missive?

Or did it include a viral worm?

Montgomery hated when there were no good answers. He was staring at the blinking cursor when Lilia returned home.

She was late, but he hadn't expected otherwise. She was dressed to adhere more or less to the Decency Code, at least, her full dark cloak covering the worst of her sins.

She'd gone to visit her mother and as much as he would have liked to have gone along, he knew their parting should be private. Lil's mother had declared the Republic too noxious for her taste, and was retreating to a northern refuge with her old friend Eva. They had resolved to take Micheline, the child in Lilia's custody, for her own safety.

Montgomery didn't doubt there'd be another argument about that, given Lil's fondness for the little girl and her sense of obligation to take care of her. Montgomery agreed with Lil's mother: Micheline had a third eye and she would be safer if farther away from the Republic's many eyes.

He expected Lil's spirits to be low on her return, but her eyes were bright with excitement. She came to his side, so full of bounce and enthusiasm that he was suspicious.

"Did you see?" she asked.

"See what?"

"The vidcast of the choice of the Oracle."

Montgomery frowned at her enthusiasm for this rite of the Republic. "You said it was fixed."

"It was," Lil pronounced with a satisfaction the situation didn't seem to deserve. "But something else happened first. Something wonderful."

She punched up the display on the official household vid, then perched on the arm of his chair. Her manner was so expectant that he was intrigued.

Montgomery's mouth fell open as a shade shrugged off her hood, took command of the ceremony, and pronounced a prophecy. Her eyes were as blue as Lilia's own, and her face had the same heart-shaped beauty. She was younger and thinner, taller perhaps, but the resemblance was unmistakable.

She looked to be possessed by angelfire, her face radiant with that strange light the angels had.

"Delilah," he whispered.

Lilia gripped his arm hard. "She's alive. I knew it all these years, but I couldn't believe it when I saw her. She's *alive!*" She gave him an enthusiastic kiss.

"What did your mother say?"

Lil rolled her eyes. "That she knew all along I'd lied to her. That she wanted the whole story, naturally."

"And?"

Lilia gave him a scathing glance. "As if that will happen."

"She can't have taken no for an answer."

"I told her I'd tell her when we saw each other next."

She sobered then and Montgomery understood the implication of her change of mood. Lil wasn't sure she would see her mother again. He took her hand in his, sensing her uncertainty when she immediately locked her fingers with his own.

"So, you won't tell me, then?"

Lil froze for a moment. Then she rose and tapped the vidscreen, manipulating the image so that Delilah's face filled the whole screen. Montgomery thought that she just wanted to really see her lost daughter, but he should have known by now that Lil was never so sentimental.

"What do you see?" she challenged.

"A young woman who must be your daughter."

She shook her head. "Look again."

Montgomery looked, but beyond the striking resemblance between the two, couldn't see anything of note. He indicated his confusion.

"Why was my child harvested from the maternity ward?" Lilia asked. "What made Max call the Society of Nuclear Darwinists?"

"She had a third eye," Montgomery remembered, then saw her point. "But she doesn't anymore. Are you sure it's her?"

"Who else could it be?" Lilia looked at the image, her expression assessing. "Someone removed it, and removed it so well that there isn't even a scar."

"That's incredible, Lil. Maybe it's not her . . ."

"Gid took care of it," she said firmly and he felt an unwelcome stab of jealousy for her dead ex-husband. "Gid took her to the Daughters of the Light of the Republic. He took her to that very Citadel. That much he told me."

"Why'd they take her in?"

"His aunt was Daughter Superior. He said she thought the shade was his child. As a Nuclear Darwinist with a promising career, he'd want her to disappear, if that was the case."

Montgomery watched Lil's expression soften as she looked at the image of her child. "My mother always watches for proof of the selection of a false Oracle: I watched in hope of a glimpse of her." Her expression was so filled with yearning that Montgomery's heart clenched.

"You never told me that before."

Her impish grin caught him by surprise. "I still have lots of secrets, Montgomery."

"That's what I'm afraid of."

She folded her arms across her chest to survey him. "It just might take you a lifetime to figure them all out."

"Speaking of which—"

Lil waved a hand, interrupting him. "Let's not argue. Not tonight." Her eyes filled with promise and her voice dropped. "Let's celebrate instead." Montgomery felt his body respond to her, as predictably as ever, and he didn't regret it one bit.

He moved to tap the screen into darkness, not yet ready to talk about the message with Lilia, but he didn't move quickly enough.

"What's that?" She was leaning over his shoulder, the silk of her hair against his cheek.

"I don't know. I'll think about it tomorrow."

"You should open it."

"I don't know who it's from, or how they found me."

"All the more reason to open it and find out." She moved to do so herself and Montgomery caught her wrist with one hand. "Still think you're faster than me, don't you?" she teased with a smile.

"Just barely."

"Sometimes that's enough."

"Sometimes I'm sure you're letting me win."

"I'll never admit to that. Open it."

Montgomery sighed. "Do you ever think about being cautious?"

Lil pretended to consider the idea, but Montgomery wasn't fooled. She shook her head almost immediately. "Not for longer than it deserves. Someone's going to take us down sooner or later, Montgomery. The timing is just a detail."

"I'd rather it be later than sooner."

"I'd rather see it coming."

He knew she was right. He gritted his teeth and tapped the screen to open the message. Just as he had suspected, that gesture launched the attachment.

Which was a vid.

It began with silence and darkness. Lil scowled at the display and leaned closer. "Can you make it brighter?"

No sooner had she spoken, than the image on the vid exploded into orange flames.

"Ask and you shall receive," Montgomery muttered.

"Very funny." Her eyes narrowed. "It's a building in the wilderness."

"A complex of buildings," he corrected. "And it's being bombed."

The vid was grainy and the view shook, as if it had been

shot from a palm. There was a second explosion and a plume of flames illuminated a bell tower with a cross on top of it.

"Wait a minute," Lil said. "I've seen that before."

There was a sound of women screaming, then white shapes began to spill out of the burning buildings. It was women or girls, in long white robes, and they clustered in what appeared to be a central courtyard in obvious fear.

"That's the Citadel, where they held the ceremony to choose the Oracle," Lil said, her voice rising in fear. "Those are the Daughters and the acolytes. When did this happen? Is there a time stamp?"

"None," Montgomery said. He felt cornered by the agenda of whoever had sent this, powerless to change the tempo of their presentation. He didn't like feeling so manipulated and knew Lil wouldn't take well to it either. "Where is the Citadel?"

"Near New Seattle." Lil was watching, her manner intent.

Dark figures emerged from the smoke and shadows. They were dressed in black and helmeted, indistinguishable from each other.

"Commandos?" Lil asked. "From the Republic?"

"Maybe they're the ones who bombed the buildings."

"But where did they come from? The Citadel is remote."

Montgomery didn't raise the issue of special ops and the secret equipment budgets they commanded. They could have even been dropped from aircraft: the secret forces had that much budget.

But why would the government care so much about the Citadel?

The men moved quickly to separate the frightened women so that each was alone. The vid centered on one such pair, recording how the woman fell on her knees before the commando. He raised his left hand over her neck, palm down.

"He's scanning her identification bead," Lil said unnecessarily.

"Only cops have scanners in their palms," Montgomery agreed. "They must be from the Republic."

"And what agency gets patched pseudoskins?"

She was right. Montgomery had no answer. Special ops had the latest and the best. He sharpened the focus but the truth was inescapable. The man's pseudoskin was undeniably cobbled and the helm was old issue. Was that just for camouflage?

The man meanwhile checked his palm, undoubtedly reading the name of the woman on her knees before him.

Both Lil and Montgomery jumped when he raised his laze and executed her.

Lil raised her hands to her face, her eyes wide. The commando held the burn until the woman was reduced to ash.

His fellows did the same thing to other women. Any who survived were trying to flee. The men hunted them down with military precision.

"They're killing all of them," Montgomery noted with horror. "But why?" He realized that they must be seeking one specific individual at the Citadel and he had a bad feeling as to whom that might be.

Hadn't Delilah just revealed her presence and her ability to give prophecies?

And she'd also suggested that the President had been murdered.

"Where's Delilah?" Lil whispered. She reached for Montgomery's arm, her fingers digging into his skin.

The vid swiveled as dogs barked at close proximity. Montgomery thought at first that whoever was recording the sequence of events was at risk, but the palm focused on a fleeing pair of figures.

A fair man carried something or someone on his shoulder as he ran for the woods. He was tall and broad and Montgomery dared to hope that Rafe had finally gotten his sorry butt to the Citadel.

It would be about time that Rafe followed his mission, and not for any lack of prompting on Montgomery's part.

Meanwhile, Lil's grip tightened on Montgomery's arm.

The dogs snarled and barked at closer range. The bundle on the man's shoulder slipped into his left arm, giving the vid a clear shot of her blue eyes as she stared over his shoulder. The man carrying her pivoted, grimaced, and fired.

"Rafe!" Lil said with relief.

The view spun so quickly that Montgomery was left with vertigo. A dog was bleeding and motionless on the ground, its teeth bared back in a grimace.

"Shade hunters and their mutts," Lil sneered.

The man with the dog pulled his laze to shoot after Rafe, but a blaze of light flashed. The hunter grunted and fell, the laze flying out of his hand. He didn't get up.

"Good riddance," Lil muttered.

The other hunters came around the end of the building with their dogs, and there was a sound of stumbling footsteps as the viewpoint swerved again.

They had a glimpse of Rafe and his burden leaping into the cover of the forest, and what looked like a teenage boy galloping behind them.

Then the image went black. Lil moved toward the display, her tension clear. He knew she was seeking a way to replay the vid.

But words in bright yellow appeared, burning against the dark display:

We worked for cash, no questions asked.

Now we have a question:
should the Oracle live or die?

The message lingered for a moment, then faded from view. Montgomery could almost see the words hovering in the darkness before him, then his desktop returned to its normal display.

There was no sign of the rogue message. He looked but he couldn't find it anywhere, or even any evidence that it had been received. He had a bad feeling that he had been targeted and nothing good could come of it.

"I don't like this," Montgomery muttered, then looked up

at Lil. Her face was pale, her eyes wide. He knew what she wanted to hear, what they needed to do, although he couldn't imagine how they would make it work. "How much cred can we pull together?"

She shook her head and he thought he saw a tear fall before she turned away. That single tear devastated him, as any sign of vulnerability could in Lil. She was so resilient, so tough, that when she revealed her fear, he knew it was overwhelming to her.

She walked across the room and picked up her discarded veil with absent fingers. Her voice was thick when she spoke and he heard her despair. "Not enough."

He rose and went to her, catching her shoulders in his hands. "Lil, we can try. We can ask . . ."

She shook her head and there was no doubt that her tears were falling then. He saw them glimmer as they dropped, and when she glanced up, her eyes were filled with a despair that unnerved him.

Lilia Desjardins was never defeated.

He'd always thought that if she did surrender, they were all doomed.

"Only governments can afford to buy wraiths, Montgomery," she said softly. "Not small-change renegades like us." She swallowed and spoke with urgency. "I would love it to be otherwise, but there's no point in kidding ourselves."

She pulled away from him and headed for the bedroom, her despondence upsetting him more than her reckless abandon usually did.

It made him determined to solve the problem. Delilah had been safe for this long, and Montgomery would do his best to ensure her safety from this point forward. He didn't miss the fact that Gideon Fitzgerald, Lil's first husband, had won her agreement to marriage by hiding Delilah in the first place.

Marriage continued to be a sticking point between himself and Lil. No matter how vehemently Montgomery argued for it, Lil insisted that it was old-fashioned and unnecessary. He understood that saving Delilah just might change her point of view.

He was one up on Fitzgerald, after all, since he knew he'd won Lil's heart already.

Maybe two up—he wasn't dead like Fitzgerald.

Yet.

He followed her, filled with purpose and determination. "Lil, you can't just give up."

"I can recognize when the odds are too high."

"Since when?"

She cast him a smile that had a little bit of her old attitude in it. Montgomery was encouraged and reassured by the return of her spark.

Then she shrugged. "Since the wraiths turned up."

"Wraiths? What or who are you talking about?"

She braced a hand on her hip, a wary glint in her eyes. This was more like it. "Sounds like you're fishing for another one of my secrets, Montgomery."

"Doesn't sound like it's your secret to me." He smiled slowly, noting how she caught her breath, and dropped his voice to a low teasing tone. If she needed strength from him, he knew exactly how to give it to her.

He slid his fingertip along her jaw and tipped her face upward, easing the pad of his thumb across the trace of her tears. "Come on, Lil," he murmured. "I promise to make the confession worth your while."

He bent and brushed his lips across the wet stains on her other cheek. She caught her breath and her lashes fluttered as her eyes closed. He saw her lips part and bent to touch his lips to hers.

"You should be classed as a lethal weapon, Montgomery," she murmured as her hands slid over his shoulders.

"I do my best," he whispered and she laughed.

Then he kissed her thoroughly, that sweet heat rising between them as it always did.

The chime of his desktop receiving a message was not what Montgomery wanted to hear.

From *The Republican Record*
February 13, 2100
Noon Edition
Download version 0.0.1

Tragic Fire Claims Hundreds

NEW SEATTLE—A horrific fire at the Citadel of the Daughters of the Light of the Republic early this morning has claimed the lives of all of the women and students in residence at the property. Tragically, the fire destroyed the facility just hours after the ceremony in which the next Oracle of the Republic was revealed.

The Daughters of the Light of the Republic use their Northwestern Citadel to train young women—known as acolytes—who have shown precognitive abilities, any one of whom might be blessed with missives from the angels. The official Oracle of the Republic is chosen from their ranks every four years, the installation of the Oracle timed to coincide with the investiture of a new president. The next Oracle revealed herself last night in a ceremony attended and witnessed by many citizens and dignitaries. The fire raged through the Citadel shortly thereafter, apparently claiming even the new Oracle.

Firefighters arriving on the scene were frustrated by the Citadel's remote location and secured perimeter. Their inability to reach the blaze quickly proved the death knell for the many residents there. Fire Marshall Dwight Peterson said that an investigation into the cause of the blaze is already under way, but suggested that a thunderstorm might be at root. "Lightning struck repeatedly in the vicinity last night," he said. "In old wooden structures like that of the Citadel, a fire lit by lightning could quickly take the whole place down."

The role of the Oracle dates from the late 2030s, when the motions were first made to unify church and state within the

Republic. The first Oracle, known only as Sophia, revealed herself at the inauguration of Thomas Montgomery in 2032, insisting that she be his advisor. Against the expectation of many, President Montgomery concurred, and came to rely upon her clear vision. He called her "the light in the darkness," and during his tenure had the official residence of the Oracle constructed in New D.C. adjacent to the White House. It is said that there are hidden connections between the two official residences to allow conferences between the two dignitaries to occur unobserved, but this is unconfirmed.

The Daughters took custodianship of the Oracle and her selection in 2051, after the untimely death of the Oracle in Seattle. Then-president Laura M. Macdonald was reportedly so devastated by the loss of the Oracle—who had come to Seattle to aid in peace negotiations with the Pacific Rim powers and was killed in a surprise bombing—that she could not formulate a plan for the Oracle's replacement. Although many earlier Oracles had official consorts, the Daughters eliminated that role, insisting that chastity in the Oracle increased the favor of the angels. Since 2051, the Republic has never been without an Oracle.

Reverend Billie Jo Estevez was among those witnesses in attendance at the ritual, and expressed shock and dismay this morning from her hotel in Hood River. "It breaks my heart that we should lose these wonderful young women, as well as the next appointed Oracle, in such a horrific incident." The reverend dismissed suggestions made elsewhere that the destruction of the Citadel by lightning was a sign of the wrath of God. "Surely, we have moved beyond the tenacious grip of superstition and do not need to dramatize what is already a tragedy for the Republic. Our prayers are with the families of these unfortunate women." The reverend also called a comedian's comment that a true Oracle should have foreseen the fatal fire as "irreverent and insensitive." The reverend will lead a live vidcast prayer service and memorial from the Hood River City Hall tomorrow at 20:00.

The membership of the Daughters of the Light of the Republic numbers five thousand women, of various ages, all of whom have taken the order's vows of poverty, chastity, and obedience. Many of their members are from affluent and influential families, so last night's losses will strike deeply into the heart of the Republic.

It is not known at this time how many other acolytes survive at other locations or whether an appropriate Oracle can be selected from their ranks in time to be trained for the presidential inauguration this November. The Daughters have requested a week to assess the damage and formulate a forward path.

Related Links:

   From the archives: <u>Union of Church and State</u>
      <u>Complete—September 23, 2072</u>
   <u>In Memoriam—Thomasina Wilkinson, Daughter Superior</u>

V

HOW HAD the news story about the fire already gotten to
Rafe's palm? The current time was before the publication
time on the article. The news story couldn't be released. Who
had written it so quickly?

And how exactly had the commandos and their execution
of the women been excluded from the report?

There had been no lightning in the area, contrary to the report.

If nothing else, the report gave Rafe new strength. He ran
with renewed vigor, dread growing in his gut. Someone was
using the remote location of the Citadel to manipulate and
manage information about what had happened there.

He understood that there would be no inquests into the
deaths of the Daughters and the acolytes, no investigation,
no record of the explosions or the murders.

He understood that he and Delilah and Ferris might be the
only living beings who could dispute the official story.

In a way, he was glad that his palm was making sure he
knew.

He hadn't seen a news vendor, let alone bought a download. Someone must have sent the news article to him in advance of publication.

Rafe punched the keypad to seek the sender's name, but
the news item had apparently conjured itself out of nothing.
There was no datatrail to the sender, or none that he could
perceive.

Whoever had sent it to him didn't want to be found.

It must have come on a pirate frequency, a signal that Rafe

knew was illegal to use. His palm wasn't set to pick up such frequencies, although he knew that bootleg software could be bought to gain that access. He'd never installed it.

Who had?

This palm would condemn him, even if his own deeds failed to do so. He remembered arriving in New Gotham the previous autumn, but nothing before that. He might not have existed before the previous October, although Rafe knew that made no sense.

His disobedient palm knew more than he did.

Then there were the scars on his back. They were odd, a pair of diagonal scars, and he'd studied them in mirrors a number of times. He knew they were enough to ensure that he was labeled as a shade, but he had no idea where he'd gotten them. It would seem that such a trauma would be memorable.

He shuddered, but it wasn't because of the chill of the rain. Rafe had been careful. He had protected his privacy. He kept his scars hidden. He had confided in no one. The only ones who knew he was in the Republic were those who had dispatched him, the ones who had given him the mission.

Too bad he couldn't remember who they were.

Or how to find them.

Or what their real motives might be.

Rafe refused to worry about problems that had yet to manifest and instead tried to focus on solving the ones he had.

They needed a refuge. He couldn't run endlessly without stopping.

They needed food and sleep.

Delilah needed a tissue regenerator to close that wound, because its presence would make the new identification bead suspect. She also needed clothes.

It would be good for him to know what her identification was. He wondered whether his palm had scanning software installed, as he doubted that Delilah would welcome a datashare with him.

Ferris certainly wouldn't stand aside for that.

The only good thing was that she was too sedated to give him any trouble.

Rafe could guess that that happy situation wouldn't last.

THE CHIME of an incoming message ended Montgomery's kiss. He stood by his desktop, his hesitation indicating that he shared Lilia's uncertainty, and she saw his expression turn more grim when he saw the display.

"Another one," he muttered. Then he passed his hand over the top, awakening it with the scan of his handprint.

There was a news item.

"This must be before publication," Lilia noted, indicating the time stamp.

Montgomery said nothing, merely opened it. They read the article about the fire at the Citadel together.

It didn't cohere with what they had seen on the vid-file. It omitted any reference to the executions. The hair prickled on the back of Lil's neck and she shivered at the reminder of who they dealt with.

"Wraiths," she whispered.

"Wraiths," Montgomery echoed, a question in his tone. His manner was purposeful and she recognized the determined glint in his eyes. She knew there would be no escape from his questions in the near future.

Not that she intended to run anywhere.

Well, anywhere that didn't include Montgomery.

And it was possible that he might find a way to overcome what she believed to be insurmountable odds.

She tossed her hair over her shoulder. "You remember that there were people in Gotham? First there was Yvan, the shade with the third eye who contacted me about Gid."

"Y654892," Montgomery agreed. "The homicide that wasn't."

Lilia shuddered. "Let's not review the grisly bits."

Montgomery smiled and caught her hand in his. He gave her fingers a squeeze and his eyes were dark. "We met because of that nonhomicide."

She smiled despite herself, surprised at his romantic con-
notation. "Then there was Johanna . . ."

He didn't let go of her hand. "Who had been Dr. Malachy's
fiancée."

Lil avoided the issue that had been coming up between
them repeatedly of late. "And was trapped in Gotham when
the nukes hit. She told me that there were lots of people living in Gotham, underground in the tunnels."

Montgomery looked skeptical. "And you believed her?"

"I didn't know what to think. And there wasn't a lot of time
to ask questions."

"What with her being killed and all."

Lil nodded. "So I asked around at the circus afterward. I
thought the shades would know if there were groups of people living in Gotham or elsewhere." She paused, seeking a
way to explain.

"And?"

"And they clammed up."

"Because there aren't any."

"No. Because they were afraid to talk about it." Lil
drummed her fingers on the desktop. "They were more terrified to talk about it than they were of the Republic or the Society of Nuclear Darwinists."

"Be serious."

She leaned toward Montgomery in her effort to convince
him. "I am. What could be more scary to a shade than a shade
hunter? Or the Society's research labs? Or the Republic's slave
dens?"

Montgomery shrugged, inviting her to answer her own
question.

"Death. Or maybe I should say execution." Lilia straightened, confident in her answer even as Montgomery arched a
brow. "They're afraid of the wraiths. That's all I could find
out."

"Wraiths," Montgomery mused, and she recognized that he
intended to solve the puzzle. His determination always made
her believe that there were possibilities.

Even for Delilah's survival.

She dared to hope.

"Who knows more?" he demanded.

"Joachim, but he wouldn't tell me more."

"Let's find out whether he can be encouraged."

"We? He won't tell you anything, Montgomery."

Montgomery almost smiled. "That's why you're going to ask the questions, Lil."

MONTGOMERY WAS as grim as only he could be. Lilia could hardly keep up with him as he strode toward the circus. It was late, later than any citizen should be on the streets, but the rules were more flexible on the Frontier.

And the cops already knew better than to mess with Montgomery. Lilia wasn't sure how he'd earned their respect or how much they knew about his doings. Maybe they simply recognized one of their own kind. Either way, Montgomery had a gift for making the city's finest look the other way.

She deeply resented that, given that her talent with law enforcement officials was the precise opposite.

Montgomery's black velvet cloak was as dark as the night, the ruff of lace at his collar making him look debonair and unpredictable. He wore his heavy-gauge pseudoskin and packed his high-power laze, but Lilia only knew that because she'd watched him dress. To a passing glance, he could have been a fashionable gent on his way to the pleasure fringe.

Instead of a man on a more urgent mission.

The lights of the circus were dimmed as it was after hours, but Lilia knew where Joachim would be. She used her palm to clear the security check, and wondered whether she imagined that hers cleared instantly while there was a delay on Montgomery's. He gave her a look, a sure sign that she hadn't imagined it, but she ignored him.

"There's nothing illicit going on here," she insisted.

"You're smarter than that, Lil. Or you're forgetting who you're talking to."

"Okay, correction. If there are illicit activities going on here, then they're well hidden."

Montgomery snorted and followed her into the circus grounds.

Lilia did have a strange sense that there was something going on. It looked a little more spare than the circus usually did, as if things had been moved, or rearranged. Tidied up. Given that the Nouveau Mont Royal circus hadn't changed a bit as long as she'd been employed by Joachim, she thought that maybe she was faked out by the darkness.

Then they reached Joachim's tent and she knew that something was wrong.

He was cleaning.

Furiously.

Joachim was only as tall as Lilia's waist, a dwarf and circus performer who had worked his way up to ownership. Although he'd been a clown for years and was sufficiently stocky that some people found the sight of him amusing even when he wasn't in costume, Lilia knew that he was one of the most cunning individuals she'd ever known.

Joachim was obviously trying to hide the evidence of some activity from their eyes. He jumped when Montgomery cleared his throat and spun to face them, his smile a little too broad.

"Gate announced us, I assume," Montgomery mused and Joachim's eyes narrowed briefly.

"That's its job."

The hostility between the two men flared as it always did when they met and Lilia was surprised as usual by its intensity. Then she was irritated by the two of them and their territorial games. They could have gotten along, if they'd tried. But no. Montgomery, for example, could have smiled once in a while when he was in the circus bounds or turned on a bit of that fatal charm. Instead he watched Joachim as steadily and silently as a hawk.

A hungry hawk.

And Joachim became flustered under that relentless stare. His occasional rude comments became louder and more frequent, which didn't improve Montgomery's assessment of Joachim's character.

He'd told Lilia once that Montgomery reminded her of Armaros and Baraqiel, the two angels she'd captured who now resided at the circus. That had made her jump, given Montgomery's history, but it was true that his watchfulness shared much of the intensity of the angels' bemused observation of humans.

The thing was that Lilia knew why.

She hadn't trusted Joachim with that bit of truth.

"I suppose you're here for a reason," Joachim said, more than a smidgen of hostility in his tone.

"A favor, if it's not inconvenient," Montgomery said smoothly.

Joachim bristled. "It's late. Maybe tomorrow."

"Maybe it won't wait."

"Maybe it'll have to." Joachim glared at Montgomery and Lilia understood that it was the fact that Montgomery represented authority to Joachim that got under the circus owner's skin. Montgomery might not still be a cop, but he looked like one, he sounded like one, and he acted like one.

"Look, Joachim, I need to ask you about something and it can't wait until tomorrow," Lilia said, trying to ease the tension in the tent.

"I'm really tired," Joachim said and made to turn away.

"It's about Delilah."

Joachim turned and glanced back at Lilia, halted by his surprise. "I thought she was dead."

Lilia shook her head.

"Safe, then."

"She might not be much longer," Montgomery said, then stepped forward. He bent, staring at the floor of the tent, then reached out one gloved hand to pick something up.

Joachim caught his breath, his alarm clear.

Lilia saw why when Montgomery held up the glass identification bead and turned it so that it caught the light. "There's blood on this," he said softly, glancing up at Joachim. "Whose neck did you take it out of, and why?"

"You don't understand," Joachim began, his words falling in a rush.

"No, I don't," Montgomery said and closed his right hand over the bead. It was caught in his fist. Joachim swallowed and Montgomery was utterly still.

Then Montgomery lifted his left hand, indicating his palm. "You know I have a scanner in my palm. Give me a reason to not scan the bead and find out whose it is."

Joachim licked his lips and turned to Lilia. "You said you want to ask me a question. Maybe I have some time."

Montgomery smiled with satisfaction.

"We need to know about the wraiths," Lilia said quickly.

Joachim exhaled. He paled and sat down heavily, his gaze flicking between the pair of them. His fear was obvious, especially when he spoke and Lilia heard that his voice was higher than usual. "They didn't send you, did they? Because you can remind them that I paid on time, I didn't ask questions, and I . . ."

"They didn't send us, Joachim," Lilia said. "They invited us to make an offer to save Delilah." She shrugged as her employer came to terms with this. "Or someone did. I assumed it had to be them, because the message left no trace of its ever having been there once we'd read it."

Joachim nodded heavily. "That's them, all right." His hands were shaking as he locked his fingers together. He appeared to come to a decision as Lilia watched. "Okay. Okay, I'll tell you what I know." He threw a look at Montgomery. "But you give me that back, unscanned, and none of this goes any further."

Montgomery held out the bead, the bit of glass pinched between his finger and thumb, holding it just out of Joachim's range. "Start talking."

"WHERE DO you think these beads come from?" Joachim asked, clearly not expecting an answer.

Montgomery had been wondering about that. He settled against a trunk, listening. He knew that Lil would ask all the questions that needed asking. She wasn't reticent in the least, especially not with Joachim.

Montgomery knew that if he asked the same questions, though, Joachim was far less likely to answer.

So he tried to be unobtrusive.

"I assumed you bought them on the black market." Lil smiled. "I was being tactful in not asking you to reveal your sources."

Joachim snorted. "It spooks me when you make uncharacteristic choices like that," he said with affection. Lil grinned, unrepentant, and Montgomery couldn't entirely suppress his own smile. Then Joachim frowned. "If you want anything on the black market, sooner or later, you deal with the wraiths."

"But who are they?"

"Norms and shades who have disappeared off the grid. They're not in the Republic's databases. Officially, they don't exist."

"Where do they live?" Lil gave Montgomery a look. "In the old cities?"

"Some of them. Others know the labyrinths of the netherzones. Still others have hidden refuges in the wilderness."

"That's pretty vague," Montgomery felt compelled to observe.

Joachim's look was cutting. "You don't ask questions of the wraiths. You pay the price they demand, you get what you paid for, and you breathe a sigh of relief when they're gone."

"How do you know that they're really gone?"

Joachim grimaced. "You don't. They're everywhere, and nowhere."

"Which is why they're called wraiths?" Lil guessed.

Joachim shook his head. "The story I heard was that the Republic's databank managers came up with the name. There's an old story from the twentieth century about the term 'bug' . . ."

"Because a hardware failure was caused by a dead moth within the computer itself," Lil supplied. "So, software glitches were called 'bugs.'"

Joachim nodded. "Right. But now, the Republic's databanks are so cohesive and so linked that some programmers think they've become sentient. And certainly, there are so many input points and self-correcting bits of software that the databanks are virtually alive in their ability to adapt and reflect new information."

Montgomery looked at the floor, knowing that his own network was responsible for manipulating a good chunk of the Republic's data.

"That's whimsy," Lil said, her tone dismissive. Montgomery guessed that she didn't want Joachim speculating any further along those lines.

But Joachim did. "The thing is that there are changes that occur both instantly and coherently, which no one on the Republic's payroll can explain."

Montgomery developed a fascination with his boots.

"These changes are said to leave no datatrail, no evidence that the info was ever any other way. The Republic's programmers began to joke that there were wraiths in the system. Everywhere and nowhere. Never where you're looking. Never leaving a trace of their passing. That the only record of the past that defied the databases is between our ears." Joachim shrugged. "And the wraiths, who know the Republic's databanks better than the Republic, liked the name enough to take it as their own."

Montgomery glanced up at that.

Joachim saw his surprise, but didn't guess the real reason for it. "Oh, yeah. They've got their fingers into everything. They can change history and shape the future, in the blink of an eye."

"Let me guess—they use their powers only for good," Lil said.

Joachim's laugh was bitter. "Be serious. The wraiths work for a price. Paid in cred or contraband, up front."

"Anything for a price?" Montgomery asked, disliking the sound of this.

"They say everything already has a price," Joachim confirmed. "The question is whether you can pay it or not." He stepped closer to Montgomery, his manner unfriendly as he put out his hand. "That answer your question?"

Montgomery offered the bead once more. Joachim plucked it from his grasp, then without hesitation, dropped it to the floor and ground it to shards with the heel of his boot.

Lil gasped in shock. "You destroyed a bead!"

"I made a wraith, Lil." Joachim's voice was so low that Montgomery had to strain to hear it.

"What do you mean?"

"It's coming time. I don't know when, but I trust the wraiths when they tell me it's time to hide."

"But where will you go?" Lil asked.

Joachim put a hand on her arm and smiled. "We've been good to each other for a long time, Lilia. Don't ask me questions I can't answer."

She nodded. "Everyone?"

"Everyone." Joachim sighed. "At least as many of us as can make it. It's not going to be easy, from what I understand."

"But why?"

"I don't know. It's part of the return to so-called family values." Joachim swallowed and his tone turned fierce. "This is my family and I'll be damned if I stand aside to watch the harvest."

Lil opened her mouth and Montgomery knew she was going to offer to go with them. He also knew that wasn't the right path for the two of them. He stepped forward and offered Lil his left hand. "Don't say any more. If we come one day and the tents are empty, we'll be as surprised as everyone else. Right, Lil?"

Her gaze flicked between the two men, and Montgomery understood that she had a choice to make. Would she choose her past or her future?

To his relief, she put her hand in his without hesitation. "Right," she said with false cheer and he squeezed her fingers. She stood closer to him, their arms brushing, and Montgomery was aware that Joachim was watching.

"You take care of my girl," he said gruffly, then offered Montgomery his hand.

Montgomery stared at the outstretched hand for a moment.

He and Joachim had never touched and he sensed a tentative accord.

"With my life," Montgomery said as he took Joachim's hand.

"Nothing less would do," the circus owner retorted. "I'll be able to find you otherwise," he said, giving Montgomery's fingers a ferocious squeeze.

Montgomery refused to wince.

Joachim might think he'd be able to find Montgomery anywhere with the help of the wraiths, but Montgomery was pretty sure he'd be able to find Joachim as well. Their gazes held in challenge for a taut moment, then they looked away simultaneously.

Keeping their secrets.

Montgomery found Lil watching him, a question in her eyes. The fundamental question remained.

How could they ensure Delilah's safety?

An intercepted message came in on his palm and one glance proved he had Tupperman to thank for it. There was no datatrail, but Montgomery recognized that it had come from police channels. It wasn't good news, but he forwarded it to Rafe.

Forewarned was forearmed, after all.

"Bad news," Lil whispered as she read the display.

"Good news," Montgomery insisted. "If nothing else, it means that Delilah is still alive."

All Points Bulletin
Imperative Update for All Law Enforcement and
Military Officials
For the Proximity of New Seattle, Hood River, and
Surrounding Area

2100-02-23
0600

A SHADE hunter from the Society of Nuclear Darwinists was shot dead in a confrontation with an unknown man in the forest in the vicinity of Hood River east of New Seattle. The hunter had no opportunity to defend himself, but was shot on sight along with his dog.

The fugitive is reported to be Caucasian, blond, approximately six foot four, and 180 pounds. He is particularly strong and fit, as well as armed with at least one laze of high power and recent manufacture. He is in the company of two fugitive shades—a young woman and a teenage boy—and it is not clear whether they are his captives or his companions. It is believed that the three fled the scene in an easterly direction.

The suspect is considered to be armed and dangerous, as well as impossible to arrest live. Law enforcement officials are advised to shoot to kill.

Law officials in the area should be aware that hunters for the Society of Nuclear Darwinists are active in the vicinity. Their premier hunter, Rhys ibn Ali, will be arriving within the hour to coordinate the hunt. Dead or alive, the two fugitive shades and the unidentified assailant will be taken into the custody of the Society.

Link: <u>Map of Area</u>

VI

IT WAS past dawn when Rafe found the homestead. He was exhausted, running on sheer will, and ready to collapse. The boy had shown surprising fortitude, following doggedly behind. The rain had stopped, but they were all soaked to the skin.

Delilah was awake—he had sensed the change in her rhythms—but pretending otherwise. He remembered how she had tried to persuade the old woman that she was slow and confused, and knew the ploy wouldn't work any better on him.

He'd put an end to that game in a hurry.

But first, they needed shelter. They needed to take a break, find some clothing, get something to eat. Hiding in the forest made them easy prey for dogs and hunters.

Rafe crouched in the perimeter of the forest, putting back a hand to keep Ferris from stumbling into the clearing ahead. The boy halted, then collapsed, obviously as tired as Rafe. He closed his eyes and looked worn.

Rafe had other concerns. He crouched in the scrub surrounding the clearing, puzzled as to the presence of a homestead. The cabin had the silence of emptiness, but he knew better than to trust appearances. The building before him was modest, the solar panels on its roof disguised with camouflage netting.

Why would a homesteader want to hide?

And who would he be hiding from?

Come to think of it, who would homestead here, amid the ash? How would they survive?

Rafe's palm chimed again, its resonant peal making him wince. When it wouldn't be silenced, he bit back a curse and pulled back his glove to read the display. His heart sank at the news that they were hunted.

Dead or alive.

He wouldn't even think about how things could get worse.

He'd strive to make them better instead.

It was a good thing he enjoyed a challenge.

The cabin was small, consisting of a peaked roof that emerged from the ground at a steep angle. It was constructed of hewn logs, their gray hue revealing that they were dead, old wood culled from the damaged forest. There were steps on the side closest to them, which led down to a door below the level of the surface. Rafe wondered whether the house was larger beneath the surface, maybe constructed that way to save energy.

The cabin was, after all, off the power grid. There were no power lines at this remote location, and no road led to its door. There wasn't even a path.

Were the occupants recluses? There were no satellite dishes or antennae, evidence that these citizens were beyond the reach of the Republic and its databases.

And its all-seeing eyes.

Interesting.

A metal vent rose from the middle of the roof and two dozen windmills surrounded the clearing. They were a bit shorter than the dead trees, painted dark, and sited closer to the lip of the forest than would be ideal for generating power.

On the other hand, they were almost invisible.

If the homesteaders were generating their own power and disguising their presence from authority, then any alarms, even if triggered, might not summon anyone.

Rafe liked that.

There was no smoke rising from the roof vent, even though the morning was chilly. There was no sound, except the quiet whirr of the wind turbines. Rafe debated his few choices as the sky grew steadily brighter. It was safe to assume that who-ever owned and occupied this residence wasn't interested in company calling. Rafe didn't intend to either rat on the occupants or vandalize their building. He just needed sanctuary.

It appeared that he'd found a good one.

Rafe looked for the trip hazards and booby traps, and saw one between himself and the doorway. He had laid Delilah on the ground and she was breathing deeply, pretending to still be drugged. The boy sat close beside her, as if guarding her.

From Rafe? Or from other threats? The hostility in his dark eyes didn't specify. Rafe wished he knew the boy's intentions before they moved on the cabin.

He surveyed the boy, who was much closer to manhood than his tattered clothing revealed. The dirt and suspicion disguised that he had good bones. He was a handsome child and obviously not mentally handicapped. Rafe wondered how he had earned his shade status. The boy watched him, his wariness undisguised.

"What do you have in there?" he asked in an undertone, indicating the satchel that Ferris carried. He didn't doubt that Delilah was listening, and was watching her closely enough to see her eyelids twitch at his words.

She was a lousy liar. That was one factor in his favor.

Meanwhile, the boy's eyes narrowed and his hand closed protectively over the bag.

Rafe smiled and tried to make a joke. "Any chance of a tissue regenerator?"

If anything, Ferris looked more suspicious.

Which made perfect sense.

Rafe couldn't believe he hadn't made the obvious conclusion sooner. He hunkered down closer to the boy and lowered his voice. "If you and the old woman really planned this out, you must have known that the bead will be suspect as long as the wound is visible on Delilah's neck."

Ferris swallowed and stared back at him, revealing nothing.

"You had alcohol to sterilize the wound, a suture and needle, and a bandage. I'll bet you *do* have a tissue regenerator. That's why you brought the bag. That's why you went back to get it."

Ferris hugged his satchel to his chest and stumbled to his feet.

But Rafe knew where one of the boy's loyalties was. Ferris' eyes told the secrets of his heart. Even as he backed away, his gaze moved repeatedly to Delilah. He didn't imagine Ferris would abandon her, not before the tissue regenerator had done its job.

Rafe thought it was time to make things clear between them—they were both trying to save Delilah, and he believed they could accomplish more by working together.

He called Ferris' bluff.

"All right. Go ahead and run," Rafe challenged, feigning indifference. "Go ahead and abandon Delilah, with the old woman's plan only half completed. Maybe it won't bother you to break your promise. Maybe it won't bother you to leave Delilah with that wound on her neck to condemn her." He shrugged. "Maybe we don't have that much in common, after all."

Ferris' eyes darkened with anger, but Rafe continued in an easy tone. "I'm going to break into that cabin, find something to eat, some clothes for Delilah. Maybe they have a tissue regenerator to heal her wound. That's the only way she's going to be safe, and even then, it's a long shot. I'm going to give it my all, though."

Rafe got to his feet, ensuring that he was close beside Delilah. He glanced back at the wary Ferris, continuing his speech as much for Delilah's benefit as for the boy's. "You can help, or you can go to the hunters. You won't even have to find them. Just head into the hills—those dogs will track you down within hours. Their best hunter, Rhys ibn Ali, should be in the neighborhood by now. Maybe you'll have a chance to barter your freedom and maybe you won't. Life is full of risks."

The boy looked resentful.

"The choice is yours," Rafe concluded with a confident smile. "I've made my choice and it's for Delilah."

Then Rafe bent and picked up Delilah, knowing that she couldn't flee from his shoulder. She started at his touch and he swallowed his smile. He hoped she never learned the art of deception from him.

He turned his back on the boy and moved toward the cabin, Delilah's weight on his shoulder. He kept one hand on his laze, even though he was certain of what the boy would do.

RAFE HAD taken three cautious steps when he heard a snarl of frustration. Undergrowth snapped as Ferris lunged after him. Rafe smiled to himself, then Ferris caught at his sleeve.

The boy tugged Rafe to a halt.

Rafe watched as Ferris fumbled with the clasp on his satchel. The boy reached inside and pulled out an ancient device, one that looked to have been salvaged, repaired, and cobbled together. He handled it with a reverence that belied its age and simplicity. He cradled it in his palms and showed it to Rafe, pride in his eyes.

"A tissue regenerator," Rafe murmured, enjoying that he had read the boy correctly.

He was, however, horrified by the instrument. It wasn't the most sophisticated unit Rafe had ever seen and he doubted its efficacy. It must have been one of the original models, discarded but painstakingly coaxed into operation again.

It was probably slow.

It might malfunction.

If they'd had time, Rafe would have tried it on himself first, but they had no time to spare.

The boy nodded, then raised a hand toward Delilah. He shook his finger at Rafe as if to admonish him.

"Yes, for her and only for her." Rafe smiled, guessing that the boy seldom heard any praise. "You really did think of everything."

A reluctant answering smile curved Ferris' lips, making him look young, mischievous, and handsome. Rafe's chest tightened at the glimpse of what Ferris might have been, and he regretted how servitude and abuse had aged the boy beyond his years.

Rafe dared to hope that they might work in unison, then Ferris tapped quickly on his own palm. He looked up through his unkempt hair then cautiously displayed what he had typed to Rafe.

Nine years.

Rafe blinked but the words didn't change. "*Nine* years?" Ferris nodded with enthusiasm. Was the boy mute? Evidently so. Rafe decided to guess. "Ever since Delilah arrived at the Citadel, then."

Ferris nodded again.

"The old woman arranged everything," Rafe guessed and the boy obviously agreed. The old woman had been prepared to act to protect Delilah from the outset. "Did she know that Delilah is the true Oracle?"

Ferris shrugged, clearly uncertain.

Delilah started.

"Did anyone else help?" Rafe asked, wanting to make the most of Ferris' inclination to share information.

Ferris shook his head, then twined two fingers around each other. Rafe guessed that he meant two people had worked together closely. Then Ferris touched those crossed fingers to his lips.

"Just you and the old woman," Rafe guessed. "Your secret." Ferris nodded once, then tapped.

Sonja.

"Her name was Sonja," Rafe read.

Ferris nodded then waited, as watchful as ever. The old woman's choice of Ferris as helpmate persuaded Rafe to trust the boy a bit more. He decided to treat him as a coconspirator. That might earn his trust.

"Okay, so here's our problem," Rafe said. "We've got to get inside that cabin. Then you can use the tissue regenerator, we can maybe find some clothing for you and Delilah, and with any luck, we'll get some food."

Ferris nodded as he considered the small building, his expression pensive. Then he frowned slightly at Rafe, as if confused by something, and tapped on his palm again.

Delilah?

"It's her name," Rafe said with conviction. He knew he didn't imagine that the woman on his shoulder stirred ever so slightly. She was listening to his every word and doing a lousy job of disguising her interest.

Rafe liked that.

The boy shook his head and tapped again.

Twenty-three.

"Is that what the Daughters call her?" Rafe asked, not hiding his disgust. Ferris nodded. "That's a number, not a name." Rafe let his tone show that he was dismissive of the idea.

Ferris was obviously surprised.

Rafe caught the boy's left forearm in his grip and turned it up, displaying the number that was tattooed there. "Didn't they call you F762698 instead of Ferris?"

Ferris grimaced. *Twenty-six* was what he typed on his palm, showing distaste of it displayed there.

"Which is your *name*?" Rafe insisted gently. The boy regarded him warily. "I would rather call you Ferris. That's a name. People should have names. Why don't I call you Ferris instead of Twenty-six? Would that be all right with you?"

Ferris blinked in astonishment—perhaps that any norm had asked his opinion—then smiled slowly as he nodded. Once again, the expression transformed him. He looked at Delilah, his heart in his eyes, and mouthed her name carefully.

Delilah.

"That's it," Rafe said, considering the cabin again. "Now we just need to keep her safe."

Ferris straightened beside him. He seemed to have grown

taller and now stood beside Rafe instead of behind him. He laid a hand on Rafe's arm, indicated himself, then the cabin. He made a circling motion with his hand.

"You're going to find a way in," Rafe guessed.

Ferris nodded.

"Are you good at puzzles?"

Ferris beamed with pride.

"Okay, there will be traps. These people don't want uninvited guests. We have to be careful." Rafe indicated a faint line with the muzzle of his laze as Ferris watched.

He was newly appreciative of his own tendency to defy authority. Every lock he had picked and every item of value he'd liberated, every obstacle that he'd considered a puzzle and a challenge to be overcome, seemed to have been training for the task of saving Delilah.

Maybe there had been a method to his madness.

"See that?" Rafe asked, knowing the boy hadn't spotted it. "It's a trip wire."

Ferris' skepticism was obvious.

"Look." Rafe fired at the trip wire, holding the burn so that the wire sparked. It burned down its length, revealing where it was concealed in the clearing. The spark collided with a hidden sensor, prompting it to fire. It only managed to click, a subtle sound of its preparation, before Rafe fried it.

He listened for the click of another sensor linked to the first. It sounded behind him, just as he'd expected, and he pivoted, shooting it out in the nick of time.

Ferris' eyes were round.

"They're arranged in pairs, each set to trigger if the other is destroyed," he had time to tell Ferris before there was another click.

Ferris pointed across the clearing in alarm. Rafe dropped to a crouch as the shot from the third sensor fired over his shoulder. Delilah squeaked as the shot passed over her, revealing her conscious state. Rafe aimed at the third sensor, cooking it to a smoking pile of detritus before it could fire again.

Ferris had fallen on his face, the tissue regenerator cradled protectively against his chest. He didn't move and neither did Rafe.

They listened for a fourth click.

Nothing.

Rafe exhaled and straightened warily.

Ferris held up three shaking fingers and almost smiled.

Rafe laughed. "Right. They're harnessed in threes. Now we know." He looked around the clearing. "At least this group was. No assumptions in this place."

Ferris got to his feet and nodded with purpose, then stood close to Rafe. He held up his hands for Rafe to stay put with Delilah and made that circling gesture with his hand.

"You still want to find a way in for us? Even knowing the risk?"

The boy nodded without hesitation, gesturing to Rafe and Delilah and Rafe's laze, then shooting with his fingertip.

He wanted Rafe to defend Delilah.

"How do I know you won't run away?" Rafe asked, suspecting that Ferris wouldn't.

Ferris frowned and pursed his lips, considering the question.

Then he abruptly offered the tissue regenerator to Rafe. Rafe put his laze in its holster and took the device. It was heavy and a bit greasy, but Rafe understood that he was being trusted.

"Thank you." He smiled at the boy, letting his pleasure show. Ferris stared at him and Rafe wondered how often anyone had ever looked the boy in the eye or acknowledged his contribution. He put the device carefully into the pouch at his belt, then pulled his laze again. "Hurry, Ferris, but be careful."

Ferris nodded. He hesitated a moment, his gaze falling to Rafe's laze, but he knew better than to ask for it. He eased toward the cabin as Rafe watched.

He straightened suddenly and pointed. Rafe saw the wire Ferris indicated and cooked it out, following the line to eliminate the sensor.

Ferris pointed at the click that Rafe had already heard, and that sensor was fried as well.

The third click came from the roof of the cabin. When that sensor was incapacitated, the pair waited again. Then Ferris turned and grinned at Rafe, giving him a thumbs-up.

Rafe grinned back, then eased forward in pursuit of the boy. He dared to believe that the two of them might manage to conquer the obstacles together.

TWENTY-THREE LISTENED to every word her captor uttered.

It wasn't just that she liked the low rumble of his voice—because she did—or that she admired his calm competence. She'd been startled by his sudden laughter, and by how much she enjoyed knowing that it was genuine. It had been a long time since she had heard laughter, and the sound was as wonderful as a beam of sunlight in the shadows.

He was confident that he could gain access to the cabin, although given its defenses, she had to wonder whether it was worth it.

He seemed to view this as a personal challenge.

He was certainly sure he could triumph.

She hoped his laze didn't need recharging before they gained admission. But then, it wouldn't have surprised her to learn that he had planned for that eventuality.

Was he lying about his determination to protect her?

Or to make her Oracle?

It had shocked her to hear her ambition on someone else's lips, then she had been dismissive of his claim. Nineteen years as a shade had convinced Twenty-three that anything sounding too good to be true was probably a lie.

Even if the hunter had gotten her out of the Citadel, away from the fire and the shade hunters. He'd defended Ferris and didn't appear to be working with the commandos. He knew how to find his way in the forest and he had a resolve that defied belief.

Maybe it was just determination that kept him moving.

Either way, he was unlike any norm she had ever known—other than Rachel. He had asked to call Ferris by his name. He was kind to Ferris, which was shocking behavior from a norm. His decisions and his words kept Twenty-three both fascinated and guessing as to his motives.

Why did he call her Delilah? She tried the name on her tongue silently, instinctively liking it.

It was better than Twenty-three.

Did he have her confused with someone else?

At least he didn't know that she was awake. She was a bit startled to find herself conscious so soon after the Ivanofor injection, never mind that she could move her body. Sonja must have given her a low dose.

Or maybe it had been a different drug with a false label. If so, she wouldn't have minded another injection of it. Twenty-three felt as if there was starlight running in her veins. She felt invigorated as she never had before. She felt vibrant and it was a glorious sensation.

This wasn't the way she usually felt when awakening from a forced sedation. She seemed to tingle from head to toe, every increment of her flesh open to sensation.

It was the way she'd felt in the presence of angels.

Maybe they were watching over her.

Again.

She was still swathed in the hunter's cloak, his grip firm on the back of her legs. The weight of the cloak was comforting. It was warm, and the faux-fur lining was the most luxurious surfaces she'd ever felt in her life.

Her thoughts flew in a way that she'd almost forgotten, questions and conclusions coming like flashes of lightning. Her dream of Rachel hovered on the periphery of her thoughts, giving her a sense of both dread and purpose. She expected to see the flicking red of the motel sign pulsing through her eyelids, or to find herself running again.

She realized that Rachel had tried to barter her body to ensure their freedom. Twenty-three would never forget the face of that shade hunter, the sight of him in the doorway of the motel with the red light flashing over him.

Rachel had distracted the shade hunter, and her submission had very nearly allowed their escape.

Until he had seen Rachel's defect.

Whatever it had been. It had obviously been on her back, but Twenty-three had never seen Rachel's bare back.

Now she'd never know what had condemned her friend.

The hunter stood and she felt the muscles of his shoulders flex beneath her belly. He eased his hand beneath the cloak and her eyes flew open as his gloved hand locked securely across the back of her bare knees.

Her heart leapt at the contact. She could feel the faux-leather against her skin—it was cool and smooth—and the strength of his hand within. She caught her breath in awareness of him and his touch, that shimmer within her body taking new urgency. Her toes curled with pleasure in a way that was foreign to her.

Rachel had distracted the other hunter with sex. Was that what this hunter wanted from her?

Twenty-three's mouth went dry at the possibility and its import. She couldn't do that. The Daughters insisted that the Oracle had to be chaste to be effective, to maintain the favor of the angels. She couldn't surrender her gift, even to be free.

Because there would be no point in being free, if she surrendered her destiny of becoming Oracle.

But there was something about the hunter that caught her attention all the same. Twenty-three had that tingling sensation in his presence, the one she felt in the presence of the angels. It was easy to see it as an endorsement of her response to the hunter's touch.

Or was it simply due to her own inexperience with men?

"Hang on, Delilah," he murmured and she nearly choked in shock. "This could get interesting."

How could he know that she was awake? She froze, realizing too late that her reaction had revealed her awareness.

"I know that you're awake and I know that you're not stupid," he said softly. "So, let's move beyond those games. We're only going to get through this if we work together."

Twenty-three said nothing. It was always better to be underestimated and she'd seen enough of norms to know that they all loved to believe in their own inherent superiority.

"I don't understand," she said finally, speaking slowly.

"Too late." She felt his concentration sharpen and he slid her weight from his shoulder. She was caught before him, his arm like a steel band around her waist, his confident gaze boring into hers.

Twenty-three looked down, but couldn't see past the hunter. She swallowed, already knowing he was more observant than most. Could he truly read her thoughts? He was hard and strong, taller and broader than she was, vital and healthy in a way that fascinated her.

"I saw you try to fool the old woman in the netherzones," he said softly, his words vibrating within her. "You're no fool and you're not sedated." Twenty-three could feel the force of his will. "If you want to be Oracle, you need to reveal your intellect. You can start right now."

Twenty-three glanced upward and he grinned at her, as if he'd never had any doubt of her response. She averted her gaze as she blushed and he chuckled again, the sound of his amusement deepening her blush.

"Better," he said, then looked over the clearing and sobered. He lifted her to his shoulder again, that resolute grip on her knees keeping her even from wriggling. "Go ahead, be angry," he invited. "Just don't pretend to be stupid."

Then he fell silent, intent upon Ferris.

Twenty-three peered past his hip, watching as Ferris moved closer to the cabin. Ferris reached to open the cabin door. He moved cautiously and Twenty-three felt the sharpness of the hunter's attention.

"Easy," he whispered and she sensed that he was as afraid for Ferris as she was.

That wasn't the sentiment of a shade hunter.

Twenty-three held her breath as the door swung inward noiselessly.

Nobody moved.

Nothing moved.

Ferris looked back at Rafe, shrugged, then slipped over the threshold.

Twenty-three caught her breath and waited for the worst to happen, her heart in her throat. Even given her trust in Ferris' abilities, she was afraid for him.

Long moments later, Ferris returned to wave at the hunter.

"That was too easy," the hunter murmured and Twenty-three silently agreed. "Now, be the eyes at my back or we'll go down together."

Twenty-three blinked, but then heard the good sense in his request. If he was shot out from beneath her, she'd be in jeopardy as well.

"You could carry me upright," she suggested.

"Takes the sport out of it," he muttered, a thread of humor in his tone.

"For you or for me?"

"Guess. This keeps you at a mild disadvantage and I need all the help I can get."

"You don't trust me."

"And you don't trust me. That makes us even." He took one last survey of the clearing and she heard him catch his breath. "Here we go."

Twenty-three braced her hands on his back and craned her neck to look behind them as he strode out of the protective undergrowth of the forest. It was overcast and there were no shadows in the clearing.

He'd taken half a dozen steps, just enough to gain confidence, when Twenty-three heard the click.

The hunter must have heard it as well. She had time to point before he spun and shot out the sensor.

She looked immediately for the partnering one.

There was a soft click.

"There!" Twenty-three said, pointing to his right. He pivoted again, and fried the second sensor.

The third fired a shot from behind the cabin, almost simultaneous to the second.

"Sneaky," the hunter hissed, then darted to one side.

The missile landed right where he had been standing and exploded, scattering the earth in every direction.

Its impact triggered a line of land mines buried in the clearing. They blew in succession, leaving a ragged hole in the ground.

The hunter swore and ran.

He ran in a crooked line, leaping and changing the length of his steps as Twenty-three clung to his back in terror. He finally lunged into the stairwell and caught his breath.

Ferris exhaled with relief. Twenty-three was shaking.

Another trio of land mines blew, then the dust began to settle in the clearing. The hunter let her slide down the length of him, and she felt every line of his body against her own before he put her on her feet.

"You could have gotten us killed!" she accused.

"I kept us from getting killed," he replied.

"So far."

He grinned, unrepentant. "True enough."

Twenty-three felt her body respond to him, his proximity and his good looks. She felt warm and strangely aware of him. She felt herself flush slightly and saw his smile turn intimate.

When she spoke, her tone was cross. "Getting lucky isn't the same as having a plan."

He laughed aloud again, untroubled by her attitude. "No, it's not. But sometimes it all works out the same."

"You can't always count on luck."

"You can't ever count on luck," he corrected. "But sometimes it turns up, all the same."

Something in his voice warned Twenty-three to look away, but she didn't manage it in time.

Or maybe she was too curious.

The hunter smiled slowly, his eyes darkening as he stared down at her. She wondered what he saw that gave him such pleasure. His cloak covered her from shoulders to ankles, its lush warmth enveloping her in a softness beyond anything she'd felt before. She could smell that clean scent and feel the faux-fur tickling her skin.

The hunter's gaze slid over her as surely as a caress. She caught her breath when he stared hungrily for a moment at her bare feet. She tucked them beneath the hem, aware of her nudity.

He touched one gloved fingertip to her cheek, easing a smudge of dirt from her skin, and his gaze locked with hers. She felt a shimmer inside herself.

And she knew then, knew without a doubt what he wanted from her.

Exactly what she didn't dare to give him.

Then he spoke with quiet authority. "I'm going to leave you two here and go inside to check for traps."

Twenty-three's heart leapt at the possibility of escape.

The hunter smiled, his expression revealing that he'd anticipated her response. "Run if you want to," he said lightly. "If you make it through the land mines, rest assured that I will hunt you and I will find you, wherever you go."

"You sound sure of your success."

"I know my own abilities."

Twenty-three knew her defiance showed in her eyes. "You hunt shades then?"

He shook his head. "No. But I'll hunt *you*." His words surprised her, as did the weight of his finger on her chest. "Don't move or we'll both regret it."

Twenty-three felt her eyes widen but before she could ask, he continued.

"After all, not everyone wants you taken alive."

He showed her the all points bulletin on his palm and Twenty-three was shocked by its content.

Why did he have that message?

Who was he working for?

"Where did you learn to read?" he asked with quiet intensity and she knew he'd tricked her into revealing one of her skills.

She saw no reason to lie, but didn't hide her bitterness. "They taught me at the mill. It was more useful for me to read the instructions and fix the equipment than to have a norm do it."

He watched her for a long moment, his gaze piercing. Again, she wondered what he saw.

Before she could ask, the hunter pulled up his hood, hiding his face in shadows, then eased into the cabin. Twenty-three jumped at the sound of his laze firing inside the cabin. She stood with Ferris in the stairwell, more afraid of the land mines in the clearing than the hunter.

The hunter made ten shots before he came back.

"I think that's all of them." He scanned the forest and the smoking holes left by the land mines, then the sky. He gestured into the cabin. "Inside now. We've got work to do."

Twenty-three didn't need to be told twice.

She did wonder, though, what "work" the hunter had planned.

VII

RAFE WAS annoyed with himself. He should have anticipated the land mines. They were an obvious obstacle for a
cabin so well defended. He blamed his own exhaustion for
his failure.

At least he had expected the image-snatchers. Each electronic eye took just one shot from his laze to blind it forever.
He'd even found the pair disguised in the woodwork. As far
as he could tell, they were in the clear.

However temporarily.

Rafe still had a feeling that they were being watched. He
couldn't see another trap or image-snatcher, but that didn't
mean that there weren't any.

The sooner they were away from this place, the better. Rafe
didn't like stopping in the first place and this cabin's security
measures didn't increase his confidence. Being away from the
eyes of the Republic didn't mean that they were safe.

Quite the contrary. He wondered who owned this cabin.

Because it had only taken one glimpse in the cabin to reveal why it was so well defended. On another day, in another
place, he might have stepped away, found another refuge,
avoided what smelled like trouble.

Unfortunately, he saw no choice for them in the short term.
He hoped that Ferris' ancient tissue regenerator could do its
work more quickly than he expected.

Once they were all inside and the door secured against the
outside—they'd have to deal with interior threats as they
presented themselves—Rafe took a slower survey. He'd already seen that the cabin was small and spare. There were a

pair of bunk beds on the right, a table in the middle, and a makeshift kitchen on the left. A door to his immediate left led to a small and basic bathroom.

Just ahead of him was the reason for the high security and he eased closer for a better look. A double doorway opened into an underground chamber, one that must have filled the far side of the clearing. The roof was buttressed with steel beams. The ceiling was thick with lights and they were burning brightly.

Which explained the wind turbines and solar panels.

The underground caverns were thick with plants. Rafe had never seen such healthy vegetation, and its lush greenery was a stark contrast to the gray of the forest above. Each plant's roots were contained in a comparatively small vial, filled with a solution. Hoses ran between the plants and there were flow regulators at the end of each line. It was an enormous operation, one entirely disguised from the surface.

Rafe knew why the owners didn't want company. Whatever these plants were, he was sure their cultivation was illegal. This cabin was not only off the grid, but it didn't exist in any records.

Its owners wouldn't summon any authorities.

They would just defend it themselves.

Rafe didn't like the sound of that.

"Plants," Delilah whispered with such awe that Rafe wondered whether she had ever seen anything grow green and healthy. Ferris made a low sound that sounded uncertain, then stepped toward the open doorway with Delilah by his side.

Rafe saw the receptacles in the floor and intuitively guessed what they were for. "Don't!" he had time to shout before Ferris stepped over the threshold.

Rafe heard metal slide on steel.

Ferris froze. Rafe leapt toward the boy, but guessed that he couldn't get there in time.

Delilah snatched at Ferris' arm and pulled him back as the steel gate dropped into place. Even so, the points of the falling gate grazed Ferris' arm and he leapt backward, clutching the scratch.

The metal gate fell, the points sinking home with force. The floor vibrated with the impact. Delilah and Ferris backed away, their alarm clear.

"No admission," Delilah whispered.

"Point taken," Rafe said, grinning at his own pun when she glanced his way. He winked at her. She stared at him, then slowly she smiled in answer. It was a tentative smile, but it lit her features all the same.

Then she blushed and dropped her gaze, sobering as if she wished she hadn't smiled.

But she had smiled at him.

Maybe there were other skills he'd mastered on his travels that could be put to good use on this mission.

Maybe this quest wouldn't be such an ordeal after all.

Once the growing space was secured from the rest of the cabin, the cabin seemed to exhaust its defenses. The pumps whirred softly on the other side and water dripped. There was a faint rustle, as if the plants were growing right before them.

"No samples today," Rafe said quietly, then shoved a hand through his hair. "Don't touch anything, all right? Let's do what we need to do and get the hell out of here."

Ferris nodded rapid agreement. Delilah, in contrast, watched Rafe. He had the sense that she was thinking quickly, and wished he could have known her thoughts. He still felt that they were being observed, but shook off his paranoia.

He pulled the tissue regenerator out of his pouch, concentrating on the most urgent business first. He tested the lower bunk, found no traps, then gestured to Delilah. She hesitated only a moment before coming to sit on it.

"You know how to set this thing, right?" Rafe asked Ferris, who came immediately to his side. Ferris installed the tissue regenerator on her neck. It sourced power from her palm, which was an old and less than ideal solution, since those who were healing needed their own strength, but one that worked. The unit hiccuped steadily under Ferris' vigilant gaze.

Delilah appeared to go to sleep.

Rafe didn't believe it.

He left the pair of them, moving to examine the stocks in the kitchen. There was only the barest minimum of supplies: several gallons of water, some lentils and dried vegetables.

Rafe supposed that a team stayed here when it was time to harvest the illicit crop.

With any luck, that wouldn't be soon.

There were no protein-paks or meal supplements of any kind. Rafe rummaged through everything with frustration, knowing it would take precious time to cook these dried foods.

Time he didn't have.

All the same, he lit the gas stove and put on a pot of water, hauling ingredients for soup out of the cupboards. Ferris watched with fascination and wonder. Where had Rafe learned to make soup? Even he didn't remember, which was just another reminder he didn't need that someone had messed with his memory.

Rafe mixed up what should pass for a decent meal and hoped for the best. The lentils might be still hard when they ate them, but it would be better than nothing. There were crackers and water as well.

He made Ferris eat crackers while a second pot of water heated, then sent the boy into the small bathroom to wash.

Ferris came back quickly, scarcely cleaner than he had been in the first place, but Rafe took him back into the room. He showed the boy how to shave, and cut his hair with the kitchen scissors. The change in his own appearance seemed to inspire Ferris. Rafe left the boy with a rough sponge and a bar of homemade soap, after showing him how to work the filth from his own skin.

Rafe turned out the single cupboard of clothing as the soup simmered, glad to find a variety of garments that they could use. The closet was filled with work clothes in various sizes, all of which were sturdy if not attractive.

For Ferris, he chose simple garments that would be long enough if too wide, and took them back to the bathroom. He found a pair of heavy boots that looked as if they'd fit the boy.

Rafe wasn't happy with the austere choices available for Delilah, but he supposed she would attract less attention in simple clothing.

He picked as well as he could, trying to ensure that she would adhere to the Decency Code. He found a faded blue dress that would do, and a long dark cloak that he liked a great deal, for both its fullness and its hood. There were black boots too, which looked as if they'd fit her.

He returned to look down at Delilah as Ferris splashed and the soup cooked. She seemed to be dozing, her breath slow and even. Even with her head shaved and her face too lean, she possessed a beauty that tore at his heart. He wanted to see her dressed in riches and gems, her beauty highlighted not compromised.

He couldn't begin to imagine what she had endured.

He hoped she wouldn't have to endure more.

She was the Oracle. He'd seen the truth of it in her vision. She had the gift.

It was outrageous that she was being hunted and discredited.

All Rafe had to do was persuade everyone else in the Republic—or a majority, or those influential enough to make things happen—to believe in Delilah's powers.

Before any of them were harvested or killed.

Rafe's customary confidence faltered at the magnitude of his task. He couldn't imagine how anyone could doubt the truth of her gift after that vision.

But he knew that he had no time for the luxury of doubts. If he'd been asked a week before, he wouldn't have confessed to believing in noble causes or anything related to the greater good. He'd seen so many—norms and shades—interested only in their own individual advantage. He'd learned that many posed or played games, and he had no patience with pretense.

But Delilah's gift was genuine. And that alone made it, and her, worth fighting for. He would do whatever was within his power to make her Oracle.

Rafe perched on the side of the cot and looked down at her. He noted the sweep of dark lashes on her fair cheeks, the vulnerability in the feminine line of her chin, the softness in her lips. She was both fragile and tough, a combination that fascinated him.

Rafe bent and slipped Delilah's arm from within the folds of his own cloak. He was pleased that she was warm, even though he again was struck by how thin she was. She held her arm stiff for a moment before she relaxed it and he knew he felt her shiver.

He smiled. She'd have to do better to fool him.

Rafe gently removed the bundle of leaves tied to her wrist, certain the old woman's last message would crumple to nothing before Delilah could read it unless he took it into his custody. He kept them in order and wrapped them in a handkerchief, stowing them carefully in the pouch at his belt.

Her palm was silent, which was a blessing. He looked at it, noted its age and simplicity. He was tempted to interrogate it, to find out what Sonja had programmed into it, but shied away from the invasion of Delilah's privacy.

There was no question of datasharing.

He turned her arm gently, intending to slide it back within the warmth of the cloak, and his heart stopped at his glimpse of her tattoo.

He knew that her shade number had once been E562008, but in the Republic's databanks, the record showed that that shade had died nine years before. He squinted and saw that Delilah's number had been modified.

Had Sonja changed the tattoo, as well? If so, she had been talented for the change was skillfully done—he had to lean close to see how it had been changed and even then, he wouldn't have been sure.

But the number on her arm was E662308.

Rafe understood how she'd become known as Twenty-three.

He frowned at what Delilah must have endured in her short life and slid her arm back into the warmth of the cloak. He forced himself to not look at her too much, to not complicate his mission unnecessarily, but he couldn't help glancing at her face one last time before he moved to stir the soup.

That was when he saw that she was watching him.

TWENTY-THREE HAD kept her eyes closed as the hunter rummaged through the cupboards. She wiggled her toes surreptitiously, enjoying the tickle of the faux-fur against her skin. The tissue regenerator hiccuped slightly as it operated, and her neck was sore. Ferris was splashing in the bathroom and she fought a smile over the hunter's terse instruction that Ferris go back and clean himself better.

Given the chance to be clean again, she would welcome it. She remembered briefly living as a norm in Rachel's care, remembered the luxury of cleanliness.

Ferris, if he had ever had the chance to live that life, must have forgotten it. Or maybe it was associated with too much pain—like the pain of losing that life. Sympathy welled within Twenty-three for her friend and she was fiercely glad that he hadn't been impaled by that gate.

The hunter had warned Ferris again.

He wasn't the kind of hunter she knew.

That unpredictability just made him more dangerous.

Twenty-three was nude beneath the hunter's cloak, its softness caressing every inch of her skin in a distracting way. She felt him come and look down at her, felt the weight of his gaze as he studied her. She fought to hide her awareness of that, preferring that he thought her asleep.

It was always easier to be underestimated.

Except that Twenty-three wasn't sure that this hunter was underestimating her. She was oddly aware of his presence and his proximity, her skin tingling with some strange antic-ipation.

It was as if the air shimmered between them.

She felt the mattress tilt as he sat down beside her. She heard his breathing. Her awareness of his presence intensi-fied and she knew he was studying her. She didn't need to open her eyes to imagine how he looked, golden and strong and attentive. He took her left hand in his, but he didn't query her palm.

It was a surprising acknowledgment of her right to pri-vacy.

Hunters didn't give shades that luxury.

She felt him untie the leaves Sonja had bound to her wrist, then he moved to slide her arm back into the warmth of his cloak. When he froze midgesture, she couldn't keep herself from stealing a peek at him.

He was studying her tattoo, his expression so filled with concern that she was touched. Was it possible that this hunter felt some compassion for shades? It was unknown as a reac-tion, so completely unexpected that Twenty-three was in-trigued.

She noted that her captor wore a white shirt and a faux-leather jerkin that was taut across his chest. If anything, he looked bigger without his cloak, more dangerous. She could see his belt and the holster with his laze, his dark codpiece and high boots. His fair hair was damp and his wet shoulders were already drying, but it didn't seem to trouble him.

He radiated warmth and vitality, and his gaze was as in-tense as a shot from his laze.

He frowned and shook his head, moved her arm back into the warm cloak, and glanced at her face. She saw him jump when he realized she was watching him, and the question in her thoughts fell from her lips.

"Who are you?"

He smiled ruefully. "I'm not even sure I know."

Twenty-three felt her lips tighten in disapproval. "You were the one who said no games."

He nodded acknowledgment, but didn't move away.

"Why did you call me Delilah?"

"It's your name, isn't it?"

"They call me Twenty-three."

He slid one fingertip down her cheek, his light touch making her shiver. "That's not a name."

"So, you're picking a name for me?"

He shook his head. "Your mother chose that name for you."

Twenty-three's heart stopped cold and she heard suspicion in her own tone. "How do you know that?"

"Because I met her and she told me." There was no emotion in his tone—he wasn't offended but simply stating a fact. Twenty-three yearned to believe him.

His eyes twinkled unexpectedly. "There is a certain irony in the fact that I was naked except for a cloak when she had me in her protective care."

Twenty-three's mouth opened, then closed again without her making a sound.

He had to be lying to her.

Mocking her.

Nobody knew who her mother was. It wasn't in the record. Neither was her father's name.

But challenging him was probably not the smartest choice, especially if she intended to earn his trust. She swallowed and looked away, not wanting him to guess how desperately she wanted to know both her mother and her own name.

She had a feeling that he wasn't fooled and his next words proved it.

"Her name is Lilia Desjardins," he said quietly.

Twenty-three flicked a glance his way. She was curious, too curious about the identity of her mother and had yearned to know more of her own story for as long as she could remember.

Had he guessed that?

Was he using her weakness against her?

The hunter smiled, his gaze sliding over her features. "I think the resemblance between you is so strong that there can be no doubt of your being her daughter."

"You're lying," she accused, hearing the hope in her own voice.

"No." He shook his head. His hand fell to her cheek again, his fingertips sliding across her skin in a slow caress. His touch launched a shiver over Twenty-three's skin, and the admiration in his eyes put a hard lump in her throat. "I met her in New Gotham, last fall. She was worried about you."

Twenty-three's breath caught.

"I told her that I'd protect you, even give you her regards." He leaned closer, his eyes gleaming, his hands braced on either side of her shoulders.

He leaned over her and she was trapped between him and the mattress, the intensity of his expression filling her field of vision. She could smell his skin, feel his codpiece pressed against her hip, see the strength of his hands braced beside her shoulders.

It couldn't be true. It was just a story, just a lie, just the kind of thing that a gullible shade would believe.

It was too tempting to imagine herself with a protector.

Twenty-three fought to free herself from the hunter's spell, but couldn't look away from him. She had to believe that her mother would have found her in all these years, if she had cared at all. She'd been greedy for these details for too long to consider them rationally.

He braced himself on one elbow, leaning down beside her to whisper in her ear. "Her name is Lilia Desjardins."

Twenty-three was entranced. She was nude beneath her captor's cloak, he was tall and hard and wide, and his eyes glittered like a starlit sky.

And they were alone.

She swallowed.

His gaze danced over her. "You look just like her. Her hair is longer and she's older, but the resemblance is unmistakable." He tapped at his palm, then pulled up the file of one Lilia Desjardins.

Twenty-three caught her breath when she read that her mother was a shade hunter and recoiled. "That can't be true."

The hunter opened the image link.

A woman with dark hair smiled back at Twenty-three, a woman with blue eyes and a heart-shaped face remarkably like her own. There was confidence in her stance and a challenge in her eyes.

And a pair of angels behind her.

Twenty-three exhaled in her relief.

Shade Hunter Captures Two Angels, said the banner beneath the image. The angels smiled benignly down at Lilia Desjardins, the affection in their expressions telling all that Twenty-three needed to know.

Her mother knew the angels.

Or more important, the angels knew her.

Her mother.

She became aware that the golden hunter was watching her. "Why are you telling me this?" she asked, unable to shake her old suspicion. "What do you want?"

The hunter's smile broadened. He leaned closer, giving her time to evade his touch. Twenty-three waited, catching her breath when his chest crushed her breasts slightly, when his breath fanned her cheek, when he lowered his mouth to hers.

"This," he whispered. "Just this."

Then his lips closed over hers with gentle purpose.

DELILAH.

It was the kind of name she'd always wanted to have. It was feminine, yet sounded old and strong. Twenty-three didn't care whether her mother had truly chosen it for her. She didn't care whether the woman whose file he had shown her truly existed or not. She didn't care whether he was lying about having met her mother.

She loved the name Delilah.

She'd take it as her own, whether it was rightfully hers or not.

She *was* Delilah.

He'd given her a name and she'd give him one kiss for that.

She didn't count on the hunter's kiss being a revelation. It was a sweet, hot kiss, one that sent fire through her veins and left her dizzy. Twenty-three knew he could have broken her, if he'd so desired, that he could simply have taken her, if that had been his urge.

Instead, his lips teased hers, leaving her shivering and hungry for more. She was unprepared for his tenderness, and it took her a moment to realize that he was coaxing her own response. His mouth moved persuasively over hers, tempting her to participate. His tongue teased and he nibbled at her lips with his teeth in a beguiling invitation to pleasure.

Twenty-three accepted. She was shocked by the unfurling of desire within her, by her body's ready surrender to sensation, but she was curious enough to indulge.

What difference could one kiss make?

Especially this kiss that made her shiver. His touch warmed her to her toes and drove every concern from her thoughts. It awakened a hunger that made her long for more.

Whatever it was. It was all new to her to enjoy sensation. She knew pain well enough, and hunger. She knew the ache that came from working hard and the dullness that came from insufficient sleep. She knew how to push her body beyond its natural limits and knew what it could do and what it couldn't.

But his kiss was all new. It felt luxurious, like something that should be in limited supply, like a treat that needed to be earned, a rare indulgence.

Yet a free one. Why didn't everyone kiss all the time?

Her captor kissed her slowly.

Seductively.

As if they had all the time in the world.

As if he was intent on mutual pleasure, instead of simply taking his own.

And Twenty-three forgot to care about who he was and what he wanted, much less what the price of indulgence might be. All she knew was that she wanted this pleasure. She wanted more of this kiss and whatever came after it. The sensations he awakened within her were as warm and seductive as he was.

The kiss made her feel alive.

Vital.

Luminous.

It reminded her of angelfire.

And as with angelfire, Twenty-three wanted more.

She told him so, with her touch. She arched against him, opened her mouth to his kiss, mimicked his ploys. She slid her fingers into the thick gold of his hair and pulled him closer. He shook when her tongue flicked against his, shuddering with his own desire.

Twenty-three had a moment to revel in her own power to arouse her captor, then he deepened his kiss and she forgot everything except his touch.

RAFE HAD never expected Delilah to be so willing or so passionate. He should have known that she would be her mother's child, should have guessed that she'd have more than intelligence in common with Lilia Desjardins, rebel shade hunter.

Yet Delilah completely lacked her mother's ability to deceive. She was the worst liar he'd ever met—he found her efforts to deceive him endearing, because the truth was so easily read in her eyes. Rafe would have bet everything he had that she was innocent.

Which meant that she had never experienced the pleasure that a man and a woman could share.

Rafe could fix that.

He had been driven to experience every pleasure of the flesh, to deluge himself in sensation. He had bought every whore he could find between New Gotham and New Seattle, and seduced every woman who was willing. He had indulged in every kind of food, in alcohol, drug, and stimulant. He had caressed every surface he could find; he had savored pleasure and terror and passion—and he had resented the abandonment of his journey of sensation to fulfill his primary quest.

But now it seemed that both objectives came together in a most enticing way, in a tempting female named Delilah. And maybe, just maybe, the greatest sensuous quest was to be pursued with one woman, with finding variety in familiarity. Maybe the greatest pleasure was found in introducing a novice to the possibilities.

Rafe knew better than to quibble over details when opportunity presented itself.

He broke his kiss and looked down at Delilah. Her eyes were closed, her cheeks flushed, her lips rosy and swollen from his kiss. She watched him through her dark lashes and Rafe guessed that she'd realized that he knew her body better than she did. He wanted her immediately, quickly, but reminded himself to take it slow.

This should just be a taste.

Or a tease.

He eased his length alongside her, slipping one arm beneath her shoulders and drawing her close. He kissed her again, easing his tongue between her teeth again. Her own tongue immediately danced with his. She was a quick study and an equal partner in this encounter, one prepared to demand as much as she gave.

That worked for Rafe. He was ready to fully explore the possibilities of mating, ready to sample every position and location, ready to thoroughly explore the nuances and degrees of one woman's responses to pleasure.

Against all expectation, he had a volunteer.

He slipped one hand through the front opening of his own cloak and swallowed her gasp when his fingertips touched her bare thigh. He let his hand slide higher, caressing over every increment of her skin, and felt her heart skip. He flattened his palm, easing his hand over her belly, her ribs, and cupping her breast. He lifted his mouth from hers and smiled at the awe in her eyes, then let his thumb move across her nipple.

She gasped and her nipple tightened immediately. He bent and caught it in his mouth, flicking his tongue against its tautness as she shivered.

Meanwhile, his hand moved down her belly again. He felt the flutter of her pulse beneath his palm, heard the way her breath caught. His fingers moved unerringly toward his goal and he loved when Delilah moaned. She clutched his head and writhed beneath him, her hips bucking slightly. Her arousal fed his own, driving him to please her even more.

Rafe's fingertips eased lower, and she instinctively parted her thighs. She was slick and hot, ready. Delilah caught her breath when he caressed her gently and her hands gripped his shoulders.

He suckled her nipple more insistently, enjoying her response. It was raw, innocent, honest. Sensation was all new to her, which made Rafe appreciate it all over again. He moved his finger between her thighs as he flicked his tongue across her nipple, hoping to drive her to distraction. Then he lifted his head, intent on watching her release.

It would probably be her first.

She writhed beneath his touch, her eyes bright and her cheeks flushed.

"What do you want?" he murmured and she shook her head with uncertainty. His heart nearly burst with affection for this alluring woman who knew so little of what her body could do. She didn't even have the audacity to ask for something that she had to know he was willing to give.

She'd had so little. She'd known only hardship and pain, but Rafe would begin to redress the balance. He'd teach her to have expectations.

Rafe let his fingers slide more deeply into her wet heat. He leaned closer, watching her eyes widen as she stared at him, and let his voice slip low.

"I could kiss you there," he murmured. "I could slide my tongue inside you . . ." He bent and eased his teeth across her erect nipple, his tongue flicking in mimicry of his offer. "Tell me what you want."

She shuddered and closed her eyes.

"All I want to know is your name," she whispered.

"Really?" he teased, his fingers sliding deeper.

Her eyes flashed even as her flush deepened. Rafe glimpsed the stubbornness that had probably kept her alive.

"Just your name."

"Maybe there's a price for that confession," he murmured, wanting only to cast her over the edge.

"There's a price for everything," she said, surprising him with her sudden bitterness.

"Sometimes the only price is admitting your desire."

Her eyes narrowed. "Liar."

The accusation came from her experience. Rafe knew it— and he knew that he would prove her wrong.

"I never lie about this." Before she could argue, he caught her clitoris between his finger and thumb.

She trembled bodily in her arousal and gasped. Her pupils were dilated and her lips parted in astonishment. She was on the cusp of her release, overwhelmed by the vigor of her own response. He was fascinated by the change in her appearance, captivated by the desire that softened her angles.

She had a moment to survey him, her doubt clear, then Rafe pinched that tender bead abruptly but gently.

Delilah cried out and arched her back, trembling from head to toe. He slid one finger inside her, prolonging her pleasure, and was delighted when she moaned aloud.

He was more delighted when she smiled. The curve claimed her lips, putting a sparkle in her eyes and deepening the flush of her cheeks. She looked as if she'd been awakened from a long sleep, as if sparks would shoot from her fingertips.

Every increment of her skin that he could see was flushed crimson, and Rafe felt tremendous satisfaction in what he had done. It never failed to astound him, this capacity of the mortal body for both pleasure and pain. Remarkably, the sight of Delilah's pleasure pleased him as much as his own release typically did, maybe even more.

The pleasure her body could savor was new to her, overwhelming and exhausting. Rafe tried to remember his own first time and failed. There had been too many times, too many impulsive matings, and the experience had blurred together. Sex had ceased to be special for him, although he sensed that a union with Delilah would be one he never forgot. Rafe watched Delilah's eyelids flutter closed as tenderness welled within him.

Then Rafe heard the minute sound of a sole on the wooden floor.

The boy.

Of course.

VIII

DELILAH HEARD a wordless cry and looked over the hunter's shoulder. Ferris leapt toward the stranger, a kitchen knife held high in one fist. He was aiming for the hunter's head.

"No!" she cried, fearing it was too late.

Ferris never had a chance to land the blow. The hunter rolled to his feet in a smooth movement and caught Ferris by the throat with one large hand. He lifted him bodily from the floor as he grasped Ferris' wrist with the other.

The hunter's expression was grim. The boy's face worked, he squirmed, then he dropped the knife.

It clattered to the floor.

The hunter picked it up, then cast him aside with disgust. Ferris stumbled to gain his footing. His face was white and he was shaking when he turned to face the two of them.

Ferris was also transformed. He was clean, possibly for the first time since Delilah had known him. He had shaved, almost certainly with the hunter's help, and his dark hair had been cropped short. It was still wet, but Delilah could already see that it had a slight curl. He'd scrubbed from head to toe and was wearing plain dark clothing that had no holes and fit him reasonably well. He looked so much better that he might have been another person altogether.

But then, she was feeling like a different person herself. What had the hunter done to her? His touch had stirred a storm, one that left her weak in the knees.

With a glow of pleasure deep inside her. It reminded her of the healing caress of angelfire, that searing heat that had transformed her once already.

She rose to her feet, holding the tissue regenerator on her neck with one hand. If the hunter moved, she'd have to intervene on Ferris' behalf.

Somehow.

She wasn't sure she could stop him from anything he intended to do.

She wasn't convinced that the hunter meant harm to them either.

He was unlike anyone she'd ever known.

Meanwhile, the golden hunter had pulled his laze and had it trained on Ferris. He was impassive and still. Too still. Delilah understood that he had chosen to not injure Ferris fatally.

Again.

The hunter could have been carved from stone. That teasing smile was gone, as was the humor in his eyes. He looked dangerous and she already knew he was unpredictable. The two eyed each other, the hunter motionless, Ferris swallowing with uncertainty.

"Don't shoot him," she said quietly. "Please."

She expected the hunter to ask what she would offer in exchange, but he ignored her.

"Are you done?" he asked Ferris, his voice low. He was daunting, impassive, and hard to read. Delilah didn't know whether to expect kindness or not when his expression was so set. He might have been a different man.

Was this the real man?

Ferris clearly shared her doubts. He waited only a heartbeat before he raised both of his hands.

"I didn't have to save your life last night," the hunter said to Ferris, his words sounding ominous even though they were softly uttered. "But now that I have done so, a debt stands between us, a debt that is not served by your attacking me."

Ferris inhaled sharply, looking as if he would have preferred to have argued the point. He glanced at Delilah and back to the hunter, accusation in his eyes.

"What happens between Delilah and me is not your concern," the hunter said, his tone silky. "I will never hurt her."

Ferris looked as dissatisfied with this as Delilah was.

"Don't you owe me a debt, Ferris?" he repeated.

Ferris' gaze dropped to the muzzle of the laze. His lips twisted and he looked unhappy, but he nodded curt agreement.

"Then let me make your choice absolutely clear." The hunter spoke with the calm assurance that Delilah was beginning to associate with him. "Until you save my life and return your debt in kind, you can serve my will. Or, if you prefer, we can end the debt now. Call it square." He removed the safety from the laze, the click sounding loud in the cabin. "Your choice."

"That's not fair!" Delilah protested.

"It's more than fair," the hunter said without turning. "I'll let him live in exchange for a promise." He paused. "Name another hunter who bargains with his prey, never mind one who sets such easy terms."

Delilah had nothing to say, because he was right and they both knew it. Rebelliousness rose hot within her, the same rebelliousness that had earned her discipline and drugs numerous times over the years. She disliked that he could change so vehemently, moving from seductive to threatening, from kind to stern. Which was his truth?

Ferris still hadn't indicated agreement.

The hunter, perhaps impatient, sighted the laze with his thumb.

Delilah saw the blinking red and stepped forward. "Ferris!"

Ferris gritted his teeth, then inhaled sharply. He looked at Delilah, then nodded, bowing his head meekly.

The hunter didn't move.

"He agreed!" Delilah said.

"I didn't hear him." The hunter didn't glance at Delilah.

"Ferris is mute," she said angrily. "You can't hold that against him."

"Is that true?" the hunter asked Ferris. Delilah was sure he wasn't surprised.

Ferris nodded.

"Show me."

It was an offensive thing to ask, the kind of display a

hunter might demand to embarrass a shade. Delilah would have argued for Ferris, but Ferris took a deep breath and squeezed his eyes shut. He opened his mouth to scream, but the only sound that came out of his mouth was a weak gurgle of a cry. He flushed, eyed the hunter, then pulled back his collar to show the scar on his neck. His pose was defiant and rebellious, his gaze challenging.

The hunter's laze lowered. "I'm sorry, Ferris," he said softly. "I wasn't sure."

The compassion in his tone must have startled Ferris as much as it did Delilah. Ferris' anger faltered. She stared at the hunter, feeling a subtle change in the atmosphere between them.

The hunter shifted his laze to his left hand, ready for anything, then offered his hand to Ferris. "Do we have a deal?"

Ferris and Delilah stared as one at his outstretched hand. Norms and shades didn't shake on agreements—only norms did. This hunter kept her challenging her ideas of how he would behave.

He wasn't unpredictable—he treated them like equals. That surprising fact explained his choices and made it hard to resent him.

Ferris stepped forward and took the hunter's hand. The two assessed each other for a long moment and Delilah wondered what the hunter was thinking.

The hunter put the safety back on his laze and returned it to his holster. "One agreement negotiated," he murmured, then eyed Delilah. Her heart skipped a beat as he considered her, then his smile turned secretive. "One to go."

There was something about the low timbre of his voice that made her shiver, that made her lips tingle in recollection of his kiss, that made her want to feel his confident caress again.

Were the Daughters right that an Oracle's loss of chastity would cost her the ability to hear the angels? Delilah wondered whether it was a lie, as so much within the Citadel had been a lie, but the price could be high if she was wrong.

The hunter was dangerous in more ways than one.

He turned away, making her wonder whether she had seen some hint of her defiance in his eyes. His manner turned brusque. "My name, by the way, is Raphael." He crossed the room and stirred the soup, taking a quick sniff and nodding approval.

Delilah didn't believe for a moment that he was so oblivious to herself and Ferris. Even with his back to them, she knew he was fully alert.

"But you can both call me Rafe." He threw her a quick glance, his expression almost playful. Her heart skipped when his gaze collided so suddenly with hers.

Rafe. The name suited him. It sounded devil-may-care, the name of a renegade and a rebel. It sounded unpredictable, surefooted, confident, and handsome.

Rafe.

But what was Rafe's cause?

And how could she find out?

RAFE DIDN'T trust the boy. He suspected that whatever accord was between them was not only tentative, but based on Rafe not touching Delilah.

It was a high price to pay for the boy's compliance.

He consigned Delilah to bed again to let her wound heal. Ferris fidgeted and fussed with the tissue regenerator until Rafe told him to stop. It began to rain again, drenching the world outside the cabin in endless raindrops.

The afternoon stretched long. Rafe leaned against one wall, his laze at the ready. The tissue regenerator hiccuped steadily, the water dripped in the room filled with plants, and the soup simmered. He itched to be away from this place, which still seemed to be infested with watchfulness.

When it was falling dark, he decided they might as well eat the soup, which had been filling the cabin with its scent. He was ladling it out into bowls when his palm pinged.

The sound echoed loudly in the small space, the ping as clear as a bell. The sound made Delilah jump and she sat up abruptly. The tissue regenerator fell heavily on the cot and

Ferris hissed his displeasure. He picked it up with care and set it lovingly in Delilah's lap.

But Delilah stared at Rafe's hand, her expression suspicious.

He was feeling pretty suspicious himself.

"You get a lot of messages."

Rafe was feeling harassed by his palm and its incessant chiming. "And you don't get any."

"Of course not." She almost laughed at the idea.

Rafe was intrigued. "What do you mean?"

"Shades don't have the ability to receive messages from anyone other than their masters. Everybody knows that."

"I didn't know that, but then I've never had a shade of my own."

Curiosity made her eyes bright. "You've never managed any?"

Rafe shook his head.

"Or owned any?"

Rafe shook his head again.

She scoffed. "Then you must be the last living norm in the Republic with no experience of shades."

Rafe grinned. "And is that such a bad thing?"

She didn't smile back at him. "No, just an improbable thing." She studied him for a moment, then glanced down at her palm. She spoke with apparent indifference. "Since leaving the Citadel, I guess I don't have a master anymore."

Rafe wasn't fooled by her dispassion. The notion of having no master had to make her jubilant.

"So, it's common to program the incoming frequencies of shades' palms?"

"Of course. Otherwise anybody could command any shade." She looked at her palm, showing a dislike of it that Rafe shared of his own. "Messages are usually reminders or commands, and they're always audible."

"Why?"

She spared him a look, one that didn't manage to disguise her resentment. "Who would teach a shade to read?"

"But you can read."

"Yes, well, it saved a norm some work."

"And Ferris reads his palm. It's also a more current model than yours."

"The Daughters upgraded his palm, because he was *useful.*"

Before she could say more, Rafe's and Delilah's palms chimed simultaneously. Delilah jumped in shock as she eyed her left hand. She peered at it, her fear tangible.

"It could be *them,* looking for me."

Them. Rafe didn't understand for a moment, then he realized she was referring to the Daughters. "I think everyone at the Citadel is dead."

"Don't count on it," Delilah muttered, her doubt clear. "Nothing there is as it seems."

"Like you," Rafe said. "Remember that you're not Twenty-three anymore." The flash of relief in Delilah's eyes made him smile. "When Sonja datashared with you, she must have made your palm identity match the identity bead."

"Of course." Delilah nodded slowly, one hand rising to her neck. The incision was healing well, given the age of the tissue regenerator. It was closed but still visible. As much as Rafe resented the delay, they'd have to wait until morning to leave, and give the tissue regenerator more time.

Rafe wondered how many of the Daughters had known of Sonja's scheme. Had they truly all died in the fire? He didn't imagine for a minute that the attack on the Citadel had been a coincidence.

Had it been preplanned, or triggered by Delilah's vision?

Delilah seemed fascinated with her palm's new abilities. "It's not displaying anything automatically. What do I do?"

"Tap the receive button." He went to her side, sitting on the side of the bed again. Ferris clanged cutlery after he moved the soup bowls to the table.

Delilah hesitated, her finger hovering above the receive button. She then took a breath and pushed it.

Rafe did the same and was surprised at the message.

Restore the Past Glory or Chart a New Course?

Does the Republic's salvation lie in a return to family
values and the proven institutions of the past,
as President Morris Van Buren insists?
Or is the Republic's future brightest with innovation and
new perspective, change and restructuring,
as candidate Maximilian Blackstone maintains?
Both candidates will meet in the only major Republican
city undamaged in the last century to share their
competing visions for our future. Witness the last great
debate between presidential candidates in Chicago on
February 19, 2100.

Excellent seats still available!

The deadline for Republican voter registration is quickly
approaching. Be sure to <u>REGISTER</u> by March 15, 2100, to
secure your right to vote.

A reminder brought to you by the Federal Party.
All donations will go directly to the
Campaign to Elect Blackstone for the Future.

<u>Vidcast of Maximilian Blackstone, the man for our future.</u>

Vote Blackstone
for the Future of the Republic

It was a summons to a political debate.

It was palm spam.

Delilah stared at the display in her palm in astonishment. There were official images of both men, both looking handsome, assured, and reliable. She read it again, incredulous.

"Vote?" she said, her doubt resonating in the single word.

"It was probably sent to everyone in the Republic."

"Every *citizen,* maybe, but shades don't vote," Delilah said, then realized the answer to her own question. "Oh, wait. Sonja got the message, not me."

"Exactly," Rafe agreed and made to push to his feet.

Delilah saw Ferris' alarm from the corner of her eye. He had his hands in his satchel, and looked as if he was about to be caught doing something wrong.

She instinctively guessed what it was. Ferris carried a number of herbs in his satchel, and could always be relied upon to help any shade who was suffering in the netherzones. Sonja had protected him, on the guarantee that he carried nothing that was poisonous. He had herbs that were laxatives and herbs that gave the opposite result, herbs that soothed rashes and sore throats, herbs that did nothing more than smell sweet. The most potent herbs he possessed were gentle sedatives.

She knew what he was going to do with the soup.

But if Rafe caught him in an act of defiance again, he might not be so kind.

She had to help.

She snatched at Rafe's left hand, catching his wrist and pulling him to a halt. He looked down at her in surprise, then blinked when she smiled at him. "Did you get the same message?"

He hesitated for a moment. Delilah slid her hand up his arm, trying to mimic his earlier caresses. She smiled up at him.

He seemed startled for a moment, then smiled.

He was confident of his own charm, at least. He sat back down beside her and let her turn his palm display to her own view. His skin was warm beneath her hand, his thigh strong beside her on the bed. She swallowed at her own audacity and willed Ferris to hurry.

"You did!"

"It's just palm spam."

"My first palm spam." Delilah laughed, feeling the quickening of his interest. "Maybe I should save it." She dared to meet his gaze, and saw the answering twinkle in his eyes. They stared at each other for a moment, then his gaze dropped to her lips.

She was sure he would kiss her again and felt a tingle of anticipation.

One more kiss wouldn't hurt.

Kissing wasn't losing her chastity. She leaned toward Rafe, felt his breath on her cheek, felt his heat close beside her. She laced her fingers into his and heard his sigh.

But then he pushed abruptly to his feet and turned away.

"You'll run out of memory in a hurry if you save every piece of garbage that comes your way," he said gruffly. "Let's eat."

THEY WERE conspiring against him.

Rafe sensed it.

The sudden change in Delilah's attitude was suspicious, as was the fact that the boy hadn't made any protest when Rafe had seated himself on the side of the bed again. She'd encouraged his touch in a totally new way, and the boy had looked the other way.

It was a trick.

Rafe eyed the pair of them, disliking his sense of their complicity. It was true that he had the laze. It was true that he was bigger and stronger.

But he was also exhausted. It was only a matter of time before he fell asleep, and he disliked that his efforts to win the trust of these two had failed as yet.

He supposed that said more about their experience than about his abilities, but still.

The two took their seats at the table, looking as innocent as lambs.

Ferris had placed the bowls of soup on the table. Delilah was quick to sit where Ferris indicated, as if she was accustomed to taking direction from a shade. Rafe didn't miss the significance of there only being one seat left for him.

With one specific bowl placed in front of it. There was an herbal smell to his soup that he couldn't account for.

He wasn't going to eat this bowl of soup.

He leaned forward and inhaled deeply, not needing to fake his appreciation. "Nothing like hot soup."

"Better than a protein-pak," Delilah agreed, more readily than she'd agreed to much of anything thus far.

Ferris gestured to her and she nodded cheerfully.

"A lot better than a *leftover* protein-pak," she amended and the boy nodded easy agreement.

It was appalling that they had become accustomed to such living conditions.

"You don't have enough," he said to Ferris, reaching for the boy's bowl. "You need more nourishment than that. This bowl is more full. Let's trade."

He swapped the bowls before Ferris could stop him.

And watched.

Ferris swallowed and stared down at the soup.

Rafe couldn't detect the herbal scent from this bowl. He took a spoonful, savoring it. "Not bad. The lentils could have cooked a bit longer, but beggars can't be choosers."

The other two stared at Ferris' bowl.

"Eat it while it's hot," Rafe encouraged. He wondered what Ferris had put in the soup. Was it poisonous? He couldn't force the boy to eat it, if there was any such possibility.

Delilah picked up her spoon and took a taste of the soup. "It's good," she said with none of her earlier animation. "Maybe Ferris has too much now."

The boy nodded with enthusiasm, indicating the crackers, and reached for Rafe's bowl.

"Don't be ridiculous," Rafe said. "You two have been in the

netherzones too long. I'm quite happy with the smaller portion." He took the bowl that Ferris had initially served to him and passed it to Delilah instead. "You need a good meal too. Yours has a bit less, so give that one to Ferris."

Delilah froze, her spoon in the air as she considered the bowl of tainted soup.

Ferris reached across the table after the tainted bowl.

"No, no, it's fine," Delilah protested. "I'll eat this one."

Ferris sat down heavily. He lifted his spoon with reluctance, his gaze fixed upon Delilah. That he would let her eat the soup proved to Rafe that its contents weren't toxic.

He supposed the boy just wanted to knock him out, not kill him.

He supposed he should be flattered by that.

It was progress, of a kind.

Delilah ate half of the soup, then pronounced herself full. Her eyelids were already drooping and her feet dragging when she headed back to the cot. Ferris scurried after her to set the tissue regenerator, then came back to the table with reluctance.

Rafe took Delilah's half-empty bowl and pushed the tainted soup toward Ferris. The boy indicated his own bowl of soup.

"No," Rafe said softly. "You'll eat this one first." He held the boy's gaze, knowing his own was steely.

Ferris sighed.

He fidgeted.

He tried again to trade bowls, but Rafe could tell that Ferris knew his trick had been discerned.

Ferris ate the rest of the tainted soup.

He practically fell asleep at the table. Rafe leaned back and considered the pair of them, listening to the hiss and wheeze in the cabin and the patter of rain on the roof.

Against all expectation, he could risk getting some sleep himself.

He picked up Ferris and deposited the boy in the upper bunk, tucking him in. Ferris barely moved, his head falling back as he snored.

Rafe then checked on Delilah first, wanting to ensure that she wasn't tricking him. Her breathing was slow and deep, so slow and deep that he knew she really was asleep. The tissue regenerator hummed irregularly and he adjusted its position. He could have looked at her all night, but he was exhausted himself.

Just as Rafe moved to turn away, he saw the glimmer of an image on her palm.

He paused to look. Delilah had her left hand nestled under her cheek, a pose that made her look sweet and childlike. And the image on the display of her palm only redoubled Rafe's sense of her vulnerability.

It was that official image of Lilia Desjardins with the two angels flanking her.

Delilah hadn't known who her mother was, not until today.

It was outrageous that a child would be cheated of such a legacy, and even without knowing the whole story or its implications, Rafe was glad he had brought Delilah some news she had wanted. She could make whatever she wished of the revelation.

He was glad to have been a part in her learning that truth.

He pulled a blanket over her, watched her stir slightly in her sleep, then turned to consider the cabin.

There was a flicker of movement on the other side of the gate that barricaded the plants from them. Rafe pulled his laze and leapt to the barred portal, peering through it into the bright light beyond.

The solution dripped.

The pumps whirred.

The lights burned brightly.

And nothing seemed to move.

He rubbed his eyes and turned away, certain he was seeing things in his exhaustion. He eyed his two companions and decided to take a chance.

He slept in a chair that he leaned against the only exterior door to the cabin, confident that they'd have to awaken him to get past him.

It wasn't much of a guarantee but it would have to do.

DELILAH SLEPT like the dead.

She had about as easy of a time waking up as a corpse would, as well.

Rafe was disgustingly bright-eyed and well rested when he shook her awake for the second time. He moved with dizzying speed, telling Ferris to hurry. It was still dark out, as far as she could tell, but he had the water boiling. He'd changed his shirt and shaved, looking as refreshed as Delilah didn't feel.

At least her neck was healed.

She sat up, forced her eyes open, and wished she knew what Ferris had put in that soup. Her tongue was thick and her thoughts were fuzzy.

Rafe snapped his fingers, urging her to hurry. "The water's getting cold and we need to leave."

"It's still dark."

"That's why it's the perfect time to leave."

"Where are we going?"

"New D.C."

That news awakened Delilah with a snap. Rafe dumped a bucket of hot water into the basin in the bathroom and she knew she'd have to go to him for an answer.

He gestured her past him into the small room, then didn't leave.

At her pointed glance, he folded his arms across his chest and leaned in the doorway. "I'm staying. Get used to it."

Behind him, Ferris stacked the soup bowls noisily. The boy was no more mute than Delilah, given his ability to communicate his thoughts so clearly.

"Why New D.C.?"

"To see you installed as the official Oracle of the Republic. Why else?"

"You said something about that earlier, about making me Oracle. Why do you care?"

"I saw you give the prophecy at the Citadel," he reminded her. "Clearly, the angels speak through you. You weren't faking that." He grimaced. "Unlike that excuse of a prophecy that the Daughter Superior tried to present as the real thing."

"You saw that too?"

"Not by choice. They locked us into the chapel to witness it."

"It was rehearsed," Delilah said, unable to hide her disgust. "I saw them, the day before. That's when I knew they were going to lie."

"It wasn't well rehearsed," Rafe said. "Someone would have to be pretty naive to believe that it was genuine." He smiled and she felt herself flush. "Especially after your vision." He pointed a finger at her. "That was the real thing."

It was wonderful that someone believed in her gift.

Their gazes met for a moment and Delilah felt her resistance to him melting away. It was too tempting to believe that she finally had a champion, but Delilah wasn't going any farther with Rafe without knowing his loyalties. Maybe he was on her side and maybe he wasn't. Maybe he'd tell her the truth and maybe he'd lie. She liked to think that she'd be able to tell the difference.

She looked down at the basin to muster her questions, then asked what she most wanted to know. "Why did you shoot the shade hunter?"

She didn't imagine his surprise.

She was shocked that he answered her so solemnly.

"It was an instinctive choice, but I don't regret it," he said and she found herself believing him. "I have to protect you and it seemed that you would prefer for Ferris to be protected too."

"You just wanted to win my trust."

"Maybe." He grinned then, and she admitted that there was something seductive about his confidence, about the ease with which he moved through the world. "That strategy doesn't seem to be working very well, does it?"

Delilah averted her gaze quickly. "Why do you have to protect me?"

"It's my mission."

She was too aware of his proximity, and the shiver it seemed to encourage deep inside her. Just hearing his voice made her remember the pleasure he had given her, and make her wonder about what came next.

"What kind of hunter are you?" she asked.

Rafe leaned in the doorway, apparently content to answer her questions. Only his restlessly tapping fingers revealed his desire to hurry. His eyes glittered too.

"I'm not a hunter." Delilah blinked in surprise and he smiled again. "Not by trade. I was just hunting you."

It wasn't an encouraging distinction. "What's the difference?"

He held up a finger and she noticed the strength of his hands. "I have one prey, one goal, one quest."

"Which is?"

"To install you as the official Oracle of the Republic. Everything else is just detail."

He *was* telling her what she wanted to hear. She turned her back on him, unwilling to be beguiled by his assurance and easy stories.

Rafe spoke with the urgency of someone intent on persuasion. "My first task is to keep you alive." She glanced up and he met her gaze so steadily that he couldn't be lying. "And that means gaining your trust, which means protecting those you care about, like Ferris." He shrugged. "The shade hunter and his dog probably deserved to die."

"That choice made you a fugitive too."

He spared a rueful glance at his palm. "True. An inconvenient bit of fallout." He seemed to consider his next words, but she knew what they were.

"The all points bulletin."

"Unfortunately, the description isn't bad, and they've nailed our location pretty well. They're not sure if you're my hostages or my companions, but the instruction is shoot to kill."

"Shoot to kill *you*," Delilah clarified, her heart in her throat.

He nodded, at surprising ease with this bad news. "Plus we're not welcome guests in this den of illicit growth."

"You think the owners will turn up."

"They aren't going to call the police, but who knows what kind of other security measures they have installed." His eyes widened slightly as he straightened. "I'm not convinced that we aren't being monitored, so we're not going to overstay our welcome." He looked as if he'd wash her down himself if she didn't get to it.

Infected by his urgency, Delilah raised her hands to the clasp of the cloak.

Then she froze. "Wait a minute. How can you know about the bulletin? Are you a policeman?"

Rafe laughed. "Hardly."

"Do you work for the Republic?"

"No." He sobered. "As you said, I get a lot of messages." He reached for the clasp of the cloak himself and Delilah took a step backward, her hands locked over it.

"If you don't work for the Society or for the Republic, then who do you work for?"

He looked briefly pained. Then he sighed and shook his head. "I don't know."

His confession was so heartfelt that she knew it was true. Even though it made no sense.

Before she could ask, Rafe raised a hand. "I don't remember. I would tell you if I knew, Delilah, I swear it, but I don't know."

He held her gaze unflinchingly. Delilah couldn't glimpse any evidence that he was lying to her.

She believed him.

But Rafe wasn't stupid or slow. He wasn't the kind of person who forgot things like the identity of his employer or the reasoning behind his mission.

Which could only mean that his memory had been wiped.

The conclusion made Delilah's blood run cold.

IX

DELILAH COULDN'T hide the terror that realization sent through her, so she turned her back on Rafe and dropped his cloak. Her thoughts flew as she scrubbed her skin vigorously. Her agitation was sufficient that she could almost ignore the fact that Rafe was watching her.

Almost but not quite.

She felt the weight of his gaze upon her, and was well aware that she couldn't be the most attractive woman he'd ever seen. Her skin was pale from her time in the netherzones and she was leaner than a woman of her height should be. No one wasted food on shades—they got enough to survive and not one bite more. Her hair was no more than dark stubble on her head, shaved down to avoid both the trouble of maintaining it and the potential of lice.

But Rafe looked.

Delilah could imagine what he was thinking. She felt her face heat as her irritation grew. It wasn't her fault that she had been condemned to the shadows—in fact, given a choice, she would have chosen just about any other life than the one she'd had. At least she was strong. At least she had survived. At least her mind was clear again. Those were no small accomplishments, given what she'd endured. She cleaned her body with quick strokes, appreciative of its power under duress.

And Delilah's mind was still intact as well. Even thinking about Rafe having a memory wipe revolted her.

It made her feel lucky.

Shades routinely had their memories eliminated with electrical "therapy." If a shade witnessed something that could condemn its master, that shade could rely upon a session with the electrodes. There would be no risk of the shadows revealing what should have been hidden.

A memory wipe was the only thing that Delilah truly feared. She endured the injections and the pills, but would trade anything to avoid the electrodes.

Her mind was the one thing she had left.

But Rafe wasn't a shade. Delilah had never heard of the procedure being done to norms, except criminals.

She hesitated for a moment. Was Rafe a criminal?

He operated well for someone who had been "cleansed," but then the technology used on norms might be more sophisticated than that used on shades. The operators might be able to target specific bits of data, instead of simply wiping all memories from the mind. They might be able to edit a norm's memories, instead of turning them into gibbering fools or silent zombies.

Maybe Rafe *was* a criminal, being given a chance to serve society as penance for his crimes. There was no telling whom he was working for, no guessing what his real alliances were. Obviously, he was supposed to win her trust, and just as obviously, she'd have to be insane to put her faith in him.

Even if that was her instinct. Maybe she could have trusted Rafe under other circumstances—but she didn't dare trust whoever had wiped his memory. Anyone that intent on remaining hidden couldn't have noble objectives.

What was she going to do? She had the gift; the angels had told her that she was destined to be Oracle. She had to prove her abilities to someone who could sponsor her.

That wasn't a renegade like Rafe.

Delilah recalled Rachel being harvested and steeled her resolve. Anything had to be better than being harvested by the Society. Even risking her gift was better than that. She had to trust in the angels. She'd pretend to trust Rafe, pretend to be cooperative, seduce him if necessary, then run for help.

Delilah glanced over her shoulder and found a surprising heat in Rafe's eyes. He *did* find her attractive. Her mouth went dry, her skin tingled in recollection of the pleasure he'd given her.

But he'd had none.

Delilah could work with that. She pulled the shift over her head, turning as she did so. She knew Rafe would look at what the sheer fabric didn't hide, and he did. In a way, she appreciated that he didn't pretend his response was anything other than what it was. It was honest.

Maybe he'd been chosen because he was easy to trust.

That told Delilah that his employer was even less trust-worthy.

She picked up the corset, pretended to be confused by it, even though she'd laced dozens of acolytes into theirs. She met Rafe's gaze with all the innocence she could muster. "What is this? Can you help me with it?"

Rafe's eyes darkened and he swallowed, then he stepped into the small room. Delilah could feel the heat of his skin and the intensity of his gaze, and felt new confidence in her plan.

She, after all, was now Sonja Andresson, citizen and Daughter of the Light of the Republic. She could escape Rafe, find a sponsor, and make her way to New D.C. All she had to do was keep her tattoo hidden, and cover her head until her hair grew in, and she could pass as a norm.

Even though she wasn't.

She knew all about things being other than they appeared, about feigned responses and counterfeit goods. In a way, her whole life had prepared her for this challenge.

Delilah was ready.

THE WOMAN was a temptress.

Rafe eyed the intriguing shadows visible through Delilah's shift and ached for the satisfaction he hadn't yet had. He could see the curve of her breasts, the rosy shadow of her nipples, the dark triangle of hair at the apex of her thighs. When he stepped closer, he smelled her skin and the perfume from her arousal.

There was something about his ward that struck his heart. Delilah was both strong and vulnerable in a way that caught his attention as no woman ever had.

Rafe cleared his throat, reminding himself that they had to run. "Sumptuary & Decency requires all adult women to wear corsets, heels of a minimum height, to have all flesh covered from casual view, as well as a number of other injunctions." He took the intimate garment in his hands. "I don't want you to get arrested on an S&D violation."

"Veils too. Women wear veils." Delilah's words fell with a haste that revealed her own awareness of him. Rafe appreciated that he wasn't the only one caught in the snare of desire.

In fact, he had definite ideas of how their relationship could proceed.

"A veil will hide my shaved head," she said, then glanced up at him. Her expression was coy, the way she looked through her lashes making her seem more delicate and feminine.

"It'll make it easier for you to pass as an older woman, as Sonja's record says she is."

Their gazes locked and held. Her eyes widened and he saw her catch her breath, watched her nipples tighten and her cheeks flush. Her lips parted, as if in invitation.

Rafe wanted to caress her from head to toe, run his fingers over the smooth pallor of her skin and feel her soft strength. He forced himself to think about moving on. There'd be safer places to indulge their mutual attraction.

"I found you a veil," he said, knowing he sounded more stern than he was. "Hurry."

She turned at his indication and lifted her arms, arching her neck. He wrapped the corset around her waist, convinced even as he did so that there wasn't enough of her to be cinched smaller. The woman needed a month of good meals, enough laughter to make her eyes sparkle again, enough pleasure to soften the line of her lips.

That probably wouldn't be his task, though Rafe wanted to do it. He wanted to take her to the pleasure fringe, watch her learn to laugh, buy her food and drink and nights in decadent luxury. He wanted to teach her about pleasure in all its varied forms, and had the strange sense that his previous fascination with sensation had been only so he could share his knowledge with Delilah. She should be dressed in brocade and silk, in lustrous colors and gems, not these sturdy fabrics of dun and faded blue.

They had to leave.

He pulled the cords of the corset tight and she caught her breath, then glanced over her shoulder. From the glint in her eyes, he anticipated a challenge and he got one.

"If you're afraid of repercussions from the people who own this cabin, what are we going to do to reimburse them? What's the price of hospitality?"

"What do you mean?"

"It wouldn't be right to just take food and clothes from their home." She held his gaze and Rafe knew she was asking about more than the clothes.

She wanted to know his morals.

Well, they might surprise her.

"I doubt they worry about a few lentils," he said, knotting the lace. He had a strange sense that the cabin had held its breath to listen to his answer, as well. It wasn't anyone's home either.

"What about their destroyed image-snatchers and fried sensors? Security devices cost serious cred."

"I think they've got it."

"Which doesn't entitle you to take it."

"True." Rafe decided that she was due for a surprise of her own. "That's why I'm going to pay them."

"With what?"

Rafe handed her the ugly dress and she tugged it over her head. He fastened the buttons up the back and was glad it was a reasonably decent fit. He tried to make her smile. "I could leave tokens from the pleasure fringe."

"There can't be one near here."

Rafe thought the owners of this cabin probably knew where to find one, as well as many other places on the periphery of the law, but held that thought.

She clearly thought he was avoiding her question, because

she began to chide him. "Just because they're not home doesn't mean that you can take whatever you want, Rafe." She trailed a fingertip down his arm, as if trying to be provocative, and smiled at him.

Rafe blinked. "I know." He lifted one stocking, intending to slide it up her leg. He was sure she would take it from him, but she halted midgesture and smiled. She perched on the side of the tub and extended her leg to him.

Her pose was so inviting that Rafe was caught by surprise.

As a shade, of course, Delilah wouldn't be used to anyone helping her to dress. Maybe she liked it. It certainly wasn't a problem for Rafe. Delilah's legs were all long lean muscle, and he savored their feminine curves.

He eased the stocking up her leg, over her knee and thigh, following it with the palm of one hand. Her eyes widened when he slid his finger across her skin and beneath her skirts in search of the garter, then she shivered.

He couldn't summon a word to his lips when his hands were lost in the fullness of her shift and petticoats, when the smoothness of her fair skin was beneath his fingers and the scent of her filled his nostrils. She stared up at him, those eyes dark with the same wonder he felt.

He wanted to pull off the faded blue dress and cast her on the bed in her corset and stockings. He wanted to run his hands over her skin, learn her shape and find every spot that made her sigh with pleasure. He wanted to indulge both of them, forget time, surrender to sensation . . .

Ferris dropped a pot in the kitchen, and the metal clattered on the floor. Rafe didn't imagine that it was an accident. Delilah jumped and Rafe lifted his hands away, reminded again of the unwelcome press of time.

"We have to hurry," she chided him when both stockings were fastened. He had a glimpse of the playful sparkle in her eyes as she reached for the boots.

Rafe straightened and caught his breath, knowing his codpiece had never felt so restrictive. He couldn't bring himself to step away from her. He could imagine her with her hair grown in. It would be like ebony silk, lustrous and soft, falling against her cheek in gentle waves. He would run his fingers through it . . .

"How are you going to pay them?" she prompted, drawing his errant thoughts back to the conversation.

Rafe smiled. "With this." He reached into the pouch on his belt and pulled out a necklace. He hoped to shock her and he wasn't disappointed.

Delilah stared.

And justifiably so. This wasn't just any necklace. It was a piece of jewelry fit for a queen. Rafe had known as soon as he'd seen it that he had to have it. It was thick with aquamarines and diamonds, and glittered like a rare constellation. It was worth a fortune by any accounting.

This kind of jewelry hadn't been made in close to a hundred years. It was a decadent indulgence, a pleasure and an expense that could be afforded by few. Rafe's determination to possess it had been odd. Even though he loved gems and sparkling items, even though he routinely borrowed or adopted them, they seldom fascinated him for more than a moment of possession. He surrendered those trinkets to those who seemed to need them, making gifts of them along his way and bartering advantage with them.

He'd felt a strange imperative to possess this necklace, one that hadn't faded once he'd claimed it. He had a sense that he had to keep it for a special occasion.

He knew that this day was that occasion.

Delilah regarded the jewelry with a horror that was as far from his own admiration as possible. "Where did you get that?" she whispered.

"I liberated it from the collection of a wife of a senator." Rafe lifted the necklace high, grinning in recollection of that night. *That* had been a tribute to pleasure.

It would be a pale shadow compared to a night with Delilah, though. The gems sparkled in the light, taunting him with their limitations. They were beautiful, but not the elusive prize that drove him onward.

He smiled at Delilah but her new amorous mood had already vanished. "You stole it."

"I admired it and she offered it." She had wanted to repay him for their night together, but Rafe thought that detail irrelevant in present company.

Delilah put her hands on her hips and her eyes flashed. "You *stole* it!"

"She gave it to me."

"You're a thief."

"An opportunist, maybe."

"Thief!"

"I admire beauty," Rafe corrected.

"I knew it," Delilah muttered incomprehensibly and reached for the heavy ivory veil he'd found. She cast it over her head, then jammed a hat on top of it to hold it in place. "Who says norms are free?" she muttered, then reached for the brown cloak. "There's no freedom in wearing all this *stuff* . . ."

Rafe offered the necklace to her. "Here, try it on."

Even through the veil he saw the furious flash of her eyes, and their fervent hue meant he had to see her in this necklace.

"I will not try on stolen goods!"

The aquamarines would make her eyes look more blue. And he'd have his sight of her in majesty, long before it came to pass.

Just one glimpse, before he left the necklace behind forever.

He realized that that glimpse was truly the only thing he'd wanted from it.

"You said that we have to go," she said and made to push past him.

Rafe caught her elbow, spun her around, and lifted the thick veil away. He fastened the necklace around her neck before she could argue. The cold weight of it settled against her skin and he saw the astonishment in her eyes at its heft. She looked toward the mirror almost reluctantly and Rafe was sure that she was standing a little taller after she saw her reflection.

She also couldn't look away. The gems did highlight her

eyes, making their color more vehement. They accentuated the pallor of her skin and her delicacy, making her look fragile.

Rare.

He wanted her with a vigor that shook him.

"It must be worth a fortune," she whispered, her fingers caressing it.

"Certainly." He stood behind her, taking her shoulders in his hands.

She met his gaze in the mirror, her own expression turning dubious. "And you're just going to leave it here?"

Rafe grinned. "It's payment. They can sell it, get their security system upgraded or repaired." He reached into his pouch and removed the matching earrings. They glittered against his hand, then he held them beside her ears. "Do you think I should leave the earrings too?"

She was shocked again, but hid it more quickly. Rafe was coming to enjoy the glimpses of her real thoughts and watch for them. "You won't do it."

"I will."

"I don't believe you."

He offered the earrings to her. "Then you leave them."

She hesitated. He opened her hand and dropped the earrings into her palm. She stared down at them as they sparkled against her skin. "I could keep them myself."

"You won't."

"You sound very certain of that." She slanted a glance at him. "Of me."

He didn't tell her that she was easily read, knowing that she wouldn't take well to that bit of information. "These gems are not meant for you," he said softly. "They're not your birthright."

"I don't have a birthright," she said with an impatience that seemed forced. "Haven't you heard? I'm a shade, a fugitive shade—"

"You are destined to be Oracle," Rafe said, interrupting her. "I see you robed in splendor and seated upon the throne of the Oracle in New D.C."

She was silenced by his conviction, then tried to hide her surprise. "Do you have the gift of foresight too?"

Rafe shook his head. "No. But I can see you there." He took a deep breath. "The Oracle sits enthroned in majesty, in a massive room of white marble, surrounded by columns. She sits like a goddess in a Greek temple and the faithful cannot mount the last three stairs before her. They fall on their knees there and are forbidden to speak in her presence, lest they distract her from her visions. She sits above them, pure and holy, untainted by their human desires. She sees into the future and into the hearts of men and shares with all what she witnesses."

"In verse," Delilah said quietly.

Rafe met her gaze in the mirror. "She is robed in white, and holds a staff of gold. She wears a a diadem that holds a single diamond and binds it like a star to her forehead. Just as the true Oracle hears the voices of the angels, so this rare large diamond is a symbol of her ability to see clearly."

"Angelfire," Delilah whispered with conviction, although Rafe wasn't sure why. He supposed so, given that the rhetoric was that the angels spoke through the Oracle.

"It's your destiny to wear the Oracle's gem." He brushed his finger across her forehead and she jumped. He was surprised, because he had touched her more intimately before, but she took a step back before meeting his gaze.

Was she so afraid to want anything for herself? Was she so dubious that she could have a dream or an ambition—or that it could be achieved?

His determination to see her enthroned redoubled.

"You will wear that diadem," he said with authority, convinced of his own words. "I will ensure it, even if it is the last thing I do on this earth."

He let his fingertip rest upon her forehead, exactly where the diamond would fall, exactly between her brows. "That diamond will look like a star upon your brow, and it will be the only gem you ever need."

She trembled then, shook like a leaf in the wind.

Was she going to have another vision?

Before Rafe could ask, Delilah fumbled with the clasp and pulled the necklace from around her throat. She lunged from the room, dropping the gems on the table.

"What's wrong?"

She seemed disoriented and disturbed, and her cheeks were flushed. As much Rafe would have liked to have taken credit for that, he knew something else was at root.

What had he said?

What had he done?

"We have to go." Delilah headed for the door. "You said so."

She was hiding something from Rafe and he knew it. He also knew she wouldn't readily confide in him. Rafe grit his teeth, his frustration rising.

Just what he needed—another obstacle.

The last thing he'd expected was obstruction from the person he was determined to help.

RAFE'S FINGERTIP on her forehead sent a shock through Delilah, a jolt that reminded her of the brilliant white light she had seen once before. He'd brushed his fingertip across that old healed scar, the one that no one could see anymore, and his touch had awakened something deep within her.

She remembered the searing touch of angelfire.

The diamond on the headdress of the Oracle was a reference to the same blinding light of clarity brought by the angels. She saw the white heat of it in her mind's eye before a vision, felt its caress upon her skin when the angels took possession of her, body and soul.

Rafe's second touch had made her see the angelfire again. The weight of his fingertip had summoned the blinding white light. Or had his touch coincided with the first hint of another vision?

Delilah didn't know.

How could Rafe summon angelfire? That was impossible, as far as she knew. She couldn't dismiss his impact upon her, though, and now that she thought about it, the pleasure he had given her had been similar to angelfire in the way it seemed to fill her body with starlight.

And leave her energized.

She needed a sponsor whom she could trust.

She recalled the gathering in the chapel at the Citadel and the glimpse she'd had of one palm held high over the heads of the assembled witnesses.

Who had it been? Rafe was so distracting that Delilah had to put distance between them in order to think.

Unfortunately, Rafe had other ideas. He was fast behind her, taking one step for every two of hers, and caught her elbow before she got halfway across the room. He spun her to a halt, catching her other elbow in his other hand and lifting her from the ground when she would have run.

Delilah panicked. She aimed a kick at his knees and missed.

Rafe's eyes flashed but she kicked again, catching his knee with the toe of her boot. He yelped, loosed his grip on her, and Delilah wriggled free. She backed away, heading for the door. Ferris watched her from behind Rafe, his pose utterly still.

Rafe looked annoyed. Delilah didn't doubt his conviction that he could catch her. He was waiting for her to make a move.

"I need answers," she said.

"Don't we all?"

"Who vidcast my vision?" She ignored his amusement. "At the chapel. Someone image-snatched with a palm."

He eyed her for a long moment, then answered. "The Reverend Billie Jo Estevez. Why?"

"She's famous, isn't she?"

"Probably the most famous vid-evangelist in the Republic." Rafe folded his arms across his chest and regarded her. "Why?"

Delilah's thoughts flew. Rafe had been persuaded that her gift was genuine just by watching her vision. Had the reverend been similarly convinced? "Did she endorse the Oracle who the Daughters presented?"

Rafe shrugged, his gaze unswerving. "It doesn't matter. That Oracle must be dead."

A horrific thought came to Delilah and she closed the distance between herself and Rafe before she thought about it. "What about the reverend? Did she die in the fire?"

"No. The witnesses were gone by then." He tilted his head to regard her. "Why are you so interested all of a sudden in the Reverend Billie Jo Estevez?"

Delilah thought for a split second. Rafe looked grim and determined, skeptical but capable. She thought it was worth a try to persuade him to her view. Maybe he could escort her to the reverend.

Maybe she had a better chance with him than without him.

Maybe he wouldn't be easy to shake.

"Because I need a sponsor to vouch for me, and it might be easier to meet the reverend than to get to New D.C. without a plan."

His eyes flashed with annoyance. "Getting to New D.C. *is* a plan."

"But not a thorough one," Delilah argued. "Who would I call once I got there? It's far and won't be an easy journey— I might not even get there alive. It would be smarter to find a sponsor sooner rather than later and go there under protection."

Rafe's lips tightened. "There's nothing saying that a fugitive shade will have an easy time getting an audience with the most successful vid-evangelist in the Republic," he noted. "She probably has dozens in her entourage."

"Ping her."

Rafe laughed. "And bring the hunters directly to us? I don't think so."

"Then I will." She fumbled with her palm, uncertain how to command it to do such a thing. It had to be easy, though, because norms used their palms all the time . . .

Ferris made his cry of agitation, as if calling Rafe to action.

But Rafe had already moved. He seized Delilah's wrists, ensuring that she couldn't touch her own palm. She fought against him, but he was bigger and stronger.

"Are you insane?" he hissed, his eyes flashing with anger for the first time. "You'd just be surrendering all of us to the hunters. It'll achieve nothing if you're condemned to the slave dens again, or sacrificed for research."

Ferris twitched, folding his arms around himself in agitation at the very mention of the Society's labs.

"But the reverend . . ."

"Might or might not be interested in having a true Oracle installed in New D.C.," Rafe said through his teeth. His gaze bored into Delilah's own. "The Daughters wanted a false Oracle enough to create one. Maybe the reverend was complicit with that plan. Maybe going to her just makes it easy to collect and eliminate you."

Delilah exhaled, hating that he made so much sense. "You don't know her and her motives."

"Neither do you." He must have realized that she wouldn't fight him anymore because he released her. He still stood close, though, filling her vision with his breadth and strength. "Besides, she's in Hood River, which is in the opposite direction from New D.C."

"How do you know that?"

Rafe caught his breath, perhaps realizing his slip too late. He lifted his left hand and smiled ruefully. "Guess." The display of his palm glinted, reminding Delilah that persons unknown had Rafe under their control.

That gave more credence to her plan to contact the reverend, a plan that Rafe obviously opposed—maybe for reasons other than the ones he presented.

Now she knew where the reverend was.

Rafe was a criminal who'd had a memory wipe. His true motives were unknown, maybe even to himself.

Rafe's soft words surprised her. "What will it take for you to trust me, Delilah? What could I do?"

She decided to give him some honesty, just to see how he liked it. She met his gaze unflinchingly, willing him to see that she was being honest with him. "I'm not even sure it's possible for me to trust anyone."

Rafe nodded and stared at his boots for a moment. He

looked up abruptly, his gaze locking with hers. "We're not going to succeed in installing you as Oracle unless we work together."

"You have to answer some questions for me first."

His eyes narrowed briefly and she knew he was anxious to get moving. She expected him to deny her request, and braced herself to make the hard choice.

To her surprise, Rafe indulged her. "Ask."

"Who are you?"

"I told you. I'm Raphael Gerritson."

"Where do you come from?"

"Paduca." He raised his left hand when she would have asked for more details. "And no, I don't remember. My palm does."

"What's your occupation?"

"I don't have one." He waved his hand. "According to my palm."

"Really?"

"It says I'm a bon vivant and pleasure seeker." His smile was quick and irreverent, so attractive that Delilah regretting its immediate disappearance. "I do like the sound of that."

"But how do you survive?"

"By my wits." Rafe's expression became so reckless and sexy that Delilah's heart skipped a beat. "I steal things. I rely upon the kindness of strangers. And I get lucky, a lot."

"As if someone is looking out for you."

He sobered and spared a glance at his palm. "As if."

"That's not very reassuring."

"It's all I can tell you. I could lie, but the truth seems the better option."

"Such as it is."

He inclined his head. "Such as it is."

In the distance, the hunting dogs began to bark again. Ferris started, then clenched his hands in agitation. She felt Ferris look at her, but she had already turned back to face Rafe.

Rafe pushed the door open wider with his fingertips. "Are we in this together, or do you and Ferris want to go it alone?"

Delilah stared at him. No one had ever given her a choice. For a long moment, her mind stalled on the possibilities.

Was this freedom? The right to choose?

The chance to make a mistake?

Delilah felt the burden of a new responsibility. She didn't believe for a minute that Rafe would abandon what he called his mission or his quest. She thought it would be easier to get away from him if he trusted her a bit. It would also be easier to evade him if they were traveling together—she'd know where he was.

If they parted ways now, she knew he'd just follow her.

And he'd probably be good at ensuring that he wasn't detected.

If she was waiting for her moment to flee, this wasn't it.

She forced a smile. "All right. Let's be a team."

The dogs barked at closer proximity and Rafe glanced to the doorway at the sound. Delilah knew she'd have to decide what to do about Rafe later.

For the moment, they all needed to run.

Delilah watched as Rafe checked that the cabin was restored to rights, even to the point of straightening the bed and ensuring that Ferris had returned the pots to their original locations. He arranged the gems on the one table, presumably so they couldn't be missed by the returning occupants.

He was the strangest thief imaginable. He seemed to take pride in making the gems look like the gift he said they were, and couldn't keep himself from caressing the cut stones with a fingertip. His admiration of their beauty was clear.

Delilah was sure he wouldn't really leave the jewels behind, that there'd be some sleight of hand at the last minute, so she ensured that she was last out the door. She looked back at the icy gleam of the necklace and earrings as Rafe pulled the door shut and secured it.

She waited, expectant, but he didn't manufacture some excuse to go back into the cabin.

In fact, he turned his back on the door and never looked at it again.

As if he'd forgotten what he'd left behind.

Could he do that with people as well? A chill touched her heart. Was that part of his memory wipe? Had he been "taught" to forget? Or to not let anything matter to him? She'd heard of shades having their long-term memory obliterated so they never imagined that there was anything else. They lived their entire life in present tense.

Rafe couldn't be one of them, could he?

The man was nothing if not a challenge to her expectations. Maybe there was another explanation. Maybe the gems weren't real. Maybe having them in his possession was dangerous.

She slanted a glance his way and found it hard to believe that Rafe worried much about what was dangerous. He seemed to enjoy defying expectation and taking risks.

She preferred to think that, like a modern Robin Hood, Rafe had left payment for what he had used, in kind if not in coin. Maybe he didn't care about possessions. The gems were lovely, but they and the riches they offered had no hold over his heart.

What kind of thief kept so little of value for himself?

A rich and successful thief, perhaps.

Or a thief who was playing for higher stakes.

Maybe in ceding to a memory wipe, he'd saved himself from execution. Delilah shivered.

Rafe couldn't tell her—he probably didn't remember. She suspected that officially, no one knew. Memory wipes had a sympathetic effect on those who administered them—no one remembered them being done, even those who hadn't been condemned to the treatment.

Truth in the Republic was a slippery commodity.

Just like the fog that had gathered in the clearing that surrounded the cabin.

X

MONTGOMERY WAS frustrated.

It had been almost a day since the offer had come from the wraiths and he was no further ahead. He hadn't found a way to reply to them, or even any evidence that they existed. He hadn't managed to collect much cred, and knew that what he had couldn't possibly be enough to ensure Delilah's survival. He sat in the darkness that night, struggling to find a solution.

It was dawn when he looked up and saw Lil watching him from the bedroom door. She looked strained and tired, and he knew she hadn't slept either.

"Who would kill Matheson?" he asked.

She shrugged. "Impossible to know without having been there, or knowing him."

"His wife maybe."

"His mistress," Lil suggested with typical irreverence.

"Someone he'd gotten the better of in the past," Montgomery said, feeling that he was grasping at straws.

Lil brightened. "Someone who didn't want him running for the presidency again."

He looked up at her tone.

"He's really popular, his reelection pretty much a fait accompli. Someone ambitious might prefer to adjust the stakes."

Montgomery frowned, knowing what name she was going to propose. "Lil, Max isn't responsible for everything that goes wrong in the Republic."

"Maybe not, but removing an obstacle in the way of his ambition would be pretty much his forté."

"What about Van Buren?"

"He's too much of a hard ass. Max can kick his butt."

Montgomery was impatient with her conviction. "You've got no proof, Lil."

"Other than how his popularity ranking jumped right after Matheson's death." She sighed and frowned. "It's like Gid's death, but we don't have any inside information or connections to work with." She ran a hand through her hair, then asked the question that he'd been dreading. "Any luck with the cred?"

"You said already that we didn't have enough." He shrugged. "I was hoping you were wrong."

"And now she might never be Oracle." She came into the room and sat down wearily opposite him, her defeated pose tearing at his heart. "I remember watching the Oracle be installed at the inaugural ceremonies for President Arthur. That would have been 2088. Remember it?"

"You know I don't."

"I do." Her voice softened. "I met Max at that vidcast."

Montgomery's ears pricked up at the mention of Lilia's former lover—and the father of her daughter—but he tried to hide his interest. He'd learned that the expression of curiosity made his partner evasive. He frowned at his interlinked hands in apparent concentration instead, as if he wasn't really listening to her.

"I thought the Oracle was just for show," Montgomery said when she didn't continue. "I thought it was fake."

"But they're supposed to be the instruments of the angels, the echo of their voice on earth." She stared at him hard, but Montgomery wasn't ready for more questions about his compatriots. It wouldn't have surprised him if the angels had more than one way to influence events in the world, even though he knew nothing about the Oracle. He kept his own gaze averted, knowing that Lil expected him to give her information, feeling a barrier between them grow when he didn't.

"I went to the live vidcast, over my mother's protest. I wasn't quite fifteen and—" Lilia chuckled under her breath "—I was probably a challenge to her."

"Probably?" Montgomery gave her a look.

She grinned. "Okay. I was a hell-raiser."

Montgomery had no trouble believing that.

"And I wanted to meet the governor."

"Why?"

"Oh, Max was one sexy beast in those days and I was, to put it mildly, infatuated with him."

Montgomery sobered and went to his desktop, ensuring that Lil couldn't see his eyes.

"The infatuation, of course, was because my mother despised him. I would never have even been aware of a politician if she hadn't ranted about his tendencies to autocracy at regular intervals."

Montgomery said nothing.

"I stalked Max and flirted with him at that party, and ended up beside him when the inauguration was on every screen. I thought that what I saw in his face as he watched was idealism." Lil sighed. "But it was raw ambition. I know that now."

Montgomery chose to keep silent.

Lil came and perched on the side of his chair. "You never saw that vidcast. It was amazing. The President gave his first speech, announcing his policies. They weren't popular—you don't remember, but Madison wanted to add more eyes to the Republic."

Montgomery folded his arms across his chest, intrigued but wary. Lil was altogether too animated for his taste in discussing her former lover.

"That policy really wasn't popular on the Frontier, and Max was a bit twitchy about his own tenure as a result. You could feel the dissent in the ranks of his supporters, even through the vid-link, and on the floor where we were watching, the mood was downright hostile. Max's bodyguards were hovering close and I wondered whether things would get ugly."

Montgomery declined to note that Lil had made her way through the bodyguards. He had a healthy respect for her ability to achieve her ends, especially when she was determined.

Lil lifted her hands. "Then the Oracle appeared in a beam of light. It was as if she had slid down from heaven on a moonbeam. She was all dressed in white, that diadem with its huge diamond right in the middle of her forehead. The hall went silent with awe and the President dropped to one knee."

"Not both knees?"

Lil smiled. "He wasn't begging."

Montgomery sniffed at that.

"The Oracle pronounced that the short-term pain of his proposals would lead to inevitable gain, that the Republic would become invincible or some such nonsense. It was all in rhyme and sounded beautiful. It sounded inevitable." Her voice dropped. "It didn't hurt that she was young and blond and beautiful. She could have been made of sugar or stardust."

She cleared her throat. "But you could feel the tide of opinion change as she spoke. I remember there was a public-approval meter on the bottom of the one screen, an instant-update on the polls, and I watched it move higher." She lost herself in some memory and Montgomery was pretty sure he didn't want to know what it was.

"Then?" he prompted.

"Then she went to President Arthur and took his hands in hers, and raised him to his feet. He kissed her hand and Max muttered that he ought to be grateful. She kissed both of Arthur's cheeks, then put her hand in his elbow as they walked up the steps of the Capitol."

"You mean she led him?"

"They walked beside each other, like a couple." Lil arched a brow. "The union of church and state, remember? At the summit, she stepped away and turned to the crowd, holding up her hands. There was a choral symphony, then a blaze of white light. A shower of white sparks spilled from the sky, tumbling over their heads and down the stairs."

"Like falling stars," Montgomery said wryly.

"It was a brilliant piece of theater. Just watching it made you feel lighter and happier, positive about the future. My mother said later that it was illusory and manipulative crap. Theater at best, hokum at worst."

Montgomery liked Lil's mother and would miss her acidic commentary. "What does she think of the Oracle?"

"She says they're all false and that the selection must be fixed. She doesn't have any basis for that conclusion, by the way, at least not beyond her own opinion."

"Not that we know anyone else so biased."

Lil pretended to ignore him, but he saw by the glint in her eyes that she'd heard. "She says that there hasn't been a true Oracle since 2051 at least."

"What happened then?"

"The Pacific Rim Conflict."

"I know that, but not anything about the Oracle."

"There were treaty negotiations in Seattle. The President went herself—that was Laura M. Macdonald—and she took the Oracle as a consultant. The Oracle hadn't moved from New D.C. before, but Macdonald had never been comfortable with the whole Oracle tradition. People thought it was a positive policy choice to include the Oracle in such important negotiations. The Oracle wasn't so positive about the outcome. She said that the Republic had been wrong to declare war in the first place. She said that Macdonald was leading the Republic astray."

"And what happened?"

"Seattle was nuked and the Oracle was killed." Lil arched a brow. "Not the President, though. My mother says the whole story of why they were separated stank from the outset. And that was when the Daughters of the Light of the Republic took sole responsibility for finding and training Oracles. The Oracles became chaste, because the Daughters run their organization like a convent. That worked for Macdonald in a big way, because she was the proponent of much of the Sumptuary & Decency legislation. My mother says the Oracles lost their touch with the divine because they sacrificed a part of what makes them human. She says it's unnatural to be chaste."

Montgomery could see the logic in that.

Lil sighed. "And my mother always notes that the President's favorite aunt was on the governing board of the Daughters at that time—and that the President owned shares in a munitions supply company involved in the war effort."

"No proof," Montgomery felt obliged to note.

"And you'll never find any now," Lil said. "It's all ancient history." She was dismissive of the relevance of her mother's opinions, but Montgomery wasn't so sure.

"So, as I was saying, the thing about this ceremony was its effect on the audience. The ceremony culminated in all this white light and glory. The President bowed, standing there humble amid a shower of sparks as the music soared to its conclusion. The crowd went completely wild in their applause."

"They'd never seen such a spectacle?"

"It was particularly well done. And Max . . . Max was enraptured."

Montgomery felt a pang. "What do you mean?"

"He said that having an Oracle in his pocket gave the President carte blanche to pass policy." She stepped aside and looked Montgomery in the eye. "He said he'd do anything to have an Oracle on his side. *Anything*. Then he laughed and propositioned me, pretending he hadn't been serious. But he was."

"And now he's running for the presidency." Montgomery thought about the Oracle presented by the Daughters of the Light of the Republic and how pallid she seemed in comparison to the passion of Lil's daughter. "Do you think he'd buy himself an Oracle?"

Lil scoffed. "That's not the question. The question is whether he could afford it."

"How much would he pay?"

"Well, one thing is for certain. If he hadn't already lost his soul by the time I met him, he tossed it aside when he called the Society to harvest Delilah."

Montgomery tapped his fingers on the desktop. "Who was born with a third eye. Isn't that supposed to indicate a gift of prophecy?"

"Well, that's just rumor and mumbo jumbo, but that's the story you hear."

"And now she's shown that she has the gift of foresight."

Lil's lips tightened. "Which is putting her in danger. Again."

"Funny that the Oracle who could thwart Max might be his own daughter."

"It's not funny at all," Lil said fiercely. "We already know he'd eliminate her without a second thought." She sobered, then eyed him with concern. "Montgomery, I think it's clear what's going on. Max is running for president and he wants to win. He's managed to eliminate the only real competition. He's bought himself a false Oracle, and will eliminate Delilah to ensure that the false Oracle, the one in his pocket, rules."

"Speculation, Lil."

She leaned toward him, intent and convinced. "Who do you think paid for the raid on the Citadel, then? They were hunting someone. Don't you think they were hunting Delilah? Don't you think they were trying to get rid of her, to silence the voice of the angels?"

He met her gaze steadily, having no doubt that they'd both reached the same conclusion. "There's no proof, Lil," he said softly. "You don't accuse a man like Blackstone without proof and live to tell about it."

"You don't let a man like Max do whatever he wants whenever he wants." Lil had her determined look, the one she got whenever her daughter was mentioned or threatened. "We need to *find* proof. And then we need to stop Max."

Before she could say more, Montgomery's desktop pinged. He wasn't expecting a message and he had a bad feeling about receiving one.

He saw immediately that it was from the same untraceable source, which didn't make him feel any better. The wraiths had his number, so to speak, but he wasn't really interested in reading another demand for ransom.

There was no question of hiding it from Lil. She stared at the screen, holding her breath, and pointed imperiously.

She was right. There was nothing to be gained in avoiding bad news.

Montgomery clicked.

There were only two words in the message, but they were enough to send a chill down his spine:

PAYMENT RECEIVED.

Lil swore. "But by who?"

Montgomery didn't know that but he did know it was time to give Rafe some more motivation. Lil caught her breath but didn't intervene.

RAFE WISHED he had a plan, but he didn't. Delilah looked more vital and alive, color in her cheeks and purpose making her eyes flash. He found her more intriguing with every passing hour. It was as if she was awakening from a long sleep, discovering the woman she was meant to be.

He was fascinated.

Too fascinated.

Delilah was an enigma, a woman scarred by her history, but valiant enough to try to overcome the past. She was innocent in some matters and unexpectedly jaded in others. She had known nothing but deception and abuse, but remained idealistic. She had been beaten but not broken. He was amazed that she had any initiative left in her, and wasn't surprised that she found it hard to trust him.

He, in contrast, was beginning to trust Delilah completely. He felt that he could read her reactions, sometimes even before she was aware of them herself.

She needed a protector, a guardian, a bodyguard to defend her against others who would take advantage of her weaknesses. She needed someone to watch out for her until she found her footing in her new role.

Rafe considered himself to be the perfect candidate.

He didn't expect he'd find it easy to convince her, but welcomed the challenge.

"Just take her," murmured a man's deep voice in Rafe's own thoughts. *"Take what you deserve and take her now. It's only right."*

Rafe jumped.

What was that?

Who was that?

A man's voice that had sounded like it was part of his own thoughts, must have really been in his mind. Delilah watched him with obvious confusion, so she hadn't heard it at all.

Had he imagined it?

Rafe didn't think so. Still, the hair on the back of Rafe's neck prickled with the certainty that someone was watching them.

Even with the door of the cabin shut behind them.

He shuddered and tried to forget about the voice. He had enough to remember and enough to do. He had the strange sense that he couldn't trust himself if they lingered. That command that he *take* lingered on the periphery of his thoughts, making more sense than it should have, a whisper that he couldn't trust. He always had control over his impulses. He never took more than was offered. He prided himself on being a gentleman.

But there had been that voice in his thoughts, a voice that insisted he claim his due and take what was his, whether it was offered or not.

Was he overtired? That wasn't a stretch of the imagination.

Or had the whisper come from somewhere else?

Someone else?

The clearing was empty, except for a gathering of white fog. The clearing was as empty as it had been, but the idea of stepping into the fog filled Rafe with dread. Had he missed a trap?

Was his a genuine foreboding or was his persistently rotten luck affecting his perspective?

That fog was rapidly filling the area around the cabin. It was a strange fog, almost pearlescent in hue and radiant in an unnatural way. Rafe didn't like the look of it. It had already pooled at the bottom of the stairs and tendrils eased over the threshold into the cabin.

Fog wasn't going to stop him. Rafe stepped over the threshold and the fog coiled around his boots, as if it would caress him. It swirled around his ankle, like a tendril that would hold him in its grasp. It felt dirty, as fog never did, and seemed to emanate a presence of its own.

He thought this and felt foolish.

They had to move.

Immediately.

DELILAH HAD an instinctive dislike of the fog. It was a silvery silken fog that seemed to glow with its own light, and she distrusted how it had gathered so thickly while they were in the cabin.

As if it had targeted them.

Which made no sense.

All the same, the fog did pose a threat. They could become lost in it, or disoriented, or not see anyone who pursued them until it was too late.

The fog swirled, hiding and illuminating details, growing deeper by the minute. The sky was brightening, but it was so overcast that Delilah couldn't see the sun.

Rafe's unhappiness with its appearance was more than clear.

"Strange kind of fog," Delilah said.

"It's unnatural," he agreed. "But it is what it is."

Ferris pointed to the house, to some burned debris in the clearing, then looked at Rafe.

Rafe frowned. "You're right. It could be some kind of defense, maybe a mist generated from the water in the growing rooms. I don't know. Let's get out of here and think about it later."

Ferris nodded agreement and climbed the stairs to the clearing. The fog danced around his ankles, spiraling up to his knees as if it would devour him. It seemed to have an intent of its own, which made no sense. Delilah was certain that it wound up the leg of his trousers like a snake, even while knowing that was impossible.

But Ferris' eyes widened in horror. He flicked a glance at her, then pivoted, but not before she saw the bulge of his erection.

Rafe cleared his throat and Delilah knew he had seen the same thing. He offered his hand to her and they climbed the steps as one.

The fog embraced Delilah's legs and slipped under her skirts. The hem of her dress billowed out and she could feel the fog moving beneath her petticoats. She felt as if it caressed her, just as Rafe had done earlier, but the fog's touch was cold. It left her feeling dirty.

But it was just fog.

Wasn't it? She supposed it could be a hallucinogen, if it had been created as a defense of the cabin, one that twisted the thoughts of those who inhaled it.

Getting away from it was the smartest plan.

"Which way are we going?" she asked Rafe.

"East." He too seemed anxious to move out of the fog. He struck a path across the clearing and within a dozen steps, the fog had swallowed them like a silvery cloud.

Delilah couldn't even see the cabin anymore and her twinge of fear became more emphatic. Rafe, however, strode onward with purpose, as confident as ever.

"And which way is that?" she asked, not troubling to hide her uncertainty. He'd put her hand in her elbow and she liked having the strength of his arm beneath her hand. Having his heat close beside her was welcome as well.

"This way."

"Aren't you afraid of getting lost in the fog?"

"I'm more afraid to sit and wait to be discovered, in a corner with no escape." His tone was grim and Delilah had to admit that he had a point. She felt better moving too.

She just wasn't as confident as Rafe. "We might stumble right across the hunters."

"We might," he agreed amiably. "But fog carries sound. That's both our ally and our enemy on this day."

"We heard the dogs already."

"And they're probably farther away than they sound."

Delilah would have preferred that there were no dogs at all.

She thought she heard the cabin door open and close then, and glanced back over her shoulder. There was only the white swirl of the fog behind them, obscuring her vision of the cabin. She could barely make out the peak of its roof.

Neither Rafe nor Ferris seemed to have heard the sound, and Delilah decided that she'd imagined it.

She walked more quickly, intent on moving through the fog.

Rafe leaned toward her and lowered his voice to a murmur that she found impossibly attractive. His whisper seemed to thrum deep inside her, feeding that tingle of awareness, and his steady gaze bored into her own. "Watch your step. We'll be in the forest within moments and it will be easy to trip."

Delilah understood his meaning. "And the sound will echo."

"Drawing them directly to us."

Delilah gripped his elbow a little more tightly and nodded. He moved his other hand, his gloved fingers closing securely over her own in a gesture intended to reassure her. It worked. The warmth of his skin penetrated both the faux-leather of his gloves and the fabric of her own. She felt safer with her hand in his, which made little sense.

She felt even safer when he lifted his right hand away from hers and pulled his laze. The warm glow of Rafe's presence and protectiveness spread through her veins, making her feel more optimistic.

Ferris too stepped with care, remaining close to Rafe's right side. Just as Rafe had predicted, the silhouettes of tree trunks suddenly loomed against the fog. The dead old trees rose high overhead, their tops lost above the fog.

Delilah tightened her grip on Rafe's elbow as they stepped into the undergrowth, aware that she could easily stumble. His sense of direction was so sure that she thought she probably wouldn't get out of the fog without him.

She wouldn't tell him he was right just yet. He'd enjoy the confession too much and whatever he did in response might eliminate her resistance to his charm.

A man's voice whispered in her thoughts then, teasing her with possibilities. *"A thief and a criminal, working for forces unknown. Was it really your vision that had brought the commandos to the Citadel?"*

Delilah started, but the voice continued its persuasive comments.

"Or had Rafe been just the first of their number? He might not even know his role, but could easily be part of a plan to eliminate you."

Delilah gritted her teeth and strode beside Rafe as quickly as she could. She didn't know where the voice came from, but it made good sense. Maybe it was the voice of reason. Maybe it was the voice of the angels.

But it was right. She had to evade Rafe.

Soon.

Maybe the fog would prove to be her ally in that.

XI

RAFE DESPISED the fog.

There was something unnatural about it. It was more than the sinister light it emanated, more than the way it made the forest appear unfathomable and dangerous. This fog had presence in a way that fog should not.

It felt dirty against his skin.

It felt sentient, even malicious. He sensed it infiltrating his mind, turning his thoughts in directions they would never have gone of their own volition.

He distrusted it.

He resented its presence with an intensity that was foreign to him.

No matter how he fought it, Rafe felt his mood move beyond frustration to a fury that was rare for him. He became angry at whoever had given him this assignment and resentful of the obstacles arrayed against him. He found himself angry at Delilah's innocence, even though he knew that made no sense, and bitter that he had Ferris to consider as well.

He wanted Delilah, that wasn't new, but that whisper in his mind suggested that he should just take her. That beguiling whisper insisted that she was his to take, that he was owed his own pleasure, that it was stupid to let anything or anyone get in the way of his desire.

He began to entertain ideas of how to get rid of Ferris, none of which were very pleasant.

But rape and murder had never been attractive possibilities to Rafe before. It was the fog.

The fog was driving him insane.

Maybe it was some kind of drug, released automatically from the cabin when its security was breached. If so, it was potent stuff. They had to get through it before it drove Rafe to do something he knew he shouldn't.

If it came from the cabin, the cloud of it shouldn't be that big.

Rafe marched more quickly, setting a killing pace through the deadened and silent forest. He jammed his laze back into his holster, intent only on getting through the woods.

He didn't even care where they emerged.

He was less careful about moving quietly, fixed only on making progress. He cut a straight line through the woods, knowing it was more or less easterly, and kept his gaze fixed on the next tree in the line he cut.

The fog condensed on his skin, leaving a slippery film of mingled perspiration and fog on his forehead, in his hair, on his back. His cloak hung damply from his shoulders and his boots were wet. Rafe kept going, hating that he was dirty.

He was always fastidiously clean, and the growing awareness of his body's state troubled him deeply.

Delilah panted as she worked to keep up with him.

"Too fast?" Rafe thought to slow down for her.

"Not for me," she said, her manner grim. He respected her determination to move quickly and was reassured that their instincts were the same. Then she hesitated. "But Ferris is too tired to travel this quickly. We should slow down."

Fury boiled within Rafe that she was more concerned with Ferris' welfare than his own. His anger was unreasonable, he knew that on some level, but he couldn't halt it.

"How dare she sacrifice your needs to those of the boy?" whispered the dark voice in Rafe's thoughts. It was louder and seemed more compelling than it had been in the cabin. *"Doesn't she know how lucky she is to be with you? Show her!"*

When Rafe glanced at Ferris, he saw a resentment simmering in the boy's gaze.

The words crossed his lips before he could stop them. They came from the whisper, but they fell out of his mouth.

"Not man enough to keep up?" he taunted Ferris.

"Good!" crowed the voice. *"Put him in his place!"*

Before Rafe could speak again, Ferris snarled. He leapt for Rafe's throat, his eyes blazing and his lips twisted with hate.

Delilah snatched at Ferris. "Your promise!" she cried, but Ferris struck her across the shoulder.

Delilah fell to one knee, her expression as astonished as Rafe felt.

The hunting dogs must have heard them, because they barked.

"Kill him!" whispered that dark voice. *"Perfect! A clear shot. It's even self-defense."*

Rafe reached instinctively for his laze, but the voice made him pause. How could it command him to act against his will? What was it? Who was it?

In that heartbeat of hesitation, Ferris launched through the air, hands outstretched like claws. Rafe lifted his hand away from the easy solution and caught Ferris by the shoulders instead.

"Fool!" raged the voice.

The boy lunged for Rafe's throat. Rafe was bigger and stronger, but Ferris had passion on his side. Ferris also was ready to kill, while Rafe was trying to not hurt the boy. He tipped Ferris head over heels and flung him to the ground. He knew the undergrowth would keep Ferris from getting more than a bruise and hoped the fall knocked some sense into him.

Ferris growled and kicked at Rafe's legs from behind, throwing his weight against Rafe. Rafe stumbled, regained his footing. He lunged after Delilah, disinterested in Ferris when Delilah's safety was at risk.

The boy jumped him from behind, showing surprising agility. He put his arm around Rafe's neck to try to choke him, then chomped on his ear. Rafe shouted in pain, spinning to shake the boy off him.

"Kill him!" shouted the voice. *"Beat him senseless. Might makes right."*

Rafe knew that was wrong. He couldn't kill the boy, didn't even want to bruise him. He knew that Ferris loved Delilah and was acting out of an urge to protect her.

Rafe shook off the boy's weight. He twisted, breaking free of Ferris' grip on his neck. The boy fought like a monkey, biting and scratching, digging his fingers into Rafe, kicking and screaming. Rafe broke free and held the boy at arm's length.

"We had a deal," he reminded Ferris, his voice stern.

Ferris bit his hand hard enough to make Rafe yelp.

Rafe swore and made to fling the boy to the ground again. Ferris clung to him, biting and scratching in an attempt to do as much damage as possible.

From the corner of his eye, Rafe saw Delilah come closer, and expected her to help him in breaking free of the jealous boy.

Instead, Delilah seized the laze from his own holster.

Rafe thought she would threaten Ferris, but she simply backed away. Maybe she was afraid to shoot the boy. He knew that they were working together, though. He cast Ferris into the undergrowth, then pivoted to claim his weapon.

Delilah held the laze, its muzzle pointed at Rafe's chest. He froze to consider her. There was determination in her eyes, and he knew he was seeing the fullness of her distrust of him.

"Faithless bitch!" cried the voice. *"You should have taught her a lesson when you had the chance."*

The dogs barked, closer again.

"Delilah," Rafe said and put out his hand.

She sighted the laze.

He took a step closer and she swallowed. He took another step and her hands shook. At his third step, she leapt backward, running instead of shooting. Rafe knew there was truth in that gesture, as well.

She wouldn't shoot him, which was all Rafe needed to know.

He lunged after her and she flung the laze over his head, back toward Ferris. Rafe snatched at her skirts, then heard the click of the laze being sighted.

Ferris made a grunt and Rafe understood that it was a command.

When Rafe slowly turned to face the boy, he saw that there would be no mercy from Ferris. Meanwhile, Delilah raced noisily into the forest, leaving both of them behind.

But there was nothing Rafe could do. He lifted his hands, and hoped he could talk Ferris out of killing him.

It was a long shot, given the resentment in the boy's eyes.

"DIDN'T I warn you that no good deed goes unpunished?" sneered the voice that had slid into Rafe's thoughts. *"You should have killed him while you had the chance."*

"Easy now," Rafe said, keeping his voice calm.

The panting boy eased to his feet and backed away, aiming Rafe's laze at his chest.

The dogs snarled in the distance. Rafe could hear undergrowth being broken and men shouting at each other.

They were closer than he would have preferred.

Ferris was obviously nervous, his gaze flicking to the forest and back to Rafe. His dark hair hung wetly against his forehead and his new clothing was disheveled from their struggle.

There was no sign of Delilah, and no sound of her passage. She might as well have disappeared into thin air.

Once again, Rafe's luck could have been better.

He tried to negotiate.

"You don't know how to use that," he said, keeping his voice low and steady. He stretched out his right hand. "You'd better give it back to me."

Ferris grinned, as if the very idea was funny, and fired.

Rafe jumped at the blaze of light and knew he was lucky that the shot missed. The kid had aimed right at Rafe's groin, leaving no doubt of the root—so to speak—of the problem between them.

"Give that back to me," Rafe insisted.

Ferris backed away. He shoved one hand through his hair, pushing it away from his forehead, and licked his lips in concentration. He was breathing heavily and his eyes were filled with animosity. He gripped the laze in both hands to steady it.

Rafe folded his arms across his chest and eyed the uncooperative boy. "So, maybe you could explain to me how this helps Delilah?"

Ferris gestured in the direction Delilah had fled.

"Sure. She's gone. But she's alone, with neither one of us to defend her."

The dogs, to Rafe's satisfaction, barked right on cue. Ferris started.

"She still has a tattoo, remember? No amount of talking on her part is going to change what that means to a shade hunter."

The boy's eyes narrowed.

"Maybe you could tell me. What *was* Sonja's plan to solve that?"

Ferris' gaze flicked from side to side in uncertainty, then he lifted the laze higher. Rafe was sure that if Sonja had had a plan, the boy didn't know it.

That wasn't particularly helpful.

"Give me the laze," Rafe said with authority. "Give me the laze, Ferris, and let's protect Delilah together. We had a deal. We can make it work."

Ferris seemed to consider the idea.

Rafe took a step toward him, his right hand extended.

Ferris lowered the laze slightly.

Rafe took that as a promising sign. He moved closer again, his boots making the undergrowth crunch.

Ferris held his ground, but some of the fight went out of his shoulders.

Rafe took a third step.

The boy dropped his gaze and sagged, letting the laze muzzle dip.

Rafe didn't hesitate. He leapt for the weapon, certain he had read the boy correctly.

But no sooner had Rafe moved than Ferris lifted the laze. His eyes shone with that primal anger again. In the beat that Rafe recognized his mistake, the boy fired.

Rafe screamed as the laze hit him.

And that dark voice laughed in Rafe's own thoughts.

DELILAH HAD to make the most of opportunity.

As much as she wanted to see whether Ferris or Rafe was triumphant, she had a pretty good idea that it would be Rafe. She had to put distance between them while she could.

She needed to be away from Rafe and his tempting touch to even think straight. As much as she would have liked to have believed otherwise, she wasn't in control of herself. The man could make her forget herself with sensation—if ever she surrendered her chastity and risked her gift, it had to be a deliberate and conscious choice.

Not an impulse.

Not a seduction she'd regret.

She ran through the forest, snagging her ankle once on the undergrowth, not caring about anything but forward progress. She needed be far from Rafe before she paused at all, far enough that there was no turning back.

At the same time, it was terrifying to run into the unknown, alone and undefended. Rafe was right that she had no means of defending herself and no plan. She was afraid he was also right that someone was trying to kill her. She felt vulnerable and fearful, but she kept running.

This was freedom.

This was choice.

She'd better get used to freedom and get better at making choices if she meant to survive.

Delilah heard the laze shot behind her and paused, afraid. Who had been shot?

"Go on, leave them to themselves," a voice murmured in her thoughts. *"What's more important than you? Aren't you the Oracle? Aren't you the salvation of the Republic? Who cares about a pair of fugitives?"*

It sounded wrong, as if she should go back, but Delilah had to admit that selfishness made some sense. Standing in the woods uncertain of what to do made no sense at all. She fought the urge to turn back, and tried to rationalize her choice.

Ferris would be fine without her help. He'd managed before.

She had to take care of herself.

"That's it," urged the voice. *"Look out for yourself first."*

Delilah had never put her own needs first, had never ensured her own goals were met independent of what other people wanted from her.

She wanted to be Oracle.

She might be destined to be Oracle, but she had to do something herself to bring her own dream to fruition. She had to make a choice in her own favor.

"Live for yourself," whispered the man in her thoughts. *"Being free means having the chance to make the selfish choice—protect yourself for the greater good."*

It sounded like a plan.

She had to get to Hood River and Reverend Billie Jo Estevez.

When the laze fired a second time, though, the shot was so long that Delilah halted to look back. The fog swirled around her, shrouding her from anything or anyone else in the forest.

Had Rafe shot Ferris dead?

She might have taken a step back in the direction she had come, but the voice gained stridency in her thoughts.

"Isn't this the opportunity you've been waiting for?" it murmured, sounding so reasonable that Delilah couldn't ignore it. *"Run while you can!"*

She hesitated, fearful of what had happened.

"Maybe you deserve to be a slave forever," sneered the voice. *"Maybe you deserve whatever they'll do to you once you're caught again."*

The hunting dogs barked and Delilah couldn't tell where they were. The shade hunters were close. Panic rose within

her at the sound of them and Delilah turned her back on Rafe
and Ferris.

She ran, even though she felt cowardly in doing so.

She leapt over fallen logs and when she found a stream,
she remembered Rafe's strategy of the night before. She ran
in the middle of it, disguising her scent. It was a long and
winding river, one that headed uphill.

How far would it rise? Delilah didn't know and couldn't
guess. What would she do at the top? She had no plan, beyond putting one foot in front of the other and moving onward.

The fog grew thinner and she could see farther into the
forest on either side. The trees were thinning and there were
more stones. Wan sunlight of pale gold burned away the last
wisps of the fog and she felt cleaner as she moved out of it.

It was a relief to be free of the fog.

As soon as she stepped out of it, the voice in her thoughts
fell silent. She was suddenly embarrassed that she had abandoned Rafe and Ferris. She paused, the water swirling around
her booted ankles, and stared downhill, into the forest and its
clutch of iridescent fog.

Could she find her way back to them?

Or was it smarter to save herself, as that oily voice had insisted? Delilah was certain that the course of such selfishness could only be wrong.

How had the fog twisted her thoughts?

Rafe's comments about her lack of a plan and a weapon
made good sense now that she had left him behind. Could
she beat the odds and gain an audience with the reverend?

Even without knowing which way Hood River was?

Delilah could have despaired of her own chances, but then
she saw a familiar shimmer of light. She heard a humming and
felt a half-forgotten whisper dance over her flesh. It seemed
that all the little hairs on her body stood up and vibrated in time
with the hum.

Her heart began to sing.

Delilah had only seen that light once before. She had only
glimpsed it in Rachel's presence. She'd been reminded of it

in Rafe's presence, but this was as vibrant as it had been only
once before. She'd never thought to see them again in her
lifetime, but its brilliant radiance meant that it could only be
one thing.

Angelfire.

Angels.

The angels were coming and she would see them again.
Delilah trusted them completely. They would help her, just
as they had helped her before.

Her doubts banished, she ran directly for that light.

"*KILL HIM.*"

The low voice in Ferris' mind terrified him. It was a seductive voice, one that seemed sensible and that he found persuasive. He struggled against its insistence, fought to recall his
own promise, even as he faced down Rafe.

He'd made a promise, and Rafe had shown him mercy
even when he'd broken it. Rafe had called him by his name.
Rafe had defended him and shown him kindness.

"*Deeds speak louder than words,*" hissed the voice.
"*Promises are for the weak. Kill him while you can.*"

Rafe took a step toward Ferris, looking dangerous. The
laze shook in Ferris' grip. Ferris forced himself to remember
that Rafe had saved him already.

"*Only to betray you later,*" the voice insisted, and Ferris'
determination wavered.

Rafe took another step and held out his hand.

"*Only to make you a pawn,*" the voice sneered. "*But then,
weren't you always somebody's pawn? Did you ever think for
yourself? Did you ever make a choice of your own?*"

Ferris felt a mighty shudder begin within him. It was
wrong to kill. It would be wrong to shoot Rafe.

Yet . . .

Yet . . .

There was something heady about having the balance of
power work in his favor for once. There was something

seductive—as seductive as the dark voice—about that glimmer of fear in Rafe's eyes as he watched Ferris.

"Maybe you were born to be enslaved. Maybe you've gotten precisely what you deserve. Maybe you shouldn't be free." There was a sound of a man spitting. *"Maybe it's no surprise that Delilah isn't interested in you, slave boy."*

Ferris fired Rafe's laze at Rafe, stunned by the power of the weapon. The kick of it threw him back a step and the brightness of its shot made him squint. He could feel the heat of the blaze in his hands, but once he pressed the trigger, he couldn't stop. He held it down, his finger locked in position.

The laze fired in one continuous lethal stream.

Ferris watched in horror as Rafe fell backward.

He was terrified when Rafe hit his head and didn't move anymore. There was smoke rising from Rafe's codpiece and a terrible smell of combustion. There was blood beneath Rafe's nose, a trickle of red that shocked Ferris to his core. Rafe's eyes were closed and he was still.

Too still.

That voice laughed with glee inside Ferris' head.

He'd made Rafe bleed.

He'd broken his promise.

He'd forgotten everything he had learned about wickedness and people who enjoyed hurting others. He'd even forgotten his own determination to never become one of them.

Ferris spun away with the sight of what he'd done and flung the laze into the forest. It smoked as it tumbled through the air, then landed with a crash in the undergrowth. Ferris didn't care. He didn't want to know where it was.

"Loser," the voice charged, disdain dripping from the word. *"You were made to be fodder for the Republic. You were made to be nothing more than a worm beneath the heel of someone better . . ."*

Ferris ran.

He ran wildly through the forest, not caring where he went. He leapt logs and ducked under low branches, his sense of direction null with the thick fog. He slipped on loose stones and tripped over brambles. Branches slapped his face and heavy raindrops fell from the boughs overhead. He panted, he sweat, but he didn't look back.

The only thing he wanted to do was get away from that voice, to get away from what he had done.

By the time he was aware that he heard dogs, they were too close and too numerous. He heard the men too, and panicked.

He splashed across a churning river, intent only on getting to the other side, and miscalculated. He fell and the riverbed disappeared beneath his feet. The river became deeper just there, the current churned, and Ferris was tumbled head over heels.

The river carried him along, spinning and twisting him, keeping him from getting his footing again. He flailed and fought, desperate to catch a branch or a rock. He needed a breath. He would drown. He fought and struggled, cutting his hand on a passing rock before the water pushed him under again. Terror rose within him, and just when Ferris thought the world would fade to black, something caught the back of his shirt.

A man pulled him from the river and held him a foot over the surface of the water. Ferris gulped for air, sputtering as he shoved the water and weeds from his face. He halfway expected that it was Rafe who had saved him, Rafe who had acted with honor and decency. He opened his eyes, prepared for a lecture.

Instead, he found a stranger holding him captive. The man's face was swarthy, his eyes dark and his hair even darker. He was dressed in a hunter's garb, and his smile was filled with malice.

Ferris struggled, wishing the hunter would drop him back into the river. Even death was better than being harvested.

Better than going back *there*.

"Let me guess who you are," the man said.

He flung Ferris to the bank of the river and a trio of men quickly bound Ferris with ropes.

"Leave his left arm free," the hunter said.

Ferris fought but he lost. He was trussed helpless in moments, twisting on the ground. The men laughed, then the hunter bent beside him. The hunter drew his knife and cut away Ferris's left sleeve. He smiled at the tattoo displayed there as Ferris averted his face and caught his breath.

"I thought so," the hunter said with assurance. He touched the tip of his knife to Ferris' chin, compelling Ferris to look at him. He spoke slowly. "I could let you live if you told me where your friends were."

Ferris held the hunter's gaze steadily. He didn't make a noise, didn't give the hunter a hint that he was incapable of answering. Having his voice wouldn't have made any difference. He wouldn't betray Rafe again, and he'd never betray Delilah.

"Cat got your tongue?" the hunter asked, then slid the tip of the knife across Ferris' bottom lip. Ferris gasped in fear and the hunter smiled.

"I've got a better idea." He lifted Ferris' left hand in his with a leisurely gesture. Ferris had a heartbeat to guess his intent before the hunter slid his dataprobe into Ferris' palm.

"Here's hoping your firewalls are intact, Rhys," muttered one of the man. The second man looked away while the third watched with grim fascination.

Ferris knew why. Norms only datashared with intimates, and that never included shades.

Then he recalled what the man had said. *Rhys.* He had called the hunter Rhys. This hunter couldn't be Rhys ibn Ali, legendary for his cruelty and effectiveness.

Could he? Rafe had said that the famous hunter would be in the area.

Ferris' heart skipped a beat.

"Recognize my name?" the hunter mused, his eyes narrowed as he punched commands into his own palm. "You should. It's an honor to be harvested by Rhys ibn Ali, best of the best." He smiled and Ferris' heart stopped cold. "Now you've got a little something to tell your compatriots in the research labs."

Ferris inhaled and shook.

"You know the research labs, then?" Rhys tapped his palm and viewed the display. "Yes, I see you do. Probably not very good memories, F762698. You shouldn't have survived that experiment. How interesting that you did." His eyes narrowed and his voice dropped low. "And this is even more interesting."

Ferris swallowed and glanced at his own palm, then had to look away in shame. Rhys had found the images Ferris had surreptitiously snatched of Delilah over the years. There were images of her sleeping, images of her working in the netherzones, images of her nude, and images of her cloaked. It was a gallery documenting the duration of his fascination for her and the depth of his love.

There were images of Delilah making that prophecy in the chapel.

He looked away from the malice in Rhys' expression and stared into the woods. He blinked.

There was a woman in the undergrowth.

Watching him.

All Ferris could see was the oval of her face. Her skin was fair, so fair that he immediately assumed that she was a shade. She must have been wearing black, maybe a cloak with a fitted hood, because he couldn't discern more of her body.

"Pretty isn't she?" Rhys mused, tapping his way through the collection of shots. Ferris jumped and blinked, and by the time he looked back into the shadows of the undergrowth, the woman was gone.

Had she even been there?

Or had he imagined her?

Rhys worked through the shots, admiring some more than others, his salacious glee making Ferris uncomfortable. Ferris hoped the hunter would get bored before he got to the latest ones, but knew from the chill that claimed Rhys' smile that that hadn't happened.

"And oh so familiar," Rhys murmured. He tapped his own palm, compelling Ferris to look up. The two interlinked palms showed different images of the same woman.

Delilah.

Captured from different angles in the moment of her prophecy.

Ferris swallowed, not needing foresight to recognize that his situation was about to get worse.

"So you know the false Oracle," Rhys mused. "And you like her a lot, judging by your tendency to document her life."

The men snickered.

Rhys pulled out the dataprobe of his palm with a rough gesture, leaving Ferris feeling violated and confused. What had the hunter done to his palm? Ferris itched to check its protocols.

"Well, this is your lucky day." Rhys knelt beside Ferris, his elbows braced on his knees. He oozed persuasiveness, a persuasiveness that Ferris didn't trust. "I'm going to make you one of those offers you can't refuse. Your record says your intellect is normal, so listen closely to me. I know you understand."

Ferris looked at the hunter, unable to hide his dread.

Rhys smiled, but it didn't reach his eyes. "I've just put you on an electronic leash. I can track you anywhere. I can harvest you anytime. Your freedom, such as it is, is an illusion from this point in time forward."

Ferris swallowed, disliking everything he'd heard so far.

"But I'm going to give you a chance to avoid the research labs this time. I'm going to let you go, and if you bring me your two friends—the killer of the shade hunter and the false Oracle—in, oh, let's say seventy-two hours, you won't have to go back to the research labs."

Ferris caught his breath.

Rhys smiled. "In seventy-two hours, I'm going to collect you, F762698. It doesn't matter where you are or how far you run. Your butt is mine. What happens to you after you're harvested is entirely your decision."

It was a lie. Ferris knew it. If the Society of Nuclear Darwinists wanted to perform research on him, they would do it, regardless of what Rhys ibn Ali promised. Promises to shades didn't count. And even if Rhys kept his word, Ferris didn't think that being condemned to the slave dens, drugged and harnessed to equipment to generate power—never mind the prospect of being used as a sex slave—wasn't much better.

On the other hand, if he didn't pretend to take the offer, he'd be sent to the research labs immediately.

Ferris closed his eyes, overwhelmed by his so-called choices.

"You have doubts," Rhys whispered from surprising proximity. Ferris opened his eyes to find the hunter leaning close to his face, his eyes shining. "Then let me change the terms. Bring them to me and I'll let *her* live."

Ferris' terror at the implication must have shown.

Rhys smiled. "Yes. Anyone having seizures of such violence as she does should have a brain autopsy, so we can learn for the future. That's what's going to happen to her, unless you help her. Your choice."

Ferris shook. They would kill Delilah. He didn't believe that she would have much of an existence if they let her live, but it had to be better than dying.

She'd have a chance to escape again if they let her live.

He nodded once, curtly.

"Smart decision. Maybe there's more to you than meets the eye." Rhys smiled, and the expression made him look both predatory and hungry. He pushed to his feet with purpose and brushed off his hands. "Untie him." As the men did his bidding, Rhys tapped on his palm, making notes.

When Ferris was on his feet, wet and shaking, the shade hunter spared him a quick glance. "Our palms are synchronized. You've got seventy-two hours, F762698." He tapped his palm once hard, and a chime sounded simultaneously from his palm and Ferris'. Ferris looked down at his hand in horror.

He *was* on an electronic leash, just as the hunter had said.

"Go!" Rhys commanded, then grinned.

Ferris didn't wait for a second invitation.

He ran. He bolted through the forest, determined to leave the hunter far, far behind him. He heard Rhys laugh and knew his reaction was foolish, but he couldn't deny his instinct. His thoughts raced, moving as quickly as his feet.

How could he warn Delilah, without leading Rhys directly to her?

Had there really been a woman in the woods?

Or had Ferris imagined her?

XII

"I TOLD you to kill him."

Rafe blinked at the sound of that dark voice. It was audible and louder, no longer in his thoughts alone.

Then he dismissed it as a figment of his imagination. After all, he'd been shot. He was lying on the forest floor, brambles crushed beneath him. The ground was unpleasantly damp. It was presumably where he had fallen when Ferris shot him.

Rafe opened his eyes, moved slightly, and winced at the pain that shot through his body. His reevlar codpiece had been heavily damaged, which Rafe hadn't thought possible. The polymer was supposed to be indestructible.

On the other hand, his was a really powerful laze.

And there was no sign of it. His empty holster made him feel naked, and the damage to the codpiece certainly left him feeling vulnerable.

Should he be grateful that Ferris had shot the only place where he was protected? Or was that reading too much into the boy's choice?

Rafe gingerly lifted the edge of the blackened codpiece and was relieved to find that everything underneath remained intact. His trousers were singed, and as much as he regretted the damage to good fabric, he could live with it. There were burn holes in all of his garments, probably from the sparks that were scattered by the blaze hitting the codpiece, but that was a small detail.

He could buy clothes.

Delilah's disappearance was a problem of a different magnitude. There was no sound of her presence and again he was assailed by a terror of the consequences if his mission failed.

But what exactly *were* the consequences? He pushed to his feet, impatient with his persistent memory loss.

"It's that pesky compassion shit," the voice continued. "You all get caught up in this selfless garbage instead of doing what should come naturally."

Rafe looked around himself then, not truly surprised that the fog appeared to have become thicker. He was startled to find a man sitting on a fallen log near him.

Not just any man. This one was gleaming black, muscled, tall, and nude. He also happened to have large, dark wings, wings that looked leathery and reptilian, which arched high above his head. He lounged on the log, his pose one of complete confidence.

He also sported a large erection, one that made Rafe think there was a theme to the proceedings.

He had to be dreaming.

Or hallucinating.

This man couldn't be real.

The man smiled, a flash of white against obsidian.

"As I was saying," he continued. That deep voice was the same that Rafe had heard in his own thoughts, which made him think that the cabin had issued some kind of powerful hallucinogen. "Whatever happened to survival of the fittest and looking out for number one?"

There was something insidious about his voice. It wound into Rafe's thoughts, leaving his mind feeling as soiled as his body felt in the fog. His words were persuasive, charming even, but Rafe felt a revulsion that went right to his core.

His words, in fact, expressed all of Rafe's doubts. The drug, whatever it was, poked in the shadows of the mind of whoever was exposed and brought doubts to light.

Rafe had to get away from its influence. Unfortunately, he was feeling the limitations of his physical body as he seldom did.

His companion chuckled darkly. "There is a downside to volunteering after all, isn't there? Taking physical form has its limitations, both in the nature of the mortal vehicle, and in the capacity of memory."

What was he talking about?

The dark man held up a hand and Rafe saw that it wasn't quite substantial. There was proof that he wasn't real.

"That's why I've avoided that last step of taking flesh. I can't imagine dying, can you?" He chuckled as he surveyed Rafe. "Maybe it's a little easier for you to conceptualize now."

"I'm fine," Rafe said, feeling foolish for answering a hallucination. He took a couple of steps away. It wasn't as easy as it should have been, but his companion watched Rafe's efforts with indifference. "Thanks for your help."

"Didn't you hear? I'm not interested in helping anyone else."

"How compassionate."

"That's exactly my point." The man leaned forward, his manner intent. "Where, precisely, has compassion gotten you in this particular adventure? Your laze has been stolen by the kid you should have killed, the woman you're supposed to protect was key to the theft and has vanished, and you've been injured." He clucked his tongue. "Looks to me like you need to change tactics."

Maybe this figment could be helpful. "Did you see where the boy went?"

The man smiled slyly. "Telling you that would constitute help, wouldn't it?"

"Not your department, I'll guess."

The dark man's smile broadened. "I prefer the big seven." Rafe must have looked blank because he continued. "The seven deadly sins, that would be. Pride, covetousness, lust, anger, gluttony, envy, and sloth. I have to admit that lust is my all-time favorite. Isn't it yours?"

Rafe peered into the forest, planning his pursuit of either Ferris or Delilah. Were they together? He had to think so. Together, with his laze.

"She is lovely, isn't she?" the man whispered.

Rafe felt a flash of anger and ignored him.

He felt his lips tighten. Delilah might have betrayed him, but he had a mission to complete.

It would have been better to have had an idea of the direction to take, and he wondered whether his chatty companion would share whatever he knew.

Rafe didn't doubt that there'd be a price.

In his current mood, he might pay it.

"Actually, I am a little out of character," the dark man said, his manner jovial. "I wanted to stop by and thank you."

Rafe glanced his way in distrust. "For what?"

"The seven deadlies, as we call them, help me to manifest on earth. The more there is, the stronger I get. I'm really flexing some manifestation these days, the strongest I've been in centuries, and you've helped." He smiled. "Thanks."

Rafe regarded the man warily. "How did I help?"

"Lust!" The man's eyes shone. "Lust works for me in a big way, seeing as it is my favorite deadly, and the lust of you and your kind—"

Rafe interrupted what was shaping up to be a lecture. "What do you mean, me and my kind?"

The dark man fell silent and considered Rafe. There was something disturbing about the glitter of his eyes. "You really don't remember, do you?"

"Remember what?" Rafe didn't appreciate the reference to that black void in his mind, never mind his sense that this abomination knew precisely what he'd forgotten.

His companion exhaled and shook his head. "You take all the fun out of it, you know? What kind of sparkling conversation can we have, what kind of witty repartee and clever exchange is possible if you don't even remember what you were?"

Rafe turned his back on the man and chose a direction arbitrarily.

"At least I remembered what I'd lost when I fell," the dark man hissed, his venom making Rafe look back. "At least I knew the stakes."

Rafe blinked, sensing that there was a truth in those words, albeit one that he couldn't remember.

It wasn't a good feeling.

"All right, let's review." The dark man unfolded himself from his casual pose and straightened to his full height. He was impressive, tall and magnificently built. His wings arched high over his shoulders, gleaming in the fog, and he spoke with evident pride. "I am Lucifer, the first and the greatest of the fallen angels, the Prince of Darkness." When Rafe obviously didn't recognize the name, he continued bitterly. "Satan. Mephistophiles. Old Scratch. Jumping Jack Flash. Mr. Smith. Ring any bells?"

They did. Rafe remembered stories of Satan and his desire to rule the world. How had he manifested a vision of the Devil himself? Was that his fear, that he served someone evil?

Rafe took a step back. "I need to find Delilah."

His companion sniffed. "Don't we all?" he mused in an undertone, then leaned closer to Rafe. "I have survived for centuries in the stories of men. I have come close to triumph over the material world of creation time and time again, but this time, this time—" he reached out one hand, palm up, and slowly closed his fingers around an invisible orb "—*this* time, triumph is within my grasp. I have found a resonance within the hearts of men. There is a darkness in these times that serves me perfectly."

Rafe could believe that.

The man smiled. "And I have found an acolyte whose progress pleases me to no end, and whose intent is so dark that my realm can come on earth. I have moved the pieces into place and this time, victory will be mine."

"So you say."

"So I know! It's inevitable now, despite the puny efforts of you and your kind to stop the tide." He leaned closer, his eyes shining, and revulsion rolled through Rafe. "I know you, Raphael." His easy use of Rafe's name sent a shiver through Rafe. "I understand you, because we were both once of the same kind."

"No!"

Lucifer continued without acknowledging Rafe's protest. "I can restore your lost memory. I can make you more than what you were before. I can empower you with immortality and strengths you've forgotten you ever possessed. I can show you that my way is the right way." He smiled again. "All you have to do is act for yourself first."

"That's all?" Rafe didn't hide his skepticism.

His voice hardened. "And bring me the girl."

"Why don't you get her yourself?"

Lucifer gritted his teeth and hissed. "That's the pesky part of not taking flesh. I can't act directly in the world. I need agents and acolytes. I need *volunteers*." He smiled and it was a chilling sight. "Like you."

Something about the way he said *volunteers* sent a shudder through Rafe. "I wouldn't be the only one."

"The latest and greatest perhaps, but not the only. You'd be in good company." He arched a brow. "Powerful company. In fact, you might be surprised by who sits in my court."

Rafe wasn't persuaded. He had to purge this hallucination from his thoughts, ignore Satan's insidious suggestions, and succeed at his mission.

"But what kind of court is it, if you're insubstantial?" he demanded. "How can you rule material world without taking flesh?" Rafe stepped closer and sneered. "Maybe you're the one who should be afraid."

He lunged at Lucifer and passed directly through him, dispersing the shadow that had given the illusion of substance. He felt cold, that same icy chill as the caress of the fog, then the air was clear again.

And when he looked back, there was no dark man behind him.

The fog was thinning as well.

He'd been right—the fog had been making him insane. Getting out of its grasp had been the smart choice.

Rafe turned, saw that the fog was thinnest in one direction, and strode that way with newfound purpose.

"This isn't over yet," Lucifer whispered, his voice resonating in Rafe's thoughts.

But Rafe turned his heart against temptation.

It was over for him, and that was all that mattered. He refused to entertain doubts. He had to install Delilah as Oracle,

which meant he had to find and protect her. He would succeed or die trying.

It was that simple.

AFTER A few moments, Rafe realized that the fog was thinner
because the land was rising. It became rockier with every step,
and the vegetation more sparse. The fog became insubstantial,
which Rafe liked a lot. He felt cleaner and more determined.

He saw that the bracken was flattened ahead of him and to
the right, as if someone had run that way recently without
caring about leaving a trail. He bent and found a snippet of
fabric caught on a thorn.

It looked similar to—if not the same as—that of the dress
he had chosen for Delilah in the settler's cabin.

Rafe grinned. He followed the trail, seeking bent sticks and
half-hidden footsteps. When he found the stream and couldn't
see any sign of passage beyond it, new optimism buoyed his
steps.

She had followed the stream to disguise her scent, learning from his choice of the night before. He marched into the
river, proud of Delilah and her quick wits.

It didn't hurt Rafe's mood that the fog was soon behind
him, no more than a memory. The sunlight was pale, but he
welcomed the normalcy of its light. He strode faster, invigorated by the touch of the sun, cheered by the signs of someone's passing that he found every ten feet or so.

Delilah had been careless.

Frightened maybe.

That worried him. Was Ferris with her? He saw no sign of
a second set of footsteps, which was troubling. He hoped he
found them before hunters did.

Rafe suddenly saw a brilliant white light emanating from
a clearing ahead of him. There were pine trees gathering in a
tight cluster, as if they had been planted in a triple circle.
They were long dead, their trunks reaching toward the sky
like dark pillars. The ground was barren, the site stark.

The silvery light emphasized that. It made striking silhouettes of the trees and radiated from the clearing. Rafe could hardly look straight at the light, it was so strong, and its silvery color seemed vaguely familiar.

He had a very strong sense of Delilah's location, one that was confirmed by her faint cry.

It was almost an orgasmic cry.

Although he wanted to help her, Rafe had a bad feeling about approaching the clearing. He didn't want to go anywhere near that light. The light made him think of pain, excruciating pain and just the sight of it gave him a sense of loss so potent that it nearly brought him to his knees.

Worse, he didn't know why he felt that way. He couldn't remember. The light's brilliance hurt his eyes, even when he narrowed them. The light ran along the forest floor like mercury, and stepping into it made Rafe shiver.

His body remembered something that he didn't.

But he couldn't lose Delilah.

He went, against his every inclination.

He stumbled toward the light, one hand raised before his face, squinting as he stepped into the clearing. It seemed to him that the light dimmed in its intensity—it remained bright but not blindingly so. Maybe he had simply become accustomed to it.

But Delilah was there. She was on her knees, in an attitude of prayer.

Rafe didn't understand why.

He peered through his fingers at the source of the light, and felt his mouth fall open.

The light came from a massive winged figure.

An angel.

There was no fog here, no hallucinogen to mess with his mind or voice his doubts. There was only an angel, one so splendid that it had to be real.

Rafe fell to his knees in turn, awed and shaken.

THE ANGEL stood before Delilah, his wings arching high over his back and his hands spread in welcome. He seemed to be made of light, but this light was nothing like the slippery luminescence of the fog.

This light was tranquil and warm, although Rafe couldn't quell his distrust of it.

The angel's smile was serene and kind, but the sight of him made Rafe's breath catch in terror. There was something familiar about him, something terrifying and unknown. The angel considered Rafe with that calm smile, then winked so quickly that Rafe thought he had imagined the gesture.

Then the angel bent toward Delilah, as if drawing her into his embrace. Rafe's heart stopped cold in his fear. Could he stop an angel? He thought not.

Why was he so afraid of angels?

The angel's radiance painted Delilah's features with white light, a light that made her look soft and innocent. Rafe swallowed, incoherent in his own dread. The angel lifted Delilah's left hand in his own. She looked up at him, reverent and hopeful.

The angel smiled with affection.

He lifted one finger, his right index finger.

Rafe took one look at that finger and shouted in terror. "No!" He leapt at the angel, not able to articulate what he feared, but knowing he had to stop whatever would happen next. He snatched at the angel, determined to stop whatever he intended to do.

The angel's eyes blazed. He moved so quickly that Rafe didn't see the blow coming, much less have time to respond. In the blink of an eye, that fingertip was pointed at Rafe. Light emanated from it with fearsome force.

It was like a laze, but more potent.

Rafe took the blow on his chest and fell stunned to the ground. His heart seemed to have stopped cold, then started again with a gallop. He couldn't catch his breath. He felt shocked and dizzy, nauseous and powerless. He lay there, blinking and shaking, betrayed by his body's weakness.

Unable to save Delilah.

He rolled over, winced, and watched with horror.

The angel had already turned his smile upon Delilah. She

stared up at him in rapture, oblivious to Rafe. The angel took her arm again, raised his finger once more, then slid his fingertip down the inside of Delilah's left forearm.

Rafe watched it cut. He smelled the flesh burn. He watched the line of fire that spread from that fingertip and felt sick. He couldn't remember why he knew this angel with his burning fingertip, but he knew the pain of that incision being made.

The lost memory tantalized him, lingering just out of his reach. He forced himself to his hands and knees, determined to help Delilah to escape.

Somehow.

Delilah cried out in pain, but the angel held fast to her hand. She shook, but didn't try to fight the angel.

Rafe was amazed. She trusted the angel, even though he obviously was hurting her. The angel shook his head in sympathy even as he finished making his mark.

Then he eased the flat of his hand down the length of the wound.

Delilah gasped and blinked back her tears. Her entire body was trembling. She looked down at her arm, smiling as she marveled.

The angel's hand had seared the wound closed, as surely as if it had never been.

Rafe stared. Delilah's tattoo was gone.

There was no evidence that it had ever been there.

Rafe was shocked. He'd never thought to rely on divine intervention to solve his problems. But Delilah had knelt before the light, as if she'd known what to expect. Had she encountered angels before? Or did she simply trust her instincts? He supposed that if she had the gift of foresight, her intuition would be strong.

And it would be right.

There were tears on Delilah's face, but her smile was brilliant. She bent and touched her lips to the angel's feet in gratitude. The angel caught her shoulders in his hands, his smile seeming to increase his radiance. Rafe saw that she was shaking, but she looked up at the angel with a joyous expression on her face.

The angel smiled, then bent to touch his lips to Delilah's brow.

She gasped and Rafe struggled to his feet, fearful of what the angel did to her now.

But the angel had set her on her own feet. He moved backward by no visible means, neither walking or flying. The angel might have willed his own movement. But his body wasn't substantial or clearly defined.

Like Lucifer, but made of light instead of darkness.

And able to make change in the material world. The angel, no matter what Rafe would have preferred to believe, was real.

Rafe was awed to see the angel join a chorus of angels that hovered just over the tops of the trees. He hadn't seen them but as the first angel rose to join them, their shapes became increasingly clear. The light they emanated grew to blinding intensity.

Rafe couldn't entirely quell his terror, although he couldn't explain it. He felt that wall in his memory again and wanted more than anything to know what lurked behind its locked doors.

The angels sang. Their song was wordless and joyous. It resonated in Rafe's veins and filled him with a familiar exuberance. He wanted to raise his own voice in the chorus. He wanted to show his love for all of creation, for all of the marvel and mystery of the world. He wanted to celebrate goodness and joy.

What did he know of angels and their songs?

The angel who had removed Delilah's tattoo smiled at him then, smiled with the fondness of an old friend. Despite his fear, that look sent joy through Rafe. What did the angels want with him? Rafe managed to rise to his feet to meet whatever destiny was his. His heart quaked, but he would stand to meet his destiny.

"You will remember, Raphael, just as you desired." The words echoed in his thoughts. *"There is a plan and it is good. Have faith in the plan."*

Rafe heard the angel speaking in his own thoughts, but the

voice didn't fill him with revulsion the way Lucifer's words had.

The angel wasn't trying to command or manipulate him.

The angel was content to leave Rafe to make his own choices.

Rafe looked at the angel, desperately searching his memory once again and finding nothing. Surely the angel wasn't lying to him? Did he dare to believe in the goodness of a divine plan?

The angel lifted his hands as the song of his fellows built to a crescendo. It seemed as if he would speak again and Rafe wanted to hear whatever the angel said.

But Rafe's palm chimed.

Rafe tried to slap it to silence, well aware of the angel's disapproval. The stupid palm chimed again, insistent upon telling him something he didn't want to know. He'd set the chime to silence, he knew it, but the device consistently overrode whatever Rafe told it to do.

Delilah cast Rafe a disparaging glance, but there was nothing he could do. To his relief, after the third chime, his palm fell silent.

But the angel shook his head, seemingly bemused. He didn't speak again. He grew brilliant in his radiance, then the entire chorus faded to nothing at all.

They were gone.

Delilah tipped back her head and lifted her own hands in an echo of the angel's pose. "Hallelujah!" she cried.

Rafe wondered whether he imagined that heavenly chorus echoing her joyous cry of praise.

Then she turned to him, her eyes shining, and he saw the red mark of the angel's kiss on her forehead.

"Angelfire!" she said, her exhilaration clear.

Rafe was less exhilarated by the realities of their situation. She had a flaw again, a visible one. Had the angel simply exchanged one defect for another? He disliked that this mark was even more visible than the tattoo had been. He wasn't happy with his palm's persistent chiming, with its collection of secure data that he shouldn't possess, with the loss of his laze and the unknown location of Ferris.

Things only got worse when Delilah began to tremble.

Rafe understood instantly that another vision was taking command of her. Here, in the woods, where no one could witness the power of her gift. Here, in the wilderness, where her vision would gain her no credibility.

She fought it, her teeth gritted and her fists clenched. "Not here," she whispered.

"Can you hold it until we find witnesses?" Rafe demanded, kneeling by her side.

She shook her head adamantly, fighting the power of it.

Rafe made a snap decision. He decided that his palm could prove itself useful for once. "Let it come. I'll vidcast it to the Reverend Billie Jo Estevez. Just like you wanted."

He had a fleeting glimpse of her smile, and his heart warmed that he could give her what she wanted. He had time to set his palm for a live vidcast, sought the address for the reverend, targeted the signal, and focused the image-snatcher on Delilah just as she surrendered to the voices of the angels inside her mind.

He had to hope that the reverend would recognize Delilah.

Something had to go right soon if Rafe's mission was going to succeed.

THE ANGEL had called Rafe by name.

More, the angel had brought Rafe a message. If Rafe knew the angels as well, was he also psychic? Did he also hear their voices? Did she have that in common with him?

Delilah recognized that the chime of Rafe's palm had interrupted the angelic chorus. Was he really unable to control his palm? Had he deliberately stopped the angels from singing?

Or had he been trying to stop the angels from telling Delilah whatever they knew about him?

Delilah wanted to know.

He had agreed to vidcast to the reverend, which gave Delilah the confidence to surrender to the vision. The tumult grew in her thoughts, the light becoming ever brighter and the concerns of the moment seeming irrelevant. She felt herself shake, saw the white flood of light in her mind, and reached to rub the middle of her forehead.

It stung from the angel's kiss. There was no room for her thoughts in her own mind. Her body was not her own, but she didn't resent the angels' claim. She felt herself to be an instrument of a higher power, and felt blessed that she had been chosen to deliver these messages.

At the same time, she was troubled by her vision as it unfolded. It was darker and more ominous than any she had had before. She could smell smoke and blood and destruction, her sense of violence shaking her to her core. She was caught in the middle of a blood-red maelstrom, one that billowed like dust and filled her with terror.

She heard the voice of the angels spill from her own lips. The voice was stern, a reprimand and a warning, and it did nothing to ease her trepidation.

> *The good book warns of dragons red;*
> *Of plagues of locusts and blood that's shed;*
> *Of a dark angel taking flesh;*
> *Casting God's creation in distress.*
> *Matheson first and then the next*
> *As Satan's spawn pursues his quest*
> *To bring the world to its dark end*
> *And see his master sovereign.*

The light faded from Delilah's thoughts, its touch leaving her strangely drained and frightened. She'd received a warning, one that shook her.

Because she knew it was personal.

She'd seen the destruction that would result if she failed to fulfil her destiny.

The angels spoke through her, but they were becoming impatient. They were warning her. They had said that the President had been murdered and now said there would be more deaths.

Unless the culprit was stopped.

"Are you all right? This vision seemed different." Rafe bent down beside her, his brow knotted into a frown.

"It was. It was darker. More ominous, and less invigorating." Delilah sighed and looked up at him, noting his concern. He had followed her. He had sent the vid of her vision to the reverend, doing as she had asked despite his own misgivings.

The angels trusted him, so maybe she should as well.

"Did you hear that man's voice?"

Rafe shuddered, showing that he shared her dislike of it. "I thought it came from the fog, but that makes no sense. The cabin's defenses must have included the release of a hallucinogen."

"I don't think so." Delilah said softly. "If there are angels at work, there can be demons too." Rafe started visibly. "That's why it felt so wicked."

"He said he was Lucifer, and becoming manifest," Rafe said with caution. "He said he was close to claiming the world as his own."

Delilah nodded at this news, not truly surprised. "I have to stop him," she said with determination. "There has to be hope."

"Alone?" Rafe asked.

She smiled at him. "I have the angels on my side."

Rafe frowned and looked away. "We should move on," he said, and she knew that he was deliberately changing the subject.

Delilah tapped a query into her palm for the first time in her life. She had to know how to go forward and she feared that she was missing something.

Her mother knew the angels. Was there a clue in that article?

There was—there was a hotlink at the bottom to an interview with none other than the Reverend Billie Jo Estevez. Delilah read the piece, which was actually a monologue from the reverend, and eyed the image.

The angels knew the reverend. That was all the endorsement she needed to be sure that the reverend could be the sponsor she sought. Again, she wondered about Rafe's alliances.

"How do you know the angels, Rafe?"

He took a step back. "I don't."

"Don't be ridiculous. The angel called you by name. And he knew about your having lost your memory. He said you would remember, just as you desired."

"Maybe the angels know everybody. Maybe it's not important." He glared at her and Delilah glared back, certain he was hiding something. "Maybe we need to move before someone follows up on the coordinates of the vidcast I uploaded to the reverend."

Then she had a thought. Maybe Rafe didn't remember the angels either. Delilah's annoyance with him evaporated. They remembered him. That should be all the credential she needed.

She smiled at him and he blinked.

"I'm going to Hood River." Delilah started to walk in what she believed was the right direction. It was the opposite direction in which Rafe had pointed. "You can come along, or not. Your choice."

"Hood River? Why?"

"You said the reverend was there."

"She's having a memorial service for the victims," Rafe said, glancing toward his palm with exasperation.

Delilah turned her back on him and walked.

She knew exactly what he would do. He was on a mission to protect her, after all, and had already gone to great lengths to defend her, justifying the angel's affection for him. Delilah knew he'd come after her.

She smiled when she heard him swear.

Her smile broadened when she heard his footfalls, and she jumped when he locked his hand beneath her elbow. "We're going to regret this," he said through his teeth. "I promise you that."

"Don't be ridiculous," she said. "Have some faith."

Rafe snorted. "I'd have more faith with my laze back."

"What happened to Ferris?"

Rafe's mood, if anything, became more grim. "I don't know."

Delilah glanced back, fearful, remembering the dogs.

"When I came to, he had vanished without a trace," Rafe said with quiet heat.

She didn't want to think about Ferris being harvested and sent back to the research labs. She didn't want to think of him being shredded alive by the hunters' dogs either, or shot dead as a rogue and a fugitive. She might have headed back down into the valley behind them, but Rafe's hand landed on her shoulder.

"I don't think we can help Ferris now," he said softly.

She closed her eyes, knowing he was right. First Rachel and now Ferris. Too many people were paying the price for her gift. She had to succeed to do justice to their sacrifices.

"Why did you trust the angel, even when he was hurting you?"

"I'll tell you, if you tell me why you frightened them away."

"I didn't."

"Your palm pinged. That made them leave."

His exasperation was clear. "It wasn't my choice . . ."

"Show me what you received."

Rafe's expression turned grim. "I don't have to do that . . ."

"You do if we're going to travel together." Delilah halted and met his gaze steadily, her vision having given her resolve. "Either that, or we datashare. Choose, Raphael Gerritson."

XIII

Rafe was shocked by Delilah's suggestion, and his surprise probably showed. "No."

Her eyes darkened and he glimpsed that well-earned hostility. "Because I'm just a shade?"

"No, no, that's not it. I don't know what's on my palm . . ."

"That's the point." Delilah rose to follow him, her lips set in such a firm line that Rafe doubted he could change her mind. In a way, it had been easier when she was sedated. In another, he appreciated that she was clever.

"You don't know who wiped your memory or who controls your palm," she insisted. "I need to know what you know before we go farther."

"No." The idea filled Rafe with horror. She had no tattoo, no scars, a chance for life as a norm and she wanted to risk infection from his unruly palm and its subroutines. It was out of the question.

He realized with some surprise that her hair had grown. It was about half an inch long all over her head and as dark as ebony. How had it grown that fast? And why?

The angel's kiss had turned to a burgundy mark on her forehead, as if a whore had left a smear of lipstain there. It was less damning than Rafe had feared.

He turned away from her and checked his palm. "We're a couple of hours' walk from Hood River. If you're so sure that the reverend will take your cause, we'll go to that prayer service . . ."

"Why do you care so much about making me Oracle?"

Her question silenced Rafe because he didn't have an

answer. "I don't remember," he admitted quietly. "I just know that I don't have a choice. I have to make you Oracle or die trying."

She didn't reply and he turned to study her, surprised to find her expression so shrewdly assessing. "You're a thief."

"I like shiny things." Rafe shrugged.

"You *take* shiny things," she corrected. "Like the necklace. That makes you a thief."

"Sometimes I end up with those shiny things," he admitted.

She tilted her head to watch him. He had the sense that no nuance of his response would go unnoticed. "Stealing is against the law of the Republic. Have you ever been caught?"

Rafe ran a hand over his his hair, disliking that he didn't know the answer to a very simple question. "I'm not sure."

Delilah came to his side, her gaze searching. "What if you got caught once?" He was snared by the question and watched her, wondering what she would say. "What if you made a deal for clemency, maybe that you'd find me in exchange for your freedom. What if you had a memory wipe to make sure you didn't remember who you were working for?"

Rafe couldn't hide his disgust at the prospect. "So you think I'm taking you right into danger, even though I don't realize it myself."

"Maybe." She grimaced. "Maybe neither one of us should trust you."

"I've given you my word . . ."

"Or maybe neither one of us should trust whoever gave you that memory wipe."

Rafe felt his frustration rise. "There's no way to know for sure. Anyone who did that would have made my palm data correspond to my memory."

"I thought it knew things you didn't."

Rafe nodded.

"Then maybe it knows more than it should. You ignore it most of the time, anyway. You might not know."

"I don't trust it."

Delilah's gaze was steely as she held out her left hand. "Datashare with me."

"No." Before she could argue, he continued. "I don't know what kind of software worms are installed on it. Something viral could infect your palm. There could be a malicious sub-routine . . ."

Her wide smile shocked him to silence. "You're saying no, not because you want to keep secrets from me, but because you want to protect me."

"It's my responsibility to protect you!"

Her smile softened as she regarded him. "Even from yourself."

Rafe exhaled, recognizing truth when he heard it. "If need be."

There was a warmth in her eyes that made Rafe think about other unions between them, ones he found more interesting than datasharing. She was changing before his very eyes, filling with life and vitality. Her skin was less pale than it had been, and her eyelashes appeared to be longer and thicker.

She looked exotic, the angel's kiss on her forehead like a mark of divine favor. She flicked a glance at him, her eyes very blue, and their gazes locked and held. Rafe felt his desire grow, just with her proximity, though he knew they had no time.

Delilah eased even closer. She tapped her fingertips on his chest, each rap making his heart leap in response. She looked up at him, so clever and coy and irresistible that Rafe feared he wouldn't be able to deny her anything. "Any chance that it was the angels who wiped your memory?" she asked lightly.

Rafe gaped at her. "That's the craziest thing I've ever heard."

She was undeterred. "It's no crazier than your insistence that your palm keeps sending you stuff that you shouldn't have."

"It's a worthless piece of garbage."

"Maybe not," she mused. "Who sends the messages?"

Rafe shrugged. He'd spent too much time trying to answer the same question, without any results. "There's no datatrail. They just come out of the blue."

"On pirate frequencies," she murmured. "The messages can't be from the Republic, then."

"They could be. Or from someone working inside the Republic's databanks." Rafe winced. "I get a lot of posts that look as if they should be on secure police servers only."

She nodded. "Or they're coming from someone who has hacked into their databases and is forwarding stuff to you."

"That can't even be possible."

She gave him a furious glance, one that reminded him of the blast from the angel's fingertip. "An *angel* just removed the tattoo that has been on my arm for my entire life, leaving no scar or sign that it was there. *Anything* is possible."

Rafe couldn't argue with that.

Delilah brushed her fingertips across the back of his left hand, sending shivers of desire through him. "What did you receive when they were singing?"

"I didn't even look."

"It interrupted them. Maybe that was important."

"Maybe it's just more of my luck." Rafe was reluctant to pull up the message, precisely because he thought Delilah might be right. He didn't want to look at the message in front of her, and find out that they were in deeper trouble than he'd already imagined.

It might be about Ferris being captured.

She obviously didn't share his trepidation. "Datashare with me."

"No."

"Then let me see the message."

"No. I'll check it first . . ."

She glanced at him, her eyes dancing. "I thought you were the carefree and reckless one."

"I'm thinking a little caution is a better strategy in this time and place."

He thought for a minute that she'd laugh. He wished she would. Instead she sobered and looked too stubborn for his taste. "I want to see what you received."

"I have a bad feeling about that message."

"I'm the one with foresight," Delilah said and gave him a nudge. "You're supposed to be the bold one. Show me."

Rafe hesitated. "What if it's about Ferris?" he asked quietly.

She inhaled and squared her shoulders, showing a determination he was beginning to associate with her. "I want to know."

Maybe showing her the message would end the discussion once and for all. If it was horrific, she'd listen to him in the future.

Rafe wasn't prepared to bet on that.

He punched up the last message received by the palm before he thought more about it. It wasn't about Ferris, but it was just as bad.

"See?" he said. "It makes no sense that I have this. It's a police record of a homicide."

"Exactly the kind of thing that shouldn't be on a citizen's palm," Delilah agreed as she pressed closer to read it.

Rafe frowned as he scrolled down the item. "No, it's a cold case," he corrected.

"Not even a homicide," Delilah agreed. "Because the victim was a shade."

"Her execution is simply a property crime against the Republic." Rafe was shocked when his palm displayed a sequence of images from the crime scene. They were gruesome, but he couldn't halt their appearance.

He stared at them in horrified silence.

He saw the scars that had condemned the shade, a pair of diagonal scars on her back. They looked just like the scars that graced his own back, the scars he'd never been able to figure out.

His mouth went dry.

Why had he been sent this file?

Was he being targeted?

Or was he being warned?

R786903
a.k.a. Rachel Gottlieb

- <u>facial image</u>
- b. ?
- harvested as an adult in 2090 in New Concord by Rhys ibn Ali
  - <u>assessment</u> of Society of Nuclear Darwinists with <u>images</u>
- abandoned labor six months later and declared fugitive
- d. October 29, 2099, in New Gotham

N.B. As this shade was masquerading as a citizen, its violent death was initially believed to be a murder. At time of death, the shade's palm had been wiped of all information by persons or subroutines unknown. Activities and interactions 2090 to 2099 remain unidentified. Reference <u>NGPD Cold Case File 99-87659-3A.</u>

DELILAH GASPED at the image displayed on Rafe's palm. "Rachel!"

It was her old friend, but she was very dead.

"You know her?"

"I did, yes. But she was alive, then."

Delilah stared wanting the image to be anything other than what it was, wanting to be wrong, but the woman was Rachel. She couldn't look at how Rachel's body had been violated, couldn't stomach the idea that anyone had committed such a violent crime against a person she loved.

"When?"

"She saved me from the mill. She stole me from my assigned labor. She was so nice to me that I was happy to go." Delilah swallowed. "I always thought she must have been my mother."

"What happened to her?"

"They took her." Delilah swallowed and straightened. "The

shade hunter came for us. She tried to protect me, she did protect me, but she was harvested herself."

He was watching her intently. "Then what?"

"I ran." Delilah shrugged. "Another shade hunter captured me—he was kinder but I fought him. He sedated me and took me to the Daughters, to Sonja." She frowned in recollection. "I think Sonja knew him."

Rafe was staring fixedly at the last image, apparently not listening to her anymore. He had paled as if he would be ill. That was so at odds with his normal expression that Delilah looked closer at his palm.

She saw Rachel's back, with those two diagonal scars.

They were so strange. What would cause such scars? She looked more closely, struggling to solve the puzzle.

Rafe slapped his palm, abruptly removing the display, and paced away from her. He was breathing raggedly, visibly upset by the images.

And no wonder. Rachel's death had been awful.

But those two diagonal scars bothered Delilah. She'd never seen anything like them and couldn't imagine what malady would cause them. Extra limbs? But they'd be unlikely to grow there.

Two long incisions in Rachel's back.

Delilah remembered the shade hunter tearing Rachel's clothing when he'd snatched after her, remembered his smile when he'd seen Rachel's bare back. She knew now what he had seen, what had condemned Rachel, what had allowed the shade hunter to harvest her.

And now Rachel was dead.

She'd never see her again. She felt tired and overwhelmed by the knowledge that Rachel was dead. She had hoped to be reunited at some point with her old friend, but that was clearly impossible.

"She took me to the angels the first time," Delilah said softly. "That's why I trusted them, because I knew."

"Even when he cut your arm?" Rafe asked, his tone dubious.

"But they did that before. I knew it would be all right."

Rafe regarded her with confusion.

"I had a third eye." She rubbed her forehead and there was an answering glimmer of light in her mind's eye. "Right there. It's why I failed the S.H.A.D.E. It's what made me a shade. But the angels removed it, and removed it so well that there was no evidence that it had ever been there at all."

"Why?" Rafe asked, the brightness of his eyes seeming to make that inner light spark.

"They said I would be Oracle. They said that I would still hear their voices, but that they had to make it harder for me to be found. They said I would be hunted otherwise."

"It only bought you time," Rafe said with impatience. "And maybe not enough of that. We'd better get moving."

That was when Delilah realized what could have caused Rachel's scars.

"She was an angel," she whispered. "They took away her wings."

The angels weren't just giving Delilah her visions—they were helping her and defending her. One of their own had helped her to escape the mill and the Society, and had ultimately paid with her own life. The angels truly had chosen her as their own.

How did Rafe fit into that?

"That's crazy talk," he said tersely, and she bristled that he could be dismissive of what seemed an obvious truth to her. She would have argued, but he pivoted to offer his hand to her. "Let's go."

"But the angels . . ."

His eyes flashed. "We're not talking about this anymore. There's no point. We still need to find the reverend and persuade her to sponsor you. That's plenty to resolve for the moment."

"You're not feeling optimistic."

"I don't like this plan, and I really don't like pursuing it without my laze." His eyes gleamed. "It's the only plan we've got, though, so we might as well get started."

Delilah acquiesced, knowing that she couldn't persuade

him otherwise. She knew that he would see soon enough that she was right. After all, the angels were watching over her. Rafe might not be convinced, but Delilah knew that was true.

The angels wouldn't abandon her when success was so close.

They just had to find the reverend and everything would be fine.

RAFE'S THOUGHTS were spinning, a thousand details pulling together into a coherence that defied belief.

Delilah was right—the angel knew him.

And Rafe had feared the angel and his burning fingertip.

He had scars on his back that matched those that would be left by the removal of a pair of wings.

And Lucifer, the dark man he had thought to be a manifestation of his own doubts, had insisted that they had once been the same thing, that at least Lucifer had remembered his past when he had fallen.

Was Rafe himself a fallen angel?

It was an incredible possibility. All the same, he much preferred it to Delilah's theory that the Republic had convicted him as a criminal, then given him a memory wipe and a second chance. He preferred to imagine that he was working for the angels in protecting Delilah.

But maybe that was what whoever controlled his palm wanted him to believe.

Maybe he *was* a criminal working for his own salvation.

Against Delilah's best interests.

The angel, after all, had left no scar on Delilah's forearm. If the angels had removed wings from Rafe's back, then there should be no scars. He couldn't imagine who else could remove angel wings. If he had been an angel like the one they had seen in the woods, a being of light and luminosity, how could anyone mortal have performed that surgery upon him?

No. The scars were frauds. He had them and this Rachel

had had them. If she had helped Delilah before, she might have been manipulated to serve some unknown agenda. He felt a union with her, and recognized the similarities in their situations.

She had been working for the same anonymous controllers.

Had she known who they were?

Feeling common purpose with Rachel wasn't the most comforting sensation Rafe could have had. Rachel had been harvested after taking Delilah into her custody, after all, and then she had been brutally killed. The ping was a warning, a portent of his own fate.

Rafe's pace quickened with his anxiety.

His body ached in places he hadn't ever felt before. His shoulders were sore and there were blisters on his feet. His legs felt heavy—he'd never walked so far in one day in his life— and he wanted to sleep through the rest of the week.

But he didn't have that luxury.

He needed a wash and a shave and was very aware of the scent of his body. He preferred to be fastidiously groomed and clean at all times, but this last day hadn't allowed for that.

Had it been only a day since he entered the Citadel?

His shirt had dirt on the cuffs, his trousers were singed, and his boots were mired. There was a smattering of small holes burned in his garments from the sparks of the laze shot hitting his codpiece. It was a scorched disgrace. The queue in his hair had come unfastened and there was mud on the hem of his cloak.

He felt like an animal and he didn't like it one bit.

His confidence and good humor were at an all-time low. He didn't know what had happened to Ferris, but doubted that anything good had come of the boy's escape. Either he had been captured again by the hunters, or he had been tracked down and killed by dogs. Rafe didn't want to think about it. Even though the kid had turned on him and broken his promise, no one deserved either of those fates.

Did Delilah blame Rafe for Ferris' fate, whatever it was?

He halfway blamed himself for not anticipating events. It wasn't as if Ferris hadn't turned on him before.

Worse, they were heading straight into danger. Rafe feared that going to Hood River to seek out the reverend was a plan doomed to end badly.

The problem was that Delilah was right—he didn't have a better plan. He had no laze anymore. The windmills of Hood River came into view long before the town itself did, their white arms spinning furiously against the overcast skies.

Rafe knew with the sight of them that one way or another, their adventure was coming to an end.

He was afraid it wouldn't be a good one.

The worst thing of all was that Delilah was thinking. She was practically humming along beside him, her movements quick and energetic. She was so invigorated by her exchange with the angels that she was almost radiant herself. She was completely convinced that the reverend would take her cause, that justice had to prevail.

It was as if Rafe's previous confidence had abandoned him for Delilah.

He hoped she was right.

He prayed she was right.

And he tried to figure out what he would do about it, if she was wrong.

Overall, it could have been said that Rafe didn't approach the town of Hood River at his best.

THEY STRODE into the periphery of the town, Delilah's curiosity and light step at complete odds with Rafe's own concerns. The towers rose high on every side, each one crowned with a spinning windmill. The persistent wind tousled Rafe's hair, refreshing him in a way that the water had not.

Hood River was the largest regional center that had escaped destruction incurred during the Pacific Rim Conflict. Its economy had recovered with remarkable speed as the town became a focus for wind generation and its export. New Portland relied almost exclusively upon Hood River's juice, and more of it went north to New Seattle. The town was comparatively prosperous, and was one that had grown in population.

The streets were filled with people, most of whom were moving steadily in the same direction. They were healthier than most citizens of the Republic, their cheeks ruddy from that wind and a bounce in most steps. Rafe realized that they were optimistic, and found himself resisting the appeal of that mood.

He reminded himself that he was probably taking Delilah to her doom.

There were bicycles and rickshaws moving through the crowd, as well as hundreds of people. They were all dressed to the letter of the Decency Code. Rafe saw a few image-snatchers, perhaps journalists, capturing the scope of the crowd. There were dozens of police officers moving steadily through the streets, their black pseudoskins and helms marking them as separate from the citizens.

And as the presence of authority.

They reminded him of the commandos who had executed women at the burning Citadel. Had any of those recruits come from here? Were they among the police officers in attendance here? Rafe swallowed his dread with an effort.

A few banners fluttered from buildings, and more from the towers of the windmills, each featuring the familiar logo of the watchful eyes of the Republic. It was a reminder Rafe didn't need.

He felt exposed, right in the thick of the place potentially most treacherous to Delilah. He wanted his laze desperately, but when he saw the police officers checking citizens, he had to cede that it might be smarter to be without it. One looked pointedly at his empty holster, then moved on without saying anything, much to Rafe's relief.

Being amid people, in a bustling town, reminded Rafe of the oldest memory he could recall. He tried to remember details of being in the custody of Lilia Desjardins. That day was hazy in his mind, filled with pain. It troubled him even to try to think of it.

But Rafe persisted. There had to be a clue there as to the truth.

He knew that he had moved through a crowd like this one, and had been naked except for someone's cloak. Who had given him the cloak? A man, Rafe recalled that, but not any more. He knew that he had been dazzled by the sound of people and traffic, yet fascinated by the city of New Gotham.

He felt a similar curiosity from Delilah.

Lilia had taken him to get clothes. She had taught him how to use his palm. She had helped him catch the train. He had known nothing of the world and she had been complicit in that.

Why?

She'd been shocked by his confession that he was to seek Delilah—or had she simply pretended to be surprised? He had to admit that he could have been easily deceived that day. Was Lilia part of the scheme against Delilah, on the side of whoever had wiped his memory?

Or did she too know the angels?

Rafe recalled the news article about Lilia the shade hunter and the two genuine angels she had brought to the circus in Nouveau Mont Royal. They were a sensation, albeit one that hadn't captured Rafe's interest. He assumed it to be promotional nonsense, but itched now to call up the article on his palm and read it again.

First things first.

A rickshaw veered around them, the driver cracking his whip over the shade in the harness. Delilah gasped, but Rafe caught her elbow in his hand. He gave her a firm look, trying to advise her to not draw attention to herself, but couldn't read her expression through her veil.

He kept his own hood up, a challenge in the stiff wind, and matched his pace to that of the milling crowd. He assumed that they were headed for Reverend Billie Jo Estevez's memorial service for victims of the Citadel fire. As the crowd gathered around its destination, he knew that his guess was right.

The building ahead of them could only be the town hall.

A platform had been raised before it, the flag of the Republic fluttering from the clock tower of the building itself. The flag was lit, the expense of juice being no object in Hood River. The stars and cross almost glowed on the flag, looking brilliantly white against the darkening sky. There were lights around the perimeter of the stage and the large white cross that hung from the front of this and every town hall in the Republic was illuminated.

The crowd's mood was festive, if quiet. Rafe guessed that their tendency to be sober at a memorial service was challenged by their excitement at a celebrity holding that service in their town. Volunteers passed out pale beeswax candles and Rafe took two. He lit them both from the volunteer's lamp, then tried to ease closer to the stage. He had no idea what Delilah would do or what would happen, but closer to the reverend had to be better.

If Delilah had a vision during the service, she was more likely to be seen by the reverend. If she simply exposed her face, she had a better chance of being recognized with proximity. She was breathing quickly, but Rafe couldn't tell whether it was excitement, fear, or a pending vision at root.

He hoped in a way that she would have a vision.

Pressed amid his fellow citizens where every word would be overheard, he couldn't simply ask. Rafe simply hoped that Delilah's conviction that the reverend would take her cause was justified. He cupped his hand around the flame of his burning candle, protecting it from the wind, and Delilah mimicked his gesture. Music began to play and spotlights swirled over the assembled citizens. The air practically crackled with excitement.

Rafe saw a helicopter descending behind the city hall and whispers slipped through the crowd as its black silhouette was spotted. Such a vehicle was an unusual sight, and the persistent chop of the rotor announced the arrival of an important individual.

A wealthy individual.

The helicopter disappeared behind the building and the crowd began to chant the reverend's name. The lights spun over the square at dizzying speed and the vid operators scanned the crowd with purpose.

"Billie Jo Estevez. Billie Jo Estevez."

Vid-screens were revealed around the perimeter of the town square as they were illuminated. Rafe knew that those screens weren't usually there, but had been installed for the reverend's appearance by the astonishment of the crowd as each was lit. Images of rapt citizens appeared on the screens, a dizzying array of faces and expressions.

The excitement was palpable. Rafe could feel Delilah's amazement and he wasn't truly surprised when she lifted her veil. She cast the fabric over the top of her hat, revealing her face and that port wine mark of the angel's kiss on her brow.

Rafe's heart stopped cold in fear.

But she wasn't alone. Many of the women had removed the veils that obscured their view of the proceedings and some didn't even wear any. Rafe caught Delilah's elbow in his hand and pulled her closer, disliking her visibility all the same.

She, in contrast, was sparkling in her excitement. "Isn't it wonderful?" she whispered, but Rafe didn't agree.

He watched the police officers move into position, noting how they secured each street entrance to the town square. They were making preparations to contain the crowd—because they knew they would have to? Or because they were simply prepared for the worst?

Rafe took that idea as a mandate and sought alternative means of escape. There had to be a netherzone here, but he couldn't see an access point. No commuter tunnels opened into this square—he could see their arches in the side streets beyond the police officers' barricades. The town square was cobbled from one side to the other. The businesses that fronted the square—primarily the offices of lawyers and politicians— were closed, their windows shuttered and doors locked. Any netherzone accesses within those offices were inaccessible.

The town hall was locked down as well.

Which meant the only way out was the path preserved for the use of the reverend herself. Rafe didn't have to like that, or the probabilities of his being able to use it with any success.

Without a laze.

There was a fanfare, then a vid-screen mounted on the door of the city hall was filled with the image of the reverend's face. She had her eyes closed in an expression of joyous ecstasy, an expression not unlike that of Delilah after the angel kissed her brow. Rafe dared to hope at the similarity.

Maybe, just maybe, this would work out all right.

"Hallelujah!" roared the crowd in recognition, using the cry that began every vidcast from Reverend Billie Jo Estevez. Delilah raised her own voice in the shout. The music soared and settled to a familiar tune, and the crowd jostled with excitement.

They lifted their candles high and sang the *Battle Hymn of the Republic* with vigor, as if their passion could make the reverend arrive more quickly. Mist roiled across the white stage, obscuring it momentarily.

And when it cleared, just as the hymn ended, the reverend herself was standing in front of the vid-screen. Her hands were raised high, her expression exactly as in the still image. She wore flowing white robes with long sleeves, and the gems on her fingers glinted in the spotlights. She looked majestic and powerful and held the pose for the barest beat.

Then she smiled, shouted, "Hallelujah!" and marched to the front of the stage with purpose. The vid-screens around the square switched to a live vidcast of the reverend, presumably the same one being presented to citizens throughout the Republic. The crowd screamed its approval and pushed closer to the stage.

Rafe let himself and Delilah be pushed. He was more reassured than he could have imagined moments earlier.

Because there had to be a trapdoor in the stage. The reverend had come from beneath the platform, which meant she had been raised to the stage proper on a trapdoor. The dry ice had been used to disguise the sleight of hand, but Rafe wasn't fooled.

An access to what laid beneath was precisely what he had been seeking. The way out of the square was straight across the stage and down through that trapdoor.

If they had to make a run for it, Rafe was pretty sure they'd have surprise on their side.

That just might be good enough.

XIV

FERRIS SLID into the crowd gathered in Hood River's town square. He didn't doubt that he was being followed, but he hoped to be less visible in such a big crowd. He appreciated the clothing that Rafe had found for him and the way Rafe had cut his hair—he was more nondescript this way and blended more easily with norms.

He yearned to be invisible, and he was closer to it because of Rafe. He tried to walk with the confidence Rafe showed, taking that man as his model of human behavior. Shades clung to the shadows, they slumped, they hunkered down in the hope that they would be overlooked. Ferris tried to walk as if he belonged, as if he was a norm and didn't care who knew it.

It worked pretty well.

At least as far as he could tell.

He was achingly aware of his palm and the deception programmed right into it. It would betray him and he knew it. He didn't want to betray Rafe and Delilah.

Still he felt compelled somehow to warn them.

Which was why he had followed them to Hood River.

He feared Rhys, though, and his electronic leash. With the crowd gathering in the main square, Ferris took advantage of the empty streets. He found a hardware store, its door locked and its owners absent.

There were hammers displayed in the window.

Ferris took a deep breath, then smashed his fist through the glass. It took five blows to make it shatter, and the alarm sounded after the second one.

He seized a hammer and ran. He dodged down alleys and turned corners, leaping between people and trying to lose himself in the crowd. He heard sounds of pursuit, but they faded, along with the ringing of the alarm.

And he had a hammer in his pocket.

Once caught in the throng and disguised by them, Ferris slipped the hammer into his right hand. He surreptitiously tapped at his palm with the hammer, making many tiny blows on the display.

He felt it crack.

He heard it sizzle.

He kept tapping, dropping little pieces of the display out of his sleeve as he walked. Destroying the palm was illegal, but that was the lesser of two evils. If his palm was inoperative, the hunters could never collect him.

And he could warn Rafe and Delilah.

If he could find them.

Ferris dropped the hammer as he moved onward, and shook the debris out of his palm. He was sure it wasn't working any longer. He began to ease between people, crossing the square and back again. He was advised by several people that he'd never meet his friends here. He nodded rueful agreement, but kept looking.

Just before the service began, he saw Rafe.

Right near the stage.

Of course.

That man had his hood up, but Ferris was sure that no one else stood as tall. Those broad shoulders couldn't have belonged to anyone else, and the way he stayed protectively close to the woman beside him spoke volumes.

To the hooded man's left was a woman, wearing an ugly hat and a thick cream veil.

Delilah.

Ferris worked his way closer with new purpose. His heartbeat accelerated, even as Rafe made better progress toward the stage. People blocked Ferris' path, thinking that he only wanted a better vantage point. They gave him bitter looks and he moved sideways, then forward again.

He hated that he couldn't excuse himself, his inability to speak seeming to become a glaring defect. His breath hitched with his certainty that he would be caught, that he would be condemned by the silence that he couldn't shatter. He feared that he would be sent back to the labs, that he would be forced to help the Nuclear Darwinist researchers torment his fellow shades.

Ferris much preferred to die.

If that was to be his fate, he wanted to warn Delilah first.

DELILAH WAS entranced.

She had never been among so many people, let alone witnessed an event like this one. Even though it was to be a memorial service, the mood was celebratory.

It seemed a perfect culmination of her exchange with the angels, the ideal way to finish her day. She had a sense that everything was leading her to the precise place she should be.

Wasn't she destined to be Oracle?

Reverend Billie Jo Estevez crossed the stage, the hem of her robes glittering in the light. Her sleeves were edged with silver thread, which made a sparkle around her wrists when she raised her hands. Delilah supposed that it was meant to evoke starlight or angelfire, although it was a distant approximation.

"We are gathered to mourn the destruction of the Citadel of the Daughters of the Republic," she said, her voice resonant.

"Amen," was the choral reply. Delilah missed the cue on the vid-screens, and the woman to her left gave her a nudge and pointed so that Delilah understood. She nodded her gratitude, noting how the woman's gaze lingered on her forehead.

That was when she remembered the kiss of the angel, the mark of his favor that adorned her skin. She pushed back her hat a little farther, willing the reverend to notice her.

The reverend stared out over the crowd. "We are gathered

to mourn the loss of so many precious women, so many bright lights who graced our lives and our Republic with their goodness." She gestured broadly. "And each light that burns in this square, each candle flame commemorates the radiance brought into our lives by the women who pledge themselves to the Daughters, who surrender their secular lives to nurture the radiance of the angels among us."

"Amen."

This time, Delilah saw the flashing word on the vid-screen and raised her voice along with the others. Rafe stood grim and silent beside her. Watchful.

"We are gathered also to celebrate the contribution of those women to our own communal wealth. Where would we be as a society without those who stand witness to the divine? Where would we wander without a reminder that there is a greater purpose to all that happens within God's creation, without the vision to guide us forward?" Her voice rose even louder. "When there is darkness in our lives, when there is disaster, when there are events that seem meaningless, where do we find our faith to go on?"

She waited, but there was no cue on the vid-screen.

Then the reverend smiled. "You all know the answer. We find our faith in Scripture, the evidence of God's love for his creation is there on every page. For is it not writ—"

Delilah saw the words displayed on the screen and lifted her voice along with the group assembled. The volume of their collected voices send a shiver through her.

" 'The Lord is my shepherd; I shall not want. He makes me lie down in green pastures; he leads me beside still waters; he restores my soul. He leads me in right paths for his name's sake. Even though I walk through the valley in the shadow of death, I fear no evil . . .' "

The words could have been chosen specifically for Delilah and they convinced her that the reverend was speaking directly to her. Maybe the reverend had expected her to be present.

Maybe the reverend also communed with the angels.

"Amen!" cried the reverend at the end of the verse, jabbing her finger skyward. "And if we believe that there will be a light in the darkness, should we not look for the sign of God's favor among ourselves? Do we not seek the sign of his light, shining as beacon into the shadows of our lives? Do we not look for some indication of goodness, even in tragedy?" Her voice rose to a roar. "Do we not pray?"

The vid-screen displayed another psalm for the crowd to recite.

" *'To you, O Lord, I call; my rock, do not refuse to hear me, for if you are silent to me I shall be like those who go down to the Pit. Hear the voice of my supplication, as I cry to you for help, as I lift up my hands toward your most holy Oracle.'* "

"Amen!"

"The Oracle," murmured the reverend as she considered the crowd. Delilah's heart skipped with the conviction that the reverend already knew that she was present. This was her moment!

"And what should we seek to find in the ash of destruction, but the angelic light of clarity?" demanded the reverend, raising a fist. "What should we seek but the Oracle herself?"

Delilah was nudging closer to the stage, so intent on getting to its lip in time that she didn't see the spotlights spin.

"I give you the next Oracle of the Republic!" the reverend roared. "Divinely revealed, miraculously defended from harm, alive and present to serve us all."

Delilah heard Rafe cuss.

She heard the woman who had been beside her hiss in disapproval.

She felt Rafe snatch at her, but shoved closer to the stage as the crowd shouted its enthusiastic welcome.

"The revealed Oracle, Teresa!"

Delilah looked up to find the false Oracle, chosen by the Daughters, standing in the spotlight. She was dressed in white, her hands outspread, her expression as demure as she was devious.

The reverend beamed at the woman who had been a schem-

ing acolyte just days before. The crowd cheered and stomped
their feet.

"No!" Delilah shouted in outrage.

DELILAH HURLED herself onto the stage, driven to new
strength by her sense of injustice. She heard Rafe bellow and
felt him grab after her but she was livid. She would not be
cheated by the Daughters and their lies.

Once on the stage, she threw off her hat and veil and pointed
at the former acolyte.

"You!" whispered the reverend, taking a step closer.

"False Oracle!" Delilah cried, pointing toward Teresa. The
crowd stirred in surprise. "The Daughter Superior trained you
to lie and deceive the witnesses!" She pivoted to face the citizens gathered, convinced that they would believe the truth.
They would be her witnesses. "She lies to you!"

The crowd murmured in consternation. Delilah caught a
dizzying glimpse of her own face, magnified on every vid-
screen around the perimeter of the town square.

"I am the true Oracle, graced to hear the voice of the angels," Delilah insisted. "I have revealed my gift and should
have been chosen."

"Liar," hissed Teresa. "Is it not writ that *'the sixth angel
poured his bowl on the great river Euphrates'*?"

" *'And its water was dried up in order to prepare the way
for the kings from the east,'* " continued the reverend. " *'And I
saw three foul spirits like frogs coming from the mouth of the
dragon, from the mouth of the beast, and from the mouth of
the false prophet. These are demonic spirits, performing signs,
who go abroad to the kings of the whole world, to assemble
them for battle on the great day of God the Almighty.'* "

Teresa advanced upon Delilah, her hands held high. "And
the apostle Mark counsels us to *'beware of false prophets,
who come to you in sheep's clothing but inwardly are raven-
ous wolves.'* "

" *'You will know them by their fruits,'* " said the reverend,
her gaze flicking between the two younger women. " *'Are*

*grapes gathered from thorns, or figs from thistles? In the same
way, every good tree bears good fruit, but the bad tree bears
bad fruit. A good tree cannot bear bad fruit, nor can a bad tree
bear good fruit. Every tree that does not bear good fruit is cut
down and thrown into the fire.' "*

"Amen!" cried the false Oracle, pointing at Delilah. " *'Thus
you will know them by their fruits.' "*

The lights dimmed and Delilah saw herself again on the
vid-screens around the square. It was the vidcast of her original prophecy. She was on her knees in the chapel at the Citadel,
grunting out her prophecy about the president's death like an
animal. She looked pale and wild, even to her own eyes, prim-
itive and unreliable.

Her heart sank when the vidcast of the false Oracle's sweet
prophecy was shown immediately afterward. The message was
bland and palatable, not threatening or dubious of authority.
The crowd fell into an expectant hush.

She looked up to find the reverend's assessing gaze upon
her. She couldn't tell what the reverend was thinking, but the
very presence of the false Oracle on the stage spoke volumes.
Delilah's heart sank with the certainty that she had chosen the
wrong defender.

She had nothing left to lose.

The angels had defended her. They had protected her.
They spoke through her. If she had to prove herself worthy
of their esteem, she was prepared to do so.

"And so it is true," she said softly, "that the Devil himself
can quote Scripture best."

"Witch!" cried Teresa, hatred marring her fair beauty.

The crowd stirred, uncertain what to make of this.

"Prove your merit," Delilah challenged Teresa. "Spare a
prophecy for those who have gathered to see whatever light
you can cast in the darkness."

There was a hush of silence, then the false Oracle took a
step closer. She dropped her voice to a hiss, but her words
were magnified and cast throughout the square.

Throughout the Republic.

"Why should I answer a fugitive *shade?*" She pointed to

the image of Delilah captured by the reverend at the Citadel. Delilah's shaved head and her somber garb were enough to cast doubt.

The image spiraled in on Delilah's left arm. Her dark robe was askew and with the magnification of the image, her tattoo was made clear.

"Fugitive shade!" someone cried in the crowd. The cry was taken up by the others, becoming a chant filled with blood lust.

Delilah looked across the crowd with horror.

The people bellowed and began to push forward. They rushed for the stage, shouting and stamping, and there were screams as people were trampled. Police officers shouted for order. She saw one fire his laze into the crowd as the celebrants turned on him.

The reverend forgot Delilah and watched chaos erupt, her horrified expression visible on every vid-screen.

At the same time, the hunters appeared on every perimeter, some with snarling dogs on leashes. Delilah heard the dogs and her gaze fell on one man pushing his way to the forefront. Her heart stopped cold.

It was the hunter who had harvested Rachel.

Come to collect Delilah.

That shade hunter looked up, his gaze locking on Delilah. She gasped when he smiled, his cold smile all too familiar to her. She'd never forgotten it, but had hoped to never see it again.

She saw too late that her trust had been misplaced, that she had underestimated the desire of some to manipulate the choice of Oracle. Had Sonja been right that optimism had no place in the world? Delilah didn't want to believe it.

But security forces vaulted onto the stage from its perimeter, moving to confine Delilah in the middle.

But she wasn't the criminal! Delilah heard the crowd roar for blood. *"Fugitive shade! Fugitive shade! Fugitive shade!"*

They roared for *her* blood.

But she was the Oracle! She pulled back her left sleeve, revealing that there was no tattoo, but it was too late.

Was this how her quest would end? By her being harvested—or shredded by hunting dogs—on live vidcast?

Where were the angels who had defended her so far?

How could they abandon her now?

Before she could panic, Delilah saw Rafe leap onto the stage behind the security forces. He caught one man by the shoulder, spinning him around and punching him in the gut.

Rafe winced at the pain and Delilah knew he'd hit reevlar. The guard buckled over all the same. Rafe tripped him then flung him over the lip of the stage and into the crowd. The others turned in surprise, but Rafe lunged between them.

He snatched Delilah's hand and ran for the town hall, practically dragging her to the back of the stage.

"Stop!" cried the reverend.

"*Fugitive shade*," chanted the crowd.

"Don't go," the reverend said, but Delilah wasn't going to be harvested if she had anything to say about it. Rafe didn't even slow down, cutting a path directly to the back of the stage.

"That's the wrong way!" Delilah shouted.

"It's the only way," he retorted.

Then she saw that he was right. No one had expected them to go that direction and there were few guards at the back of the stage.

One of the security guards fired a laze shot. It grazed Rafe's shoulder, only missing because he ducked in the last minute.

Delilah was sure they were trapped, between the firing guards and the solid brick of the town hall. But Rafe shoved Delilah onto a square marked on the stage. He stamped his feet in demand and the square began to slowly slip lower, dropping below the level of the stage.

A trapdoor! Delilah realized belatedly that this was how the reverend had appeared so dramatically.

To her astonishment, the reverend stepped between them and the security guards. She held up her hands, giving Rafe a chance to flee.

"No bloodshed on my vidcast," the reverend said, her

voice low but authoritative. Her words didn't carry to the audio system, but they left Delilah wondering.

Was the reverend protecting her for the sake of appearances? Or did the reverend believe in her abilities?

There was no time to consider it.

The guards fired again, and the reverend shouted in protest. Rafe shielded Delilah with his body, bending over her as the trapdoor descended.

She was pretty sure he missed having his own laze.

"They ought to feed their shades," he muttered, obviously impatient with the door's speed.

They were barely three feet below the stage when Rafe jumped into the darkness below. Again, he pulled Delilah behind him and she stumbled to get her balance on the cobblestones below.

An astonished worker stepped backward, raising his hands as if he feared what they would do.

Rafe didn't linger. He pivoted, then sprinted for the only visible light. Delilah was right behind him, her heart pounding. She could hear the security men leaping into the space under the stage, heard their shouted questions and the murmur of the reverend on the stage behind them. The security guards fired from behind them, and Rafe hugged the shadows along the wall.

They emerged behind the city hall, in too much darkness to get their bearings. The helicopter's rotors were audible and Delilah raised a hand against the wind that buffeted them. Rafe ran directly into it. A pair of spotlights illuminated a landing pad behind the town hall, and gleamed off the helicopter that had brought the reverend.

Its rotors were turning, and all of the guards in the vicinity were looking toward it. Rafe led Delilah into the darkness ringing the area and moved quickly around the perimeter. The guards that had pursued them emerged noisily into the area, but whatever they called to their fellows was lost in the din of the rotors.

Three figures ran to the helicopter, one of them large enough to be the reverend. No sooner were they inside than the dark silhouette of the helicopter lifted from the landing pad, awing Delilah that anything that big could fly. She stared for a precious moment.

"Perfect," Rafe muttered.

Before she could ask what he meant, he jumped a guard and dragged him into the shadows. The man's cry was lost in the noise. Rafe slammed him into the wall and decked him. The man fought back but Rafe had surprise on his side.

And in a heartbeat, he had the guard's laze.

"Surprise," Rafe said to the astonished guard, his irreverent smile flashing in the darkness.

The guard opened his mouth to shout, but he never made a sound.

Delilah winced as the laze fired red in the shadows. The man fell silently and didn't move again.

"You killed him!" Delilah accused.

"You don't think he would have killed us?"

"It doesn't make anything better."

"We're already fugitives. We officially have nothing to lose."

"I think the reverend believed me."

He gave her a look. "Let's survive this first, then talk about the reverend."

The other guard saw the light from the weapon. A cry rose from the far side of the landing pad as the helicopter whipped up a whirlwind. Rafe bolted to the far side, taking advantage of the distraction offered by the craft.

"Where are we going?" Delilah demanded as he led her down a dark and empty street.

"Into the netherzones. It's our only chance."

He was right. Delilah put her hand in his and they ran. He turned down a side street, then took another.

Even though the choice was a sensible one, Delilah dreaded returning to that hidden space. She felt as if she had had an opportunity to be visible, to follow her dream and become Oracle. Returning to the netherzones and hiding felt like sacrificing her only chance.

She feared that she'd never emerge from that darkness again.

"And then where? The netherzones don't go all the way to New D.C."

"I'll figure it out once we're safe," Rafe said through gritted teeth. They rounded a corner, and Rafe slammed their backs into the wall. They stood for a moment, each holding their breath, until a pair of guards ran past.

"That's not much of a plan," Delilah whispered.

He gave her a look. "It's looking better for our health than yours was." His eyes were sparkling despite his supposed resentment, and Delilah suspected that fleeing authority was what Rafe did best. He peeked around the corner, then led her back in the direction they had come.

"All we need is an access," he murmured.

"You can't get anywhere from the netherzones," she said, not hiding her bitterness. "It's a trap with no escape."

"Don't be ridiculous," Rafe said, flashing that grin that made her heart skip. "You can always get to the pleasure fringe from the netherzones."

Delilah smiled despite herself. "Why am I not surprised that you know that?"

"Because you're an astute judge of character," he mused, glancing down yet another side street. He frowned. "What is it with these people? Where do they get into the netherzones? The accesses can't all be locked up at night."

There was a hiss, like that of an irritated cat. Both Rafe and Delilah looked.

Delilah started at the sight of a woman looking back at them from the next alley. She must have been dressed in black, because only the pale oval of her face was visible. They inhaled as one and then she was gone.

"Did you see her?" Delilah whispered.

Rafe took the safety off the laze. He moved ahead of Delilah, cautiously approaching the corner where the woman had been. Delilah watched behind them, but there was no sign of pursuit.

Rafe sprang around the corner, leading with his laze.

There was no one there.

Rafe and Delilah waited, each wary of a trap about to be sprung. It was quiet in this area, although Delilah could hear the distant roar of the riot in the town square. She winced with every laze shot she heard.

The hiss came again.

Delilah pointed when she saw the pale oval of the woman's face. It was there for only a heartbeat, then she disappeared again. Rafe led the way again, and again, she wasn't there by the time they rounded the corner.

Delilah looked back at the main street, feeling trepidation. They could easily get lost in a network of alleys in the night. "Where's she leading us?"

Rafe chuckled.

Delilah turned in surprise, and found him bending to pick something off the pavement. It glittered in his hand like a patch of moonlight. He handed it to her, his satisfaction clear, then scanned the shadows ahead.

It was one of the earrings he had left in the cabin.

"I'm guessing," he murmured, "that she's leading us exactly where we need to go."

"Honor among thieves?"

"Something like that," Rafe agreed easily and pointed. "There she is."

THE WOMAN met them at a gated entrance to the netherzones, her pseudoskin patched but dark as midnight. She had a dark hood, one that disguised her hair and covered her ears in sleek black. She was gloved and booted, sheathed in black polymer.

Her eyes were a vivid orange, their pupils vertical slits like those of a cat. Rafe knew she was wearing filters on her eyes, and was impressed by how little of her physical characteristics he would have been able to identify with any certainty.

She was short and slight, and those eyes, even with their

disguising filters, were clearly filled with suspicion. There was a telling bulge beneath the neck of her pseudoskin.

She was wearing the aquamarine necklace he had left in the cabin. Rafe knew its shape well. He had a sudden understanding of why he had felt as if they were being observed there.

The grate behind her couldn't have covered anything but an entrance to the netherzones. Beyond the grill, Rafe could see stairs descending into darkness. He smelled dampness and sewage.

The girl pulled a laze and trained it on them—it was mucky and had a new dent on one side, but Rafe recognized it all the same.

"That's mine!"

"Afraid not," she said. Her voice had the strange resonance of automated speech. There was a bulge on the side of her neck, some device hidden beneath her pseudoskin.

"Nice voice-box modifier," Rafe muttered.

The girl smiled and gestured them toward the gate to the netherzones. She pulled a key from the pouch on her belt, and unlocked the access silently. The grate slid open, revealing a set of stairs that wound down into the shadows.

Then she put out her hand in silent demand, holding it between Rafe and the netherzones. Rafe knew what she wanted, but wasn't that ready to surrender his only advantage.

"It's a nice set," he admitted.

"And it's mine."

Rafe tried to negotiate. "Give me back my laze."

"Finders keepers."

There was a sound of sirens coming closer. The hunt was expanding and Rafe knew it was only a matter of time until the police reached this corner of the town.

"You don't have a lot of time," she noted. Those orange eyes were unsettling, making her look alien and unfriendly.

"Who are you?" Rafe asked, thinking about that cabin and its secrets once again.

She smiled.

"What's the crop growing there?"

She took the safety off the laze. Rafe understood she wouldn't tell them.

"Contraband," Delilah guessed.

"Revenue," the woman corrected.

Rafe pulled the earring from his pocket and displayed it on his palm. It sparkled ever so slightly in his hand, and he was struck again by its beauty. "Anything for a price?"

"Everything has a price," she corrected, then scooped the earring from his hand. "You've paid for what you've had."

She lifted her head, glancing over Rafe's shoulder. He saw her nostrils flare, though whether it was because she sensed something or because she was afraid, he couldn't have said.

He doubted that this cold-eyed woman was afraid of much.

"Move now, Raphael, or you never will," she whispered.

Rafe stared at her in shock. "How do you know my name?"

Her smile was broad and fleeting. "We wraiths know everybody's name."

Running footsteps echoed in the streets and a man shouted.

"Hurry!" Delilah said, and Rafe knew good sense when he heard it.

Rafe and Delilah held hands tightly, feeling their way down the dark stairs as quickly as they could. There was no light in these netherzones and Rafe missed the ambient light of the city above. His other senses seemed sharper in the absence of sight, but he feared they weren't sharp enough.

The darkness in the netherzones was silky against his skin, damp and chilly. He shivered, felt Delilah shiver beside him, and he had a moment's fear that the wraith had led them into more danger.

Then to Rafe's relief, he smelled the sweet scent of perfume coming from the right.

The pleasure fringe.

He pivoted, smiling. "Thank you," he whispered, but there was no one at the top of the stairs anymore.

The grate was closed.

Rafe leapt up the steps and rattled it, not really surprised that it was locked against them. He heard the sirens, saw flashing lights as the pursuers ran across the end of the alley, and hunkered lower into the protective shadows.

"She's gone as surely as if she was never here," Delilah murmured beside him.

Rafe nodded and turned back to the blackness that yawned below them. "We'd better move while we can."

Delilah nodded and they descended the stairs together once again. Rafe turned to the right, toward the pleasure fringe and the opportunity it offered to disappear.

Wraiths.

What were wraiths?

Who were wraiths?

Did they know who had given him his mission, or who controlled his palm?

How would he find them again, to have his questions answered?

Or would they find him?

Rafe wasn't sure he liked the sound of that.

XV

RAFE WAS as surefooted as a cat. He could have been a resident in Hood River for years. He navigated the labyrinthine netherzones quickly and silently, pausing every few moments to decide his course, but never taking long.

The darkness closed in on Delilah, reminding her of the years she had spent in the netherzones at the Citadel, crippling her with a sense of failure. The shadows and the smell suffocated her, made her desperate to escape. It sapped her strength and left her feeling helpless and captive.

The netherzones of Hood River weren't as vacant as they had initially appeared, nor were they as dark. They passed chambers of shades who were undoubtedly sedated, working in darkness and probably shackled to the equipment. Delilah saw many with eyes so glazed that they weren't even aware of her and Rafe. They were naked in the dampness, their pale bodies gleaming against the shadows.

They finally reached the perimeter of the pleasure fringe and she knew it offered no pleasure to many. The shades in the netherzones here were more dramatically mutated and damaged by radiation poisoning. The victims of botched back-alley surgeries were here as well, consigned to the darkness by failed attempts to make them look normal.

She saw shades with extra fingers and toes, shades with the distinctive bump of the third eye on their forehead, shades with lesions and humps and those red scars of keloids that always made her squirm. They looked raw to her, and painful.

These shades regarded her and Rafe with indifference or cynicism. She found herself resenting the cool gazes of the shades they passed, feeling accused of not doing more, feeling guilty for appearing to be a norm. She couldn't explain to them that she was one of them, that she had lived something like their lives, not without taking too much time when Rafe sought haste.

The shades of the pleasure fringe were less likely to be sedated, more likely to be consigned to these shadows as much by their own will as by their damaged bodies.

They knew there were worse places.

So did Delilah. She felt a commonality with them, a similar dread of the world of norms and the power of norms over shades. That sense of common ground was all the more bitter because they regarded her as alien.

Their situation was horrific and it was wrong. Delilah pulled her veil down over her face to hide her tears of compassion. And she kept her hand in Rafe's, trusting him to guide her to safety.

Even if he didn't guide her to safety, she was past caring. She only wanted to get out of the stinking shadows of the netherzones.

Angelfire never reached into this darkness.

She wondered whether it could.

And with that idea, a spark of hope lit within Delilah. Maybe she could make a difference. Maybe she had been chosen to become Oracle because she understood the plight of the shades enough to eliminate it. Maybe there was a divine plan to all she had endured.

Maybe believing it was possible was enough.

RAFE TOOK a number of rapid turns, then chose a staircase. Music floated down from the street level above, but he kept close to the wall as he led Delilah up the stairs. This entrance had a grate, just like the one the wraith had unlocked for them, but it was standing open.

It had started to rain again, a gentle patter that made the pavement gleam. The rain splashed on the umbrellas over the empty patio of the bar on the opposite side of the street.

It had also driven most people in the streets of the pleasure fringe to enter the establishments. Two or three men hastened down the street, their collars turned up against the rain and their hat brims pulled low.

Rafe stood completely still for long moments, only his eyes flicking as he surveyed the scene. Then he unfurled his cloak and cast it over Delilah's shoulders again.

"Pull up the hood," he advised and she heard anger in his tone. "You could be recognized anywhere now."

"I had to go to the reverend," she protested.

Rafe flicked her a potent look, locked his hand over hers, and strode into the rain. His mood was grim, but he was both purposeful and vigilant. She felt him scanning the street and the windows that overlooked it. She sensed that he was taut, ready to shoot first and ask questions later.

She decided it was a bad moment to argue with him.

He chose a woebegone inn on a side alley, one that had seen better days and was clearly desperate for business. Rafe asked after the rate and the man on the desk didn't even glance at Delilah. He named a price and Rafe paid it in tokens immediately. Delilah watched the man's eyes light at the sight of the tokens.

He could be bought.

Rafe took the key and headed for the stairs, ushering Delilah to the room on the third floor at the back. She felt the gaze of the man on the desk follow them and dreaded what he would do.

"I don't trust him," she whispered to Rafe.

"Neither do I," he said flatly.

On the threshold of the room, he pulled his laze, and made Delilah stand to one side of the door. He unlocked the door and kicked it open, then moved into the space. She watched him go through the cupboard and closet, look behind the drapes, under the bed and in the bathroom, all without turning on the light. He checked the locks on the windows, pulled the drapes shut, and then turned on one lamp.

He beckoned to her, his expression solemn. Delilah hurried into the room and locked the door behind herself. At his gesture, they worked together to move a small bureau to block the door.

"That won't stop anyone," she whispered.

"It'll make noise, though, maybe enough noise to give me time to respond."

"But nobody knows we're here."

Rafe looked unpersuaded. "That situation might not last." He surveyed the room with dissatisfaction, shaking out the covers on the bed in poor temper. He muttered to himself about the obscenity of the price he'd paid, then marched into the bathroom. Delilah heard the tap running, then Rafe swear.

"Cold," he said and the water stopped. "I should have guessed."

Delilah followed him, pausing in the doorway to watch him. He looked larger and more unpredictable than he had thus far. He looked strained and irritated.

Delilah kept her voice low, knowing that they might be overheard. "If you think he'll call someone, we should go somewhere else . . ."

Rafe spun to face her, his eyes flashing. "And where would we go?" he demanded. He flung out one hand, nearly hitting his knuckles on the far wall of the small tiled room. He kept his voice low as well, but she could see the effort it took to keep his temper in check. "This town is crawling with hunters and police, all of whom are looking for you. Your face has been on every twenty-foot-wide vid-screen in the Republic, and seen in glorious detail by every single citizen. It'll be a miracle if we get out of here alive."

Delilah refused to respond in kind. "We could go to the reverend—"

Rafe interrupted her with impatience. "Since that plan worked so well earlier." He leaned against the wall to regard her. "Going right into the heart of trouble is never a good plan."

"While walking to New D.C. was a stroke of brilliance."

He pointed a finger at her. "It would have been safer—"

"It's no better to starve to death in the forest than to be

surrounded by enemies," Delilah said, interrupting him for a change. "I need a sponsor and the reverend is the best candidate."

"Even if her minions want to harvest you." Rafe shoved a hand through his hair and lowered his voice as he stepped closer. "Delilah, don't you see? A lot of people want you dead. You could have been harvested right on live vidcast and no one would have intervened to save you. No one would have helped you! You could have been killed, or worse, sent to the Society's labs, and no one, not even the reverend, could have or would have done anything to change your fate."

Delilah's annoyance with him melted. He was angry because she had put herself at risk. She didn't think it was just because his mission's success was in peril.

Then she realized that it was very likely that her plan had gone badly awry because of Rafe. He didn't know who had programmed his palm or wiped his memory—but they knew whatever he did.

Delilah was beginning to fear that they were the ones who wanted her dead.

Rafe continued to defend her, to save her and protect her, regardless of the cost to himself. Was that what they intended? That he would be collateral damage when they captured or killed her?

The prospect sent a chill through Delilah.

She saw his anguish and knew that if he ever realized that he had led danger to her, it would destroy him. His own nature was honorable. He wanted to defend her. He wanted to ensure her safety. But he might unwittingly betray her.

She had to leave him, because she didn't want to see him realize that he had been the agent of her destruction.

That brought her back again to Rachel's scheme.

And the knowledge that she had to risk her gift to survive.

She had to seduce Rafe, escape him, and live with the consequences, whatever they might be. She chose to believe that the angels wouldn't abandon her.

"Your shoulder was hit," she said softly and reached for him.

Rafe pushed her hand away. "Don't touch me. Not now. Not here."

"Why not?"

"Because I don't know what I'll do." He fixed her with a hot look, and Delilah, in contrast, knew exactly what he'd do.

She chose another tactic. She was in the doorway, blocking his departure, and the room was small. She lifted his cloak from her shoulders and folded it, to put it aside. Then she unfastened her jacket and added it to the pile. She saw Rafe swallow.

"What are you doing?"

"Well, at least we can get clean and have some sleep."

He looked from her to the tub, then he licked his lips.

Delilah pretended not to notice his agitation. "That my plan didn't work is no reason to be angry. Any risk was mine . . ."

"That's every reason to be angry," Rafe said, his voice rising. "I listened to you and I shouldn't have."

"I wasn't going to walk to New D.C.," Delilah said calmly and smiled at him. She turned her back on him and braced her hands on the door frame, casting a glance over her shoulder. "Unlace me, please?"

He glared at her, his fists clenching. "I should leave."

"Maybe I won't let you until you help me with the laces."

"This is no time for games."

She smiled.

Rafe spoke with heat. "I should have tossed you over my shoulder and forced you to go east, instead of coming here."

"Laces," she reminded him lightly, bending her neck.

There was silence in the bathroom, but a silence charged with electricity. She was keenly aware of Rafe's gaze upon her, knew he looked at her neck, the curve of her waist, and her hands on the door frame. She thought for a moment that he would push her aside and leave the room, thought he might decline what she offered.

She was sure she didn't imagine his growl of assent. She smiled to herself, knowing he was attracted to her. She didn't understand why or how, but she recognized her own power in this transaction. Plus Rafe's admiration made her feel attractive as she never had before. She tingled in anticipation of what they would do, of feeling his sure touch upon her once again, and had a hard time waiting for him to make the next move.

She felt the heat of his presence immediately behind her and felt his breath on the back of her neck. He took a moment to steady himself then bent and touched his lips to the back of her shoulder. He whispered her name and the low word sent shivers through her.

He'd given her a name.

He'd given her a chance.

He'd given her hope.

She would give him the pleasure he obviously desired, then she would leave him before he could unwittingly betray her, before the knowledge of what he had been compelled to do broke his heart. She felt a tear slide down her cheek, her chest tightening with her admiration of the kind of man he was.

In another time and another place, she could have loved him.

In another time and another place, they could have loved each other, maybe.

But in this time and this place, they were doomed to either part or destroy each other.

Delilah swallowed, hating that the choice was no choice at all.

That was when she knew that she loved Rafe already, regardless of the time and place. He had captured her heart in a matter of days, but it would only be bitter to tell him that truth.

"Are you sure?" he murmured, only his lips touching her skin.

She nodded, glad that there was no pretense between them. The honesty they could share only made the control of his palm even more cruel, pushing him as it did to betray his own intent.

To betray her.

She turned her head slightly, found that intense blue gaze

close to her own. The question in his eyes was clear, as was his desire. He was tired and disheveled, at far less than his best, but his sincerity tore at her.

She would never forget this night, as long as she lived.

She wanted just one memory of Rafe to take with her.

Delilah smiled and lifted one hand to touch his jaw. He had a day's growth of stubble, the dark whiskers making him look even more rakish.

"Absolutely," she whispered, letting him hear her conviction.

Rafe didn't give her a chance to reconsider. His hands locked around her waist and he bent his head with purpose, kissing her with a desire that echoed her own.

THE WOMAN was intoxicating.

Delilah kissed Rafe with a hunger that surprised him. There was a sincerity in her passion that he'd seldom tasted before, a joy in the union that couldn't be bought or bartered. She pressed against him, her fingers in his hair and her breasts against his chest, and kissed him as if she'd devour him whole. She dissipated his anger and made him forget practicalities. In a heartbeat, in one kiss, there was only Delilah and Rafe's desire for her.

He broke their kiss with an effort, knowing that he had to take things more slowly. She was an innocent and he was responsible for introducing her to the pleasure they could share. She pouted, her eyes twinkling in a mischievous expression that would have been out of the question for her just days before.

Rafe found himself smiling. Her skin was still too pale and she was still too thin, but he found grace in her supple strength. She kicked off her skirts and turned to face him again, her sheer shift doing little to hide her charms. He could see the dark peaks of her nipples above her corset and fitted his hands to the neat indent of her waist again. He would have unlaced the corset, but Delilah was too impatient for that.

"Come here and kiss me," she whispered, her eyes filled with an irresistible devilry. When he didn't comply quickly enough, she locked one hand around the back of his neck and pulled his mouth down to hers.

This time, she kissed him, nudging his mouth open with her tongue, stretching to her toes to taste him more deeply. She ground her hips against his codpiece in silent demand, and Rafe cupped his hands beneath her buttocks, lifting her higher. Her cheeks filled his hands and he squeezed their fullness, gasping when she wrapped her legs around his waist.

His heart was already pounding, his senses flooded with Delilah.

Rafe was shocked that she was already so demanding in her passion, but it was a shock he could live with.

He could even get used to it.

Maybe he was teaching her well. Maybe she was a quick study. Maybe they made a good team.

Maybe he'd just enjoy the moment and worry about details later.

Delilah slipped her hand around his neck to pull him closer and locked her mouth on his, teasing and tempting him to distraction. He could feel the erratic pace of her heart and the sweet curve of her breast. Rafe closed his eyes and kissed her back, wanting this woman with an intensity that should have frightened him. He forced himself to remember that she was an innocent, but her kiss wasn't that innocent.

He leaned back against the door, content to let her have her way with him. She kissed his ear, his jaw, his throat, her fingers running through his hair and down his neck. She unfastened his jerkin, and slid her palms across his chest. She nudged open the collar of his shirt and slipped a hand inside, bending to touch the sweet of her lips against his skin.

Rafe groaned. Her busy hands found the fastening of his trousers and he felt her fingers slide beneath the lip of his damaged codpiece. She wasn't wasting any time in her exploration of him and of pleasure, and Rafe appreciated that he wouldn't have to hold out for long.

He didn't think he could have done it anyway. Being in

Delilah's presence had stoked his desire to a fever pitch and he was too hot to take it slow.

The second time would be different.

Admiration surged through Rafe that Delilah wasn't shy or uncertain. She had grasped her opportunity to live fully with both hands. She was learning and adapting, making choices and embracing life. She was pursuing her ambition with the forthright determination of one who has learned that opportunity can't be taken for granted. He respected that and wanted to ensure that she achieved her goal.

But first, there was pleasure to be shared.

He lifted his lips from hers and carried her to the bedroom, casting her playfully across the bed. She bounced once and laughed, the sweetest sound that Rafe could have imagined. He shed his jerkin and his codpiece, perching on the edge of the bed to pull off his boots.

The pouch on his belt hit the floor with a solid thud, followed by Delilah's laced boots. He grinned when he saw her stockings flutter over his shoulders to land on the floor. He shed his trousers by the time Delilah jumped him from behind, pulling him back in only his shirt. They rolled together across the bed, kissing and touching until they came to a halt with Rafe on top.

"You still haven't untied my corset," she complained, her eyes filled with stars.

"You haven't given me a chance."

"All I do is give you chances you don't take," she teased.

Rafe smiled slowly, letting his hand cup her breast. He slid his thumb across her nipple and watched her catch her breath. "That's about to change," he murmured.

"Promises, promises," Delilah whispered.

Rafe rolled her over abruptly, then unknotted the laces quickly. He pulled the lace out of the corset and freed her from the garment, casting it to the floor with everything else. She rolled to one hip, regarding him over one shoulder, her lashes long and dark. She couldn't have looked more seductive, to Rafe's thinking, her expression mingling curiosity and desire.

She gazed downward and he smiled at what she was curious about. He rolled onto his back, as if surrendering, and let her look. "Go ahead," he invited. "Have your way with me."

Delilah's eyes flashed and then she sat up beside him. She flattened her hands on his stomach, then slid them down, her palms smooth against his skin. Her fingers closed around him, tentatively at first, then with more purpose, and Rafe closed his eyes in pleasure.

The woman was adept at making the most of opportunity.

And he was only too willing to be the object of her desire.

RAFE WAS magnificent.

Delilah had seen boys nude, but they had been other shades. Although she understood the basics of anatomy, she had never seen such a splendid specimen of masculinity as Rafe. He was muscled and lean, so strong and healthy that she doubted anyone could find his equal in all the Republic. His skin was tanned to a warm golden hue, and the hair on his body was a medium brown. There wasn't a single defect in his shape and she marveled at the perfection of his body.

His erection was large, and just the sight of it fed her own desire. She knew how norms mated, knew that Rafe's sure touch had been only part of that biological ritual. She had a feeling that she wouldn't need that much stimulation to be ready for him on this day.

She welcomed the chance to examine his body, anticipating that this might be her only chance to do so. She would be leaving Rafe when he slept afterward and she doubted that any other man would be able to compete for the place Rafe already held in her heart.

The Oracle, after all, was supposed to be chaste.

Delilah would have only this one taste of pleasure.

And of Rafe.

She was going to make it count.

He watched her, his eyes shining, intent and observant. His was a stillness that she would always remember, and one that could still make her blush. She pushed his shirt open and slid her hands across the breadth of his chest, feeling his breath beneath her hands. His nipples were flatter than hers but just as sensitive to touch. She slid her hands down the length of him, liking the feel of his body hair against her hands, then ran her hands over his pubic hair.

She touched his erection, first with caution then with greater boldness. She let his reactions guide her choices, a quick intake of breath telling her that she went too far, and low growl of approval indicating that she had it right.

When she caressed him and he practically purred, she knew she had it exactly right. He grew beneath her hands, becoming impossibly larger, then whispered her name with such taut urgency that she looked up.

"Come here," he murmured, his eyes as dark as midnight.

She straddled him, then leaned down to kiss him. He caught her face in his hands, pulling her closer with gentle power. His kiss reassured her, encouraged her, and fed her confidence. He slid his hands under her shift, his fingers dancing over her flesh like feathers, then he lifted the garment over her head. He threw it aside, smiling with a satisfaction that warmed her heart.

She bent to kiss him, and her nipples tightened when her breasts collided with his chest. He placed one hand on the back of her waist, his other hand slipping between them to touch her again. Delilah gasped when his fingertip found the sensitive spot, her pulse jumping at his caress. She was wet already, anticipating the pleasure he could give her.

He moved his fingers against her, coaxing her reaction with a confidence that Delilah found so attractive. Her hips rolled of their own accord and he chuckled into their kiss.

Then he caught her waist in his hands and lifted her over him. Delilah braced her hands on his shoulders, uncertain what to expect. But Rafe smiled at her and she trusted him completely. She smiled back.

He lowered her on top of him. Delilah gasped as his strength eased inside her, filling her in a way that was more satisfying than she could have imagined. Rafe seemed to holding his breath as he eased deeper inside her. She felt her fingers flex against his shoulders, thought she couldn't accommodate any more of him, and learned that she was wrong.

In moments, she was sitting atop him, his heat buried inside her. She moved and he gritted his teeth, closing his eyes in rapture.

"Slowly," he said, his voice filled with strain. He lifted her so slowly that Delilah gasped, then lowered her again. Delilah smiled at the tingle that danced through her veins. She moved, watching Rafe catch his breath in pleasure.

She wanted him to find the same pleasure she'd felt the other day. She wanted to reciprocate in kind. She stretched her length over his, caught his face in her hands, and kissed him.

Rafe groaned and caught her close, one arm locking around her waist as his other hand slid between them again.

His fingers moved and Delilah jolted at the pleasure that shot through her body. She caught Rafe's wicked grin and knew that she wasn't the only one determined to ensure her partner's pleasure.

They moved together, intent on each other's reactions, staring into each other's eyes. They moved faster and slower, coaxing the heat between them to burn higher, urging desire to greater heights. Delilah felt herself flush, felt the demand increase to a fever pitch, watched the glitter of Rafe's eyes in the darkness.

This sparkle in her veins was like an earthly variant of angelfire. It was just as potent. Just as addictive. And she suspected, it was just as critical to her own happiness and survival. She refused to think about leaving him, refused to shed a tear, refused to admit that this time, this only time, would also be the last time.

She simply moved with him, feeling desire build, hearing her pulse race, feeling her blood rush, and watching Rafe's own reaction. He became harder and thicker, moving more and more quickly. Their breath came faster, mingling between them. Their hearts beat against each other, and the pleasure became more than Delilah could bear.

Then the heat of release rolled through her, searing her old wounds and illuminating the darkness. Delilah fell against Rafe's chest as his arms locked around her, her mind filled with a single thought.

Rafe's touch was like angelfire.

Maybe that was why she had been destined to love him.

RAFE WAS exhausted.

He stayed in bed, content to remain entangled with Delilah for the moment. He wanted more, another encounter with her, but knew that she'd be sore for a day or two. He contented himself with the fan of her breath against his skin, the sweet curl of her fingers within his. She slept, as trusting as a child, sated and savored.

And their journey together had only just begun.

Her lashes were dark crescents against her skin, which made her look both fragile and feminine. Rafe knew better than to underestimate her, though. Delilah was a formidable force, one that grew stronger every day.

He couldn't wait to see her with the Oracle's star on her brow.

He'd figure out how to solve that later, after he'd slept a bit.

He eased her to the mattress beside him and gazed down at her, letting his admiration blossom. She had been an innocent, but one determined to learn, and learn quickly. She was showing him new facets of the deed he thought he had fully explored, and he knew they'd discover even more together.

Unlike his other encounters, one interval with Delilah hadn't been nearly enough. He doubted he would ever have enough of her. He wanted to hear her laugh again.

He realized that this was the pleasure he had been so restlessly seeking.

She was who he had been seeking. An expected wave of tenderness rolled through him, making him feel protective.

Blessed, even. Rafe bent and pressed his lips to her forehead.

And, against all expectation, he remembered.

RAFE *REMEMBERED*.

A door opened in his mind, letting memories that had been locked away tumble into his thoughts. He blinked, astonished by the barrage of recollections.

His memories.

They crowded each other, jostling for space in his mind. His name wasn't just Raphael. He was the Archangel Raphael. He had lived for eons, but in an angelic state. He had walked the earth once before, accompanying the son of Tobias, and still could taste the dust of that pilgrimage. That had been an austere journey, one filled with hardship and duty, one devoid of the pleasure he so actively sought this time.

His own objective suddenly made so much sense. He was driven to experience what he had missed on that previous mission upon earth, to learn what he had missed.

Because few angels made the sacrifice and no angel made the sacrifice twice.

Except Raphael.

And there was more, so much more. Rafe was dizzy with the sudden torrent of memories—of his angelic state, of his decision to make the sacrifice again, of all he had experienced and all he had lost. He was dazed by the detail and number of his memories, as astonished by their reappearance as the fact that Delilah had conjured them.

He knew that he was not supposed to remember.

He remembered now that he had asked to have his memory left intact and that his request had been declined. He knew too much, as angel of knowledge, and it had been feared that the volume of information would distract him from the simplicity of his task.

He had argued and lost.

But Delilah had given him his heartfelt desire, without

even knowing what it was. He had kissed her brow and she had fulfilled his yearning, perhaps in exchange for her own.

That redoubled Rafe's determination to succeed.

It was potent to have his mind filled with the past, but distracting as well. His thoughts were a jumble of past and present, a joyous chorus of all he had endured and experienced. As much as he wanted to savor the details, to review their rich complexity, he didn't have the luxury of time to do so.

The press of time was new to him, a facet of earthly life that he didn't entirely welcome. Once time had had no meaning for him. Immortality destroyed urgency. Days and years had stretched to eternity in every direction.

Now Rafe had a deadline and he didn't like it. But the only way to return to the luxury of timelessness was to complete his mission successfully and regain his wings. The completion of his mission was key, yet it seemed that the path to success was strewn with obstacles.

His traditional task was to heal the world, to help humanity find its spiritual path. Installing Delilah as Oracle was the key ingredient to that healing. He understood why he had volunteered for this labor of labors.

And the memory meant that he was newly determined to fulfil his quest. He wanted to ensure that Delilah gained her rightful place.

Even if success meant that he would be condemned to leave the earth, and leave Delilah. Fulfilling his mission had a price.

He would regain what he had lost but lose what he had found.

But he had to do it, for Delilah.

She dozed against him, her features relaxed in sleep. It was probably the only time she let down her guard, and he didn't blame her for that.

He admired her for her ability to survive.

Rafe could have watched her sleep all day and night. He felt an affection swell within him, a warmth toward this particular human that was only an echo of the angelic love that had once filled him. He felt protective of her, but it was more than that.

He would forgive her anything in exchange for this gift.

Even her attempts to lie to him and to trick him. They were learned responses to all that she had endured and he knew that she trusted him more than might have been expected. He understood that she could learn and change.

That was only one of the qualities that made her so remarkable.

He eased away from her side and left her sleeping.

He was going to take advantage of this room's lack of prying eyes and wash. It would give him a chance to plan their next step, to plan clearly away from the temptation she offered.

He might have been an angel once and, if all worked well, he would become an angel again. But for the moment Rafe was a man, and a man susceptible to earthly temptation.

Especially one temptation named Delilah.

He kissed her again and left her sleeping.

XVI

ONE THING Rafe could not become accustomed to was the overwhelming scent of being human. He loved the visual feast of being mortal, and his keen awareness of sensation was a constant delight. He enjoyed the sounds of earthly life, and the tastes of the world were a constant voyage of discovery. He liked the feel of his body flexing—even though it was far less powerful than it had been previously, he was more aware of it.

But Rafe found scent distracting and disturbing. He particularly disliked when he himself emanated scent.

And now, now that he had remembered his previous existence, its purity and cleanliness, he felt filthy. His scent was a pungent reminder of what he had sacrificed—and of the price of failure. He smelled mortality in his own perspiration—mortality and finality and death. He saw Rachel's violated body in his memory and shuddered.

He had to wash, immediately and thoroughly. He had to shave. He had to make his body most resemble the form he had sacrificed in order to best concentrate on what had to be done.

He didn't think that either the bedroom or the bathroom had any peepholes or cameras. There were advantages to the deep pleasure fringe, in that the Republic's gaze didn't always penetrate this far. Rafe wasn't positive that he was safe—no one could ever be truly certain of that—but he would be quick.

The water was cold and the soap was floral in scent, but Rafe didn't care. He pushed the door so that he could just see Delilah through the slit, then peeled down.

He filled the basin as he shaved, delighting in the smoothness of his skin after each stroke of the blade. The water eventually got hotter, a sign perhaps that his luck was changing, and the mirror fogged with steam.

Rafe scrubbed himself down, enjoying how the water turned darker. He felt clean for the first time in days and he reveled in it. Being clean clarified his thoughts and honed his sense of purpose.

There had to be a solution.

He just had to find it.

DELILAH ONLY pretended to be asleep.

She listened to Rafe washing and knew the time had come. Her reluctance to leave Rafe was irrelevant. The reverend would probably leave Hood River soon. Delilah intended to go with her.

She was tempted to punch a query into her palm, the way she had seen Sonja do, but didn't want to reveal her conscious state to Rafe. Besides, her palm was a substandard version, old and with limited abilities.

On the upside, without a palm to rely upon, she'd learned to think for herself and to remember details herself.

She thought of the hunters and the pursuit of her from the town hall. They would come this far eventually, and maybe they would find Rafe.

But Rafe was adept at fending for himself. He'd be fine. He'd talk his way out of whatever trouble he found—or shoot his way out of it.

Rafe was a survivor.

For all she knew—for all Rafe knew—he was working for the hunters, for the Republic, or for the Society. They might welcome him as an old comrade, maybe give him his memory back.

That would be the good ending to his story.

He'd left the bathroom door open slightly and she could see him checking it at intervals. It was annoying that he

didn't trust her, but she had to wait. She kept her eyes closed
and breathed slowly, feigning sleep.

How was she going to move the bureau without Rafe hearing it? The window had been sealed so long that it had probably rusted in place, and again, it would make a revealing noise.
There were only the two ways out, as far as she could see.

She was just about ready to risk the window when the paneling opened to one side of the bed. Ferris crept into the
room. He eased toward the bathroom, crouching low.

Delilah kept silent, still pretending to sleep.

She almost gave herself away when Rafe erupted from the
bathroom in a furious flash of strength.

RAFE WAS bent, drying his feet, when he heard a noise. He
pivoted to find a face pressed to the crack of the door, dark
eyes wide with astonishment.

Ferris!

And he was staring at Rafe's bare back.

Rafe lunged for the boy, kicking the door open. Ferris ran
for an open panel on the far wall, but never made it. Rafe
caught Ferris by the shirt collar and lifted the boy to his toes,
holding fast as Ferris struggled.

Rafe glimpsed stairs descending to darkness and cursed
himself for not checking the room more thoroughly. Of course,
there would be a portal to the netherzones. He'd been so awed
by Delilah awakening his memory that he hadn't thought of it.

It wasn't the kind of mistake he should be making. Delilah,
fortunately, was sound asleep, curled up in the middle of the
bed and breathing deeply.

Rafe hauled the boy back into the bathroom, tossing him
on the floor with disgust. He kicked the door shut and leaned
against it, his arms folded across his chest.

Ferris swallowed, his gaze moving over the room then back
to Rafe. He appeared to be resigned, which meant he knew
there was no other way out of the small room.

Apparently not even a hidden door to the netherzones.

Rafe saw no reason to pretend that the situation was other than it was.

"So, you've seen," he said.

Ferris scrambled to his feet cautiously. He straightened only when Rafe didn't move. He displayed the wreckage of his palm and Rafe wondered what had happened to it.

"You're saying you won't tell. That you can't tell."

The boy nodded.

Rafe looked down at Ferris, not troubling to hide his irritation. "You could still tell someone what you've seen."

Ferris shook his head.

"Why should I trust you?"

Ferris touched his own throat. Rafe had already seen the boy's scar and understood immediately. Shades were often characterized by their low intelligence, a result of radiation exposure while in utero. Others—like Delilah—were harvested at birth because of their birth defects.

He guessed that Ferris hadn't been either kind of shade.

He kept his tone calm, so as to not spook the boy. "You weren't born a shade, were you?"

Ferris shook his head. He gestured as if holding a large lump against his throat.

"A tumor?" Rafe asked. "A cancer?"

Ferris nodded.

"Radiation induced?"

Ferris nodded again, then made a slicing gesture across his throat with his index finger.

"And it was removed." Rafe touched Ferris' left forearm. "By the Society?"

Ferris shook his head, then mocked rocking a baby in his arms.

"By your parents." The boy nodded at Rafe's guess. "To keep you from being found a shade."

Ferris nodded again. He took a furtive stance, as if creeping through an unauthorized zone, and held a finger to his lips as he looked over his shoulder. He pretended to be holding someone's hand and Rafe guessed that he was recalling the clandestine journey with his parents to the surgeon. He mocked opening a door, straightened as if relieved, then made the slicing gesture again.

"An illegal surgery," Rafe guessed. It was common for parents with children in danger of being harvested as shades to break the law, to buy backstreet surgeries for their children in an effort to ensure their safety. "But the surgeon made a mistake and damaged your vocal chords."

Giving the boy a different malady than the one he had had. One that was just as obvious.

Ferris nodded and sighed.

"What happened to your parents?"

Ferris ran his fingertips down his cheeks, mocking tears, then jerked his head over and closed his eyes.

"One died of grief," Rafe guessed. "After you were taken."

Ferris looked Rafe in the eye. He held his finger and thumb like a gun and put the tip of his index finger into his mouth.

"One committed suicide." Rafe knew that there were thousands of stories of similar desperation in the breadth of the Republic. He felt sorry for Ferris and for the boy's parents. "And what did the Society do to you?"

Ferris grimaced and stepped backward, shaking his head.

Rafe put out a hand. "Nothing good. You don't need to remember, Ferris, I understand. I won't be summoning them to collect you, I promise."

The boy's eyes brightened.

"And you, I'm hoping, won't be summoning them for me."

Ferris shook his head emphatically, his alarm making it difficult for Rafe to follow whatever the boy was trying to tell him.

"Slow down, slow down. Calm yourself or I'll never understand."

As soon as Rafe closed the bathroom door, Delilah was on her feet. She dressed in haste, abandoning the corset that she couldn't fasten herself, grabbed her boots and some tokens from Rafe's small pouch. She leapt into the dark stairwell that led to the netherzones.

She closed the door silently behind herself. With any luck, the latch would be well hidden. Even if Rafe found it, it would take him time to pursue her, time that Delilah could use to advantage.

She held up her palm and found her way silently down the stairs in its faint blue light. She pulled on her boots at the base of the stairs, saw that the empty corridor stretched both to the left and to the right.

It looked the same in either direction, but the left corridor seemed to snake downward. Unfortunately, there were never any maps of netherzones. Shades didn't need them, because they were taught the small local area they needed to know. It was believed that maps would simply allow norms with nefarious schemes or help fugitive shades. Delilah was certain that the Republic must have maps for its own uses, but they weren't readily available.

She guessed and ran to the left.

IN THE bathroom, Ferris scrambled to his feet, then wrote in the steam on the mirror.

Raziel.

Rafe recognized the name immediately as an angelic name. He had a vague recollection of a bright light volunteering for a dangerous duty.

Had Ferris known another volunteer?

Ferris, meanwhile, tapped the name, mimed being led by the hand into the sunlight, blinking and smiling. He parted his wrists abruptly, as if breaking shackles, then ran in place.

Rafe understood. "Raziel freed you from the slave dens."

Ferris nodded with enthusiasm. He returned to the mirror, tapped Raziel's name again, then drew two diagonal lines in the steam.

They made a V that wasn't joined at the bottom.

They were precisely like Rafe's scars.

Raziel had been a volunteer, just like him.

Rafe studied the boy's obvious approval, recognizing that he'd gained credence with Ferris because of the similarity of his scars with those of Raziel, the boy's savior.

He wondered what Raziel's assignment had been. Had saving Ferris been part of it? Or had she simply taken him along? He sat on the side of the tub and considered the boy. There was only one way to find out how much Ferris knew.

"Did she tell you why she saved you?"

Ferris nodded again. He jabbed his thumb at himself, then mimed pulling a knife and jabbing it at an assailant.

"You were supposed to fight."

Ferris shook his head. He pointed toward the bedroom where Delilah slept, then indicated pushing someone behind himself and fighting again.

"You were supposed to protect Delilah."

Ferris nodded.

"You've done a good job," Rafe said. Ferris blushed and dropped his gaze. "We have the same job," Rafe added and Ferris glanced up. "I'm supposed to protect Delilah too."

Ferris nodded slowly. He tapped his own scar and let his hand curve to the shape of the tumor that had been removed. Then he tapped those two lines he'd drawn in the steam on the mirror. He lifted his hands, his confusion obvious.

What had given Rafe and Raziel those scars?

Rafe decided to take a chance. He stepped forward and drew two wings in the mist on the mirror, wings that arched high from the diagonal lines. He watched Ferris gasp in understanding.

The boy hesitated for a moment, then drew a halo overtop.

Rafe grinned. "Something like that." He ran the flat of his hand through the steam, removing the drawing.

Rafe turned to find Ferris on his knees on the bathroom floor. The boy looked as if he was praying. To Rafe's astonishment, he kissed Rafe's foot with reverence. Rafe touched the top of the boy's head, knowing that he'd won the boy's loyalty.

By revealing his own vulnerability.

He was relieved that he had one ally at least.

He wondered then whether Ferris was giving him the opportunity to find another. He could use the resources of another volunteer, especially one who understood the system well enough to liberate shades.

One who knew about Delilah's destiny.

"What happened to Raziel, Ferris?"

The boy looked up, mouthed Raziel's name, then put a finger over his lips and frowned.

"That name was her secret," Rafe guessed. Ferris nodded with enthusiasm. "What name did she use?"

Ferris got to his feet, then frowned at his destroyed palm.

Rafe held out his own hand to the boy. "If we can find her, she might be able to help us as well."

Ferris grinned. He typed, then tapped the rim of Rafe's palm impatiently, so obviously hoping that Rafe would know the location of his savior that Rafe's heart wrenched. He smiled at Ferris, then caught his breath when he read the name that the boy had typed.

Rachel Gottlieb.

The assassinated shade in New Gotham.

Again he wondered whether his palm was receiving information intended to help him or to terrify him. Was someone hunting angels? Was Rafe on the list of targets?

Ferris scowled as he watched Rafe's response and he tapped his palm again.

"She's dead, Ferris." Rafe put a hand on the boy's shoulder. He hid his palm, not trusting it to keep from showing the dead Rachel to the boy. For all he knew, it would search on the name Ferris had typed and display all associated files. "I'm sorry. I just heard."

The boy's face crumpled and he fought his tears. They fell anyway, cascading down his cheeks, and Rafe knew he couldn't tell Ferris the truth of how Raziel had died. He put

one arm around Ferris and hugged him tightly, then opened
the door to the bedroom.

He saw instantly that Delilah was gone. The window was
sealed, the door to the hall was locked on the inside, and the
panel that had opened to the netherzones was smooth against
the wall again.

He knew which way she'd gone. He had time to take one
step into the room, intending to grab his clothes and pursue
her.

But Rafe got no further.

THERE WAS a shout from the hallway and the sound of
feet running up the stairs. The lock on the door was incinerated in a laze blast, then someone kicked in the door. Before
the smoke could clear the bureau had been shoved out of the
way.

Rafe found himself looking into the muzzle of a laze for
the second time in rapid succession.

"Don't even think about going for the laze," the hunter
said. "Toss it on the floor and raise your hands."

The shade hunter was as large as Rafe. His hair was as
dark as his eyes and he was deeply tanned. There was malice
in his smile, which made Rafe quickly consider and discard
options. At least half a dozen men crowded the hallway behind him.

Could he reach the window? Rafe wondered whether the
hunter would shoot him in the back, whether running was
worth the risk.

"One fugitive found," the hunter said and Rafe saw the blink
of the laze sighting. "No longer armed, but probably just as
dangerous." He winked and Ferris caught his breath. "Good
job, kid."

"What are you talking about?" Rafe demanded.

"He led us right to you, just like I asked him to." The shade
hunter's smile turned more sinister. "I guess the price was
right."

Ferris snarled, shaking his left hand beside Rafe. The display was smashed and no light emanated from the device.

"They put a tracking device in your palm," Rafe guessed.

Ferris nodded, his outrage as clear as his fear.

Rafe understood that the boy had believed he had disabled the palm and thus eliminated the trace. "You tried, Ferris," he said softly.

The only good thing was that Delilah was gone.

Rafe slowly raised his hands, easing to one side so that Ferris was behind him.

"Turn around slowly," the shade hunter commanded. "I can take you in dead or alive. The choice is yours."

Rafe held the hunter's gaze for a long moment, letting the man see that he wasn't afraid. He was naked, though, and his scars would be evident when he turned.

He had to think that his chances of survival would be better with an obvious defect like that.

He had to hope that his fellow angels wouldn't abandon him to the Society's research labs.

He didn't know, though.

If nothing else, he guessed that Ferris wouldn't fare very well in the labs. He'd ensure that the boy got away before he was taken down. And maybe, just maybe, Ferris would be able to help Delilah.

It wasn't much, but it was the best Rafe could hope for.

He dropped his head as if defeated, keeping his hands high. He began to turn slowly, easing back toward the bathroom door.

"That's it," the hunter said, stepping into the room. "Nice and slow."

Rafe turned an increment more, keeping Ferris behind him. The boy looked unhappy, his hands opening and closing as he looked between the two men. Rafe took another step, turning his back to the hunters, and heard the shade hunter inhale.

"What the hell is that?" one of his fellows asked.

"I've seen those scars before," the hunter said with satisfaction. He took another step into the room.

Rafe spun and grabbed Ferris.

"Run!" he whispered as he shoved the boy into the bathroom. He kicked the pouch from his belt into the bathroom, knowing Ferris would need the tokens in it. He slammed the door and came up fighting. He kicked the shade hunter right in the face, then landed a solid punch on another.

The men shouted. Rafe elbowed a third, making chaos of their ranks, and a laze shot grazed his shoulder.

"No! This one comes in alive!" shouted the shade hunter.

Ha! Rafe could work with that. He punched and kicked and fought as if his life depended on it, slamming one man into the wall and breaking the nose of another. He took all comers until he could dive toward the hidden panel to the netherzones.

He never made it, but then it had been a long shot.

The shade hunter struck him from behind. Rafe stumbled, then felt a needle slide into his belly. He had time to roar in frustration before the drug slithered through his veins. His body refused to respond to his command, a frightening lethargy claiming his limbs.

He fell, unable to do otherwise, and found himself looking up at the shade hunter's satisfied smile.

"Let the kid go," the hunter said to his bleeding fellows. "We can pick him up anytime with that electronic leash." He leaned closer and leered at Rafe. "And maybe, just maybe, he'll lead us to the girl."

Rafe closed his eyes against the hunter's leer. He understood now what Delilah had endured and why she had hated it so. His mind was untethered, racing at full speed, but his body wasn't his to command. The powerlessness was horrific. He was completely at the mercy of men who had no mercy.

And there was nothing he could do about it.

He thought of what he had been and what he had surrendered and knew that it would be worthwhile if Delilah had her chance. If she became Oracle, his efforts and his sacrifice would not have been in vain.

If she simply survived, he would count his mission a success.

The hunters loaded Rafe onto a stretcher. He enjoyed that

they had some trouble doing so, given his size, and that the leader was irritated with their incompetence.

He would have traded that in a minute for freedom, though.

He would have traded it in a minute to help Delilah.

Rafe kept his eyes closed, ignoring the curses of the men and the gloating of the desk clerk. He focused his thoughts on one command, hoping he could send the force of his will to help Delilah. It might not be possible, but it was the only thing he could do. He had to hope it could make a difference.

Run, Delilah, run.

EVERY SECOND was another second Delilah had to use to put distance between herself and Rafe. She didn't doubt that he was a terrific stalker. She had to evade him. She had to find the reverend, without being found by shade hunters.

Where would the reverend be?

She had to find out, which meant she had to abandon the netherzones. No shade would know—or no shade who knew would be likely to confide in her.

Delilah took a deep breath and chose a staircase. It proved to lead to a kitchen, which was in the back of a whorehouse. The cook leaned against the counter smoking, and if she was surprised at the emergence of a stranger from the netherzones, she hid that response behind indifference.

Delilah sidled through the front room, smiling at each waiting customer, then out into the street. One gentleman followed her, trying to negotiate a better rate than the house price. Delilah had some difficulty in evading him, but finally ducked down several side streets to do so.

In her haste, she stumbled over the threshold of a quiet café. The man who was wiping tables glanced at the wall clock, clearly surprised to have a customer so close to midnight.

"The kitchen is closed," he said primly.

"I don't want food. What's the best hotel in town?" Delilah demanded.

He straightened, his gaze flicking over her in assessment.

"You're not pretty enough to work that bar," he said, then his eyes narrowed. "Haven't I seen you somewhere before?"

Delilah tossed him a pair of tokens from Rafe's stash.

He caught them out of the air with dexterity, examined them quickly, then pointed to Delilah's left. "The Mountain View. It's on First Avenue, maybe six blocks past the town square."

"I'll bet it has a heliport."

His smile was more calculating than friendly. "You'd be betting right." Then he shook a finger at her. "I know who you are . . ."

Delilah didn't wait to hear what he said. She leapt directly at him, using Rafe's trick of surprise. She pushed the man out of her way so hard that he stumbled. She was in the kitchen before the waiter could stop her.

"Hey!"

Three shades worked in the kitchen, cleaning the dishes and floor. Their quick glances in her direction revealed that they weren't sedated, although they moved with despondence. They stepped aside so that Delilah could slip between them, then closed ranks against the man. Their move could have been choreographed, but had the appearance of a sleepy accident.

"Hey!" he shouted again, but Delilah was leaping down the stairs to the netherzones.

At the foot of the stairs, she paused to orient herself, then ran toward the hotel. She heard a clock chime midnight in the distance, which only reminded her to hurry.

For once, she felt safer in the shadows. This was familiar to her. The smell of sewage and rotting garbage seemed to sharpen her senses and her vision adjusted quickly to the darkness. Her sense of direction was as keen as ever—no matter how the tunnels twisted and turned, not matter how they forked, she knew which path to follow.

Hers was a convoluted path, all the same, and she guessed that Hood River's netherzones had been added piecemeal. The tunnels were all finished in different materials—some tiled, some bare earth, some of stone—and they varied enormously in height and width. She assumed that people had built their own tunnels, maybe beneath their own homes, and that the network had been linked together over time. Making it consistent throughout wasn't enough of a priority for the citizens of the town, so it remained erratic and inefficient.

It was still useful.

The paths became wider and more uniform, and she knew that she had left the pleasure fringe behind. The tunnel was wide enough for two to walk abreast, albeit on either side of the sewer ditch that ran down the center. The path was sloped, the sewage flowing to the river, and Delilah headed upward.

She climbed a set of stairs, ready to emerge on the street, but found a grate locked over the exit.

The street beyond was empty.

She remembered the grate that the wraith had unlocked and began to panic. Were the unsecured accesses only in the pleasure fringe? Had she made a mistake in choosing the netherzones? Delilah trotted along the stone floor to the next exit.

It was locked as well.

She checked half a dozen exits, her panic rising as she discovered that each and every one was locked down. Was this done for the night? Or were they always locked?

It didn't matter. She had to find the reverend. She pivoted to retrace her steps to the netherzones, disliking that she was heading directly back toward Rafe.

The town seemed much quieter, even when she looked through the grate at the streets. Too quiet. Did they have a curfew in Hood River? Would she be arrested simply for being on the street?

Delilah began to run again, fearful that her plan was doomed to failure. Precious time was slipping away. When the condition of the tunnels revealed that she was back in the pleasure fringe, she tried exits again.

The first one was locked down with a heavy grate.

So was the second.

Delilah panicked.

She checked every exit, her heart racing as she found no escape. The sewage was less well managed in this area and the floor of the tunnel gleamed wetly. The slope was also steeper. She could hear the current of the river, closer at hand.

There was no music from the pleasure fringe above. In fact there was no sound of civilization at all. Each glimpse she had of the town above was of shuttered windows and empty streets.

She slipped on the wet ground in her frenzy to get back to the access she had used in the restaurant. It was too close to Rafe for her to avoid him finding her, but she didn't care anymore. She smiled in recognition of the crooked alley that led to the restaurant kitchen and leapt up the stairs in her relief.

There were bars across the door at the top of the stairs.

The kitchen was empty. Every surface shone, pristine, but there wasn't a shade to be seen.

"Help me!" Delilah shook the gate in frustration, then heard a footstep on the floor.

The man who had taken her tokens appeared in the kitchen before her, a set of keys in one hand. His smile didn't reach his eyes. "Help you?"

"Unlock the grate, please." Delilah rattled it for emphasis. "I need to get to that hotel—"

"No," he said, interrupting her plea. "You're a fugitive shade, and you're exactly where you belong."

And he shut a heavy metal door over the netherzone access. Delilah heard the lock turn and a bar drop, even as she was plunged into darkness.

She was locked in the netherzones.

Again.

Just when she thought things couldn't get any worse, she heard a footstep echo in the darkness below.

Delilah eased down the stairs, silent and cautious. Was there another shade trapped with her? Would the other person help her?

Or would that person betray her?

Was it Rafe? Her heart leapt at the possibility. The truth was that she would have been glad to see Rafe at this point in time. He never got himself into corners like this one. He always seemed to have a plan—or to make one up as he went along.

Maybe he just got lucky.

Delilah decided she could use a bit of that kind of luck.

She reached the bottom of the stairs and strained her ears to listen. The darkness was more complete than it had been, or maybe despair was affecting her perceptions.

She heard a footfall to the right.

She decided to take her chances and follow it.

At least then she'd know whether the other person was friend or foe. She took two silent steps in pursuit, then listened again.

There was a splash ahead. The sound echoed in the tunnel, and she assumed that someone had dropped something into the open sewer. She darted toward the sound of the splash, hoping to surprise whomever it was.

She managed three steps before she was jumped from behind.

XVII

DELILAH FELL under the weight of her assailant but she fought all the way down. She hit her shoulder on the wall of the tunnel, but rolled so that her attacker took the brunt of the fall. It was a male, she could tell from the shape of him, and he was wiry.

That individual wore no reevlar or helm, which meant she had a chance.

It also meant he wasn't a policeman or a shade hunter.

And he certainly wasn't Rafe.

Her tried to trap her arms against her sides, but Delilah wriggled her right hand free. She punched in the direction of his face, then dragged her nails across his skin.

Something about his cry of pain was familiar.

"Ferris?"

He flung her to her back and held her wrists together, holding her captive with his weight. Then he slapped her palm on the ground so it illuminated. He held her wrist high and the palm cast a pale blue light over the pair of them.

"Ferris!"

He looked disgruntled and dirty, and Delilah winced at the four long scratches she'd left on his cheek. They were starting to bleed and she knew his dislike of the sight of blood. Ferris stood up, then rubbed his sleeve across his face impatiently.

"I'm sorry," Delilah began, but he practically spat at her.

He was furious, shaking with his anger. He shook his head and drew a fingertip across his own mouth.

"Silence," she mouthed and he nodded.

And she looked at him, amazed by the transformation. It was more than Rafe having trimmed his hair. He stood taller and moved with more assertion. His eyes flashed with a fervor she hadn't known he possessed. His palm was smashed into darkness.

He squatted down beside her and removed something from his satchel with curt gestures, then thrust the bundle of leaves at her.

Delilah recognized it immediately. It was the prediction Sonja had made, the one she had given to Delilah at the Citadel before killing herself. Sonja used the old method of divination: each fall she had prepared a selection of dried leaves, each embossed with a single letter. In her meditative state, she would choose leaves in order, then present them to the querent.

Sometimes they were acrostics, needing to be reorganized to be understood. They always protected the seer, though, as they could be reorganized into gibberish at will.

Delilah sat up and took the leaves with reverence. This had been Sonja's last gift to her, and she regretted that she had never had the opportunity to thank the older woman for her help. She'd forgotten about them, forgotten that Rafe had them. She unlaced the bundle and with the light of her palm, examined them in order.

The letters upon them spelled GLEAN.

Delilah glanced up at Ferris, surprised to find him still scowling at her. She shrugged her lack of understanding. He pointed to her own palm with impatience.

She would eventually get used to its abilities. She sought the meaning of the word:

To gather or collect slowly. To harvest what has been overlooked or rejected.

Delilah shivered at the double entendre in the second meaning, but was unable to guess the point of Sonja's prediction. Sonja was quite accurate as a seer; Delilah had thought that the Daughter Superior had been slightly afraid of Sonja not because of her feigned madness but because of the power of her gift.

"Glean," she whispered. She supposed it could apply to the identification bead that Sonja had given her. She supposed it could mean the building of energy she felt before having a vision. Both of those were thin, though, and unlikely candidates for the meaning of a vision Sonja had been so intent to give her.

Ferris exhaled with irritation and seized the leaves. He reorganized them quickly, then lifted his hands away.

And they spelled ANGEL.

Angel. The angels had helped Delilah. She knew that. Their angelfire prompted her visions. They had removed her third eye and her tattoo, healing her skin with their radiant touch.

"*I know about the angels,*" she mouthed to Ferris.

He shook his head and held up a single finger.

One angel. The word wasn't plural.

One angel was particularly important.

Well, she knew who that was, as well.

"*Rachel,*" she mouthed. Rachel had been an angel, albeit one without wings. She had defended Delilah and freed her from the mill. Delilah assumed this meant that Sonja had known it too.

But Rachel was dead. Again, she couldn't understand the importance of the message.

Ferris gritted his teeth and shook his head, his annoyance clear. He leaned forward, putting his face close to hers. The blue light of the palm made him look ghoulish and otherworldly. He mouthed the single word so deliberately that she couldn't misunderstand. "*Rafe.*"

Rafe? Delilah knew her surprise showed.

Ferris nodded and turned, indicating two lines on his back. "*Rafe.*"

Delilah blinked. Rafe had the same scars as Rachel had had. Rafe had been an angel, which was why he couldn't remember his past, which was why he was so lucky, which was why he had a mission to protect her.

It was the angels who were sending him the information he needed, the information necessary for Rafe to protect her.

She should have trusted him and whoever guided him.

She looked down at the leaves, wondering how Ferris had gotten them. Had Rafe sent Ferris to retrieve her? It seemed unlike Rafe to delegate something of such importance.

Delilah stood up, determined to return to the man who had been protecting her. Rafe would know what to do.

But Ferris seized her arm and pulled her to a halt. He shook his head at her inquiring glance.

"Why shouldn't I go back to him?" she whispered.

"Because he's not there," a woman with a reverb on her voice said.

Both Ferris and Delilah jumped.

The woman in the patched pseudoskin stepped out of the shadows, her laze trained on the pair of them. "The Society just harvested him. This one got away only with our help."

"What?"

"His palm is infected with a tracking device," she continued calmly. "He led the hunters right to the hotel, and those scars did the rest."

Ferris shook his head adamantly. He drove his right fist into his palm, indicating that he had damaged it.

"They have better software than that," the wraith said with scorn. She raised the laze and her strange eyes widened slightly. "Drastic times call for drastic means," she murmured and fired.

THE RED light of the laze hit Ferris' left hand. He jumped and made an incoherent cry of pain. The wraith held the trigger down, keeping the beam focused on Ferris' left hand.

Delilah understood. "She's destroying it," she said. "Hold still and there'll be less collateral damage."

"Exactly," said the wraith.

Ferris whimpered and extended his left hand, palm toward

the wraith. The tunnel filled with the scent of burning flesh, but she held the shot. Ferris' palm crackled and snapped, the display blowing, then small sparks flying from the device.

When it was cooked and blackening, Ferris collapsed with a moan. His eyes closed. He was pale and his hand jumped as the wraith held the burn.

Long after Delilah thought the damage must be complete, the wraith stopped. She strode to Ferris' side and examined his hand dispassionately. "We might be able to save it."

"He has a tissue regenerator . . ."

The wraith snorted. "We have better ones."

She bent over the unconscious Ferris then, turned his head, and bit into the back of his neck. Her teeth flashed as if they'd been sharpened or had metal augmentations, and she sucked audibly for a moment. Delilah took a step backward, fearful of what kind of being she'd encountered.

Then the wraith spat Ferris' identification bead into the trickle of sewage. It glinted for a moment before it bobbed and disappeared.

"That'll give them something to follow for a while," the wraith said. She wadded up the hem of Ferris' jacket and pressed the cloth to the wound, then her amber gaze locked on Delilah. "Choose your path, Oracle."

"But what about Ferris?"

"He's ours now. It's his only chance."

"That's not very reassuring."

The wraith's smile was cool. "Choose your path, Oracle."

There was no decision to be made. "I have to help Rafe. I can't let the Society take him to their labs."

"Even if it means sacrificing your chance to be Oracle?"

Delilah nodded. She couldn't continue to pursue her own ambition, knowing that Rafe had paid for helping her with his life. "That price is too high."

The wraith nodded and straightened. She moved so quickly to Delilah's side that Delilah had no chance to evade her. The wraith grasped Delilah's neck and bent it, scanning her identification bead with her palm quickly then releasing her.

"I just won a bet," she mused as she eyed her palm display,

then she glanced at Delilah again. "You have fourteen minutes to catch the Nuclear Darwinists' train before it leaves for Chicago."

"He's on the train?"

"Cargo car B." She checked her palm again. "Cell 16. Taken down with 150 milligrams of Ivanofor. By a rough guess, he won't be able to move at least until the morning." She shrugged. "Maybe not even then. Talk to Big Ted, who runs the kitchen shades. He's one of ours. Tell him Theodora sent you."

"Why are you telling me this?"

The wraith slanted a coy glance at Delilah. "Maybe we're helping you."

Delilah didn't believe that for a minute. "Why?"

"The tall one has an outstanding credit." Theodora touched the lump in her pseudoskin, the circle around her neck that Delilah knew was the jewelry Rafe had left in the cabin.

She cocked her head as if listening to some distant sound, one that Delilah couldn't hear. "Tonight's the night then," she murmured without surprise, then eyed Delilah again. "Thirteen minutes. Maybe less."

Delilah swallowed the lump in her throat. "How much credit?"

The wraith smiled and bent over Ferris. She picked him up, showing surprising strength, and cast his limp body over her shoulder. Then she shot out the lock on the grate over the exit from the netherzones.

"Run, Oracle, while you can." Her words were softly uttered and Delilah had to strain to catch them. "There's a bounty on your head and it's against my mandate to leave cred unclaimed."

Delilah ran.

And while she ran, her palm pinged.

From *THE REPUBLICAN RECORD*
February 14, 2100
Download version 1.02

Pleasure Fringes Closed

NEW D.C.—Pleasure fringes throughout the Republic were closed in a surprise move at the stroke of midnight this morning. Law enforcement officials throughout the Republic moved in a coordinated effort to impede access to the pleasure fringes. Streets entering and exiting pleasure fringes in all cities of the Republic were gated and secured. Additionally, netherzone accesses around the perimeter of each pleasure fringe were locked down. Those individuals within the pleasure fringes are being documented and processed by law enforcement officials. Once the geographic regions are depopulated, the areas will be cleansed and redeployed as economical housing for deserving citizens.

The action was the implementation of secret legislation passed by President Van Buren in a special session, reportedly held last week. Van Buren has vowed to bring his program of encouraging family values to the national forum if elected. In his presidential campaign last fall, Van Buren stressed the need to eliminate temptation throughout the Republic in order to "better focus the energies of our citizens," and cited his own history as an example of what could be done to "clean up the Republic."

As governor of the state of Louisiana, Van Buren introduced legislature and "sin tax" policies that effectively led to the closing of casinos, pleasure fringes, and whorehouses. He contends that these policies vastly reduced crime and increased revenue for the state. His critics claim that such policies simply drove those transactions underground and devastated local economies. The citizens of Louisiana showed no such doubt: Van Buren won a majority in three subsequent state elections, showing a clear mandate from the people. Analysts suggest that Van Buren is using his unexpected tenure as president to show citizens what can be expected from his administration if he is elected in November.

The abrupt closing of pleasure fringes caught many citizens by surprise, but was greeted with overwhelming approval. "It's about time they shut those filthy places," said Gerta Morganson, a resident of New Gotham. "People should stay home and spend time with their families, instead of wasting their time and cred in such sinful areas." Mrs. Morganson's opinion is shared by many, as evidenced by the rapid overnight gain in President Van Buren's popularity in the polls.

Even his opponent, candidate Maximilian Blackstone, applauded the move, saying that it was long overdue. Blackstone sounded the sole warning, however, wondering aloud about the fate of those citizens who were trapped in the pleasure fringes when the access was secured. There has as yet been no response to this question from the administration.

Other Stories in Today's Download:

Popularity Polls for the Presidential Candidates:
    Neck and Neck
All Eyes on Chicago and the Upcoming Presidential
    Candidates' Debate
Concurrent Netherzone Lockdown: A Challenge
    in Management
History of the Pleasure Fringes
Circuses Disappear throughout the Republic

LILIA AWAKENED suddenly, certain that something was wrong.

Her heart was leaping, although the unit was still. Montgomery slept beside her, his breathing deep and regular. She strained her ears but heard nothing. It was midnight.

She slipped from the bed carefully to avoid disturbing Montgomery and went to the window in the living room. She opened it quietly, taking a deep breath of the cold wind that was blowing in from the north. The city was quiet and dark, sleeping.

There'd be snow by morning; she could smell it. The clouds were thick overhead, obscuring the stars, but the snow would shine the next day like a carpet of diamonds.

Or fallen stars.

And that was when Lilia knew what was wrong.

The calliope at the circus was silent.

She could usually hear the faint lilting strains of the music from her window, and that had been part of the appeal of the unit, which had few other merits beyond its perfunctory services. And there should have been music at this hour—the circus would be open until two in the morning, since Nouveau Mont Royal had no curfew. It was Saturday night, or early Sunday morning, usually the busiest night of the week for Joachim.

But the calliope made no sound.

There was only darkness where the twinkle of circus lights should have been visible.

Lilia knew why.

If Joachim and the shades from the circus had gone into hiding, there was trouble coming. She could have hidden as well, but it wasn't in her nature to avoid trouble.

She had to try to make a difference.

Lilia pivoted with purpose. She eased past Montgomery's sleeping form, undecided as to whether to wake him. He wouldn't approve. He might try to stop her. They might have the final fight that would end it all, the one she'd been dreading since he'd come home with her.

She knew he didn't fully trust her, and while she blamed herself for that, she couldn't relinquish her secrets that easily.

She still feared his judgment.

She feared his departure.

She went to the closet and put on her pseudoskin. She dressed quickly, layering conventional street clothing over the protective suit, pulling on her favorite boots, packing her helm into her bag and checking the charge on her laze.

She wasn't truly surprised to find Montgomery, naked and leaning in the doorway when she was ready to leave. The man could move with the silence of a cat. He watched her, his expression unfathomable.

"Going somewhere?" His voice was low and silky, just the way that drove her crazy.

"Chicago."

He arched a brow, leaving it for her to explain.

"The music is stopped, the circus is gone. The night that Joachim told us about is this one."

There was no change in his impassivity. "And what does that have to do with Chicago?"

"I have to go to the Society."

"You're not a member anymore, Lil."

"But I have to talk to Blake."

"Patterson?" Montgomery filled one word with more skepticism than should have been possible.

Lilia found herself talking more quickly than usual. "I have to talk to someone and I think I can persuade Blake to my view. If the Society decides to eliminate shades, I have to do something to make a difference." She took a breath, disliking that Montgomery was so still and watchful. "I have to *try*, and I have to believe that I have a better chance of persuading Blake to change policy in person."

"He didn't get elected to the Society presidency yet."

"But he knows people. And he believes in change from the inside." Lilia heard the futility of her plan. She didn't need Montgomery to tell her that it was crazy. She knew it, but she couldn't sit aside and wait for bad news.

"Montgomery, I have to try. They're going to capture her—" She heard her voice rise. "And I have to do something."

"Go to Chicago." His skepticism of the merit of her plan was clear and Lilia hated that she felt like agreeing with him.

She flung out her hands. "I don't know what else to do. I can't stay here. You know they'll come for me too."

Montgomery frowned and looked at the floor for a long moment. He was splendid in his nudity, so muscled and trim. His thoughtfulness, though, was daunting.

And when he looked up, she saw the doubt in his eyes.

The sight shattered her. She had vowed a long time before that she would never be locked in a marriage again where there was doubt and distrust. She had known that Montgomery had uncertainties about her, which was why she'd declined his insistence that they marry.

She wanted to pledge her life to being with him, but she never wanted to see that doubt in her husband's eyes.

"Blackstone is having that debate in Chicago," he noted softly. "Is it really Blake that you're going to see?"

Lilia was shocked that he could imagine she had any feelings left for Max, the greatest snake in the history of mankind.

She was stunned that Montgomery could be jealous.

"Max is a part of my past," she began angrily. "I can't change my history—"

"But is he truly in the past, Lil?" Montgomery's quiet question stopped her cold.

"I haven't seen him for years."

"But your voice softens when you talk about him, and you're not dispassionate in your judgment of him." Montgomery shrugged. "He's a handsome man. Charming. Powerful. Wealthy."

"He's evil! I think he's trying to destroy the Republic!"

Montgomery's eyes narrowed. "I thought that would be your favorite cause. You are a rebel, Lil."

"Correction: I think he's prepared to destroy every norm and shade in the Republic to serve his own ambition." Lilia heard the bitterness in her own tone. "I know he'll sacrifice anybody and anything in his path, without a moment's remorse." She took a deep breath. "Just for the record, I think he's the one that you're here to stop. I think he's the manifestation of evil in the world and if he takes the presidency, well, maybe that will bring on the Apocalypse." She glared at him. "We should be working together on this, Montgomery."

"Just because he's your ex doesn't mean he's the Antichrist."

"Just because he's my ex doesn't mean he's *not* the Antichrist."

Montgomery smiled then, smiled that slow smile that dissolved Lilia's resistance. He even chuckled as he shook his head, and her anger was instantly dissipated. It was frightening how much she cared for this man, how easily he could manipulate her feelings, how terrified she was of the idea of losing him.

By some miracle, she managed to hold her ground.

"You just want me to go along to keep you out of trouble," he mused.

"As if!" Lilia scoffed. She blinked back her tears of disappointment and made to push past him. "In your dreams, Montgomery."

"We've already been over that." He caught her upper arm in one hand, holding her captive against his side. He pulled her closer, his scrutiny telling her that the subject wasn't closed. Lilia tipped back her head and held his gaze, letting him see her determination.

And maybe her disappointment.

She swallowed. "I thought your gift was the ability to read the truth in the hearts of men," she whispered, knowing her heart was in her eyes.

Montgomery's smile turned rueful. "What does that have to do with you?"

"Man, mankind—"

"No, Lil," he interrupted quietly. "You're an enigma to me." He arched a brow, his eyes seeming even more dark than usual. "Maybe you like it better that way."

Lilia couldn't deny that she liked having her secrets. But at what price? She averted her gaze with an effort and looked down at her boots, fearing that her own nature would destroy the best chance at a relationship she'd ever had.

Could she change?

Could she trust anyone fully?

Could she do it in time?

"I love you, Adam. I'm trying—"

He interrupted her again. "Maybe you just want me to come along and get you out of whatever trouble you manage to find," Montgomery suggested. His hand slid up her arm in a deliberate caress, one that left her yearning for him.

But a physical union wasn't good enough. She wanted him body and soul, no doubts, no hesitation.

Which meant she had to open herself fully to him.

Lilia pulled away and marched across the room with her bag. She paused on the threshold to look back at Montgomery, knowing that this journey would make or break their relationship.

If he joined her on it.

"Maybe you'd better come to Chicago and find out for yourself," she challenged, trying to hide her fear.

Their gazes locked and held for a potent moment, then Montgomery reached for his pseudoskin. "I have a better idea," he said with the decisiveness and authority she so admired. "Chicago is too risky and I'm unpersuaded that even you can change Patterson's mind. We could waste a lot of canola, just heading into deep trouble."

"What then?"

"We'll ask Armaros and Baraqiel. They have to be at the circus for a reason, and maybe it's time they shared whatever they know." He came to her side and caught her arm in his hand again, his gaze fierce. "You'll only go to Chicago over my dead body, Lil."

She caught her breath and forced a smile. "Let's hope it doesn't come to that."

THE HOOD River train station was empty.

There was a slight fog gathering, and the night's darkness pressed through the roof. Both the departure board and the arrival board were unlit. The fog tingled as it touched Delilah's ankles and she shivered in the chill.

It was odd to be in a public place that was so devoid of life. Delilah felt vulnerable and visible as she seldom had before. She feared that she was being watched, but she didn't have much time.

Delilah strode through the main hall, listening intently for some sounds of life. Her footsteps stirred dust that hadn't moved in years and the grime on the windows was thick. Glass panes were broken in the doors and windows, and the silence was oppressive.

Menacing.

That low fog shimmered as it crept over the floors, making the station look unreal and desolate. She thought she glimpsed the dark silhouette of a man ahead of her, but he moved quickly out toward the platforms. When she hurried through the arch, she should have been able to see him.

But he was gone.

Like a shadow dispersed by the light.

She surveyed the railyard, not seeing a train that could be the one Theodora had meant. Defunct trains were parked on the tracks, shadowed and dusty like ghosts of the past. Some tracks were empty, weeds growing in the gravel between the rails. The platforms were barren, but there was a persistent hum.

Delilah moved toward the sound with caution. The clatter of metal on concrete from the same area made her steps quicken. A faint light emanated from the far side of the last parked train on her right, casting a pale glow onto the platform.

Delilah clung to the shadows, painfully aware of the press of time. She moved from train to train until she reached the last silent engine. She heard the tread of booted feet then, mens' voices, and a bustle of activity.

She held her breath and peeked.

Hidden behind the hulk of this old still engine was a sleek, low, silver train. It shone in the light cast by a trio of lanterns, and hummed as its generators were juiced up. Delilah saw the overhead cables and guessed that it had batteries, so that electricity could augment the coal usually used for trains.

There were two engines and only three cars, the whole of it narrower in diameter and lower than typical trains. There were wider wheel carriages mounted on either side so it could use the regular tracks, but it rode low in between. Delilah wondered where else this train was designed to travel.

The gold logo of the Society of Nuclear Darwinists was the only embellishment on each car. Just seeing that insignia made her heart skip.

She had less than four minutes to get herself on board.

The engines were closer to her, presumably so they could access those heavy electrical cables. The men were working around the engines—Delilah could tell by the volume of their voices as they conferred. There weren't many of them, maybe four. As she listened, one engine began to hum louder.

She pivoted and ran down the dark side of the train that wasn't going anywhere, using it as a cover. At the far end, she leapt down onto the tracks and crossed them, remaining in the shadows between the two trains. She crossed the tracks to the departing train, moving into the gap between two of the cars. There were two cars still to her left, one to her right with the two engines beyond it.

The juncture was designed so that there was a narrow walkway between the cars, one with side railings but no roof. The doors to both cars were sealed and dark. Delilah climbed the juncture and slipped over the railing. She tested each door silently, but they were locked. There was a digital pad for the lock, but Delilah knew that guessing the code would only reveal her presence and trigger an alarm.

There had to be another way in. She moved carefully over the other railing to the opposite side and stood between the cars, on the track. The train was boarding from this side, and she could hear voices. The coupling between the cars was vibrating steadily, a persistent reminder that the engine was preparing for departure.

She looked around the end of the train and drew back in alarm. They were loading a stretcher into the last car, far to her left. She caught a glimpse of Rafe, strapped to the stretcher, his fair hair hanging loose, his chest bare.

He looked to be dead, and the sight made her heart clench. Delilah caught her breath. Rafe wasn't dead. He was under the influence of Ivanofor, but that wasn't fatal.

Unless fallen angels had physiological differences from humans.

Delilah decided not to think about that.

She heard a man's laughter echo through the quiet station. It was deep and filled with malice, familiar. The sound made the hair stand up on the back of her neck. It reminded her of the voice she'd heard outside the cabin.

Rafe had been wrong about it being due to a hallucinogen. There was a palpable sense of wickedness in the air, as far as possible from the joy the angels brought.

She knew what, or who, it was.

She knew why Lucifer was laughing.

And she knew that the angels were counting on her to stop him.

She had to get on the train.

Delilah steadied herself and looked again, hoping to spot the wraith Theodora had told her to seek. What would she say to him? How would she argue her case?

She'd worry about that when she saw him.

A pair of workers stood with their backs to her, at the end of the last car. Both were small and lean, clearly not the cook in question, and moved with the swagger of norms. She heard dogs barking, then saw Rafe's attendant disappear into the car.

He returned moments later, and the trio of norms walked down the platform. Delilah ducked under the lip of the platform as they passed her and heard them enter the car to her right. There was a burst of male laughter, then the doors to the car were audibly sealed.

The second engine hummed to life.

It was now or never.

Delilah hauled herself up, but only got one one knee onto the platform before someone snatched at the back of her clothes. She was hauled off her feet and pulled over the railing onto the coupling between the cars.

She barely yelped before she was slapped to silence. She struggled, but was hauled into the back of the left car so roughly that she hit both elbows and her knee on the door frame. She was flung against the wall hard, but scrambled to her feet to fight.

A heavyset man stood before her, each of his hands larger than her head. He wore a black singlet and his head was shaved bald. His dark pants had a drawstring waist and looked like surgical scrubs—they were jammed into tall black faux-leather biker boots. He had his arms folded across his chest and every increment of skin that Delilah could see was covered with whorling tattoos. He had a pair of gold earrings in his left earlobe, the metal gleaming against his dark skin.

Big Ted had found her.

XVIII

"ABOUT TIME you showed up," he drawled and his tone was surprisingly congenial. "Theodora said you were coming, but even I can't make this baby wait." He shook his head. "You nearly got left behind, kid."

The train began to move, vibrating beneath Delilah's feet that very moment. He winked at her and she dared to hope.

"You're Ted?"

He grinned, revealing that half of his teeth were capped in gold. "That's me. Get naked and toss all that stuff out the door pronto. They'll seal the locks by the time we leave the station, and you don't want any identifying garments on you. You're a worker that I picked up in New Portland if anyone asks. Got it?"

Delilah nodded, then realized he had no intention of leaving while she stripped. She was glad that she'd never had a chance to develop any modesty in the netherzones. She peeled off her clothes and flung them out the open door, managing to stuff the last boot out the gap as the door automatically closed.

There was a rush of air as the seal was secured, then a red light illuminated over the door.

"Chicago, here we come." Ted handed her a dark singlet and pants much like his own, as well as a watchman's cap.

"Chicago?"

He snorted. "Where else do you think the hunters take their prizes? We're going right to the Institute with this one."

Delilah fought to control her heartbeat and look nonchalant. They were headed directly for the place she'd been avoiding for nine years. That was why the train had different wheel chassis, so it could ride the rails of the underground chambers of the Society of Nuclear Darwinists.

A netherzone from which shades never emerged. She pulled on the clothes under Ted's knowing eye and tried to hide her panic.

"Welcome aboard, kid." The car rocked slightly as the train shunted to another track, then changed direction. It began to accelerate and Ted turned to walk away.

"Wait a minute. Can you help me?"

"I already did."

"Did Theodora tell you . . ."

"Don't condemn yourself, kid," Ted said genially. "Keep your head down, do what I tell you, and you might get to Chicago alive." He shrugged. "After that, it's anyone's guess."

Once Delilah would have taken that chance and been glad of it, but she wasn't as ready to cede now. "I want more than that."

Ted didn't appear to be surprised.

"Then you'll have to negotiate it." He turned and walked down the corridor on one side of the car, leaning to keep from hitting his head. Delilah knew he was leaving it up to her to name the terms of negotiation.

She wanted Rafe free.

But she remembered all too well Theodora's assertion about everything having a price. "I don't have any cred!"

Ted paused, then cast a glimmering glance over his shoulder. "What do you want?"

"Him free."

Ted pursed his lips. "That's big."

"I'll do anything. I can't let them have him."

Ted smiled. "True love?"

Delilah blushed despite herself, but said nothing.

Ted surveyed her for a long moment, his gaze lingering on her forehead. Delilah assumed that the mark from the angel's kiss was still there. "I tell you what, kid. I'll make you a deal."

"Why?"

Ted grinned. "Because I'm an idealist deep down inside."

Delilah didn't believe that for a minute, but she listened. Ted shook a heavy finger at her. "But a realist too. You gotta remember that."

Delilah's heart sank. "There's a bounty on my head."

"And it's big," Ted agreed ruefully. "Somebody wants you bad, kid. But here's the thing—if you really are the Oracle, then money's no object."

"Well, I am."

"Well, I'm a disenchanted idealist. Prove it to me. Gimme a prophecy in forty-eight hours and I won't claim the bounty."

Delilah noticed the omissions in his promise. "And what's that really worth? Are there other people working on this train who might claim it?"

"There are always people ready to claim a bounty." Ted smiled. "But for the next forty-eight hours, I'll protect your skinny butt. That's the best offer you're going to get, kid, guaranteed." He sobered and tipped his head to watch her. "Unless, of course, you're not really the Oracle."

"I am!"

Ted smiled, then turned away again, his challenge echoing in Delilah's ears without being said aloud.

Prove it.

A prophecy.

Delilah had had two of them in rapid succession. She should be able to do this. She would be able to do this.

She had to do this—for Rafe.

And for everyone, shade or norm, in the Republic.

In the meantime, she'd do what Ted told her to do and keep her head down. Ted ambled down the train and she hurried after him, bumping her head more than once along the way. She rubbed the place on her forehead where her third eye had been and felt a spark of light as a result.

One way or another, she had to conjure a prophecy in time.

THE NOUVEAU Mont Royal circus was more like a morgue.

It was silent and dark, empty. Lilia shivered as she and Montgomery passed the dead eye of the security link. There

was no juice, no music, no bustle, or hustle. The colored banners flicked in the breeze overhead, the eyes of the Republic
emblazoned on each one.

But there were no eyes here.

Joachim and the shades were gone. Even knowing it would
happen didn't make the reality any easier to face.

She wondered where they had run, whether they would be
safe, how many of them would survive. She wondered how
much worse things would get before they became better, and
then she worried about Delilah.

Lilia shivered, folded her arms around herself, and walked
toward the tent that Armaros and Baraqiel occupied. She had
a bad feeling, given the darkness of the entire circus, but she
had to know for sure.

They walked together in grim silence and entered the tent
together.

There was no sign of either angel, no radiant gleam of angelfire, no shimmer of heat or electrical charge in the air.

"Gone," Lilia whispered.

Montgomery surveyed the perimeter of the tent, sliding
his hands across the places they had favored. Lilia took the
other direction, and slipped through the flap to the part of the
tent with the stage. There was a vid-screen on one wall of
the tent, one that was often used to display images of the pair
to a rapt audience just before their appearance.

The vid-screen shimmered ever so slightly around its
perimeter.

It had juice.

Lilia headed straight for it, saw instantly that it was in its
energy-saving mode. She touched the display, bringing up
the last viewed item, and a single word flashed in brilliant
white on the dark screen:

NOW.

She had a heartbeat to see the word before it faded and disappeared. The vid-screen fizzled, its last bit of juice spent, and
went dark.

"They were Joachim's signal," Montgomery said from behind her.

"They delivered a message, although I'm not sure it was from God."

"It was, if it was the only one they were assigned to bring."

Lilia disliked the uncertainty that seemed to follow her every step. "Where would they go, Montgomery?"

"Back," he said simply.

It wasn't much of an answer, and certainly wasn't one that pleased Lilia. If Armaros and Baraqiel had come to earth to warn Joachim to take the circus into hiding, she thought they might have hung around to share a bit more of what they knew.

Before she could figure out how to complain without offending Montgomery, she saw him bend.

He picked up something from the floor then pivoted, his gaze locking on hers.

He held a single white feather. It was so perfect and luminous that Lilia knew exactly what kind of feather it was.

She'd never seen an angel feather before. Montgomery looked strained, and she knew he was remembering the loss of his own wings. The feather shimmered, then seemed to dissolve into dust motes made of light.

And it was gone.

"They stayed," she whispered in awe.

"At least one of them." Montgomery was looking, scanning the perimeter of the tent, peering into corners. "I should have been told, but maybe Tupperman . . ."

His palm chimed and he stared at it, his brow dark.

"What's wrong?" Lilia asked, fearing the answer. It couldn't be good if it troubled Montgomery so much. He was the most composed individual she'd ever known. She went to his side when he didn't immediately respond. "Montgomery? What's wrong?"

He spared her a glance that shook her to her core. "He's gone."

"Who? Raphael?"

Montgomery nodded. "His palm isn't responsive at all. I

can't even get a root ping. It's like he's dead. Or more like he never existed. He's just gone."

Lilia felt sick at the implications of that. "They got him," she said softly, knowing there was no point in evading the truth.

Montgomery's gaze was piercing. "What do you mean?"

"The Society. They got him." She heaved a sigh. "First item of protocol is disabling the palm." She licked her lips. "If he's in a cargo hold, the cells are sheathed so that no signal can be sent or received."

"No stays of execution," Montgomery said, drumming his fingertips on the windowsill. "No reprieve."

"It's effective. You've got to give them that." She waited but he didn't answer the question he had to know she had. "Delilah," she whispered, fearing the worst.

Montgomery winced. "It's what I was trying to send him."

She went to his side, anxious for the news. "Let me see."

"Lil. You're not going to like it."

She held his gaze for a moment, hoping he was wrong, then looked at his palm.

But Montgomery, as usual, was right.

The man just knew her too well.

Bounty Offered for Fugitive

- F
- 19 years of age
- Caucasian
- Dark hair and blue eyes, shaved head.
- Distinctive port wine mark on forehead.

The Society of Nuclear Darwinists has requested this fugitive be captured alive for research purposes. The identification bead installed in this shade may or may not be correct, and it is possible that its tattoo number has been modified. Identification will be made on physical appearance alone.

If you have seen this fugitive and can point authorities in its direction, half of the bounty will be paid on successful capture. If you capture this fugitive alive, the full bounty will be payable to you. If the fugitive is killed during capture, one third of the bounty will be paid.

Contact: <u>Rhys ibn Ali</u>, shade hunter, or <u>Ernestine Sinclair</u>, Society President, for further details on collecting the bounty.

IN THE rocking rhythm of darkness, Raphael dreamed.

Or maybe he remembered.

Maybe the distinction wasn't important.

He was in a place of such luminosity that it could only have been made of light. Space seemed infinite and time had no meaning at all. His body was so weightless that it might have had no substance at all, and he could see the beams of light pierce the silhouette of his own hand.

His wings were lush. Their feathers shone and he could arch them effortlessly above himself, feel himself smile as the light touched them.

Was he radiant? Or was he surrounded by light? Raphael

didn't know and he didn't care. He felt optimistic, beyond the burdens of the flesh, ageless and timeless.

It was seductive to feel such power again.

And yet . . .

And yet, he remembered. He remembered the brush of lips on his own. He remembered his shiver at Delilah's breath upon his skin. He remembered the smooth sweep of her pale skin, the vivacity in her eyes, and the determination in her stance. He remembered a woman who had strength despite her tests, and despite the frailty of her body, and he felt the blossom of love within him.

It was different from the affection he had known for all of creation. It was more specific and more intense, more linked to sensation and mortality.

More precious because it was fleeting.

And he yearned to feel it again. Raphael knew he had taken flesh before and regained his wings, that he had thought it was sensation that drew him back to the earthly sphere, but in his dream, he knew otherwise.

Delilah. They complemented each other—her solemnity with his playfulness, her youth with his age, her impulsiveness with his need to plan ahead. She pursued her personal ambition with what might have been called selfishness, but in truth, she was driven by a selfless desire to serve her fellows. She understood sacrifice.

He understood it too.

He was surrounded by radiance and joy, the tranquillity that could be his in the completion of his mission, but Raphael found his gaze turning earthward. His own reward was less important to him than Delilah's success. He would give anything to see her become Oracle.

Even his wings.

Forever.

He turned earthward in his mind's eye, plummeting again toward sensation and possible destruction, his choice made. And as he fell once more in his dream, for the third time in all of his existence, he heard a woman's voice.

"Once there was the *Sefer Raziel,* and it was the greatest

treasure held by the angels," she said, her words at once coming from everywhere and nowhere. "The *Sefer Raziel*, or the *Book of the Angel Raziel*, was the compendium of all knowledge. Everything known by the angels was recorded there and secured on high."

Her voice was low and wry, innately appealing, but Rafe couldn't see her. He halted to listen, scanning all around himself in what he thought was a futile effort to find the woman who spoke.

She was within his own thoughts.

As Lucifer had been.

But she was not wicked. Raphael knew that there was no risk in listening to her words.

The angels might even help him.

"It was called the *Book of the Angel Raziel* because that angel compiled it. She felt the compulsion to ensure that the great knowledge of the celestial host was never lost. And so she compiled the book, and so, in a sort of pride, she believed herself the custodian of it. She believed that she had the right to do with the book as she desired."

Raphael watched the clouds begin to swirl before him, forming a whorl of light. He couldn't tell if there was anything in the center of the spiral or not, but also couldn't tear his gaze away from its increasing speed.

"So when man and his mate were wrought of earth and given the divine breath, the angel Raziel believed that they had need of this knowledge for their own. And she bestowed the *Sefer Raziel* upon Adam, that he could look upon it, marvel, and learn the majesty of creation. But the other angels, seeing this, responded in anger. They seized the book from Adam and cast it into the sea. And Raziel feared that she had erred.

"But God chastised the other angels, and insisted that the book be fetched from the depths of the sea. He commanded that it be returned to Adam and his descendants, proving that Raziel had been correct in assessing his favor of men.

"And so Raziel took it upon herself to constantly defend man's custody of that precious book, ensuring that in times of trouble it always came into the possession of those men who can change the tide of history. So it was that Enoch had the *Sefer Raziel* when he wrote of the Watchers aiding men—Raziel being one of those angelic guardians and teachers—and so it was that Noah used the *Sefer Raziel* to guide his construction of the ark, and so it was that Solomon consulted the *Sefer Raziel* to construct the Temple."

The cloud spun faster before Raphael's eyes and he was certain that there was something spinning in its vortex.

"Every secret is resident within the *Sefer Raziel*. Every answer can be found within its depths. Every issue can be resolved and every conflict can be defeated."

The item in the center of the spinning dervish flashed and shone, reflecting the light from all sides. It was a gem, he knew it. It sparkled like sunlight on ocean waves and Raphael wanted to touch it. He wanted it because it sparkled. He needed to hold it in his hand and admire its beauty. The desire for faceted jewels that had possessed him since volunteering was redoubled in the presence of this prize. He moved closer and reached out.

"And so it was, and so it is, and so it always will be," the woman continued. The spiral spun faster, the light growing to blinding brightness. "The *Sefer Raziel* is the light in the darkness. It is the star in the brow of the Oracle. It carries the voice of the angels into the most shadowed corners of creation." Her voice became louder. "The *Sefer Raziel* brings knowledge and vision—and with knowledge and vision, comes hope. This is the gift of the angel Raziel."

Raphael plunged his hands into the whorl and snatched at the source of the flashing light. He felt a faceted gem in his left hand, opened his fingers, and found nothing there.

Nothing.

And he wasn't in the place of radiance anymore.

His eyes were open and he was alone. He was lying on his back in a closed metal tube that rocked gently. The only light was the faint blue coming from his palm.

And the official image of the murdered shade, Rachel Gottlieb, was displayed there. Her gaze seemed to hold his, even though it was a still image, as if she would compel him to make sense of his dream. He scrolled down, reviewing the image of her scars and the brutality of her death, and understood fully the stakes before himself.

Raziel had sacrificed her wings to aid mankind, and had been murdered while on earth. She hadn't regained her wings, hadn't returned to their celestial abode, but her voice could still be heard by those who listened.

But the *Sefer Raziel* existed. Her legacy survived and it was her desire that it be used to aid mankind.

And he knew already that it was his task to heal humanity. The solution to both missions was to install Delilah as Oracle, so that she could be the light in the darkness for the president of the Republic.

Rafe reviewed what Raziel had said to him. He thought of how Delilah rubbed her brow, and her story that Rachel had taken her to the angels to have her third eye removed.

Rafe had a very good idea not only where the *Sefer Raziel* had been secured, but why the angels were so protective of Delilah. It was contained in a gemstone, a small faceted gem that had been surgically inlaid into Delilah's brow.

She carried the repository of all knowledge, celestial and earthly, in her brow.

And his own desire to possess and protect all gems was no accident either. He had taken flesh to help her and he wasn't going to stop trying to do so.

He was still alive.

He had to help Delilah.

He tried to check the date and time on his palm, but it was unreceptive to satellite data. He could only access what he had downloaded before being captured.

Presumably that meant that he couldn't either summon help or be tracked by anyone intending to aid him.

And whoever had been feeding Rafe information didn't know Delilah's new identity. Rafe didn't even know her location.

He had to get himself free somehow.

Rafe set to exploring his prison, with no clear idea of how

much time had passed or what he was going to do once he
escaped. His control over his body had returned and he had
to act before they drugged him again.

Delilah needed him.

And the people of the Republic needed Delilah.

DELILAH STRAINED for a vision, but came up empty.

Maybe it was the press of time. The hours ticked down
with relentless speed, seeming to disappear with even more
haste as Ted's deadline drew closer.

Maybe it was exhaustion. She washed dishes and cleaned
floors and did prep work for Ted, managing to catch only a
few hours' sleep each night. The kitchen was an oppressive
environment, all steel and low lighting. The only bright lights
were over the counter where Ted worked, obsessively fussing
with the presentation of the meals he sent into the front car.

The only thing that came back were dirty plates and the
occasional sound of laughter.

There were no windows in the service car and it was hard
to tell the time of day. Delilah had to keep checking her palm.
The train rocked with a relentless rhythm, one that told her
they were making fast progress toward Chicago.

That only increased her anxiety about summoning a vision.

Four shades worked for Ted, all of them sedated and simple. They wouldn't have noticed much in their state, and
Delilah wasn't even sure they were aware that another had
joined their number. Ted was rough and jovial, a demon for
detail in his presentation. He was merciless in his pursuit of
cleanliness in the kitchen and could find a stray molecule of
grease on a dish with terrifying speed. Otherwise, he said
nothing.

The hunters never came back into the service car, much
less into the cargo car at the end of the train. One shade routinely took buckets forward and Delilah assumed he cleaned
latrines in the first car.

The accommodation in the service car was minimal—four

hammocks were slung in the space at the back of the car beside the latrine. The largest and lowest hammock was Ted's, while the others were shared by the shades and Delilah. At first, she had been repelled by this, but exhaustion had made her less fussy.

On the second night, she laid in her hammock as the train moved eastward. She rubbed the middle of her forehead but had only a glimmer of light. There was nothing on her mental horizon, and she panicked that Ted would toss her to the hunters.

The worst part was that she would be condemning Rafe as well.

She interrogated her palm, having grown more proficient at using it, and worked through Sonja's files. Sonja had dumped the entire contents of her own palm into Delilah's, and Delilah hoped that there was some kernel of information in there that would help her. She'd checked all of the obvious places and file names, and was poking through a file of what appeared to be administrative details.

Sonja had once been the Daughter Superior at the Citadel and there were a lot of memos and meeting agendas, propositions and action plans.

Then Delilah saw a file entitled *Gideon Fitzgerald*.

She hesitated over it. She had a vague memory of that name, and when she opened the file and saw his image, she caught her breath.

This was the shade hunter who had taken her to the Citadel.

She quickly learned that he was Sonja's nephew, and wondered at his plan. He'd taken her to the Citadel instead of the Society's labs, and Sonja had protected her all these years.

Why hadn't he done what shade hunters and researchers usually did with shades?

The answer was in two linked files.

The first was a wedding announcement, sent to Sonja, for the marriage of Gideon Fitzgerald and Lilia Desjardins. It was dated after Delilah had arrived at the Citadel.

She flicked back. Was Gideon her father? The dates indicated otherwise—her mother must have gone to the Institute for Radiation Studies after Delilah's birth, and she'd met Gideon there.

But they'd married.

The second linked file was a research proposal. Delilah read it with dawning horror, a lump rising in her throat when she saw her old shade number in the list attached to the end.

She asked her palm about the individual Nuclear Darwinists listed in the proposal and came up with a good idea of why Lilia had married Gideon.

Her mother had seen this protocol and sent Gideon to save her.

Rachel had gotten to Delilah first, but when she was harvested, Gideon had found Delilah—and taken her to his aunt for her safety.

And Lilia had married him, maybe out of love, maybe out of gratitude.

Delilah stared at the ceiling of the moving train, coming to terms with the realization that her mother had cared for her, if only from a distance.

Maybe that had been the best Lilia could have done.

Society of Nuclear Darwinists Internal Memo
Research Proposal 14249
Submitted by Dr. Paul Cosmopolous and Dr. Liam Malachy
November 3, 2089

An Investigation into the "Third Eye"
Executive Summary

THE "THIRD eye" is a skin nodule located in the middle of the forehead, directly above the brows and nose. It appears as a large wart, often as big as the subject's thumbnail. Anecdotes about the "third eye" and the powers it supposedly gives to those born with it are persistent in our society. (Ref: *Man and Myth in the Postnuclear Republic,* Dr. Wilhelmina Olsendatter, Institute for Radiation Studies Press, Chicago, 2078, pp. 34–56 for a thorough discussion.) Popular stories and mythology associate the "third eye" with the ability to predict the future. This was believed to be baseless, until research into the pineal gland in birds was recently reviewed. The avian pineal gland is located the front center lobe, directly behind the "third eye." Because birds' skulls are thinner over the gland, it has long been believed that the pineal gland is light sensitive and triggers the birds' migratory urges.

The goal of this experiment is to more precisely define the function and ability of the pineal gland in humans, as well as to assess any link between its activity and the presence of a "third eye." We believe that this area of research has been overlooked for too long.

It is proposed that 160 shades—of various ages and ethnicities—all identified in the Society's databases as having been born with the "third eye," will be subjected to the test and stimulus protocol attached. The tests will take two years to complete, and will be conducted at the Society's labs in Chicago. The final step will be the physical examination of the brains of the subjects for evidence of any effects of the prolonged stimulus.

It is entirely feasible that the test results will lead to a greater understanding of brain function and hormone effects, possibly leading to additional drug research and patents. Additionally, it will provide a cohesive and valuable experience for graduate students at the Institute for Radiation Studies, preparing them for further work in the Society's labs.

Please see the attached budget. Note that this includes any fees that will be incurred by transferring shades in the possession of the Republic or private sector to the experiment. Also attached is the list of proposed graduate students and their specialities, as well as a beginning inventory of shades eligible for the experiment. (Note that there appears to be a slightly greater incidence of the defect among females than among males.)

Proposed List of Participating Graduate Students:

Cecil O'Donnell—Tracking & Collection
Mike MacPherson—Laboratory Protocol &
    Experiment Management
Gideon Fitzgerald—Statistics Compilation
Ernestine Sinclair—Dissection & Vivisection

Proposed Shade Inventory

D324675—F. b. 2056
W674839—F. b. 2042
S780095—M. b. 2078
M764839—M. b. 2085
. . .
E562008—F. b. 2081

BY THE next night, Delilah was beginning to panic.

There was no sign of a vision in her thoughts, no hint of a prophecy. Had she lost her gift of foresight with her virginity? The Daughters had been adamant that the Oracle must be chaste, although Delilah hadn't been thinking of that when she'd been with Rafe in the pleasure fringe. And it was hard to regret something that had been so wonderful.

So much like the touch of angelfire.

Delilah caught her breath in realization and froze in the middle of cleaning the galley.

It made so much sense.

Rafe was an angel.

He was working for the angels.

She had had her first vision in the chapel of the Daughters of the Light of the Republic in his presence. She remembered the sense of an electrical current sparking through her when she'd met his gaze.

She'd also had a blinding flash of foresight when he'd flicked his fingertip across her brow in the cabin. The gathering of the angels shortly afterward had brought that vision to fruition.

Rafe's presence, his touch, his kiss, were all tinged with the power of angelfire, which was why they all awakened the foresight within her. In the absence of the angels, she could use a fallen one to summon her gift.

She had to see Rafe.

She had to touch Rafe.

Which meant she had to persuade Ted to take her into the cargo car. Delilah assumed that wouldn't be easy, and she was right.

TED WAS doing his final survey of the kitchen, running his fingertip over the surfaces and squinting into the cracks where grease could hide. Two of the shades in his service stood dully at the end of the space, waiting for his approval or further commands. He barely spared Delilah a glance, but she sensed that she had his attention.

"I'm curious," she said, leaning against the counter at the opposite end of the galley to the two shades.

"We all are, kid."

"But I'm curious about things you know about."

He looked at her. "That's dangerous talk." He turned and nodded to the shades, watching as they retreated to the hammocks. He was motionless, fixed on the two shades for so long that Delilah assumed he'd ignore her from that point onward.

Then he turned a stern look on her. "You know I can't tell you anything, kid."

"Someone's trying to kill me. I'd like to know who."

Ted grimaced. "You've got to understand. Among my kind, indiscretion is really the only sin."

"I think I have a right to know. And I think you should tell me."

He almost smiled. "Because I'm your only chance?"

Delilah smiled. "Pretty much."

"Everything's got a price, kid."

"You know I've got no cred." She stepped forward and touched his arm. He looked down at her hand in surprise. "I have to be sure, Ted. What if I prove to you that I'm the Oracle and you're working for whoever is targeting me?"

"Anybody can be bought, kid." He shrugged. "In fact, pretty much everyone has been."

"No," Delilah insisted. "No. I think you really are an idealist. You're good to these shades, better than most. You're on this train because you're working for the Society on the surface but against them in reality."

He started and gave her a sidelong glance, one that persuaded Delilah she'd guessed his true intentions.

"I need more than a few days of protection to become Oracle. I need to survive, and to do that, I need to know exactly who is hunting me."

Ted pursed his lips and moved away. He strolled to the end of the galley, surveyed the small space, then turned on the dish sanitizer with a decisive flick. It ran noisily, filling the galley with its clanking and hissing.

Delilah understood that whatever happened next wouldn't be overheard.

Ted came quickly back toward her with purpose. His eyes gleamed and he looked bigger, his sudden resolve making her uncertain of what he'd do.

"You've got five minutes," he muttered, his gaze fixed on the door to the passenger car. "Make it count, kid."

Delilah didn't hesitate. "Who ordered the destruction of the Citadel?"

"Van Buren's people." Ted nodded approval. "Nice, profitable piece of business."

Delilah was shocked. "People died!"

"That was the point." At her obvious exasperation, he told her more. "Van Buren only wants an Oracle who does what she's told. Blackstone too, although it was rumored to be Blackstone who paid the Daughters to set that up."

"You don't know?"

"Not our piece of trade. But you hear things. Often they're true. Anyway, Van Buren was on board with the false Oracle, and the word was that your vision spooked him. You had to be eliminated."

"But I got away."

He grunted assent. "With help."

"From Rafe."

Ted's expression turned sly. "I'm not the only idealist living on the edge, kid. Don't forget that."

"But Teresa lived too."

Ted nodded. "Yup. Blackstone had sunk good cred into her selection, from what we'd heard. We liberated a bit more from him to let her live." Ted shrugged and grinned. "We thought it might even look like divine intervention for her to be the only one spared. Good PR in that."

Delilah knew that time was slipping away. "What about my prophecy?" she asked. "Who killed Matheson?"

"We did, of course. We do anything for cred, kid."

"But who paid you?"

Ted's smile was sly. "Guess."

"Van Buren or Blackstone."

"Duh. Had to be one of them." Ted eyed the door behind Delilah again and dropped his voice an increment lower. "It was Van Buren. The only way he could get the Heartland Party nomination was to get rid of Matheson."

"But it looked like a natural death."

Ted grinned. "In our world, you get what you pay for, kid."

"Well, there has to be justice . . ."

"Says who?"

"There must be evidence! People can't just get away with crimes like this . . ." She sputtered to silence when Ted put his hand on her arm.

"There is no evidence. No one in this game is dumb enough to leave any chance of getting caught." He shrugged. "Maybe I'm even lying to you."

"No, you're not." Delilah saw that Ted was shocked by her conviction. "But don't you see? They should be punished. There should be repercussions. That's what's destroying the Republic. There has to be *justice*."

"Justice? That's another thing altogether, kid."

"What do you mean?"

His smile flashed. "We take cred, anybody's cred, and you know, what goes around usually comes around." The sanitizer came to a noisy halt and the kitchen seemed suddenly very silent. Ted smiled and his voice dropped low. "That's five." He turned away, ambling toward his hammock.

But the transaction wasn't finished. "I need to see Rafe," Delilah said, her words bringing Ted to a halt.

He turned slowly to survey her. "You have no idea what you're asking."

"I know who I'm asking. Maybe that's good enough."

He blinked, then turned away again. He retreated to his hammock and Delilah feared that she had failed.

Was Rafe still sedated?

Was he okay?

What if the Ivanofor had killed him?

She slumped to the kitchen floor, letting the train rock her while she thought. She rubbed her forehead and prayed for a vision.

She also prayed that Ted would change his mind.

The sound of his snores soon filled the car, and that wasn't encouraging at all.

XIX

WHEN TED rolled out of his hammock hours later, Delilah was sure he'd decided to turn her down. She was instantly awake, her gaze fixed on his face. He paused beside her, looking torn, his gaze moving to the end door.

"Now," he said softly.

Delilah scrambled to her feet so hastily that she nearly fell. Ted caught her elbow and released her as soon as she'd gotten her footing, turning then to the back door of the car.

He retrieved a bulging bag from a cabinet and handed it to her. It was the same kind of storage bag they used for the kitchen waste, the half-eaten protein-paks and leftover extruded food product. There was neither incinerator nor drain on the train and Delilah assumed that the waste was sealed for disposal in Chicago.

She'd never seen anyone take it to the cargo train, though.

She kept her mouth shut and followed Ted.

He hesitated at the back door and cast a furtive glance over his shoulder, eying the door at the other end of the service car. The light over that door remained red.

Delilah followed his glance, as his trepidation was contagious. She understood that Ted was breaking a rule for her and that nothing good would happen if they were caught.

He pulled on a pair of latex gloves, presumably to ensure that he left no fingerprints. He didn't offer her a pair. He hurriedly punched in a code, shielding the number pad from Delilah's view with one meaty hand.

The door slid open in silence, admitting a bracingly cold draft. Ted strode onto the coupling between the cars and

Delilah followed him. She stood in the middle, gripping the rails and breathing deeply. Then she shivered.

The air was cold and there was snow on the ground, glittering white in every direction. The sky was clear enough that she could see a few stars between the clouds. It was dark, darker than she might have believed possible. The land was flat and empty in every direction, only the silhouettes of spinning windmills on their towers filling the view.

She saw a star fall in the distance and caught her breath at its unexpected beauty. She heard a chopping sound then, and sought the source of that sound in the sky. A helicopter was moving in the same direction as the train and she peered around the car. There was a city on the horizon ahead.

Chicago.

She watched the helicopter, wondering how many of them there were in the Republic. Could it be the reverend? Was she foolish to hope?

The other door slid open while she was looking skyward and Ted slipped inside the cargo car with surprising agility for his size.

Delilah was right behind him. Her heart leapt when the dogs snarled and barked at the bars of their kennel to one side of the corridor.

They were the hunting hounds of the shade hunters, and she'd forgotten all about them. The flash of their teeth and the frenzy of their barking drove Delilah back against the door in fear.

It had already closed behind them.

The bars that contained the dogs offered no consolation, as they jumped against them in their urge to be free. Their eyes gleamed and some fit their snouts between the bars in their desperation to reach her.

It was as if they knew she was a shade.

"Quick!" Ted said. "Empty the bag."

Delilah opened the kitchen waste bag and flung its contents into the kennel with shaking hands. Some of it fell on the floor, but the dogs pounced on whatever they could reach.

They wolfed down the food, not taking time to chew. They

slobbered as they ate, growling slightly. A pair wrestled over one protein-pak that was more full, snarling at each other until one was triumphant.

But they quieted.

Delilah bent and gathered the bits of waste on the floor, dumping every morsel she could find into the kennel.

She'd been right—they were kept hungry.

To her amazement, they settled once they had sniffed out the scraps. There were about a dozen of them, all different-colored mongrels. The floor of their kennel was mesh and there must have been some automated system to remove their waste. The kennel was clean and the cargo car didn't smell.

Despite their earlier competitiveness, the dogs moved to pile together in one corner of the kennel, nestling against each other for warmth. Several remained near the grate, sniffing with optimism. A brindle hound reached through the bars and licked her fingers, much to her surprise. They licked their chops and watched Delilah as they settled, clearly hoping that she had more.

She wished that she did.

A hiss from Ted made her hurry after him. She followed him, looking about herself with curiosity. The cargo car's interior was all shaped steel, like the service car, but the narrow corridor was in the center of this car.

The two sides were lined with long horizontal doors, each with a digital lock. They were three high on either side. Ted moved down the car, peering at each illuminated info panel. He paused beside one and threw Delilah a look.

"Sixteen," he said, and she caught her breath in understanding of what the panels concealed.

Rafe was in there. She looked around herself, counting quickly. There were fifteen such panels on either side, three high and five long—were there thirty captives riding sedated in this car?

Shades, after all, would be cargo to Nuclear Darwinists.

And she doubted the shade hunters would take well to losing their carefully collected prizes.

Delilah couldn't swallow the lump in her throat. Ted tapped

in a code and it seemed far too long before there was a resonant chime. She heard metal move in the panel of number sixteen, then the panel slid out. Ted had moved to the far side of the panel so was out of the way when it revealed itself to be a large drawer.

With Rafe lying in it.

So still that he might have been dead.

His head was toward Delilah and his feet toward the back of the train. His trousers were as disheveled as she recalled, but he had shaved and retied the queue of his hair. He wore only his trousers and boots, the tanned golden perfection of his body looking wrong in this place.

It was strange to see him motionless and unanimated.

Sickening.

On the lip of drawer number sixteen glowed several images. One was the all points bulletin released for the three of them, with Rafe's description highlighted. The second was a grainy shot of Rafe in the chapel of the Citadel, his manner impatient and intent. The third was an image snatched of the scars on his back.

They were just like Rachel's, just as Ferris had said.

Rafe couldn't be dead too. His breathing was so slow and so deep that she could barely discern it. Delilah held her left hand in front of Rafe's face and his breath fogged the corner of her palm's display.

Had they given him something other than Ivanofor? He should have been motionless, but awake under the influence of the Ivanofor. Delilah watched him for a minute, confused, but Ted gestured with impatience.

"Move it."

She eased into the gap between the lip of the open drawer and the opposite panel of drawers. She laid the flat of her right hand upon Rafe's chest and felt the slow thunder of his heart. The pulse was stronger than she'd expected, which reassured her. She spread out her hand, increasing the contact between them.

Delilah wished he'd open his eyes and look at her, the way he'd looked at her in the chapel. She glanced at the image of him on the lip of the drawer, and felt a twinge of that angelfire. She rubbed her forehead with her other fingertip and the spark grew in intensity. Leaning closer, willing the vision to come, she bent over Rafe.

She smelled him, the scent of soap mingled with his own clean scent. She felt the smooth heat of his skin, the sheer strength and vitality of him, and the tingle of angelfire grew in her thoughts.

Delilah bent and kissed Rafe's cheek, wanting him to awaken, wanting him to be whole and free again. She touched her lips to his, a chaste kiss befitting a Daughter of the Light of the Republic, and whispered his name. His mouth didn't move in response to her caress.

Delilah was afraid, afraid that someone else had paid the price for her gift, afraid that she would fail and betray those sacrifices. Would the angels continue to favor her if their own emissaries kept dying in trying to help Delilah?

She couldn't imagine the world without Rafe.

She couldn't imagine her world without Rafe.

She brushed her lips across his, willing him to wakefulness. "I love you," she murmured, doubting that he could hear her but hoping it was so.

His eyes flew abruptly open. His gaze blazed into hers, a vehement blue that sent a jolt through her. She recognized that he was fully awake but had been disguising his state.

Joy leapt through her veins, but she struggled to hide his secret.

More important, the fire in his eyes jolted through her thoughts, igniting the angelfire in her mind. She kept her head low, hiding Rafe's face from Ted, and stared into his eyes. She felt the light grow whiter and brighter, heard the chorus of the angels and their demand to be heard.

They had come to her.

She could save Rafe.

Exultant and filled with their power, Delilah straightened and pivoted to face Ted. She noticed that Rafe had closed his eyes as soon as she lifted her lips from his.

Then the tingle of electricity passed through her, driving

all else from her thoughts. She felt the power of the angels claiming her body, every sinew humming along with their song. It was joyous and exhilarating and Delilah knew she was fulfilling her own destiny in surrendering to their summons. She felt as if sparks were flying from her fingers as she met the doubt in Ted's gaze. She knew he would soon be convinced of her power.

She opened her mouth and the prophecy of the angels spilled from her lips.

> *Compassion alone can halt the loss*
> *of the world to fatal chaos*
> *Wickedness is fed by selfish schemes*
> *But love defeats evil's dark dreams.*
> *Within each of us lies the power*
> *To turn the tide in this dark hour.*
> *Love your enemy has oft been writ*
> *It's past time to live that edict.*

"How trite," a man said behind her.

Delilah spun to find the man who haunted her nightmares standing in the open door of the cargo car. Rhys ibn Ali pointed his laze directly at her and grinned. "Nothing like a little more bounty. Shall we split the cred, Ted?"

Delilah spun to look at Ted in horror. He was not surprised.

"We all have our price, kid," he said with a shrug, his tone unapologetic.

Delilah sputtered in outrage. "You lied to me!"

"Pretty much." Ted smiled. "Do yourself a favor and go down easy. This doesn't have to be ugly."

Delilah had no intention of doing any such thing. There were only two ways out of the cargo car, and one man blocked each access. She was cornered, without a lot of room to maneuver.

"What do you think, Ted? A hundred milligrams of Ivanofor?" Rhys asked lightly.

"Let's go with a bit more," Ted mused as he filled the syringe. "She could use a good sleep." He held the loaded syringe aloft. Its contents shone in the half-light as he looked at Delilah expectantly.

"I thought you were an idealist."

"Maybe I got over that." Ted took a step closer.

Rhys grinned at Delilah as he moved closer, so confident in his scheme that she wanted to injure him. "You want the pod above lover boy? Just for old time's sake?"

Delilah leapt toward Rhys and away from the Ivanofor. Rhys stumbled backward, surprised by her choice. He shot at her feet, but Delilah went for his eyes.

"This is for Rachel," she whispered. He swore and stumbled backward as she dug her nails into his face.

"Hurry!" Rhys shouted and Delilah knew he was supposed to take her down alive.

She'd just have to inflict as much damage as possible before they sedated her. Her nails dragged down Rhys' face, drawing blood.

He dropped his laze and it clattered on the floor of the train. She had no chance to go after it because he slapped her face hard. Delilah's head snapped to one side, but she went after him again.

Ted made to kick drawer number sixteen closed again so he could move closer but his foot never connected.

IT WAS time.

Rafe moved like lightning. He would either stop them from capturing Delilah or die trying.

He leapt to his feet and attacked the tattooed man.

The burly man lost his balance in his shock, but Rafe gave him no time to recover. He decked him, the man faltered and his head slammed into the steel drawer opposite. Rafe snatched the syringe, then jabbed it into the other man's belly.

The tattooed man moaned as Rafe emptied the syringe. It probably didn't contain enough sedative to knock him out completely, but it would slow him down.

Rafe punched him again, then tripped him so that he fell

into drawer number sixteen. The tattooed man landed heavily, his weight making the mechanism of the drawer clang.

"Hey! You can't do that . . ." he protested, the drug already slowing his speech. "You shouldn't do that . . ."

"Watch," Rafe said and kicked the door shut. The lock clicked, the insulation on the drawer muting the man's struggles.

Rafe looked up to find Rhys holding Delilah before himself like a shield. He was backing toward the door. Delilah bit him and kicked him, but he made steady progress.

Rafe picked up the fallen laze, checking its load. It was fully charged.

The dogs snarled as Rhys came close to the kennel and Rafe had an idea. One brindle dog put its muzzle between the bars to snap at Rhys, its lack of affection for the shade hunter more than clear.

"Shaddup, mutt," Rhys snarled, taking another step back. "You can't shoot me without hitting her," he said to Rafe, his tone taunting.

"You sure?" Rafe asked calmly, then lifted the laze. He saw Delilah's eyes widen, and she went completely still. Rhys paled and held her a little higher in front of him.

The angle wasn't the best and Rafe didn't trust Rhys not to move in the last second.

After Rafe had aimed and fired.

Rafe smiled, knowing his confidence would disconcert the shade hunter. "Is it legal to use a shade as a shield?" he mused. "I'd think that would count as damaging federal property."

"It counts as self-defense." Rhys took another step back.

He was just in front of the kennel.

Perfect.

"Let's see if it works," Rafe suggested, his tone amiable. He sighted the laze, then in the last second, changed his aim.

Rhys jumped as the blaze went straight past his shoulder. Rafe shot the lock off the kennel. The animals retreated from the light and heat. Rafe pinched off another pair of shots, incinerating the hinges, and the kennel door fell onto the floor.

The dog with the brindle coat that had snapped at Rhys was the first one to jump out of the kennel.

It went straight for Rhys. He flung Delilah at them, but she ducked.

The dogs went right over her.

The shade hunter swore as the dog leapt on him. He stumbled over the fallen kennel door in his haste to avoid the attacking dog.

Delilah ran toward Rafe.

Rafe had a clear shot.

He sighted again and fired. He got Rhys right in the chest and the shade hunter fell with a shout. Rafe would have fired again, but the dogs had blocked his shot. Since they'd not injured Delilah, he was inclined to repay them in kind.

He was glad when the brindle hound ripped out Rhys' throat.

Delilah averted her face from the sight and ran to his side. Rafe caught her close, glad she wasn't injured.

"Okay?" Rafe asked quietly, retreating to the back of the cargo car.

"Okay enough."

Rafe was surprised to find her alone. He'd been sure that the boy would track her down and help her. "Where's Ferris? Didn't he find you?"

Delilah frowned, then leaned her brow on Rafe's chest. "She took him."

"Who?"

"The wraith," she murmured.

Rafe was alarmed. "As a hostage?"

"I don't think so. She incinerated his palm and bit out his identification bead. He passed out and she took him, saying he was theirs now." Delilah shuddered and Rafe closed his arms more tightly around her. "I hope he's okay."

Rafe wondered whether there was a way to be sure, but knew he had more immediate concerns. "At least you're all right," he whispered to Delilah.

She pressed her lips to his throat, her kiss the only answer he needed, just as the train changed sidings.

Rafe braced his feet against the floor. The train dropped

then, dipping down with alarming speed. It began making more noise on the tracks. It rocked more vehemently, turning sharply at intervals. Rafe and Delilah looked around, but without windows, there was nothing to be seen.

"Chicago," Delilah whispered. She took a deep breath. "The research labs of the Society of Nuclear Darwinists."

"Out of the frying pan and into the fire," Rafe murmured. His palm pinged. He glanced down at it with some irritation, then read the incoming message.

It was another message from out of the blue, but one that was shorter and more blunt than usual:

WHERE ARE YOU?

This time, there was a datatrail allowing him to reply.

"We need a map of the netherzones of Chicago," Delilah said, reading his display. "And a way out of the Society's labs."

"You sound as if you have a destination in mind." Rafe watched her, intrigued by her animation and sense of purpose.

"I do. We're going to find Reverend Billie Jo Estevez."

"How do you know she's even in Chicago?" Rafe asked, knowing he had to be the voice of skepticism. If they got into worse trouble, they might not escape. "And if so, how do we find her? It's a big city and if we manage to get out of the labs, we'll be hunted. It's probably inevitable that we trip an alarm or two."

Delilah looked momentarily defeated.

Rafe nudged her. "You're the one who likes better plans. Let's make one. Tell me what you know."

Delilah frowned with concentration. "I saw a helicopter heading toward the city. It wasn't close enough to be sure, but it might be hers."

"If so, she's probably making an appearance somewhere." Rafe queried his palm, while Delilah did the same. His, which was a faster model, came up with the answer first. "You're right. She's scheduled to appear at the candidates' debate to-night and make an endorsement at the end."

"That palm spam. Maximilian Blackstone and Morris Van Buren are going to debate tonight." Delilah clutched his arm. "Wherever it is, we have to go there."

"We?"

She grinned at him and his heart skipped. She was almost luminous after her vision, the angelfire clinging to her fea-tures and giving her an otherworldly animation. "How could I go straight into danger without my guardian angel?"

Rafe exhaled, realizing that the completion of his mission would mean leaving Delilah. He didn't want to think about that, especially as the end must be close. "You're going to get us killed with this plan."

She poked his shoulder. "I thought you were going to make me Oracle or die trying."

Rafe nodded ruefully. "And I'm not dead yet. But are you sure about the candidates' debate?"

"We need witnesses, lots of them, too many to be easily silenced. That means a big event on vidcast." Her eyes shone. "I think she'll endorse me."

"Well, you're the one with second sight."

Her quick smile made his heart skip. "We have to get there, Rafe. We have to get out of here."

Rafe was irritated that the car had no windows. The train was still moving, but had slowed down, as if shunting into its final destination. "If the labs are underground, they must feed into the netherzones."

"But we need help getting through the labyrinth. We don't have much time."

They both looked in unison at his palm.

"We'll have to trust them," Rafe murmured, disliking how little information he had.

"They're on the side of the angels," Delilah insisted. "Your side. Answer it."

Rafe exhaled, then punched the request into his palm. He received a reply so quickly that they both jumped.

Open your audio. Lilia will guide you out.

"Lilia," Delilah breathed. "I knew she was helping us."

Rafe typed quickly, telling his unseen helper to ditto the aud to Sonja Andresson. "Set up your palm," he said to Delilah. "You're going to talk to your mom."

Delilah blinked back her tears of anticipation as she followed Rafe's instructions. She put her left palm to her ear and Rafe did the same. The shine of her eyes when the woman's matter-of-fact voice came through the audio made him smile.

"Watch your ass in the train station," Lil said. "It's all automated and thick with sensors. What car are you on?"

"Cargo," Delilah said. "It's the last one. We have to get to the Ernest Sinclair Memorial Arena in time for the debate."

"Not there," Lilia argued.

Delilah spoke firmly. "Yes, there." She paused and swallowed, her gaze locking with Rafe's. "Please, Mom."

They both heard the woman's sharp intake of breath. "Call me Lil," she said, her words hoarse. "Otherwise you'll throw my game. Let's get your asses out of there before we get sentimental."

Delilah grinned.

"You're sure about the debate?"

"Positive," Delilah said.

"Okay," Lil said. "When the door unseals, you're going to look for the platform number. I need to know exactly where you are."

Before she could say more, the train screeched to a halt, jerking one last time before it stopped. The door at the far end of the car opened then, one man leaning around the lip. "Move it, Rhys, we're here already—"

He fell silent at the sight of Rhys' body, his gaze shifting to Delilah and Rafe.

"Hey!" he had time to shout before the dogs lunged at him.

The door at their end unsealed and Rafe pushed Delilah out of the car. "They know about us," Delilah said as the alarm began to resonate throughout the train station. A red light began to flick regularly and a low drone of warning sounded from deeper within the labs.

"I would never have guessed," Lilia said wryly. "Run straight down the tracks behind you and take the first siding to the right. And I mean *run*!"

REVEREND BILLIE JO Estevez sat in her assigned dressing room at the Ernest Sinclair Memorial Arena and watched the vid on her palm again. The rogue signal had come directly to her, circumnavigating all of her firewalls and filters with startling ease. She had almost shut down the signal when it fed straight to her display, but then she'd seen something that had stopped her.

Someone.

That girl with the kiss on her forehead. She kissed a man who laid in a stainless steel drawer, then had a vision, right there. A shade hunter who looked familiar tried to harvest her, the person uploading the vid seemed to be a part of that plan, but the subsequent action had the uploader locked in the drawer.

He whispered "Ivanofor," under his breath, his words slow and slurring, then said no more. The display was black.

There was a sound of laze fire, barking dogs, the regular click clack of a train on tracks.

Then silence.

The reverend replayed the vid one more time.

That girl had been a shade at the Citadel.

She had also starred in the vision uploaded to the reverend earlier, the one with the shaky vid that had occurred in the forest. That one had almost been lost behind the firewall, but the sender's name had caught the reverend's eye.

Raphael. Not just the name of an angel, but that of an archangel, one with the power to heal both man and mankind. The reverend was seldom whimsical but she had felt a compulsion to open that e-mail when her filters would have preferred she didn't.

It had contained vid of the young woman's second vision.

Then she had come to the rally, but had run before the reverend could talk to her.

Now this, a vid from a source so well disguised that the reverend couldn't have guessed who had sent it to her.

But she was glad they had.

The vid was shaky, obviously captured by a palm and done surreptitiously so that none of the players were aware of it. The aud was perfect, but the vid left much to be desired. A single glimpse of the young woman, though, was all that the reverend needed.

It was *her*.

Her hair was growing in. It had to be an inch long and dark all over her head, showing an unnatural rate of growth. And she had that mark on her forehead, the one that looked like a kiss burned into her skin.

The reverend was struck by her similarity to Lilia Desjardins, the evasive shade hunter who had captured the angels Armaros and Baraqiel. The young woman's vitality made her almost radiant, and the reverend couldn't deny her own impulse to believe that this was the true Oracle.

She recalled Teresa's hiss of hatred and was troubled anew by the lack of compassion in the selected Oracle.

There was truth in this young woman's visions.

But where was she?

The reverend reviewed the vid slowly, replaying it and freezing the images that showed the surroundings of the pair. They were in a train car, a cargo car of some kind. The reverend eyed the long drawers and realized what the cargo was. She considered the expense of stainless steel, the presence of the shade hunter she'd seen before, and knew.

The Society of Nuclear Darwinists had harvested the young woman and her companion. There was a link at the end of the vid, one that she hadn't noticed before. She opened it and her eyes widened.

It was an addendum to an old research protocol. It included a copy of her own vidcast from the Citadel, the incredible sequence of the shade's vision. The addendum told her precisely what the Society would do with this young woman whom the reverend believed was the true Oracle.

Billie Jo wasn't going to let that happen.

She checked the guest list and saw the one name she wanted to find. Ernestine Sinclair, the president of the Society of Nuclear Darwinists, was also scheduled to attend the debate and publicly endorse a candidate at the end.

If she waited until the end of the festivities, it might be too late. She heard a tone, a five-minute warning of her entry on the stage, followed by a rap on her door. She expected the assistant who did her makeup and called for him to enter, her thoughts consumed with strategy.

Somehow during the debate, the reverend would have a quiet word with Ernestine Sinclair. If necessary, she'd buy the young woman with the kiss on her brow.

The Oracle had to survive.

Society of Nuclear Darwinists Internal Memo
Addendum to *Research Proposal 14249*
Submitted by Dr. Paul Cosmopolous

THIS RESEARCH project did not result in any conclusive <u>conclusions</u> in a promising area of study and third-eye inquiries have been abandoned for several years. One weakness noted in the initial protocol was that there was little data of the proven foresight of the subjects tested. The shades were selected on the basis of their having the third eye.

Given developments in recent days and the extraordinary performances by the nameless shade from the Citadel of the Daughters of the Light of the Republic, it is proposed that we begin again, this time with shades proven to have some foresight. <u><vid link></u> The shade in question is a prime candidate for this research, which will conclude with a brain dissection as done in the previous study. Even a single shade's results may be used reasonably for comparative purposes with the body of data already collected.

This study would also be economical for the Society to pursue in these times of fiscal restraint. All equipment has already been acquired and graduate students from the Institute for Radiation Studies could, as previously, complete the lab work as part of their studies. All that is required is that the shade in question be harvested alive and delivered to the Society's labs in Chicago.

Submitted February 15, 2100
Approved by Ernestine Sinclair, February 15, 2100

THE TUNNELS of the Chicago netherzone were low and wide, each with at least one pair of train tracks running through them. The Society had covered the walls in white tiles and every sound was magnified as it bounced off the hard surface. Rafe and Delilah both used their palms for light when they needed to tell Lilia where they were, but otherwise ran in a darkness filled with odd reflections.

Delilah didn't like it. She still felt buried alive, confined and forgotten. She knew that she and Rafe could disappear in this maze of corridors and never be heard of in the Republic again. She knew that their existences could be erased as easily as their lives.

The prospect terrified her.

At intervals, Delilah heard the bubble of liquids in labs, the hiss of climate control, the clang of steel. Lilia led them through the labyrinth, ensuring that they avoided the major locus of activity, but the pervasive smell of blood and formaldehyde made Delilah keenly aware of the risk they faced.

They saw no shades, but they heard them moaning.

Mostly they heard the sounds of pursuit and the regular pulse of alarms. They dodged electronic eyes and motion detectors, slipping over barriers and under arches as silently as possible. They ran down tunnels and dodged trains and ducked down corridors that looked as if they hadn't been used in years.

It smelled wet to Delilah and she realized that Chicago was beside a lake. If the tunnels were underground, did they go under the lake? She didn't want to think about being buried that deeply.

"Almost there," Lilia said as they took the turn she indicated.

"Stairs!" Delilah breathed in relief.

"That's it," Lilia said. "That's the way out."

Both Rafe and Delilah ran faster, with their goal in sight. Beyond the stairs, there was a steel door, so this tunnel had no other escape.

They were halfway down the length of the tunnel when the rumble started.

Delilah clutched Rafe's hand. They ran faster, fearful of what was happening, then Rafe pointed.

"There's a door!"

A steel door descended from the top of the tunnel. It was before the stairs, and would lock them into a tunnel with no escape. Rafe swore and ran faster, but Delilah feared it was too far.

The door fell like a guillotine, slamming into the bed of the tunnel so hard that Delilah's teeth were jangled.

Rafe was running his hands over the door in desperation. It was a sheer wall of metal, buttressed with bolts and bands of steel. It was smooth and offered no place to get a grip.

"Wrong way," Rafe said. Rafe spun and let his palm illuminate the steel door. Lil swore softly at the other end of the connection and Delilah understood that the door hadn't been there before.

"Go back to the last junction," Lil said. "I can get you out there." Delilah heard the desperation in her mother's voice and knew it was a harder choice.

That was why Lilia had sent them this way first.

Before they could move, there was beep that made Delilah catch her breath. She and Rafe froze, staring back into the darkness.

The beep settled into a repeating rhythm, becoming more frequent. There were footsteps in the tunnel behind them, the sound of someone making steady progress closer.

More than one someone.

Delilah put her palm to her ear. "Trapped," she tapped into her palm. The reply was instant.

1. **Sensor panel waist level, either left or right.**
2. **Lock opposite bottom corner.**
3. **Shoot them out.**
4. **Run like hell.**

Rafe and Delilah exchanged a look. Delilah knew she wasn't the only one aware that the laze would eliminate any doubt of their presence. But then, they were already trapped in a dead end.

It was their one chance.

The footsteps sounded louder, then Rafe winced. He raised his laze and fired at the panel on the left side. Sparks flew, then the sensor shorted with a thunk.

Someone shouted and started to run toward them.

Rafe incinerated the opposite corner, cooking out the lock. It failed with an audible click. Delilah was on her knees, burning her hands as she pushed up the door. It was heavy and hot, and she had a hard time getting a grip on it.

Rafe bent and put one hand where hers were. He thrust his laze at her, then used both hands to coax the door up a few inches. Delilah aimed the laze into the shadows behind them. She could hear their pursuers but not see them. The door creaked, then rose another increment. Its weight was intended to make it fall back into place automatically and Rafe gritted his teeth as he held it up. Delilah could see the strain in his muscles.

"Go!" Rafe said and Delilah rolled beneath the door.

She grabbed the door from the other side, hoping she could hold its weight. Rafe, though, kept one hand braced against it as he moved quickly beneath it.

As soon as he was on the other side, they both let go and the door fell with a resonant thud.

There was a shout from the other side, and a curse as someone tried to use the access panel. The door moved and Delilah saw a man's fingertips appear beneath it. She leapt for the stairs, looking back when she realized that Rafe wasn't immediately behind her.

He was considering the steel door that was another twenty feet along the corridor. This door had a seam in the middle and hinges so that it would open inward.

Delilah hissed at Rafe, urging him to hurry. All their pursuers had to do was get a laze under the door to hurt Rafe. The door lifted again and this time a brace was slid beneath it.

"Rafe!" Delilah mouthed in fear.

Rafe put his hand on the locked pair of steel doors and listened, then he smiled. He winked at her, even as her fear grew, then shot out the lock. The men on the far side of the disabled door shouted, but Rafe lunged for the base of the stairs, grinning with triumph.

Then Delilah knew why.

There was a gurgle and an ominous rumble. She stared at him and the doors, then followed him up the stairs.

Lake Michigan suddenly shoved open the pair of doors. A torrent of dark water slammed against the other door, roiling furiously as it was funneled beneath it and splashing up the stairs.

Delilah and Rafe ran for the summit as the water churned beneath them. The men shouted once, then Delilah heard no more.

At the top of the stairs, she saw a glimmer of angelfire limning the edge of the steps. The light came from above, beckoning her onward, and she instinctively hurried toward the angels and their light.

They were back.

It was only when she was on the street that she wondered whether they'd come to help her or to collect Rafe.

XX

RAFE SHIVERED as they climbed toward the street. The air was cold, and he was still without a shirt.

He supposed he wouldn't have to endure physical discomfort for long, not with that angelfire glimmering in the cracks.

There was no possibility of slowing down though. Delilah was far from being installed as Oracle, and every moment counted.

Even if every step took him closer to his own departure.

The stairs led to a locked grate that faced a tattoo parlor, its neon light blinking red in the darkness. Delilah seemed to catch her breath at the sight, then she jiggled the gate.

"Locked," she muttered in frustration.

"Stand back." Rafe shot the lock, noting that the charge on his laze was becoming dangerously low. If nothing else, he'd go down fighting. He kicked the damaged gate and it swung open.

They crossed the threshold as one.

"We're on the street," Delilah said into her palm. "Across from the tattoo place with the red—"

"I know exactly where you are," Lilia said, her relief evident in her voice. "My old haunt. Head right."

Delilah turned to do her mother's bidding, then a plaintive cry filled the air. Rafe glanced left and saw that they had emerged near the pleasure fringe.

And that there was a gate locked across the street access. The pleasure fringe behind was darkened and dead, except for the cluster of brightly dressed shades gripping the gate.

They stood in silence, suffering but not expecting to be helped. They would stand there, waiting for compassion that would never come, until they died.

No one would acknowledge them even then.

The injustice of it was almost enough to destroy Rafe's faith in the innate goodness of mankind.

"Give me your laze," Delilah said abruptly. He surrendered it to her, trusting her resolve. She aimed it toward the gate, her hand shaking under its weight. She braced one hand with the other and sighted it.

The shades looked momentarily alarmed and more than a few of them eased backward.

"Move away from the lock!" Delilah cried. As soon as they did, she fired at the gate.

Her aim could have been better, but Rafe was proud of her all the same. The lock broke and fell, the shades eying it with uncertainty.

"Push the gate open!" Delilah shouted. "Be free!"

One shade pushed tentatively on the metal. The others looked around, expecting a trick. There was a creak of metal on metal as the gate was pushed open.

They hesitated again, then the one who had pushed the gate first stepped over the line. When nothing dire befell him, the other shades followed. Rafe saw optimism flicker on their faces, perhaps for the first time, and he was proud of Delilah.

This Oracle would make change in the Republic.

"We're going to the debate!" Delilah cried. "Come and be acknowledged!"

The shades hesitated before following her.

Rafe felt doubt. He understood Delilah's desire to liberate the shades and believed that she was right, but these individuals bore the scars of their own histories. Few would heal as quickly as Delilah had done and some would never achieve her confidence. Simply unlocking their shackles would not be enough—they needed more help than that.

Who would give it to them?

Who would give them the time and the tools to heal?

He had a sense that the journey to a compassionate Republic was only beginning and that the hardest length of the road was still ahead. He didn't express his fear, for Delilah was jubilant and he loved how her newfound confidence had transformed her. She had that radiant smile again, that one that reminded Rafe of angelic joy.

Of the love for all beings he had once felt throughout his entire being.

"What are you doing?" he asked as she returned his laze and she laughed. The sound of her laughter made his heart skip a beat.

"The angels don't go into the darkness to heal, so I'll bring the darkness to them." She was confident, vivacious, and so beautiful that he couldn't resist her. He caught her close and kissed her, much to the appreciation of the shades. They were gaining confidence, following their champion more closely.

"Angelfire," she whispered, when he lifted his lips from hers. Her gaze slipped over him as she sobered. "You're leaving, aren't you?"

"I have to once my mission is done," he admitted, not liking that truth any more than she did.

She loved him.

He loved her.

Was it possible to stay?

Her eyes flashed and she caught the back of his neck in her hand. She pulled him closer and kissed him with all the urgency and passion that he felt. When she broke their kiss, he tasted a reluctance that echoed his own, and saw her own regret that things were as they were.

Then she turned and headed right, just as her mother had demanded. He understood that she wouldn't ask him to stay, that she wouldn't ask him to deny his own nature just to be with her.

But Rafe wondered whether it was possible.

The angelfire glimmered along the curbs and he knew exactly whom to ask. He caught her hand in his and they ran together toward their fate, Rafe shooting out every gate locked over the netherzones that he could find. The shades ran behind them, their numbers surging with every block.

And the angelfire burned brighter with every step.

LILIA AND Montgomery went to the town square of Nouveau Mont Royal, where a large group of citizens had gathered to watch the live vidcast of the presidential candidates' debate. It was cold enough to make Lilia's breath catch in her chest, but she didn't want to go back to their unit.

She didn't even want to be inside a restaurant or caffeine stop.

She wanted the ability to get lost in a crowd. Lilia wasn't at all confident of how things would work out. She was terrified for Delilah, fearful that stepping out of the shadows would only condemn her daughter to the darkness again.

Or worse.

Montgomery stood silently behind Lilia, his arms around her waist. He was warm, as always, and she welcomed his heat at her back. She also liked his calm manner, knowing that it was fed by his confidence that all would work out in the end.

Lilia had a hard time matching that conviction.

The pseudoskin was a good insulating layer and she was glad to have it on. She was also glad that they were both packing lazes. She found herself checking the crowd as they waited for the vidcast, looking for familiar faces. She sought Joachim, even knowing she wouldn't find him, and the other shades from the circus. She looked for Armaros and Baraqiel, even though she was equally certain that they were gone.

She certainly kept an eye on the cops.

The crowd milled, stamping their feet, their breath hanging white in the cold air. The vid-screen illuminated finally and there was a cheer from the citizens gathered there.

The candidates were introduced, each man looking wealthy and confident of his success. Van Buren was older than Max—or less well maintained—and he looked shifty to Lilia. She kept that observation to herself, as well as the conviction that Max was a snake-oil salesman made good.

One never knew who was listening, even on the Frontier, even in a crowd.

"The eyes of the Republic are everywhere," Montgomery said softly into her ear and she knew he was reminding her.

"Prudent, that's me," she whispered and felt his chuckle.

The celebrities gathered to ask questions and make their endorsements at the end of the vidcast were presented in order. Lilia stifled a hiss as Ernestine Sinclair strode across the stage, representing the Society of Nuclear Darwinists, to a tepid cheer. She was followed by Clive MacGillian, the editor-in-chief of the *Republican Record*. He was bearded and moved with less verve, and was someone Lilia had never seen live before.

"I didn't think he really existed," she whispered.

"Maybe he doesn't," Montgomery replied.

It was true. Who would have known if a substitute had been sent in for a man whose face wasn't well known?

The chief of police for Chicago was introduced, and his presence was greeted with a louder cheer. He was followed by the new Daughter Superior for the Daughters of the Light of the Republic, one Gertrude von Maier. She was solemn, her face lined and her manner joyless. Finally, the Reverend Billie Jo Estevez was presented. She bounded onto the stage, moving with surprising ease for her majestic size, and lifted her hands to the crowd.

They responded—both on site and remotely—with a resounding cheer. She gestured to the wings and the acolyte chosen by the Daughters to be Oracle appeared, looking shy and fragile.

The applause faded and the Daughter Superior fell to her knees, worshipping at the feet of the supposed Oracle. Ernestine examined her nails, MacGillian made a note on his palm, and the police chief was impassive.

"All the usual suspects," Lilia murmured.

It appeared that MacGillian was intended to be the master of ceremonies, because he stepped forward with purpose, but the reverend didn't surrender the spotlight. Lilia found herself smiling at the reverend's familiar autocratic manner.

She strode to the front of the stage, practically pushing MacGillian aside, and addressed the crowd. "You have heard the rhetoric and examined the party platforms. You have studied the histories of these men, both their personal and public records, but none of that tells you how they will lead the Republic. I want to know about their faith. I want to know what they believe. And so, I will ask the first question."

The reverend spun, her gown spiraling and floating, in an effect that had to have been calculated.

She addressed the candidates, gesturing to Teresa. "Here is the chosen Oracle, selected by the Daughters of the Light of the Republic to be the helpmate of the next elected president. In recent years, the Oracle and her role have lost authority in the Republic. Tell me if you support the Oracle, and tell me why."

Max went for the spotlight first, which Lilia thought was predictable. "The Oracle is an honorable tradition," he said, his voice resonant. "The Oracle is emblematic of the bond between church and state that makes the Republic as great as it is, and the Oracle's position must be secured for the future . . ."

"He talks with conviction but says nothing," Lilia muttered. "The man could beguile a serpent."

"Like he beguiled you?" Montgomery's question was soft. "Did he lead you into temptation?"

"Yes, but it was my own fault what choices I made once I got there. I just don't want Delilah to pay for my sins." She tipped her head to look up at him. "It was a temporary spell, Montgomery. I'm older and wiser now."

His smile was quick. "I know."

There was nothing that could silence Max when he had an audience, even less that could intervene when he was working for his own ambition. Lilia checked her palm for the time and sighed, wishing that the reverend would show some of her characteristic dominance.

But it wasn't the reverend who drowned out Max.

There was a dizzying panorama of the crowd as the image-snatchers spun to focus on a new arrival. A young woman strode down the center aisle, heading from the back of the stadium directly for the stage. Rafe marched beside her, half naked, golden and determined.

A host of shades trailed behind the pair, filling the aisle with their quiet presence, their haunted eyes making Lilia's mouth go dry.

The crowd fell silent, shocked by the sight.

Delilah smiled, completely confident of her place in the festivities. She wore a black tank top and black baggy pants, both of which only made her look more pale and frail to Lilia. Her hair had grown a remarkable amount, and bristled darkly around her face. One image-snatcher focused tightly on her face, tossing the image to the vid-screens in Nouveau Mont Royal as well as the rest of the Republic.

In the silence of the Chicago stadium, Lilia thought a person might hear a pin drop.

What she heard was Max's quick intake of breath. "Lilia," he whispered, his horror clear.

"If he hurts her, I'll kill him," Lilia whispered to Montgomery.

He tightened his arms around her and said the only words that could have made her smile. "Not if I get to him first." The view widened, zeroing in on the shades and the striking sight of Rafe.

His customary smile was notably absent.

"Although," Montgomery noted, "it looks as if Rafe will get to him first."

Lilia held tightly to him, her gaze locked on the screen.

DELILAH PUSHED through the doors to the stadium, energized by the prospect of success. She was aware of the company of shades behind her, the tide that had been loosed from the shadows and trailed her steps. She was aware of Rafe striding right beside her, his laze at the ready. She halfway thought that the sight of his scarred back had persuaded the shades to trust her.

And follow.

The new arrivals surged down the aisles, moving like a quiet tide toward the stage, a tide that carried Delilah closer to her destiny. The crowd assembled for the debate stared in silence. Van Buren frowned and Blackstone stared at her as if he'd seen a ghost.

Delilah didn't care.

The Reverend Billie Jo was the first to recover from the shock of Delilah's appearance. She smiled at Delilah. "You!" she said and Delilah savored her acknowledgment. Then the reverend held her hands high in the air and shouted, "Hallelujah!"

Delilah reached the edge of the stage as confusion began to erupt behind her. The crowd began to murmur, but the shades weren't violent.

They'd spent their lives learning to wait for whatever they were given and to be grateful for it.

She had to end their suffering.

She had to use her experience to speak as one of them, to speak for them. Delilah felt the tingle of an approaching vision and rubbed her forehead, drawing it closer. That one was coming in this moment was the best possibility. She'd prove her gift again to the observers.

There were too many witnesses here for her truth to be silenced.

Rafe put his laze in its holster, then bent. He locked his hands together, offering her a foothold to get on the stage.

"Wish me luck," she whispered as she put her foot in his hand.

"You don't need it," he said with complete confidence. "You're the Oracle and in moments, everyone will know it."

Their gazes met for an electric moment and Delilah's heart clenched with the realization that this might be their last exchange. There was so much she wanted to say to him, so much she wanted to do with him, so much to share.

But she feared he'd be gone by the time she left the stage.

She intended to leave it as Oracle.

And there was no time to linger now. She touched his cheek

as he lifted her to the stage. He smiled and turned his head to kiss her palm.

"Go," he said and she knew to trust the command of those sent by the angels to help her.

She supposed that just having known Rafe should be good enough. She supposed that he had taught her to be bolder, to be assertive, to bring her dream to life.

She knew that wasn't enough, but it would have to do.

Delilah blinked back her tears and focused on the final challenge. She turned to face the crowd, feeling the light of the angels in her veins, and lifted her arms.

"My name is Delilah," she said. "I am the true Oracle."

Some of the crowd began to applaud, then the sound swept through the stadium. The applause rose to a crescendo, then fell into expectant silence.

"Prove it," said the Reverend Billie Jo Estevez, her tone revealing that she expected exactly that.

Delilah smiled. She rubbed her forehead, saw the light of angelfire, and heard the hum of bees. She felt the electrical charge of their presence fill her until her body seemed to shimmer.

Then she surrendered and let the angels tell the people what they needed to know.

DELILAH WAS radiant.

Rafe eased away from the stage, letting the people gather closer. They were fascinated with her, drawn to her magnetism, her truth. She appeared to be a conduit for angelfire, the brilliant light illuminating her and radiating from her fingertips.

The angelfire made her almost luminescent, standing as she did in her black pants and top, her hair cut short and her eyes blazing with passion. The mark of the angel's kiss on her forehead appeared to be blood red, and Rafe thought he could discern the sparkle of the *Sefer Raziel* in the very center of it.

Either way, Delilah gleamed. She raised her hands and

sparks flew from her fingertips, casting the light of angelfire over the rapt audience.

She could have been an angel, one who had chosen to walk the earth and mingle with humans.

The idea made Rafe smile.

There was pride in his smile too.

She had welcomed the reverend's challenge, he'd heard that truth in her voice, and knew she must have felt a vision coming close. She stood with her eyes closed, her radiance building, then abruptly threw back her head and spoke.

> *The silent are not always meek,*
> *And now the shadows begin to speak.*
> *Hidden does not mean forgotten;*
> *Darkness sees only lies begotten.*
> *Our debts cannot be left unpaid;*
> *Justice can no longer be waylaid.*
> *The time has come to right our wrongs.*
> *The time has come for angels' song."*

"Amen!" cried the reverend. She gazed over the crowd and Rafe wondered what she saw. He glanced back and saw thousands of shades filling the aisles of the stadium.

They had followed Delilah.

They stood silently, waiting to be acknowledged. As Delilah had said, they wouldn't always be silent. A woman beside him wiped away a tear and he knew that whomever she had been compelled to hide wasn't forgotten.

"The Oracle is the light that shines in the darkness," the reverend said. "What brighter light could we find in our times than the light of angelfire in the netherzones? Where else should we look for divine favor than in the darkest shadows?"

"Fugitive shade," hissed Teresa, the false Oracle.

This time, no one listened to her.

And no one took up her cry.

Perhaps because of the number of fugitive shades at hand, Rafe felt a ripple of unease in the crowd, but the shades weren't violent.

"And so it was that Saul was on the road to Damascus when he saw the divine light," the reverend said. "Just as we see the light among us on this great night. Saul tells of his conversion in the Acts of the Apostles: *'I saw a light in heaven, brighter than the sun, shining around me and my companions. When we had all fallen to the ground, I heard a voice saying to me "Saul, Saul, why do you persecute me?"'"*

She paused and surveyed the crowd. "*'Why do you persecute me?'* Why do we persecute those of our number for being as God made them to be? Why do we cast the weak into darkness, and turn aside from this gift of God's favor?" The crowd stirred, more than one glancing guiltily at the shades standing in the aisles.

The woman whom Rafe had seen wipe away a tear was openly weeping. She reached into the aisle and offered her hand to the closest shade.

That shade hesitated to touch her for a moment, then tentatively reached up and put his hand on hers. The woman smiled through her tears and locked her hand over the shade's, drawing him to her side. "What is hidden is not forgotten," she repeated fiercely. "What is stolen is not lost."

Rafe looked up to see that an image-snatcher had noted the exchange as well—it played repeatedly on one of the large vidscreens. Not everyone was persuaded though: there were skeptical expressions on faces all around Rafe.

The reverend's voice gained in volume. "For as God said to Paul, *'I will rescue you and your people, and open their eyes, so that they may turn from the darkness to light and from the power of Satan to God, so that they may receive forgiveness of sins and a place among those who are sanctified by faith in me.'*" She gestured to Delilah. "This woman brings the word of God among us. She speaks with the voice of the angels, and yet we spurn her message of compassion."

The reverend moved to stand beside Delilah, put one arm around her shoulder, and lifted her other hand to the crowd. "Did Luke not tell us of Zachariah's prophecy? That by the tender mercy of God, the dawn from on high would break upon us, to give light to those who sit in darkness and in the shadow of death, to guide our feet into the way of peace?" The reverend paused for effect. "Yea, verily, it is so written!"

"Amen!" replied the crowd, and the reverend smiled.

"Is it not written that the meek shall inherit the earth? Is it not said that the burden of our brother is not too much to bear?"

The crowd assented, their conviction growing.

"Is it not time to carry the burden of our fellows, to treat our fellows with kindness and repent of our ways?" the reverend cried.

The image-snatchers were capturing moments of union from throughout the stadium, norm after norm reaching out to a shade. The images of entwined hands spilled from the vidscreens in dizzying variety.

The reverend's voice boomed. "Is it not time to acknowledge that there is merit, that a jewel can be found in the dung heap?"

"Amen!" roared the crowd.

The reverend beamed. "It is time for change and this Oracle brings the good news to all of us. Join me in welcoming the beacon sent into our darkness." The applause began at the front of the stadium and spread like a ripple, growing in volume with a speed that amazed Rafe. The reverend had to bellow to be heard. "All hail the new Oracle of the Republic!"

Delilah smiled. The crowd roared approval, many rising to their feet as they applauded. The shades even began to clap and optimism lit more than one pale face.

President Van Buren looked uneasy with this show of fervor and several of the guests were making frantic notes. Maximilian Blackstone stared fixedly at Delilah. The Daughter Superior was clearly displeased.

And the Daughter's appointed Oracle was livid.

"No!" shouted Teresa, and flung herself at Delilah.

Rafe leapt for the stage, his laze at the ready.

But the angels were already intervening.

THE REVEREND couldn't believe her eyes.

The angels descended from the sky in brilliant fury, their

chorus drowning out the sound of the crowd. There were hundreds of them, their collective light so bright that she couldn't begin to count their number with any accuracy. Their radiance was blinding in its intensity.

The other guests cried out and fell to their knees before the angels' brilliant light. The Daughter Superior also dropped to her knees and shielded her eyes. The candidates were on their knees, heads bowed.

Delilah stood as straight as an arrow, her arms uplifted and her face tipped to the descending chorus. She had her eyes closed, her lashes thick on her cheeks, and that strange kiss on her forehead almost glowed. The angels' light slipped lovingly over her features, painting her with the radiance of their favor.

And Billie Jo knew she had chosen rightly in defending the Oracle.

The song of the angels was both wordless and beautiful beyond expectation. It filled the reverend's heart with a joy of forgotten innocence and power. It made her feel lighter and stronger, more potent and more optimistic.

She kept her arm around Delilah's shoulder, letting the angels see her alliance. Their light flowed over her and through her, casting illumination and purpose into every facet of her body, her life, and her memories.

She was so beguiled by the vibrancy that it took her a minute to realize that not everyone shared her experience.

Teresa was screaming.

The reverend turned, blinking in the light, and saw the false Oracle fall to her knees. One angel descended directly toward her, his light so bright that the reverend had to shield her eyes.

"Turn away," Delilah said and the two women turned away as one. The reverend heard the crowd gasp, she smelled burning flesh, and she knew the price of the angels' disapproval.

She felt the skin burning on her shoulder and the back of her neck and didn't dare to look. She certainly couldn't intervene.

When the brilliant light faded and Delilah turned, the reverend dared to follow suit. Delilah's skin was red, the kiss on her forehead even more crimson. She stared at the angels in adoration.

There was nothing left of Teresa but a pile of ash on the stage.

The angel who had shone so brightly just moments before blew and the ashes scattered. His smile was bemused when he turned to the crowd, his manner reminding the reverend of Armaros and Baraqiel. He let his light fade further and she recognized the extraordinary power that those two angels had held in check.

"Hallelujah," she whispered, awed and shaken by what she had seen.

The angel turned and smiled at her, his expression filling her heart with joy. He raised one hand to his mouth and blew her a kiss.

She felt it strike her brow, as surely as a hot slap. It burned momentarily, then she knew what had put that strange mark upon Delilah's brow.

An angel's kiss.

The angel rose from the stage, the features of his body dissolving into the light of the company of angels. They sang, their chorus rising to a jubilant crescendo. When their song halted, the crowd stared after them, rapt with wonder.

The angels rose steadily into the night sky, fading as they gained altitude. The crowd stared in silence until the light disappeared, then erupted into spontaneous applause.

The reverend knew what she had to do.

"You have seen the favor of the angels." The crowd cheered and hooted, compelling the reverend to shout. "You have witnessed the assistants of God and you know who they grace with their song."

"*Delilah,*" came the chant from the crowd. "*Delilah. Delilah.*"

The reverend turned to the candidates. "I asked you a question earlier," she reminded them.

Van Buren smiled. "I embrace the chance to consult with the Oracle Delilah, the light in the darkness."

The crowd roared approval.

"As do I," Blackstone said, smiling with his trademark charm. "For there is not a one of us who can argue with the choice of the angels." The crowd began to cheer, but Blackstone raised a finger. His presence was sufficient that they hushed at his command. "And may I be the first to suggest that it is past time for the Republic to reconsider not only the Sub Human Atomic Deviancy Evaluation, but the status of shades throughout the Republic. Good government requires forward thinking and the active pursuit of new solutions. It may be that the S.H.A.D.E. served the Republic in the past, but it is clear that the future demands change."

There was nothing that could be said after that. It wouldn't have been heard. The crowd was chanting Delilah's name, stamping and clapping and hooting. The only thing that silenced them was the appearance once more of the angels' fiery light.

RAFE RECOGNIZED that the victory achieved by the reverend was a precarious one. The candidates might have been compelled to endorse Delilah as Oracle, but neither liked the situation.

And the wraiths, Rafe knew, could always be bought.

He felt the ripple of unease that persisted among the citizens gathered and knew that the battle for the Oracle's endorsement had only truly begun. It was easy to imagine that either of the ruthless candidates could buy the wraiths again—and that the assassination of Delilah could be the result.

Lucifer was manifest in the world, Ferris had been captured by the wraiths, and Delilah's future was far from secure.

Rafe knew what he had to do.

He knew what he had to ask.

He wanted to finish what he had begun, regardless of the price.

He saw the light of the angels descending and wondered whether they would intervene again. He waited, not truly surprised that they targeted him.

It was time.

Once again, he felt that it had come too soon.

The angels surrounded him and Rafe closed his eyes against

the power of their radiance. He wasn't afraid of them anymore, just welcomed their brilliant familiarity. Their light touched his skin, caressing it and making his blood sing. He felt his mortal body respond to their presence, and heard their joyous song within his every sinew.

"Your quest is complete, Raphael. Congratulations." Rafe heard the low voice in his thoughts, and smiled at the serene confidence that filled every word. *"We have come to take you home."*

Home. Rafe had no desire to return to his former life and his former state. He didn't want to stand apart and observe. He wanted to make a difference. He wanted to make more of a difference than he already had.

There was no question of lying to the angels.

He answered in kind, in his thoughts, and hoped he was heard. *"Neither the Oracle or the* Sefer Raziel *are entirely safe."*

"No one is ever entirely safe, Raphael. We do what we can in this sphere. Come and be glad of all you have achieved."

"I don't think my quest is done," Rafe argued.

There was a moment of silence and Rafe sensed that the angel was exploring all of his motives. He had no secrets from those who had been his own kind, and let them see his love for Delilah.

"She is only one mortal, Raphael."

"I'll stay for this one mortal."

"Are you certain? There is no reprieve from this choice."

Rafe stood tall. *"I believe it's the only choice possible."*

He felt the angels' consternation as keenly as his own. He sensed that they conferred but he was no longer able to hear that rapid exchange of thoughts. He knew what he was surrendering, he knew that he was making his sacrifice permanent. He understood that he was trading immortality for death and pain and sensation.

And love.

He knew that the benefit of being with Delilah outweighed the cost.

"One last gift for you, then," the angel said and Rafe rec-

ognized the voice of the surgeon. *"Let us make your burden easier to bear."*

Rafe felt the angels' light become brighter and hotter, felt it press closer against him. He was enveloped in light, aware of the soft brush of a thousand feathers.

He cried out at the touch of the surgeon's hand on his back. The angelic caress smoothed from one shoulder to his waist, tracing a diagonal line. It seared his flesh, cauterizing and—Rafe knew—eliminating that old scar. He welcomed this pain, this agony that would remove his chance of being condemned to slavery.

The second touch was easier to bear. Rafe stood tall and raised his arms in triumph, recognizing the merit of the gift he was being given. He felt invigorated and strengthened by the angels' touch, powerful and potent.

"Thank you," he said in his thoughts and he felt the surrounding angels smile.

"Be blessed, Raphael. We shall miss you forever."

The light began to fade as the angels rose heavenward. Rafe heard the murmur of the crowd around him, smelled the scent of mortal bodies pressed together, and felt the heat of humanity. He opened his eyes and watched the angels disappear into the darkness of the sky overhead.

When they were gone, he looked at the stage, at Delilah.

There were tears on her face, the wetness shining in the spotlights. Disbelief filled the blue of her eyes, and he smiled to reassure her.

She laughed, then vaulted off the stage, running toward him at full speed. The crowd cheered and the reverend watched with a small smile. Rafe caught Delilah in his arms and swung her high, laughing at her enthusiasm.

"You stayed!"

"I stayed," he agreed, watching the joy light her features.

Her laughter was the only reward he needed.

XXI

LILIA AND Montgomery lingered downtown for hours. The streets were thronged with citizens, celebrating the endorsement of the Oracle. Many had put red lipstain marks on their foreheads in the shape of kisses, showing their support by mimicking the port wine stain on Delilah's brow.

It seemed that only Lilia and Montgomery weren't participating in the festivities. Lilia didn't understand why Montgomery didn't want to go home—or to celebrate—after all they had seen, but he was absorbed with his palm.

She supposed he was trying to find out from Tupperman about the new angelic arrival. He wasn't inclined to talk or answer her questions and she resigned herself to his mood.

She was too happy to quibble.

Delilah was alive!

Lilia watched the celebrants in the streets, her own heart singing that her daughter was safely in the custody of the Reverend Billie Jo Estevez. Lilia trusted the reverend, especially as the Oracle would be good for the tel-evangelist's vid ratings. Lilia yearned to see her daughter again, to touch her once again, but she had learned not to expect too much.

It should be enough to know that Delilah had survived.

Even if it wasn't quite.

Could she go south again, to the heart of the Republic, to see Delilah in New D.C.? Could she risk it? She couldn't ask Montgomery to risk his own life in so doing. Both of them would be prudent to remain on the Frontier, or even to follow

Lilia's mother into the wilderness, but Lilia's heart had never counselled prudence.

She wanted to hold her child.

Just once.

It was too much to hope for, and that tempered Lilia's happiness with her daughter's fate. Joachim and the circus had disappeared, which also was a sobering development.

She pushed to her feet, impatient with the direction of her thoughts. "I'm cold, Montgomery. Let's go home already."

He glanced up but didn't move, the unexpected mischief in his dark gaze making her heart leap. "Not yet, Lil."

"It's late and I'm tired and . . ."

"And you'll miss the best part if you leave."

She eyed him in confusion, noting the new curve at the corner of his mouth. His legs were outstretched and crossed at the ankles, his dark collar turned up, his eyes gleaming. He was motionless and watchful as always, but looked like a man with a secret.

That mysterious smile made her curious.

She found herself smiling in anticipation of whatever was giving him such pleasure, her mood lightening just with the promise of his smile. "What's the best part? I thought that was what would happen at home."

Montgomery's smile flashed, then he glanced skyward.

Lilia didn't know why. She looked. She listened. She turned to him again, intending to ask, then she heard the distinctive chop of a helicopter rotor in the distance.

There couldn't be two helicopters airborne in the Republic on this night of nights. She held the sparkle of Montgomery's gaze and knew why they had been waiting, what he had been arranging with his palm.

She raised a hand to her mouth, astonished. "You did it."

"I made a deal," he admitted. "Town square. Go, Lil."

She flung herself at him, covering his face in kisses so that he chuckled. He stood and straightened, kissing her thoroughly, then put his hands on her shoulders as he broke their kiss. "Run, Lil. I don't know how long they can stay."

"Thank you!"

He smiled, then Lilia ran. Her heart thundered that Montgomery had given her the only gift she truly wanted.

He had seen the truth of her heart, after all.

THE REVEREND had taken Delilah into her care, hustling her toward the humming helicopter. Rafe had been collected from the jubilant crowd and the two of them sat together, peering out the window. Delilah was tired, but excited all the same.

Rafe had chosen to stay.

And she was Oracle.

The pilot flew over the stadium, giving them one last look at the cheering group. The sight nearly stopped Delilah's heart. She looked for the shades in the crowd, mingled with norms, and a lump rose in her throat.

"Your supporters," Rafe whispered and Delilah slipped her hand into his.

"This is going to work," the reverend said, raising her voice over the loud chop of the rotors. "You have a lot of training to do, but I'll help you." She eyed Rafe, the angel kiss burning bright red on his forehead. "Are you here to stay?"

"He is," Delilah said firmly and Rafe squeezed her fingers in agreement.

"Then I'll have to research the role of the Oracle's consort. At least we have precedence for this." She began to tap at her palm, organizing and delegating as the helicopter rose high in the sky.

Rafe's palm pinged an imperative. He spared it a glance filled with such irritation that Delilah wanted to laugh.

"It probably knows best," she said.

"I don't like it knowing best," he muttered. "I don't like the sense that it knows more than I do."

"Maybe you should get used to that." She eased closer to him. "Maybe you should ask it what you want to know."

He gave her a look, and slowly smiled. "You're right." He then tapped at his palm, his eyes widening as he obviously began a dialogue with someone.

Delilah looked between her two companions, each rapt upon their palm displays. She listened to the steady chop of the rotors, the persistent tap of fingers on palms, and felt exhaustion claim her body.

It was safe, safe for her to sleep.

And she did.

She awakened when the helicopter was descending, the night still black beyond the windows. There was a city spread below them, wavering lights of thousands of candles gathered in a town square. The cluster of golden light was like a beacon, the buildings dark all around it. Delilah could see upturned faces as they descended, and felt an excitement in Rafe that echoed her own.

She found the reverend's gaze upon her, that woman smiling broadly. "Is this New D.C.?"

The reverend shook her head. "Nouveau Mont Royal." She arched a brow at Rafe. "A short stop here, by request."

Nouveau Mont Royal? Wasn't that where her mother was?

Delilah turned to Rafe to find him grinning. She knew she'd never get used to the irreverent sparkle of his blue eyes, the way he could make her heart leap with just one look.

It was his angelfire for her.

"I asked what I wanted to know," he murmured.

The helicopter descended into the town square then, policemen gesturing to hold the crowd at bay. Delilah saw people protect their faces from the wind the rotors raised, and gasped at how many of those faces were marked with a red kiss in parody of her own. There were thousands of people gathered, many of them sheltering candle flames with their hands.

Then the helicopter touched the ground and the rotors slowed. "I don't have a lot of canola," the pilot said. "Make it fast."

The reverend frowned briefly. "Can't you get any?" she demanded.

The pilot's eyes narrowed. "My contacts are currently unavailable." The reverend's lips tightened as she exchanged a hard look with the pilot. He shrugged.

Rafe inhaled sharply. "Wraiths," he whispered, so quietly that only Delilah heard him.

Then Delilah saw a woman stride out of the crowd and she didn't care about anything else.

Delilah caught her breath and clutched Rafe's hand. The woman moved with confidence, which was less notable than the fact that she wore a black heavy-gauge pseudoskin that had obviously been made for her. She wore high black boots and there was a holster slung around her hips. Delilah could see the laze, positioned just below the woman's right hand. Her hair was long and as black as midnight, and it hung past her hips, the ends flicking in the wind from the helicopter.

Delilah couldn't look away. This was nothing like a still image. Delilah caught her breath in the similarity between that heart-shaped face and her own. She moved with grace and conviction, her presence enough that the crowd stood back. Delilah might resemble her mother, but she couldn't compare with her mother's verve.

"Go on," the reverend said kindly, but Delilah had already reached for the door.

And then she was running, running across the pavement toward the mother she had never known. She was vaguely aware of the cheering of the crowd, of the regular chop of the helicopter, of the reverend leading a cheer. She felt Rafe behind her and saw the dark haired man standing sentinel behind Lilia. But none of it mattered, none of it mattered when Lilia's arms locked around her tightly.

"Chère," Lilia whispered, kissing Delilah's cheek.

"Mom," Delilah replied.

The two women clung to each other for a long moment, then Lilia pulled back. She ran a hand over Delilah's face, her own cheeks stained with tears, and her breath uneven. She smiled, her eyes dancing. "My mother—your grandmother— is going to kill me," she said. Hers was the same voice that had guided Delilah and Rafe through the Society's labyrinth.

"Why?"

"Because she missed this." Lilia exhaled and grinned.

"Oh, there's going to be hell to pay." She didn't sound as if she was dreading the confrontation much and Delilah smiled at her obvious affection.

She had a family, a family who loved each other.

She wanted to know them all.

Lilia indicated the tall man who was recording the reunion with his palm. "At least Montgomery thought to get vid for her." She dropped her voice to a whisper, her eyes sparkling. "Sometimes I think she loves him more than me."

Then she winked. "Other times, I know it."

She turned to face the crowd before Delilah could reply, her arm locked around Delilah's shoulders, and raised her voice. "As many of you know, I am Lilia Desjardins, shade hunter and Nuclear Darwinist Third Degree."

There was a patter of applause and the glitter of palms held skyward as people captured the proceedings. Delilah held tight to her mother's warmth, inhaling deeply of her perfume. She was both exotic and familiar.

And her rib-breaking embrace was so very welcome.

Lilia continued. "And you also know that we now have a true Oracle for the Republic."

The crowd cheered and hooted, many holding up their fingers in a V symbol. Delilah was struck again by the number of red kisses on foreheads.

"Already an old story, Lilia," said a man with an image-snatcher. Delilah assumed he was a journalist.

Lilia laughed. "But you only have half of the story, Stephen. I'm going to tell you the best part."

He looked up, curious.

"The Oracle is my daughter," Lilia said with resolve and a ripple of surprise passed through the crowd. "And I am so proud to finally be able to claim her as my own." She smiled at Delilah. "It's been a long nineteen years since they took her from me." She shook her head slightly and Delilah saw the tears in her mother's eyes. "I had no idea whether she had survived, where she was, what she thought." Lilia's voice broke.

That journalist stepped forward, tapping at his palm. "Wait

a minute. Your own record says that you bore a child, harvested at birth by the Society of Nuclear Darwinists. A shade child."

"Yes," Lilia said, lifting her chin with pride. "She was born, here on the Frontier. Her name was supposed to be Delilah Desjardins, but I never had the chance to give it to her. She was harvested and I didn't know where she was taken. A friend found her for me, and hid her, then I wasn't sure where she was or if she was alive." She sighed and swallowed as she met Delilah's gaze again as her voice dropped. "Until this past week." She squeezed Delilah's shoulder in her excitement and Delilah knew she should never have doubted the strength of her mother's love.

Lilia had fought for her survival as determinedly as the angels had.

"Who's the father?" asked the reporter.

Lilia granted him a look of such pity that Delilah wanted to laugh. "No comment."

"How can we confirm this story?" he asked. "How can we know that this truly is your child?"

Lilia faced him, her resolve making Delilah's heart leap. "I will undergo blood and DNA tests. I will do whatever is necessary to prove that her identity is established. Delilah is my child."

"But—" the reporter persisted.

Lilia interrupted him with a determination Delilah could only envy. "She is whole and she is norm, and the angels speak through her. Delilah is the true Oracle of the Republic." She raised her free hand. "All praise the true Oracle!"

The crowd went wild in their enthusiasm, drowning out any questions the reporter might have asked. Lilia embraced Delilah again, and Delilah whispered. "Thank you for—"

"The eyes of the Republic are everywhere," Lilia said, interrupting Delilah before she could refer to their escape from the netherzones of Chicago. She gripped Delilah's shoulders and looked into her eyes. Delilah saw both wariness and intelligence there. "We will see each other again, somehow, and we will talk for as long as we please. For now, you have

defenders I would trust with my life." Lilia smiled and her
eyes glazed with tears again. "Hell, I'm trusting them with
my lifeblood."

"Hurry!" called the reverend and the rotors of the helicopter turned more quickly. Lilia kissed Delilah's cheeks, her
fingers tightening briefly before she stepped away. Her reluctance to part was obvious.

"May the angels be with you," Delilah said and her mother
smiled.

"They're with both of us, chère," she whispered with heat.
"All the time."

The two women's gazes locked for a moment, and Delilah
understood that the tall man who awaited her mother shared
the same legacy as Rafe. She caught the glance that Rafe
and Montgomery exchanged and Montgomery's slight nod.
Delilah liked knowing that the angels were watching over
both of them and knew her pleasure showed.

"I want to meet my grandmother," she said and Lilia rolled
her eyes.

"I think that's inevitable at this point," she said and laughed.

The reverend shouted again and Delilah ran back to the
helicopter. Rafe offered his hand to her, and she slipped her
fingers into his warm grasp as she climbed into the helicopter. His eyes were glimmering, filled with that beguiling
starlight.

"You arranged this," she accused.

"I asked a favor and it was granted." Rafe nodded at the
reverend. "The reverend gave the order to make it happen."

"I always knew Lilia wasn't telling me the whole story,"
the reverend said with satisfaction.

Delilah waved to the crowd as the helicopter took off,
amazed at the rapid change in her fortunes. The sound of the
helicopter let her talk softly with Rafe, as the reverend continued to plan on her palm.

"We have to find Ferris," she whispered.

Rafe nodded. "I've already asked about that."

"Asked who?"

"Montgomery. He was the one who greeted me, when I first

met your mother. I hadn't remembered. And he's the one who has been sending me messages."

"There's a hidden network?"

Rafe slanted a glance at the reverend who seemed absorbed in her work. "I've joined the team," was all he said.

Delilah smiled. She knew Rafe had simply reaffirmed his membership on an old team. He was still working with the angels. There were more of these norms with diagonal scars on their backs, more angels who had chosen to sacrifice their wings to aid humanity in the world. She would need their help and more to fulfil her destiny.

She would need Rafe's help.

"Your mother gave you a name and an identity," Rafe said. "She claimed you."

Delilah was worried then. "Doesn't that put her at risk? It's not legal to hide shades from the Republic."

Rafe smiled and interlaced his fingers with hers. "I don't think that it's the first time your mother tempted fate." When Delilah might have argued, he squeezed her hand. "She lied for you. She lied for me. That's why we're both here. And I think that's why the angels will take care of her, too."

"I know they do." Delilah smiled as their gazes met. She caught her breath when Rafe leaned closer and touched his lips to her forehead, matching his kiss to the mark of the angels. The brush of his lips sent a surge of angelfire through her.

Or maybe it was the desire that Rafe himself could awaken. She couldn't wait to find out.

She looked up at him, confident of what the future would bring, and his smile made her heart leap. Rafe had not only helped her become Oracle, but he had stayed. She would be the first Oracle in decades to have a consort, a consort whose touch kindled her ability to hear the angels. They would work together for the good of the Republic and of all those resident within it, and they would have the everend and Lilia and the angels on their side.

Delilah liked that portent of her future just fine.

* * *

LIL AND Montgomery were walking through the quiet streets of Nouveau Mont Royal, marveling at what they had seen. Montgomery could almost hear Lil thinking and was content to let her sort out her response to the evening.

He was filled with an old joy, a conviction that good would triumph over evil, and that in remaining on earth, he had contributed to the salvation of mankind. The angels had revealed themselves twice in public in rapid succession, proving their existence and their favor. Although that meant that the situation was dire, Montgomery was encouraged at their involvement.

He felt optimistic.

Lil slid her hand into his elbow, her breast nudging his arm in a way that would always fire his blood. "I have to thank you," she said quietly and he glanced her way in surprise. "For this. For helping Delilah."

"Helping Rafe's mission was my obligation."

"No. You and your team, you former angels, you brought her out of the darkness." Lil frowned and slowed her pace. "Gid gave Delilah a hiding place, and for a long time, I thought that was good enough. But you and Rafe gave her a life. Gid saved her temporarily, but at a huge cost."

Montgomery looked down at Lil and she smiled. "Your team made her happy. You helped her be what she wanted to be." Her eyes clouded with tears. "It's far more than I could ever have given her. Thank you."

Montgomery put his arm around her, holding her tightly against his side. It wasn't like Lil to show her vulnerabilities and he knew better than to make a show of it. They walked together for a few minutes, their arms locked around each other.

"We should go and visit your mother," he said finally, sensing that she'd regain her strength in her mother's presence. "I'd like to see how she and Eva and Micheline are doing up there."

"You want to give her the news."

"Well, she is off the grid and curiosity has to be killing her." He smiled at her. "Don't you want to share?"

Lil sighed and smiled ruefully. "Even knowing that she'll demand the whole story."

"We'll stay a few days."

"But how? Contraband supplies will dry up now that the circus has gone to ground . . ."

"I stocked up earlier."

"Delilah's the one with foresight," she teased. "Unless you're hiding a third-eye mutation from me."

"I'm an open book, Lil, you know that." She fell silent at the truth in that and he gave her shoulders a squeeze. "I thought we might have to go to Delilah, and I wanted to be ready."

"You said I was wrong to want to go to her."

"That doesn't mean you aren't persuasive."

Lil laughed. "I have to have some admirable qualities."

"More than one," Montgomery said without smiling. He stopped and turned to face her, catching her shoulders in his hands. "I would have taken you to Chicago, even, for just one promise."

She immediately looked wary. "Not that."

"Yes, that." There was no doubt in his tone and he knew she heard it. "Let's get married, Lil."

She frowned and looked away, swallowing as he watched. She looked at him, her eyes telling a thousand stories.

Including the one he wanted to hear.

"I love you, Montgomery, but I'm afraid."

He smiled slowly, noting how her gaze clung to his. "Since when has that stopped you from doing anything?" he teased. She blushed a bit then smiled.

"I guess you have shown the patience of an immortal," she said, her tone flirtatious.

"But I'm not immortal anymore, Lil."

She studied him, her smile broadening as she did so. "No," she finally said quietly. "No, you're not anymore, and I guess that should have told me everything I needed to know." She stretched up and put her hands on her shoulders. "What the hell. Let's do it, Montgomery."

He kissed her then, right in the street, not caring who saw.

He held nothing back in his relief and Lil was—as always—ready to meet him halfway. They parted long moments later, their breath fogging the cold air and their hearts pounding. "You need anything from the unit before we leave?" he asked.

Lil's smile was radiant. "There's nothing I need, Montgomery, but you."

And that was all he needed to hear.

From THE REPUBLICAN RECORD
April 3, 2100
Download version 2.3

Inauguration of Oracle Exceeds
All Attendance Records

NEW D.C.—The inauguration of Delilah as official Oracle of
the Republic last night drew record crowds and instantly
became the most downloaded vidcast in history. Reverend
Billie Jo Estevez officiated at the ceremony, attended by virtually every celebrity and politician in the Republic. With the
election so close and the house closed to new legislation, it
was decided that the Oracle would begin her official function
of consulting with the president after this fall's elections. The
news that Delilah and her consort are expecting their first
child was greeted with joy by the celebrants.

Happy citizens—many with the red angel kiss temporary
tattoos on their forehead—thronged the capitol in a peaceful
demonstration, timed to coincide with the new Oracle taking
her role. The mood was jubilant and there were no acts of
vandalism or violence reported.

Delilah's past history in the shade dens of the Republic, as
well as her luminous presence, has captured the hearts of the
nation. Her persistent messages of compassion and peace
have won her many devoted followers, a high percentage of
whom made the pilgrimage to New D.C. this week. "I don't
care if I even see her," said Tonya Erikson of New Galveston.
"Just being here for her inauguration makes me happy—and it
wouldn't hurt to see angels either." Mrs. Erikson was not alone
in expressing her hope that the angels would make another
appearance at this historic event, but thus far, there have been
no angel sightings.

For the first time in decades, the Oracle has taken an offi-

cial consort. Raphael Gerritson of Paduca is the husband of
the new Oracle Delilah. The two exchanged wedding vows
last week, in a private ceremony reputedly attended by the
Oracle's family. A spokesperson for Delilah asked for the
public's understanding in the Oracle's decision to not offer
the wedding as a vidcast, saying that the Desjardins family
wanted a private moment for their reunion. Delilah's mother,
Lilia Desjardins, had not seen her only child for nineteen
years, but has been cleared of any charges associated with
hiding a shade from the Republic.

Delilah's story has touched the heart of citizens and
launched a controversy. Her visions have prompted calls for
a reconsideration of the S.H.A.D.E., as well as the living conditions of shades throughout the Republic. Share your views
in this important debate, with the links below.

Related Articles in Today's Download

- Vidcast of the Inauguration
- Ernestine Sinclair, president of the Society of Nuclear
  Darwinists, on the Danger of Ignoring Reality
- S.H.A.D.E. Status Reevaluated—Your Questions and
  Comments
- Official Biography of Delilah
- A History of the Role of the Oracle
- Polls Show Steady Gain for Blackstone after His
  Endorsement of the Elimination of Netherzones

TOR
ROMANCE

Believe that love is magic

Please join us at the Web site below
for more information about this
author and other great romance
selections, and to sign up for our
monthly newsletter!

www.tor-forge.com